DOGS

BOOKS BY NANCY KRESS

Prince of Morning Bells (1981)
The Golden Grove (1984)
The White Pipes (1985)
Trinity and Other Stories (1985)
An Alien Light (1988)
The Price of Oranges (1989)
Brainrose (1990)
Beggars in Spain (1993)
The Aliens of Earth (1993)
Beggars and Choosers (1994)
Oaths and Miracles (1996)
Beggars Ride (1996)
Maximum Light (1998)
Stinger (1998)
Beaker's Dozen (1998)
Yanked (1999)
Probability Moon (2000)
Probability Sun (2001)
Probability Space (2002)
Crossfire (2003)
Nothing Human (2003)
Crucible (2004)
Nano Comes to Clifford Falls (2008)

NON-FICTION

Beginnings, Middles & Ends (1993)
Dynamic Characters: How to Create Personalities That Keep Readers Captivated (1998)
Characters, Emotion & Viewpoint (2005)

Dogs

a novel by

NANCY KRESS

TACHYON PUBLICATIONS
SAN FRANCISCO

Dogs

Cover design by Ann Monn.
Interior design & composition by John D. Berry.
The text typeface is Kingfisher, designed by Jeremy Tankard.

Tachyon Publications
1459 18th Street #139
San Francisco, CA 94107
(415) 285-5615
www.tachyonpublications.com

Series Editor: Jacob Weisman

ISBN 13: 978-1-892391-78-0
ISBN 10: 1-892391-78-3

Printed in the United States of America
by Worzalla

First Edition: 2008

9 8 7 6 5 4 3 2 1

"Brothers and sisters, I bid you beware
Of giving your heart to a dog to tear."

—RUDYARD KIPLING, *The Power of the Dog*, 1909

DOGS

» 1

The kitchen was too warm, and Dan wanted to open the door to the blessed winter air outside. However, if he did, Sue would complain. When she'd been his wife, she'd complained about everything, and now that she was his ex-wife, she complained even more. Dan tried to keep these brief meetings when he picked up the kids as non-confrontational as possible. It wasn't easy.

"Don't forget to put on her snow pants, not just the parka, when you bring her home," Sue said. She tied the bunny cap on two-year-old Jenny's head. "Last weekend you took her to the movies in just her parka."

"She only had to go as far as the car," Dan said.

"I don't care. Just listen to me, for once. You never listen to me."

"She'll wear everything. And Donnie will, too."

Donnie, slumped in a corner over his Game Boy, said, "No, I won't. It's not cold out."

"It's February!" Sue whined. "Why doesn't anybody listen to me?"

"Sue, it's February but it's forty degrees out."

"That's right, Dan, just undermine what I say. You always were an underminer. Donnie, do you have your math homework?"

"Yeah, I...hey, *there* she is!" Donnie leapt up and opened the kitchen door to the welcome cold. The family dog, Princess, sped in. "Dad, she's been missing since yesterday and now here she is!"

"Hey, Principessa, hey, old girl." Dan bent to stroke the golden retriever, whom he missed. Memories flooded back: Princess curled at his feet during *Monday Night Football,* running at his side while he jogged, catching a Frisbee while Donnie laughed and laughed in his port-a-swing. Good old Princess!

Princess snarled deep in her throat, a sound such as Dan had never heard her make before.

"Hey, Princess..."

The dog snarled again. Her hackles rose and her ears strained forward. Her tail lifted into the air.

Sue said, "She's never done that before!"

"Hey, Princess, down, girl, good dog – "

Princess growled loudly, lips pulled back over her teeth. Dan moved to grab her collar. He was too late. The dog sprang at Jenny.

Sue screamed. Jenny screamed, too, and Dan looked frantically around the kitchen. He grabbed a frying pan from the dish drain and whacked Princess on the back, as hard as he could. Her body shuddered but she didn't let go of Jenny. The little girl's arms flailed in her pink parka. Dan saw with stunned, sick disbelief that Princess had her by the neck. He swung the frying pan again, this time on the dog's head.

Slowly...so slowly, it seemed to take hours...Princess's grip on Jenny slacked a little. But the dog did not let go, and the child was no longer screaming.

THURSDAY

» 2

Tessa Sanderson was awakened by the phone. She glanced at the clock: 6:30 A.M. Well, the alarm would have gone off in half an hour anyway. Sleepily she groped for the receiver. Probably it was Ellen, her sister often called too early, Ellen's infant son got her up at some God-awful hour...but maybe Tessa had better check the Caller I.D. anyway. There were so many people she did not want to talk to.

Caller I.D. said the call was from the Hoover Building.

Immediately Tessa snatched her hand off the receiver. No way. No more condolence calls, no more rehashes about why she quit, no more arguments with Maddox, her former boss. *No more.*

Now she was irreversibly awake. Minette, the world's most spoiled toy poodle, was curled tight against Tessa's thigh and growled as Tessa pushed aside the blankets. Minette was supposed to stay on her own dog pillow at the foot end of the bed, but she never did. When Salah had been alive...

None of that. No self-pity.

Tessa padded into the kitchen of her new house and put on the water for coffee. It was important, she had decided, to stick to a routine as much as possible. A routine filled the days, accomplished worthwhile goals, kept her from firing her Smith & Wesson into her left temple. A routine, as Ellen pointed out every morning, was vital to a regulated life. Ellen was big on regulation. Tessa was big on getting through the day in one piece.

The phone rang again. The FBI once more, but this time Bernini's direct line. Ellen stared at Caller I.D. The Assistant Director himself, at 6:30 in the morning? Didn't seem likely. Bernini had already made his condolence call, lacking either the courage or the foolhardiness, or maybe just the grace, to show up at Salah's memorial service. Of all the FBI personnel Tessa had worked with until her resignation, only two field agents and the secretaries had attended the funeral.

Tessa let the phone ring until the answering machine picked up. "This is 240-555-6289," her own voice said. "Please leave a message."

"Tessa, this is John Maddox. I very much need to talk to you. It's not about any of the things you think it's about. Please pick up." Pause. "Tessa, pick up." Longer pause. "I'm going to keep trying, so please call me this morning. It may be urgent."

And if that wasn't a typical Maddox message, Tessa would eat her new living room rug, which lay still rolled on her new hardwood floors. As she prepared her coffee, Tessa dissected the message, getting angrier with each mental point.

Point one: *"It's not about any of the things you think it's about."* How the hell did Maddox know what she thought his message was about? Did he think that she assumed the message was about her resignation from the Bureau three weeks ago, after she'd been passed over yet again for promotion despite a sterling record in counter-terrorism?

Damn right she assumed that.

Or did Maddox think she assumed her non-promotion was due to her late husband's ethnicity? Salah Mohammed Mahjoub, citizen of Tunisia until she'd met and married him in Paris.

Damn right she assumed that, too.

Point two: *"Tessa, I'm going to keep trying."* He'd have his secretary keep trying, long-suffering Mrs. Jellison, the Rosemary Woods of her generation. Maddox would sit in his office and go on with his work until Mrs. Jellison said, "Mr. Maddox, I've got Agent Sanderson on the line." By then he might even have forgotten that he'd wanted Tessa.

And for what? Point three: That *"It may be urgent."* What a weasel word, "may." *Anything* may be urgent under the right circumstances. A lemon drop may be urgent if it's stuck in your trachea. Tessa was no longer interested in Maddox's lemon drops.

She sipped the last of her coffee, put the cup in the sink, and opened a living room window. Cold February air rushed in, bracing and sweet. Tessa liked winter if it wasn't too cold, and Maryland had been having a mild run of sunny days in the 40s. The window looked out on a small backyard, the first Tessa had ever owned, edged with what the realtor had promised would be lilacs. Now, however, they were just more bare bushes, looking curiously naked and vulnerable. There were also what the realtor promised would be lilies of the valley, but Tessa planned on digging those up. They could poison a small dog. Tessa, who'd never before lived outside a city, had carefully researched all floral threats to Minette.

Beyond her yard and the little town of Tyler rose the Appalachian foothills, dull green with pine, crowned with snow. Somewhere up there Maryland turned into West Virginia.

In T-shirt and panties, Tessa sat down on her meditation mat on the hardwood floor, assumed the lotus position, and faced the brass statue that was the first thing she'd unpacked.

The phone rang again.

Breathe in, breathe out...

"This is 240-555-6289. Please leave a message."

Breathe in, breathe out...

"Tessa, John Maddox again. Listen, I need you to pick up. Now. We just received a second classified report. There's a lot of intelligence chatter, and it's very specific."

Breathe...

"It includes your name, and your late husband's."

Slowly Tessa turned her head toward the phone.

"If you don't pick up, I'm sending two agents out there to bring you in immediately."

Tessa got up off her meditation mat and picked up the phone.

» 3

Jess Langstrom walked into his office at 7:30 on Thursday morning to find six of Suzanne's pink "While You Were Out" slips on his desk. He poured himself a cup of coffee, but before he'd had even one sip, Suzanne herself emerged from the bathroom, even more breathless than usual. "Jess – did you see? Did you?"

"See what? What've we got, a whole herd of deer hit on the highway?" The way commuting was picking up, Jess wouldn't have been surprised. More and more people living in northern Maryland, or even over the state lines in West Virginia and Pennsylvania, and commuting to D.C. to work. Three or four hours a day in the car. Crazy.

"No deer. They're all dog bites!"

"Dog bites?"

"Six! Dogs! That bit!"

Suzanne, always inclined to hyperbole, had now puffed up with it, taller and, somehow, even bigger busted. Which was saying a lot. Twenty-two and gorgeous, Suzanne was the first member Jess had ever met of that fabled group, cop groupies. Not that an Animal Control Officer was exactly a cop, but Suzanne was resourceful enough to work with what was at hand. So far Jess had resisted her blandishments. She was twenty-two to his forty; she was his subordinate; she was an airhead. Enough said.

That she turned up in his wet dreams was not said, nor would it ever be.

He studied the six slips of paper. Suzanne was an airhead, but she gave good message: who, what, where, when. Four people had left messages overnight reporting bites from dangerous dogs; two more had called in the last twenty minutes. In all six cases, someone had sought medical attention, and in all six cases, now someone wanted Jess to do something about the dangerous dogs.

He scowled at the pink bits of paper. Four point seven million people in the United States were bitten by dogs every year, and seventeen percent of those went for medical attention. In fact, medical help was sought for a dog bite every forty seconds somewhere in the country. But six bites within twelve hours here in his own small jurisdiction – what were the odds of that?

It didn't matter what the odds were. It only mattered that he took care of each out-of-control animal. "Okay, where's Billy?"

"Not in yet."

"*Get* him in."

"You want me to call him, Jess?" Suzanne took one step closer to him.

"Yes, I want you to call him! And tell him if he's not here in ten minutes, he's fired. God, he only lives across the street."

"Tough guy," Suzanne murmured, gazing up at him from under her lashes. Jess retreated to his car.

Three minutes later Billy Davis – at thirty-eight, he still didn't want to be called "Bill" – tumbled into the car beside Jess. His shirt was half-buttoned and he smelled of sex. "Hi, Jess. Sorry about being late. This little lady from the Moonlight Lounge – "

"I don't want to hear about it," Jess said, and hoped that Billy knew he meant it. Both of them knew that Jess tolerated Billy, his lateness and unreliability, only for old-time's sake, although Billy was a very good animal handler when he settled down to it. One look at Jess's face and Billy settled now, buttoning his shirt and saying professionally, "What we got?"

"Six dog bites since closing last night."

"Six?"

"That's what the man said."

"Who? Give me the slips."

Jess did, starting the car and peeling out of the parking lot, a bit of juvenile acting out that only made him irritated with himself as well as with Billy. "You were supposed to be on call last night, Billy. How come you didn't answer any of these?"

"Never got the calls," Billy said blandly. "Telephone system must be screwed up again. You know last month it didn't route to my cell, either."

Jess said nothing, and Billy knew enough to shut up. He started making the call-backs while Jess drove to Susan Parcell's place out Old Schoolhouse Road.

It was a small country farmhouse gussied up to look a century older than it really was: new fieldstone chimney, cast-iron coach lights, faux Federalist detailing. As Jess pulled up, a man raced outside, carrying a plastic garbage bag.

"Wait!" Jess said. "We're from Animal Control, we received a call that – "

"You're too late," the man said brutally. "I shot the bitch!"

Jess and Billy glanced at each other. The man looked distraught, unshaven, wild-eyed. Billy's hand rested lightly on the gun at his hip.

Jess hoped suddenly that "bitch" referred to a female dog.

The man resumed his rush toward his car. Deftly Jess stood in front of the driver's door and said soothingly, "Look, this will just take a moment, I promise. We need some basic information. Are you Mr. Parcell?"

"No, Parcell is my ex-wife's maiden name, she took it back after the divorce. I'm Daniel Kingwell. Look, I have to go back to the hospital, I just came to get some of Jenny's things, Big Pink, she never goes anywhere without it – " Abruptly he looked away.

Jess could just discern the outlines of a pink stuffed animal of some sort bulging within the plastic bag. "Jenny is your daughter, Mr. Kingwell? The dog-bite victim? Please tell me briefly what happened."

The man seemed to respond to the tone of voice. It was Jess's chief asset, that voice. Deep and soothing, it could calm when others failed, elicit information others could not. Billy was a better animal handler and, Good Ol' Boy that he was, a better shot. Jess handled that most difficult animal, *Homo sapiens*.

The man talked in quick, agitated bursts. "I came last night to pick up my kids for the evening... Sue decided she wanted to live all the way out here in the country, even though driving up from D.C. is...never mind that, I'm sorry, I'm a bit...we were in the kitchen when Donnie, my son, let in Princess. He said she'd been gone for a day or two, she's been the family dog for years, and she was always such a sweet...she's old, too! Nearly eleven! She attacked Jenny and bit her neck and face and...I tried to get her off. Princess just wouldn't let go. Then Sue tried and I ran out to my car and got my gun from the glove compartment and shot Princess. We called 911 and an ambulance came and – I have to go!"

"Of course you do," Jess said. "Just three more fast questions, sir. Do you have a license for that gun?"

"Yes!"

"Was Princess up-to-date on her rabies vaccinations?"

"Yes!"

"And where is the dog's body now?"

"Inside!"

Billy, making Jess's promised three questions into four, said, "Can we go in? Do we got your permission?"

"Yes!"

Jess and Billy mounted the steps. Jess could get the rest of the information he needed from 911, county records, and Tyler Community Hospital.

The kitchen matched the outside of the house: tasteful, ersatz Early American. Copper pans hanging overhead, farmhouse table, pie safe in distressed oak. Princess lay on the kitchen floor, a hole in her side, blood and tissue spattered over the faux plank floor. Jess could imagine how the scene had looked last night, everybody screaming, the little girl's head in the dog's jaws. He pushed the picture away.

Billy said, "Funny."

"What is?"

"Female golden retriever, nearly eleven years old, spayed, no sign of foam on the mouth, winter months...she don't fit the profile for a biter."

This was true. Male dogs were six times more likely to bite than females, unneutered more likely than neutered. Among serious bites, over half were inflicted by pit bulls, Rottweilers, and German shepherds. Even the season was unusual; most bites happened between April and September. The only thing that fit the profile was that fifty percent of all dog attacks were on kids.

Jess said, "What do you make of it?"

"Don't make nothin' of it," Billy said cheerfully. "I'm no vet. Let's get a tarp and get this ol' girl out of here. Doc Venters is gonna want a look at this one."

They went back outside. Daniel Kingwell had not left for the hospital after all. He stood slumped by his car, his cell phone in his hand, the tears freezing on his face in the morning winter air.

» 4

If you are an FBI agent, you cannot marry an Arab.

This was not official policy. No one at the Bureau would publicly endorse it, advocate it, or admit it. *Cowards*, Tessa thought as she parked downtown in an overpriced, nearly full commercial lot. She'd lost her parking privileges at the Bureau, of course, when she quit.

She'd lost a lot of things in the last three months.

In December, Salah had been killed by a drunk driver who failed to navigate DuPont Circle at midnight. No covert international plot to terrorize agents by knocking off their spouses: the scared and achingly remorseful drunk had been a seventeen-year-old celebrating his high school's basketball win. His blood alcohol level was 0.12. Nonetheless, the Bureau had investigated, and had come up empty. Tessa believed it. Salah had not even been Muslim. He was a lackadaisical Catholic, a convert during the long, expensive Parisian education provided by an old and rich Tunisian family who had cooperated with the West since the French ruled North Africa.

They'd met while Tessa was on vacation in Greece, a ten-day tour sponsored by the Smithsonian. He'd spotted her in a taverna, asked her to dance, and made off with her heart. This was something no one had done in thirty-five years. Tessa usually went very slow with men, postponing the inevitable, messy end so as to savor the sweet beginning. It was different with Salah; everything was different with Salah. She danced with him, made love with him, and ran every possible deep-background check on him, his family, and his friends.

It all came up clean. Two months later, she married him. He moved to D.C. and took a job at the World Bank, who were overjoyed to hire a native speaker from one of the few Arab countries friendly to the United States. Suddenly money was not a problem in Tessa's life. Salah and she bought a townhouse on Capitol Hill. They redecorated, gave dinner parties, made love. Tessa was happy. The only fly in the truffle was that she kept being passed over for promotions she deserved, promotions her outstanding record had earned.

But not, of course, because she had married an Arab. There was no such official policy.

She hiked up E Street to the Hoover Building, thinking for the thousandth time that it looked like an ugly, lopsided fortress, and stopped at Security. "Hello, Paul. John Maddox called me back in."

"Yes, ma'am, he called down about it. Good to see you back, Agent Sanderson."

"It's not Agent Sanderson anymore, Paul. But thank you."

"I'm afraid you have to go through the metal detector. And can I have your bag and coat, please?"

Tessa submitted to having her purse and jacket searched, and to walking through the metal detector. Paul said fumblingly, "You're looking good, ma'am."

"Thank you again." She made for the elevators.

Well, she *was* looking good. She'd planned it that way. New coat in her favorite dark red, short skirt, red lipstick, shine gel in her black hair. No way she was coming back here looking either like a whipped frump or like an agent wannabe, in dark pantsuit and no make-up.

"Hello, John," she said to Maddox; Mrs. Jellison had waved her right in. "What intelligence chatter concerns me?"

"Right to the point, as always," Maddox said. "Sit down, Tessa. How are you doing?"

"Fine. What intel chatter?"

He grimaced, a weird movement of mouth and eyes she'd come to know well over the years of working with him. It meant he didn't like what he had to say but was going to say it anyway. "I can't show you the direct translations, Tessa, not anymore. All I can say is that your name and Salah's have been reported as turning up in conversations with overseas agents. In Paris, in Tunis, and in Cairo. So I need to run some other names by you, people we're watching, and see if you can put any of it together. Hakeem bin Ahmed al-Fulani?"

Tessa shook her head. "Never heard of him."

"Aktar Erekat?"

"No."

Maddox went through more names; Tessa had heard of none of them. She said, "What else has been consistent throughout the reports? Anything?"

Maddox hesitated, then said, "Nothing."

"Uh-huh," Tessa said. The hesitation meant there was more but Maddox couldn't officially say so. Not to her, not anymore.

"Does the chatter look amateur?" Amateurs babbled – before, during, and after attacks. They bragged to family, colleagues, friends. Pros said nothing. In terrorism, silence was the mark of the truly dangerous. The FBI hadn't known the Oklahoma City bombing was coming until it happened.

Maddox said, "I can't tell you that, either."

"What are you doing looking at Arabic-language intel reports, anyway?" That was not within Maddox's area.

"I wouldn't be looking at them if your name and Salah's weren't in there."

"Bernini is taking it that seriously?"

"He is."

"So are we about to go Code Red because of me?"

Maddox let that one go by.

Tessa leaned forward. "Are *you* taking this seriously?"

Maddox seemed to realize that they were now talking about more than a few Arabic/English transcripts. He said carefully, "We investigated Salah pretty thoroughly when you married him."

"And has anything happened to make you change your mind about him since then? Has it? You know the goddamn answer is no!"

"Calm down, Tessa. Take an even strain."

She didn't want to take an even strain. She didn't want to be sitting here, didn't want this stupid fucking slur on her dead husband's name. Salah had loved his adopted country. And he'd been a peaceable, sweet-natured man. He had never, not once in his prematurely ended life, had anything to do with anything destructive, let alone terrorism. To even *imply*–

"Have a tissue," Maddox said.

"I don't need a tissue, damn it! And if you wanted to be so fucking sympathetic about Salah, you should have come to his funeral!"

Maddox stood, walked to the window, walked back, sat again.

"I'm sorry, Tessa. I wanted to go. More than you can know. But – and I'm not telling you this, please, you didn't hear it here – there was a memorandum. From Bernini."

"The A-DIC said for people to stay away from Salah's *funeral?*"

"He was thinking that so many agents massed in one place...especially so many from counter-terrorism...it would have been a perfect target for an incident."

"I was *domestic* counter-terrorism!"

"I know," Maddox said. Of course he knew – he was Special Agent in Charge for domestic counter-terrorism. "I tried to argue Bernini out of it."

"He always was a prick," Tessa said, something she never could have said if she still worked here. She stood. "Is that all?"

"I have to ask you one more question. Please don't get mad, and please consider it carefully. Is it at all possible, under any circumstances, that there was more to Salah's life *after* you married him, after both you and the Bureau finished clearing him, than he might have told you?"

Shock held her immobile for a moment. That Maddox, who had known Salah personally, who had sent them a wedding gift, who had brought his wife Jennifer to dinner at the Capitol Hill townhouse, could even suggest...even Maddox....

She managed, with dignity from God-knew-where, "No. It is not possible. I knew everything important about Salah's life. Good-bye, John."

He stood, too. "I don't have to tell you not to say anything about this to anyone or – "

"Eat it," Tessa said, which wasn't fair, because Maddox was basically a good guy. It was Bernini that she wanted to curse at, but she couldn't reach him.

"Take care, Tessa," Maddox said, holding out his hand.

She ignored the hand. But at the door she turned. "John, you asked me a hard question, and now I'm going to ask you one. *Was* I passed over for promotion all those years because I was married to Salah? The truth, between old colleagues."

He gazed at her, said nothing. The silence stretched on.

"I thought so," Tessa said, held her chin high, and left the Hoover Building. Good riddance.

But in her car, she allowed herself to rest her head for a moment on the cold steering wheel. Bright sunlight poured through the windshield, deceptively warm. Horns honked and cars streamed through downtown D.C.

Who was talking about her and Salah in Paris, Tunis, and Cairo? And why?

» 5

Steve Harper didn't like dogs, and never had. They were messy, noisy, potentially dangerous. Like all cops, he'd seen a lot of trouble caused by dogs: *Your dog shit on my lawn. Your dog's barking keeps me up nights! Keep that dog away from my garbage can/flower bed/kids or else! Officer, I'm calling to report a loose dog. The dog bit the mailman.* The world would be a better place if people kept cats, and kept them inside.

Then he and Diane had Davey, and suddenly dogs were a part of Steve's world. Davey seemed to have been born loving dogs. If a dog existed within three blocks, Davey knew it. He lurched upward in his stroller and shouted "'Oggie!" and the dog always ran to him, licking his face in a germ-laden mutual love fest. Steve didn't like it but Diane just laughed. "It's in his genes," she said. "He's probably part terrier himself. Look at that sharp little face and wet nose."

Steve hadn't thought that was funny. He still didn't.

"Come on, Davey-Guy, we're going to Grandma's. Daddy's got to get to work."

"'Oggie!"

"No 'oggies. *Grandma.*" Steve tried to keep the frustration out of his voice. None of this was Davey's fault. The little guy couldn't help it that his whore of a mother had run off with another man, or that his father was so stressed out juggling his job with full custody. Not that Steve would ever turn Davey over to Diane, that cheating bitch.

He got Davey into his snowsuit and drove across town.

Steve's mother took Davey from him at the front door. "Here's my little angel...you have time for coffee, Stevie?"

"Can't, Ma, I'm already late." He pushed the stroller, laden with a huge bag of diapers, clothes, bottles, toys – God, the *stuff* a two-year-old needed!

"Leave the stroller on the porch here, we're going to the park. Can you believe this weather for February?"

"Yeah, it's great, 'bye, thanks." Steve escaped to his patrol car. His mother was great, and God knows what he'd do without her, but she never shut up.

He had started the ignition and pulled away from the curb when the brown mastiff raced around the corner.

Fast – faster than possible! – the dog sprinted to the porch and leapt up the steps. Steve slammed on the brakes and grabbed his gun. His mother screamed. She tried to maneuver around the stroller to back through the front door, but with Davey in her arms she wasn't quick enough. The mastiff sprang, knocking her backward over the stroller.

Steve tore toward the house. By the time he reached the doorway, the mastiff had dragged Davey from his grandmother and was shaking him violently in his jaws, like a terrier with a rat. Steve fired at the dog's hind end, to avoid hitting Davey, again and again, until his nine-millimeter was empty.

There was a spun-out moment when the brown mastiff raised its head and looked straight at Steve. A single long string of saliva and blood hung from its mouth, obscenely connecting the dog to the child. Then the mastiff toppled sideways.

Steve grabbed Davey. It was too late. Davey's eyes stared, sightless, at his father. Steve's mother went on screaming, a shrill ragged sound, but Steve barely heard her. All he could hear, in a strange bubble of silence and disbelief, was Davey. His son, joyously crying "'Oggie!"

» 6

"Another one?" Cami Johnson said disbelievingly.

"Yes," the charge nurse said, the phone still in her hand. "They're coming in red, ETA five minutes. Six-year-old boy, unstable, set up the trauma room with the peds cart. Dr. Kirk is still in OR, and I've called in Baker and Olatic. Move, Nurse!"

Cami moved. The charge nurse at Tyler Community Hospital scared her, but that was all right because the other nurses had reassured Cami that Rosita Perez scared them, too, and they'd been here a lot longer than Cami's two weeks. However, not even Rosita was as scary as what was happening in the ER this morning.

Three dog bites, and a fourth one in an ambulance on the way in. And one, the little Kingwell girl, had died.

Cami had seen her when she came in, bleeding and torn up…her poor little face...why did people *own* vicious dogs like that? Especially people with little children? Cami had no kids, she was only twenty-one and this was her first ER duty, but she had a dog. A very gentle half-collie, Belle. Cami would never own any breed that could hurt anyone. She –

"Move, move!" Rosita. Cami was moving as fast as she could, but Rosita never let up. Well, maybe that was okay, even if the other nurses didn't like it. The Tyler Community ER was very well run, everybody said so. Last year they'd gotten an award for it.

A mini-van pulled up under the portico and Cami rushed over.

This patient was an old lady and the bite was on her leg. Blood and shredded flesh obscured the depth of the wound. She had to be in pain, but old people so often tried to not display it. Instead her wrinkled face showed enormous bewilderment. "He *bit* me," she kept saying. "Dragged himself over to my chair and *bit* me. Older than I am practically, no trouble all these years, and he *bit* me."

"We'll get you all fixed up, Mrs. Carby," Mary Brown said soothingly. She was good at soothing patients, Mary was. Cami admired her.

"But he *bit* me! I called 911 right away, but...why on God's green Earth would he bite me?"

"I can handle this, Cami," Mary said. "You wait for the peds patient."

Cami hurried over to Rosita just as Dr. Olatic, Chief of Medicine, walked into the ER. Probably Dr. Baker would arrive soon. Rosita had the phone in her hand again. She addressed Dr. Olatic. "Two more dog bites coming in, one possibly fatal. Pit bull. 911 is sending them here by car now, no more ambulances are available. That makes six bad bites this morning."

"Six?" Dr. Olatic said. *"Six?"*

"Six."

Dr. Olatic questioned Rosita about the patients and then said, "Where are the animal control people?"

"Jess Langstrom called to find out if *we* knew what was going on, Doctor. His team is out following up and collecting dog bodies."

"Collecting?" Olatic said sharply. "Are the dogs dying?"

"I don't know. But apparently some owners have shot them after they bit, and some are shut up in houses, and –"

The phone rang again.

Rosita stared at it a fraction of a second, picked it up, and listened. When she hung up, her usually sharp black eyes held an expression Cami had never expected to see there: fear. "Another two, Doctor. Both teenagers bit by the same dog. 911 told their parents to bring them here."

"Jesus." For a moment nobody spoke. Then Dr. Olatic said to the wide-eyed secretary, "Call Public Health. Get Alec Ramsay on the line and tell him I said they should call the CDC."

» 7

Jess and Billy had two dog bodies in the truck, Princess and a dachshund named Schopenhauer, who had also been shot. The dachshund had left its own property, which the shaken owner said it never did, and attacked a woman shoveling her driveway. The woman's husband heard screams, rushed out with his hunting rifle, and shot the dog.

"I don't understand it," the owner said. He was a very thin middle-aged man who, he said, lived alone. "Schopenhauer never leaves our property, never. And he is – was – so good with people!"

Not this time, Jess thought grimly. He'd collected the information from the owner, and it followed what was by now a familiar pattern: unprovoked dog suddenly goes berserk for no reason and bites the nearest person, snarling like there was no tomorrow. Eight cases this morning.

Billy, after a stretch of uncharacteristic silence, said, "What the hell do you think is going on, Jess?"

"I don't know. Maybe some kind of dog sickness spreading…I'm no vet. That's Dr. Venters' territory."

"Doc Venters couldn't find his ass with both hands. I wouldn't let him treat me for a hangnail."

"I don't think dogs get hangnails," Jess said, and Billy laughed. The laugh was one of the reasons he'd hung in there with Billy all these years. Straight from the belly, full and large and unfettered, the laugh of a man who enjoyed life.

"Well, shoot, sure they – "

"Jess?" came Suzanne's voice on the dispatch. Billy grew attentive.

He'd been after Suzanne since she'd been hired. And she went after Jess, who went after nobody, an endless little game of musical chairs with no movement and one chair empty.

"Yes, Suzanne," Jess said.

"New call, you better take it right away." No flirtatiousness in her voice, no teasing. "Pit bull attacked two kids. One of them might be dead. Kids and parents are on the way to Community, but the dog's still in the house, got an older kid cornered on top of the sink."

"Christ," Billy said.

"It's the Wright place again, 1649 North Edmond. Are you near there?"

"Not far. Thanks, Suzanne." She sounded scared. Jess didn't blame her.

All Billy said on the ride over was, "Some weird shit going down, Jess." Jess didn't answer.

1649 North Edmond, unlike their previous calls, was not out in the country. A small dilapidated house surrounded by a chain-link fence, it was part of a neighborhood that had once passed for Tyler's industrial section. At the end of the street stood a cluster of empty buildings, once a small factory and associated warehouses, long since closed. The site was endless trouble, a magnet for vandals, drifters, and teenage pot parties. The Wright house was endless trouble, too. Jess, like the county sheriff and Tyler town police, had been here before. He parked outside the fence, where a knot of neighbors had gathered. Inside the house a dog snarled and barked.

"What's going on, Officer?" asked a woman in a duffel coat over a nightgown.

Good question – Jess wished he had the answer. Before he could speak, another woman said shrilly, "It's clear what's going on! That damn dog finally killed somebody! I filed complaint after complaint and you people never did nothing so now – "

Jess shut her out. He and Billy went through the gate, latching it carefully behind them. They'd worked together so long they didn't even need to talk. Billy, the better shot, went first, Jess behind him. On the porch, they looked through the windows. One gave onto the kitchen.

A boy, maybe twelve or thirteen, stood on top of the sink with his back to the wall. The sink wasn't designed to support his weight. Old, porcelain, free-standing, it was basically a basin and drain board on three metal legs, the whole connected to two pipes. On the floor a pit bull jumped and snarled, reaching as high as the front rim of the sink.

Pit bulls were always the worst. Many were sweet-natured, but the breed had originally been developed for bull-baiting and dogfighting, and it still showed. Many pit bulls would attack without provocation, warning, or noise, and they would keep at it no matter how badly they hurt themselves. They bit, held, shredded, and tore, and very little would make them let go.

The boy saw them through the window. "Help me! Help me!" he screamed at them. Evidently the dog, too, sensed they were there; he turned briefly and snapped in their direction, then returned to the boy.

"Jesus," Billy repeated. "That bastard got blood on his jaws already. Come on, Jess."

Abruptly the sink sagged to the left. The boy screamed and tried to grab at a shelf beside him. It tore loose from the wall and crashed down, sending Palmolive and sponges to the floor.

Jess and Billy tore open the front door and sprinted to the kitchen. The boy, balanced precariously on the tilting sink, screamed nonstop and kicked at the pit bull, whose lunge just missed his ankle. At their entrance, the dog turned and leapt for Billy, who fired once and got him square in the brain. The dog dropped and the sink crashed to the floor with the boy, who screamed once more and lay still.

"Son, you all right?" Jess said. "No, don't move, let me see that nothing's broken."

"I'm...I'm good," the kid said, tears in his eyes, so much bravery in his voice that Jess was moved. But then the boy snarled, "Let go of me, fucker!"

So much for boyish self-control. Jess said, "You got it. Can you sit up...good. Now tell me what happened. We're from Animal Control and 911 said that a dog bit two kids."

"He did?" The boy's eyes grew wider, his tough-guy stance abandoned again. "Duke bit the twins? Are they all right?"

"I don't know," Jess said. Suzanne had said one of the kids might be dead. "What's your name, son? Do you live here?"

"A.J. Wright. Yes. That's my dad's dog, he's not supposed to be in the house, Mom says so, but Dad likes to bring Duke in and show how he can control him. Where's my mom and dad?"

"They took the twins to the hospital. You weren't here?"

"No, I was sleeping over at Bobby's, I just came home and went in the house and..."

"Steady now, it's all right." Now Jess remembered seeing the rusty bike propped inside the fence. A.J. had come home, heard the dog inside, and assumed his dad was putting the pit bull through its paces, showing off his leader-of-the-pack authority in front of his young kids. After the dog went crazy and attacked, nobody had given a thought to A.J. Their only concern had been to get the bite victims to the hospital.

Billy had expertly wrapped the dog in a tarp – they were going to run out of those soon – and now he said cheerfully, "Okay, Jess, grab the other end of this and – oh, oh, we got company. Bit late, huh?"

Police sirens screamed outside. Sheriff's department, most likely Ames and Hatfield.

"Better late than never," Billy said, "but boy am I going to rile ol' Paulie for this one. Here when the action's all over. Boy oh boy."

"*I'll* talk to them," Jess said, and Billy grinned.

"Guess you're right. I can deal with Fang here alone – ain't like the son-of-a-bitch's going to attack anybody else. Right between the eyes. Damn, I'm good."

» 8

When Tessa got home from D.C., Minette greeted her amid the mess of unpacked boxes in her new house. Tessa had moved in less than a week ago. The townhouse on Capitol Hill wasn't even sold yet; all this had been an impulse move, borne of the intense need to get out of D.C. after she quit the FBI. Away from her anger at the Bureau, away from her memories of Salah, away from her raw grief. Unfortunately, it hadn't worked.

Still, the Cape Cod on Farley Street, a few blocks off Main, was comfortable and pretty, and Tyler still retained enough small-town character to seem worlds away from Washington. A bridge loan from the bank was carrying her over the transition between house deals. And real-estate prices being the insane thing they were in D.C., she would come out with enough money to live on while Salah's will cleared probate and – more importantly – while Tessa decided what to do with the rest of her life.

"Hey, Minette, hey, good dog. Did you miss me?"

Minette, not a well-trained beast, jumped on Tessa. The tiny poodle reached only to her knees and weighed seven pounds, an elegant little bundle of silvery fur and huge black eyes. Tessa dropped to the floor and ran through the pantomime of attacking, retreating, growling at Minette. The dog loved it. No one else ever saw this side of Tessa – except Salah, who had been enormously amused.

Tessa tired of the game before Minette did. The poodle followed her to the bedroom, also filled with boxes, and watched as Tessa changed into jeans and sweater. Then Tessa tackled a pile of cardboard, but her mind wasn't on the task.

Why were her name and Salah's on intel chatter in Paris and North Africa? She'd been pummeling her brain during the long commute home, and had come up with nothing.

They hadn't even had many Arabic friends. Salah, so cosmopolitan, so at home in three languages on just as many continents, had adjusted easily to becoming an American. In fact, it sometimes seemed to Tessa that, except for his mother and sister in Tunis, Salah had shed his old life as easily as a bird shedding feathers. He had enjoyed parties with her friends. He had developed an interest in the Yankees. He was passionate about jazz. He –

The phone rang; Caller I.D. announced Tessa's sister, twenty miles away in Frederick. "Hey, Ellen."

"Hey yourself. Are you getting settled?"

Tessa looked around at the total chaos. "Sort of."

"Can I help?"

"I think you've got your hands full enough." Tessa said. Ellen, although two years younger than Tessa, had three children, a husband, two cats, and an amazing collection of gerbils to care for. Nonetheless, after Salah's death, Ellen had consigned the entire menagerie to her mother-in-law and come to stay with Tessa for two weeks, helping her pack and listening to her cry. This was all the more astonishing because Tessa and Ellen, who looked enough alike to have often been mistaken for twins, had never been close. Maybe because they'd looked too much alike. Tessa had wanted to be unique, and probably Ellen had, too.

Over the last three months they'd kept the fragile, tragedy-born intimacy growing, nurturing it like some delicate rose. That wasn't always easy; they had such radically different lives, perceptions, and personalities.

"How's the baby?" Tessa said.

"He's a vomit machine. Twice today already, and it's *projectile* vomiting. I tell you, this is absolutely the last baby."

"Well, three is probably enough." For Tessa, zero was enough.

"Amen. How are *you* doing, Tessa? No, wait, I forgot – you don't like to be asked that. I'm sorry."

"It's okay."

Awkward pause. Then Tessa said abruptly, "Can I ask you something?"

"Sure." But Tessa heard the surprise and hesitation in Ellen's voice. What was Ellen expecting?

"After you and Jim got married, did he sort of...I don't know, drift away from his old life? In favor of yours?"

Ellen laughed. "Yes. Not all at once, mind you, but over the years I sort of turned into the social director for both of us. Except for a few golfing buddies, if I don't arrange for us to see people, it doesn't happen. I don't think Jim's in contact with any of his old friends, not since the last time we moved, anyway. I think that happens with a lot of married men."

Tessa hadn't realized that. She said, "Oh," unable to think of anything else. *People aren't really your forte,* Maddox had always told her.

Ellen said, "Look, if you want to – oh, God, he's upchucking *again!* Gotta go, Tessa, bye!"

What a life. Ellen, however, seemed fine with it. Tessa returned to the living room and dug through boxes until she found Salah's laptop, the only kind of computer he'd liked. When she'd packed to move, she'd given away all his clothes, but not the laptop. She couldn't. Not yet, maybe never. She set up the computer on the edge of a kitchen table ninety percent covered with plastic bags of food and a huge box containing her grandmother's Wedgwood china, which Tessa would probably never even unpack.

She knew Salah's password. Was it right to use it? It felt like a violation. Although that was silly; Salah had never kept anything from her. She logged on and carefully, methodically, searched through his emails, outgoing and incoming, for any names she didn't recognize. She discounted all the emails with the World Bank address. Those would be professional, and subject to perusal by anyone at the organization. Tessa wanted only personal missives. She began with the day of his death and worked backward.

Most of the personal email was either to Tessa herself or to his mother and sister. Salah, faithful son that he'd been, had written his widowed mother once a week, and he and Tessa had visited Tunisia every October. Fatima had not been thrilled with Salah's choice of bride. In fact, she'd been appalled. Conservative, still veiled when she left the house, she blamed Tessa for taking her only son away from his native country, and away from her. She had never said as much, but she treated Tessa with icy courtesy, never so much as smiling at Tessa's attempts at friendliness in her stumbling schoolgirl French. For Salah's sake, Tessa had never made an issue of this. Besides, Fatima's disdain had been made up for by his sister, Aisha.

As much the new Tunisia as Fatima was the old, Aisha was a doctor with the World Health Organization in Geneva. Aisha was wonderful, as lighthearted and adventurous as her older brother. Aisha had especially loved the emailed pictures of Minette. Salah wrote to Aisha in French and to Fatima in Arabic. His laptop was equipped with software to handle the Arabic characters.

Among all the emails, Tessa found only three, all in Arabic, with addresses she didn't recognize. Two were from pennj@amserve.net, a United Kingdom ISP, dated a few days apart last August. The other was from dkd78@vvvmail.com, received two days before Salah died. If Salah had replied to either, he hadn't saved the replies on his computer, nor entered the addresses in his address book, although he was sloppy about that, anyway. Tessa had no idea who either recipient was.

Nor did she know if they spoke English. Querying them in French might be safer, although many younger Tunisians, especially those not rich, no longer learned French. France had, after all, pulled out of Tunisia in 1956. Still, it wasn't as if Tessa had fluency in a dozen languages to choose from. Salah had been the one with the natural linguistic ear.

"What language do you dream in, Salah?"

"It depends on the dream. If it is of you, I dream in poetry."

Her English-French dictionary was packed somewhere unknowable. Tessa settled for a scratch job, hoping whoever was on the other end would overlook her mistakes in grammar and vocabulary.

> Je suis la femme de Salah Mahjoub, avec qui vous avez communiqué l'année dernière. Peut-être vous avez apprendé que Salah est mort, depuis décembre. S'il vous plait, voulez-vous écrire à moi cette qu'avez-vous écrit avec lui l'année dernière? C'est tres important. Merci beaucoup. Aussi, pardonnez-vous mon francais; je suis americaine.
>
> Tessa Sanderson Mahjoub

Did that say what she wanted, which was, essentially, *"Tell me what you and Salah emailed about last year?"* God, she hoped so. What if the correspondents weren't even Tunisian? After all, one of the addresses was in the UK and the other could be anywhere. Well, then they'd email back "Huh?" and she'd take it from there.

As she sent both emails, Minette whined to go out. The Cape Cod had no fence, although Tessa was planning to install an electric one eventually. She threw on a coat, fastened Minette's leash to her collar, and left the house through the front door.

Mrs. Kalik, her new neighbor, was hauling her garbage out to the curb. She took one look at Minette and shrieked.

"Don't let your dog out!"

"No, it's fine, Mrs. Kalik, she's harmless and she – "

"Get her away from me!"

Nobody but a true phobic reacted that way to a toy poodle. Tessa picked up Minette, who squirmed to get down and piddle.

Mrs. Kalik glared at her. "Don't you know? If your dog is okay, don't let it go outside and catch the plague!"

The what? The woman must be a hallucinatory schizo. Or maybe a religious nut. Tessa tried to remember if there were any canine plagues in Revelations. She took Minette around the back of the house to piddle, while Mrs. Kalik slammed her garbage on the curb and sprinted inside as if pursued by a bear.

Apparently even Norman Rockwell small towns had their paranoid crazies.

» 9

A mile and a half from Tessa's Cape Cod, Allen Levy looked up from his and Jimmy's snow fort as his mother's blue Chevy screeched to a stop at the edge of the road.

"Wow," Jimmy said, "your mother's a fast driver."

But she wasn't, usually. Allen and Jimmy watched as Mrs. Levy leapt out of the car, waved her arms at the edge of the empty field, and screamed, "Boys! Get in the car now!"

"Why?" shouted Jimmy, who was always in trouble for not doing what adults told him to.

"Because I said so!"

Allen could have told Jimmy that's what his mother would say. He looked reluctantly at the snow fort, which had taken an hour to build because there wasn't actually much snow on the ground and they'd had to haul it over from the woods and from ditches that didn't get much sun. But there was no arguing with Allen's mother. "Come on, Jimmy."

"What if I don't want to?" Jimmy said, but not very loud, and he followed Allen to the car.

His mother hurried them into the back seat, climbed in, and turned to look at them without even starting the engine. "Listen, boys, because this is very important. Something happened. There's some kind of...of disease spreading among dogs that makes them attack viciously. Two children have already been killed. I'm going to take you both home and – Jimmy, are your parents home, for once?"

Jimmy shrugged. "I dunno."

"Then you're coming to our house," Allen's mother said. Allen wasn't allowed to play at Jimmy's house ever since she'd discovered that Jimmy's father owned a gun. The Levys didn't approve of guns. She continued, "And both you boys are staying inside until this thing is under control. Do you hear me, Allen?"

"Yes. But – what about Susie? Where is she? Does she have the disease?"

His mother started the car. "Susie's locked in the basement. She's got food and water and I'm sure...I'm sure she'll be fine. But you can't go down there until I or your father say so. Allen, do you hear me?"

"Yes. But, Mom, what if she does have the disease? How do dogs get it?"

"Nobody knows. I guess from other dogs."

"Susie was outside all day yesterday, and when she does that she could play with lots of other dogs!"

"I know. The sheriff's department is saying to keep all dogs locked up and away from people until they know what to do, and to keep all people safe inside. Do you hear me, Allen?"

"Yes," Allen said. Jimmy put his hands over his ears, shook his head violently, and grinned.

The Levy house was only a little way down the country road. As soon as they were inside, Allen could hear Susie. The cocker spaniel was at the top of the cellar stairs, scratching at the door and whining.

Allen said, "She never got put in the cellar before, Mom. She doesn't understand."

"Neither do the rest of us," Mrs. Levy said grimly. "Boys, go upstairs and play."

"At my house we just have cats," Jimmy said.

Allen knew about Jimmy's mom's cats. They were nasty and mean, living outside on scraps and mice, scratching if you tried to pet them, dirty all the time. Dogs were better, and Susie was the best dog ever. What if she really was sick? Wouldn't she be afraid and upset and lonely, all by herself in the cellar?

"Cats are better," Jimmy said. "C'mon, let's play Nintendo."

INTERIM

The man in the Dodge Caravan lit a cigarette and rolled down the mini-van's window. Night air rushed in. Above, the stars glittered, pinpricks of cold light, barely visible above the bright floodlights of the hospital parking lot.

Another ambulance raced past him on the approach to the Emergency Room, followed by a car driven wildly by a distraught woman.

A few minutes later, another racing car.

Then another ambulance.

The man finished his cigarette and crushed it in the ashtray. He rolled up the window, started the engine, and he left the parking lot, then the town.

He smiled. His work was done here. And it was good.

FRIDAY

» 10

Early Friday morning a huge van followed by three cars arrived in Tyler from the Centers for Disease Control in Atlanta, rolling into town like a miniature, very antiseptic rock tour.

"Musta driven all night," Billy said to Jess as they stumbled into the town hall for the emergency meeting called by the mayor. "Pretty damn quick."

Billy was right, Jess thought – and why was the response that fast? The CDC didn't investigate infections unless invited by local governments. Somebody must know somebody, and one of the somebodies was in a tearing hurry.

Jess wished *he* felt that energetic. He and Billy had gotten maybe three hours sleep each. The frantic dog bite reports had poured in all day yesterday, then fallen off by evening as the word spread and people isolated their dogs in basements, garages, and laundry rooms. Throughout the deserted streets of Tyler echoed a background howl and barking. School had been canceled for the day, and many businesses had not opened. Tyler was a ghost town populated only by trapped dogs.

But not all pets had been inside when their owners heard about what whole neighborhoods were now calling "the dog plague." A few dogs roamed the street, and Billy and Jess had spent the night following up on reports of vicious strays, reports of attacks, and at least one more death. There had even been a dog killed by an infected dog; a Malamute had killed a Jack Russell Terrier, sixty pounds lighter, that had been valiantly trying to defend its yard. Animal control officers had been recruited from nearby towns. All sheriff's deputies were on the streets.

And so far nobody had any answers. Maybe this meeting would provide some.

The Tyler Town Hall was an historic brick building housing the town court, tax office, county clerk, and various miscellaneous municipal offices, none of them large. The building's utilitarian interior didn't match its lovely neo-Georgian exterior. Mayor Hafner held his meeting in the empty court, a bleak space with Congoleum floors, folding chairs, and a raised dais for the twice-weekly court sessions, most of which featured traffic tickets. Anything serious was handled at the county seat.

Except that this was serious.

"I'd like to welcome our guests from the CDC," said Lou Hafner, who owned Hafner Lumber. A big, rumpled, genial man, he and Jess occasionally went fishing together. Jess liked him but didn't have a high opinion of his intelligence or administrative skills. Those weren't what got you elected small-town mayor.

"Let me take a minute to introduce everybody," Hafner continued. "Dr. Joseph Latkin from the CDC, an epimed...epidemiologist and his, uh, team. Jess Langstrom and Billy Davis, our animal control off – "

"We're not really here," Billy said, "just stopping by on our way to another call."

"Well, uh – " the mayor began, but the CDC doctor cut in.

"I'd like at least one of the animal control officers to stay. They're the ones with the most direct information on the dogs' behavior, and we'll need to ask them questions."

Jess said to Billy, "You go on. I'll stay." Billy nodded, clearly glad to escape. Meetings weren't Billy's thing. Jess just hoped Billy didn't screw anything up out there alone.

The mayor said, "Dr. Olatic from the hospital, Dr. Ramsay from Public Health, our county vet Dr. Carl Venters, and Sheriff Don DiBella. Now I'll, uh, turn it over to Dr. Latkin."

Joseph Latkin was slim, small, maybe forty-five, intense. Jess thought that he looked competent but accustomed to having his way, like a lot of doctors. He had odd eyes, very pale blue, almost white. It made his gaze disconcerting, as if he had no irises at all and his eyeballs were a solid reflective surface, giving you back nothing but yourself. Despite his small size, he commanded the room without even mounting the judge's dais.

"Please call me Joe. We're here from the CDC to find out, first, if a pathogen is causing this canine behavior. There are other possibilities, such as an ingested environmental. The speed of onset in the dogs and the relatively confined geographical area suggest that could be the case, so we'll start by examining the dogs' stomachs."

Jess considered this. The dogs all ate something that turned them into killers? What could something like that possibly be?

Latkin continued, "However, what you've told us so far is consistent with a certain class of brain pathogens that can turn animals very aggressive. We won't know for sure until we dissect a few infected animals and examine their brains. To that end, some of us – " he nodded toward the twelve people seated to the left of the room " – will be working here in the portable lab, some with Dr. Venters, and two at the hospital and morgue, examining samples from victims. We'll also have a constant, two-way flow of information and samples with Atlanta. I want to emphasize that if we determine that this animal behavior *does* have a disease-based cause, it will be absolutely necessary that we move fast to contain and neutralize the pathogen."

Jess voted silently for a brain disease. A pack of well-behaved family dogs, living peaceably for years side by side with their human pack, sleeping on kids' beds, chasing balls and sticks, part of the annual Christmas picture. Then all of them, *all at once,* attack those same beloved owners. Something infecting their brains was the only thing that made sense to him. But, then, he wasn't an epidemiologist.

"Let me ask a question," Dr. Latkin continued. "Why don't I see anyone here from the Army Veterinary Corps in Frederick?"

No one spoke. Jess could guess the answer: Nobody had thought of the Army Veterinary Corps, a tiny outfit based with the Army Medical Research Institute for Infectious Diseases at Fort Detrick, twenty miles away. Certainly Jess, busy putting out fires for most of the last twenty-four hours, had not. The CDC was here probably because someone at the hospital had thought of them. Lou Hafner, small town mayor, didn't think in terms of federal agencies.

Dr. Latkin spoke over his shoulder to one of his people. "Julie, call USAMRIID and request the Veterinary Corps." Julie rose and glided silently from the room.

Latkin talked on, clarifying CDC procedures, stressing the need for information sharing. When he dismissed the meeting, Jess rose.

"Wait a minute, doctor. What about quarantining Tyler?"

Dead silence.

Mayor Hafner said, "Jess, I think that's a bit premature." He looked panicky.

The sheriff said, his eyes narrowed, "What do you mean, Jess, by 'quarantine'?"

Jess wasn't used to addressing a crowd. But he was used to animals. "Dogs wander. If this thing is a disease, a parasite or a virus or something, it seems to transfer pretty easy from one animal to the next, judging by the quickness that the whole thing blew up and – "

"How quick?" Dr. Latkin interrupted.

"No dog bites at close of business Thursday, forty-six since then."

Dr. Latkin turned to Lou Hafner. "*Forty-six?* You didn't tell me that was the incident curve!"

"I didn't know it," Lou said. "But look here, Jess – "

"Animals don't respect town boundaries," Jess said, "dogs no more than any others. You get infected dogs wandering over to Linville and Flatsburgh, you'll never get this thing contained. You'll get people leaving town, taking their dogs with them because Spot isn't infected yet and they want to get him away before he is. But maybe Spot *is* already infected – Dr. Latkin here said they don't have any idea yet how long the incubation period of this disease might be. I think we need to close off the town now."

"Jess, do you know what you're saying?" the sheriff said.

"I'm saying we have six people dead, four of them children."

Lou Hafner said, "But there's been no new bites since last night! None at all this morning!"

"It's early yet, people are staying inside, and a lot of dogs are locked up. But Billy and I glimpsed at least one in the woods by Randolph Road, and we heard another someplace behind Wal-Mart. There are a lot of loose dogs out there."

"You can't cut off the whole town," Hafner said angrily. "We have all the commuters leaving for work in D.C., people and goods coming and going...this isn't bubonic plague, Jess! It's just a bunch of bad-behaved dogs."

The CDC doctor stared incredulously at Hafner. Then he said, "Jess Langstrom may be right. This was a topic I was going to introduce after we had a bit more data, but that was before I heard how abruptly this pathogen – if it is a pathogen – emerged. That suggests very easy animal-to-animal transmission, possibly even the worst-case scenario, which is an airborne, species-threatening hot agent. Plus, the disease may even have an alternate host, just as avian flu uses both birds and swine. I think we do need to quarantine Tyler."

"And how the hell do you propose we do that, doctor?' Lou Hafner demanded. All traces of his usual geniality had vanished. This was a weak man pushed into belligerence by fear. "Dogs don't respect yellow police tape, you know. Maybe living in a big city like Atlanta, you don't happen to realize how much woods and open land we got here. Tyler township is nearly thirty square miles. We can't just put a huge barbed-wire fence around all of it!"

"No," Joe Latkin said, unaffected by the mayor's sarcasm. "But FEMA can, or at least an approximation. I'm calling them now. Mayor, your office will need to draft a statement for the citizens of Tyler and another for the national press, because it won't be long before they're here. Outside the quarantine cordon, of course."

"Outside? No *people* can come in and out?"

"Yes, people can move in, but no animals of any kind. And no one who enters should be allowed back out, except for necessary crisis-related movement. We can issue special passes for that. We need that containment until we determine that this pathogen, if it *is* a pathogen, is not capable of human-to-human transmission."

The mayor said, "Does that include commuters who live here?"

"I'm afraid it does."

"But the dog bites have goddamned stopped! And you're declaring martial law, that's what you're doing! I don't think you have the authority to do that, doctor."

"I'm not declaring anything. I haven't the authority. These are best-practices recommendations for you to act upon."

The sheriff and the mayor glanced at each other, and Jess saw them both relax. Until Dr. Latkin said quietly, "Until FEMA gets here. Then federal authority trumps yours. Mr. Langstrom, could I ask you some questions, please?"

Jess made his way through the angry buzz of Tyler's officials toward Dr. Latkin. Jess had some questions himself. "*Alternate host*" – did that mean some other animal could have the plague, too, going berserk and attacking people? What animals: groundhogs, rabbits, raccoons? Raccoons carried rabies more often than dogs, even. And no quarantine from FEMA or anybody else was going to confine Tyler's rabbits to Tyler. Not going to happen.

A hard knot was forming in Jess's stomach. Even if there was no secondary host, even if it was only dogs that got this thing, that meant any dog in Tyler could be infected. "*Very easy animal-to-animal transmission*," the doctor had said. Latkin had also mentioned avian flu, and Jess knew what they were doing in Asia to try to control that. They were destroying all the chickens that carried it.

All the dogs in Tyler.

And, if it came to that, Jess knew who would have to carry out the order.

» 11

Ed and Cora Dormund had had a bad night. Ed remembered the fight only vaguely. He guessed he'd drunk too much but jeez, what was wrong with that? The way Cora carried on, you'd think he was an alkie or something. And Cora could pack away the Buds, too, no matter what she pretended. What had happened last night – whatever the hell it had been – wasn't all his fault, not by a fucking long shot.

Ed staggered from bedroom to bathroom. It was too early to be up, but the pressure of his bladder woke him. He scowled at the bathroom window: barely dawn.

In the living room Cora snored heavily on the sofa, surrounded by beer cans, a shattered glass vase, and the torn remains of the roses that she'd squandered on eighteen dollars they didn't have. Now the fight came back to Ed. She'd thrown the vase at him, the bitch, just because he thought they should economize now that he was laid off. It was all her fault. She'd practically forced him to hit her.

Outside, the dogs barked. Ed lurched to the kitchen. Cora hadn't even let the dogs in last night, he couldn't count on her for anything. He closed the door between kitchen and living room so that Jake or Petey or Rex wouldn't step on shards of glass.

Opening the kitchen door to the outside, he suddenly paused with his hand halfway to the latch of the old screen, which he hadn't gotten around to replacing last fall with the storm door. Something was wrong.

The three Samoyeds – "*Stupid to keep sled dogs in Maryland!*" Cora's voice nagged in his head – stood bunched by the door, waiting for him to let them in from the fenced backyard. Nothing unusual in that. But a low noise came from the dogs, rumbles in the back of their throats, that sent cold sliding down Ed's spine. Rex and Petey stared directly at him, tails high and bristling, ears forward. Jake, usually the leader and Ed's favorite, stayed further behind. His lips pulled back and forty-two long, sharp teeth gleamed in the light from the kitchen.

"Hey, guys," Ed tried to say, but the words came out a croak. All at once a picture flashed into his mind from some movie, primitive men crouched close around a fire while in the darkness beyond, creatures moved with firelit eyes and drooling jaws. But these were Ed's pets, his protectors!

"Hey, guys –"

All at once Jake snarled and sprang over Petey. Ed slammed the door. He heard Jake hit the screen and heard the wire mesh, soft as cloth from so many summers, rip away from the wood frame. All three dogs howled and snapped. Ed locked the door and leaned against it, panting as if he'd run a mile. His stomach lurched.

What the fuck had just happened?

Next door, Del Lassiter was wakened by the Dormund dogs barking. 5:46 by the bedside clock. Those awful animals! Still, they usually weren't outside this early.

Silently Del slipped out of bed, careful not to wake Brenda. Once he was awake, he could never get back to sleep. Something to do with getting older, he supposed. At twenty-two he had been able to sleep through a fire alarm; sixty-seven was a different matter.

Del padded to the kitchen, where Folly slept on her little bed. The Chihuahua liked to be near the heat register. Folly woke, too, and gave him a friendly bark and tail wag, all two pounds of her.

Putting on water for coffee, Del could still hear the Dormund dogs snarling and barking. He tried to catch sight of them through the window, but apparently they were in back. The barks sounded...enraged, somehow. What could have upset them like that? Well, whatever it was, Del would have to talk to Ed about it. Brenda needed her sleep; the chemo was hard on her. Yes, he'd call Ed later, at a decent hour, even though everything in Del recoiled from the idea. He hated confrontation of any kind.

Folly yawned, stretched, and wandered to her water bowl.

Two blocks away, Ellie Caine stirred in her warm bed. One of the Greyhounds in the kitchen, it sounded like Song, whimpered. Probably had a bad dream. Ellie shuddered to think what Song might be dreaming.

She'd rescued the four Greyhounds from a race track, where conditions were horrifying. Dogs were trained to run by starving them and then forcing them to chase a piece of meat on a mechanical arm that moved faster and faster. Sometimes, even though it was supposed to be illegal, the meat was replaced by a live rabbit with its legs broken to make it scream. If a Greyhound couldn't run fast enough, or after its racing days were over, the poor dog was killed.

Ellie wished she could rescue more Greyhounds, but even four were a tight fit for her small house and yard. She was passionately determined to make up to Song, Music, Butterfly, and Chimes everything terrible that had been done to them. She rushed home from work at noon to spend her lunch hour with them; she took them every day to the dog park; she stayed home with them every night. They were her friends, her companions, and so much more reliable and loving than people ever were.

Song still whimpered, and Ellie decided to give him five more minutes. Then if all wasn't quiet in the kitchen, she'd leave her cozy bed and go to the greyhounds.

Just five more minutes.

Steve Harper sat on a sofa at the Webster Funeral Home. He couldn't have described the sofa, or the room, or the funeral home. Nothing registered, nothing except the mental picture of Davey, in that spun-out moment when *the brown mastiff raised its head and looked straight at Steve, a single long string of saliva and blood hanging from its mouth –*

"Mr. Harper?" someone said.

Hanging from its mouth onto Davey's body...

"Mr. Harper!"

Slowly the funeral director came into focus. The man, the room, the purpose for this terrible visit. And then one thing more.

"As I was saying, Mr. Harper, FEMA's temporary regulations make it impossible for us to go forward with little David's viewing, service, or burial just now. But we can still choose the casket and make –"

The thing sat on the fireplace mantel. A statue, china or glass...

"– all the other arrangements for the eventual –"

A statue of a dog.

The brown mastiff with a single long string of saliva and blood hanging from its mouth onto Davey's body...

Steve jumped from the sofa, seized the obscene decoration, and smashed it as hard as he could to the floor.

» 12

Cami Johnson dropped the IV bag on her way to her patient's curtained corner of the ER, caught it just before it hit the floor, and banged her head on a metal linen shelf while straightening up. The fall wouldn't have hurt the sealed plastic bag, but the bump hurt Cami. She blinked back tears even as she looked around to see if Rosita Perez had noticed.

The charge nurse noticed everything. "You've been on duty how long, Camilla? Sixteen hours? Go home."

"It's all right, ma'am, I'm fine, I just slipped, I think there's a bit of water on the floor..."

"Then wipe it up, hang the bag, and go home. You look like shit."

Probably true, Cami thought wearily. Sixteen hours, and the dog bites had just kept pouring in. They wouldn't *stop.* The hospital had every available doctor, resident, and intern seeing patients, and still stretchers were stacked in the hall, people sat bleeding in the ER waiting room, and ORs had been commandeered from Maternity, so that women were delivering babies in their rooms. Nobody, the older nurses told her, had ever seen anything like it. And so many of the patients were children! Children and dogs, a boy and his dog, how much is that doggie in the window...Cami's tired mind had been going around and around with that silly tune for the last hour.

Rosita was right; Cami needed to go home for a little while. And even if Rosita hadn't been right, nobody argued with Rosita.

She was surprised to find a police officer in the underground staff parking area. "Can I see some I.D., ma'am?"

Cami showed him her driver's license and hospital pass. He inspected them, unsmiling, and then said, "All right. Drive straight out with your windows rolled up. Don't roll them down to talk to any reporters, or anyone else, who may be outside the hospital. Drive straight home. Do you have a dog at home, ma'am?"

Cami hesitated. If she said yes, would he give orders to take Belle away?

All the while she'd been working on the terrible dog bites flooding the ER, Cami had had Belle in the back of her mind. Cami had had one course in public health during nursing school. If there was an animal-borne plague, an important step was to eliminate the animal hosts. That's what WHO had tried (and failed) to do world-wide with malaria in the 1970s: eliminate the host mosquitoes. Eliminating mice had helped to bring hantavirus under some control in the Southwest. And, of course, all those poor monkeys in Reston, Virginia in 1983, carriers of Ebola from the Philippines – every single monkey had been killed. Wasn't that eventually what might happen here?

But Belle was different. She was so old, and so gentle. With her arthritis, even walking was a chore. If she were infected – and Cami *had* let her off the leash in the dog park last weekend, with tons of other dogs – Belle could hardly even *hobble* over to someone to attack. By the time Belle got there, the "victim" would have been able to escape to the next county.

Anyway, Belle would never attack Cami.

There were no reporters outside the hospital, after all. Cami drove slowly home, so tired that it was a chore to keep her arms raised to the steering wheel. The streets were weirdly deserted, even for February. But she saw a lot of police cars.

At her apartment complex, she pulled into the long garage built beneath her building. Each renter was allotted one garage slot and one outside parking place, and all the indoor slots were filled. In the SUV next to her Ford, a German shepherd barked ferociously, lunging at the window and snapping as if he could tear through the glass and get at her. He couldn't, of course, but – this garage was supposed to be communal! How dare the dog's owner put everyone else at risk...but, of course, what else could they do with the dog if there were children in their unit?

Cami flung open her car, hurried across the garage, and closed the stairwell door on the frantic barking.

At 2-B she paused and knocked. "Mr. Anselm? Are you okay? It's Cami Johnson."

Slow footsteps punctuated by the tapping of a cane. The door opened on Mr. Anselm and his seeing-eye dog, Captain. "Cami? How nice of you to stop by. Would you like a cup of tea?"

"No, I can't stay," Cami said, so exhausted that the words had trouble rising past her lips. "I just wanted to make sure that you heard about the dogs and don't go out. Did you hear, Mr. Anselm?"

His wrinkled old forehead wrinkled even more above the filmy, unfocused blue eyes. "Heard what, my dear?"

"Some kind of plague is affecting dogs, Mr. Anselm. Nobody knows what it is. Captain hasn't snapped at you or anything, has he?"

"Captain? No, of course not. He's too well-trained for anything like that, isn't he, ol' boy?"

Cami nodded, even though he couldn't see her. Seeing-eye dogs were superbly trained. And Mr. Anselm hardly ever left the house anyway. She wanted to say more, but she was just too tired. She managed, "Take care, Mr. Anselm," staggered to her own door, and let herself in.

For just a second, as she pushed open the door, Cami felt a frisson of fear: *What if Belle*...But the collie met her at the door, tail wagging, gentle old eyes shining with pleasure that Cami was home.

In a blur of exhaustion Cami put down food and water for the dog, took off her scrubs, and fell into bed in her underwear. She hadn't taken Belle out...how *could* she take her out, anyway? Let Belle pee, and even shit, in a corner of the kitchen, as she'd had to do once or twice before when Cami had worked a double shift. Cami could clean it up later. Right now sleep, sleep, *sleep*...

But just before she crashed, she pulled herself up off the duvet and closed the bedroom door, leaving Belle on the other side. Just in case.

» 13

Tessa, who'd spent all of Thursday and much of Friday morning unpacking boxes in her new kitchen and bedroom, looked around her living room, which still seemed to be full of boxes. How did she own this much stuff? She'd given away, it seemed to her, entire roomfuls of stuff before she left D.C., calling the Goodwill and Salvation Army to haul away truckloads of chairs and books and frying pans and throw pillows. Yet here was all this stuff.

It wasn't the most restful site for meditation, but Tessa nonetheless unfolded her mat. She hadn't meditated this morning; it would make a nice break now. She opened the window to the bracing cold air, faced the brass statue, and sat on her heels, hands on knees, spine straight and relaxed. Breathe...

The doorbell rang. Minette started her insane barking, and Tessa picked her up as she opened the door. Minette was always thrilled to see anyone. A visit from the FedEx man could send her into orgasm.

"Hi, I'm Pioneer Cable," said an impossibly young workman. "You had a one P.M. call for a new cable hook-up, but I got started early today so if it's okay with you..."

"Fine," Tessa said. "Want some coffee?"

"No, thanks, ma'am. I'm sort of in a hurry. Running behind schedule."

Tessa left him with his time contradictions in the living room, tethered the yipping Minette to the kitchen table, and made herself coffee. Then she checked her email for the third time today. One of Salah's unknown correspondents had answered her: pennj@amserve.net.

> Dear Tessa,
>
> I write in English for your convenience. I have heard not of Salah's death and it is very great shock to me. We have shared rooms at the Sorbonne, perhaps you know this. Also I have known him since a long time, when we were boys in Tunis. I am very sad to hear of his death. How has this occurred? Please tell me, if it is not too painful for you.
>
> I have written Salah last year because our classmate has written to me to ask for Salah's email address. I have written to Salah first to see if this is okay for him. Salah said yes, so I have given the address to our classmate, Richard Ebenfield, American. Richard writes not any Arabic. Neither Salah nor I have seen Richard since many, many years.
>
> I live now in London. Salah and I have promised to write to each other again but somehow we have not done this. Again, I am very sad to hear of this death. Please tell me what has occurred.
>
> Sincerely,
> Ruzbihan al-Ashan

Tessa closed her eyes. Salah had spoken occasionally of Ruzbihan. They had been great pals as children and at the Sorbonne but then, like many college friends, had drifted apart. No overt break, just living in different countries with different activities. And they were both still young, in their early forties only, there was lots of time. Until time had run out.

She wrote back to Ruzbihan, giving him the bare details of her husband's senseless death and adding a bit about their former life together.

Then she turned to Salah's laptop, still set up beside her own Toshiba, and scanned his files for "Richard Ebenfield." Nothing. Salah had evidently not referred to his old roommate specifically by name when he wrote back to Ruzbihan, or he had transliterated the name into Arabic. And Ebenfield, who would write in English, had apparently not contacted Salah even though he'd asked for Salah's address.

That left the other Arabic email correspondent to wonder about. He (she?) hadn't yet answered. And, of course, it was entirely possible that neither email had anything to do with Salah's and her names turning up on intelligence chatter in the MidEast. Tessa had been trained to follow all leads, but 95% of all leads turned out to be crap. Always. If Salah –

"All done, ma'am," the cable guy said, holding out a fistful of brochures. "You have all network stations, local station KJV-TV, plus – "

"That's okay, I'll read it later," Tessa said.

"If you don't mind my asking, what's that statue on that little table under the open window? I ask because it's, like, the only thing unpacked in there."

"It's a god, Natraja," Tessa said. "Shiva Dancing."

"What are you, Islam?"

Tessa stared at the nasty expression on the face of this bigoted, ignorant, probably racist kid. "No. Shiva is a Hindu god, one of many. Hindu, as in 'India.' Islam has only one God."

"Oh," he said, losing interest. "That'll be fifty-four dollars for installation plus the – "

"Just give me the bill. I can read," she snapped, and he blinked. They finished the transaction in silence and mutual dislike.

No chance of meditating after that. Not that Tessa hadn't gotten used to the attitude, ever since 9/11. The glances at Salah as he walked down the street in his beautiful business suits and Arab headdress. The murmur in restaurants. A certain kind of silence when Salah came home from work, his usually cheerful face clouded. She'd learned not to ask; he didn't like to discuss it. It was hardest when the silent attitude came from people that they'd considered friends, people who should have been sophisticated enough to know not only that not every Arab was a fundamentalist terrorist, but also that Tunisia had a long alliance with the United States. But, then, the fucking *FBI* hadn't seemed to know any better.

Now there *really* wasn't any chance of a quiet meditation. Not until she cleared her mind. She threw on her coat and untethered Minette. "Let's go for a walk, baby. Too bad you didn't bite that cable bastard."

Minette, hearing no word but "walk," went into paroxysms of joy.

The afternoon was clear, windless, still in the forties. Minette trotted forward on her short legs, thrilled to be outside. A dog's life was so simple: If you like it, lick it. If you don't like it, growl at it. If it smells interesting, pee on it.

A few early crocuses poked green shoots above the earth. Winter sunlight touched the treetops with pale gold. Tessa breathed deeply of the crisp air. Maybe this move would be okay, would help her "adjust." Whatever that meant. Tyler was a pretty place, and so peaceful after D.C. No traffic on her side street, no people crowding her, nothing moving anywhere at all, which now that she thought about it seemed a bit odd –

A police car rounded the corner and the patrolman rolled down his window, his face exhausted and incredulous. "Ma'am – what are you doing?"

"I'm walking my dog," Tessa said. At the Bureau she'd joined in all the usual jokes about inept locals, the run-of-the-mill assumption that federal agents were superior to small-town cops. She hadn't really believed it. Some locals were good, some weren't – just like agents. Still, for this guy to ask such an obvious question –

He said, "Return home immediately with that animal, ma'am, and keep it inside. The mayor has issued an off-the-streets order for all dogs, effective immediately. I guess you didn't hear about it."

"An off-the-streets order? Why?"

He stared at her, and Tessa realized what he saw: a person so out-of-it, so friendless, that no one had called her to tell her whatever this was about. She said in her most professional voice, "I just moved here from D.C., officer. Please tell me what's happened."

"Some kind of disease turning dogs vicious. The CDC is here. Get inside *now*."

Tessa saw that was all she was going to get from him. She walked the half-block home; he didn't move until she'd closed her front door. Tessa turned on CNN, sat on her meditation mat, and watched for ten minutes, Minette on her lap.

Nothing. But hadn't the cable guy mentioned a local station.... She fiddled with the remote until she found it.

" – since this morning. This is Tyler Community Hospital," said a carefully made-up blonde in an unbuttoned parka, a large building behind her, "where the worst of the dog bite victims are being treated. Ten people have already died, seven of them children. Four more are in critical condition. Law enforcement authorities admit to being stymied. Specialists from the CDC in Atlanta, KJV has just learned, have now arrived in Tyler. Stay with us as we follow this breaking story. Meanwhile, the Truman High School Scorpions last night edged out the – "

Tessa stared at the television. A plague among dogs? *Dogs?*

She made a move toward the phone, then stopped. She was no longer an FBI agent. She no longer had access, or rights, to breaking knowledge about threats to the public welfare. She had made that choice.

Bag that. This was her town, as of three weeks ago. And she didn't need the Bureau to find out what was going on in it. Her coat was still on; she closed and locked the window, grabbed her keys and gun.

Minette, quiet now, watched sadly as Tessa left.

» 14

Ed Dormund peered out the kitchen window. The Samoyeds weren't visible anywhere in the fenced yard. They'd gone either into their dog house or around to the west side of the house, which had only one small window set into the wall of what Cora called her "crafts room." Ed didn't know what she actually did in there, and he didn't care. But he cared where the dogs had gotten to.

Cora sat slumped over coffee at the dirty kitchen table. "Stop pacing, you're making me sick."

"That hangover is making you sick."

"Like you should talk. You drink more than I do. And if you ever hit me again I'll – "

"You'll do what?" Ed was barely listening; this was old ground. Where the hell were the dogs?

The phone rang and Cora answered. "Yeah?... Oh, hi." She listened, laughed shortly, and said, "Yeah, right, whatever."

"Who was that?" Ed finally said when it was clear she wasn't going to tell him, just to make him ask.

"Old Man Lassiter next door."

"What'd he want?"

Cora smirked, making him wait. Eventually she said, "He said he heard from somebody that there's some kind of plague going around, a disease that turns dogs vicious, so we should keep ours locked up. Ain't that a hoot? Some people will believe anything. Probably afraid that little Spic mutt of his will bite his finger."

Despite himself, Ed laughed. Then he scowled at Cora and went to see if he could spot Jake and Petey and Rex from the craft-room window.

Del Lassiter hung up the phone. Brenda had gone back to bed after lunch. The chemo really tired her out. Del was glad she hadn't woken when Rod Gregory had called to tell Del about the dog plague.

A *dog plague*...How could such a thing happen? Was it even true? Dogs?

Del gazed at Folly, chewing on a miniature rawhide bone on the floor. All at once the Chihuahua looked up and sniffed the air. As she rose to her feet, her entire fawn-colored body started to quiver.

"Cold, girl?" But the kitchen wasn't cold. Ever since Brenda had been diagnosed, Del kept the house at 78°, day and night. Chihuahuas shivered when cold, but also when excited, nervous, or scared.

Folly sniffed the air again and began to howl.

Ellie opened her bedroom door. The Greyhounds rushed up to her, Butterfly jumping to lay paws on Ellie's shoulders and lick her face, the other four crowding close.

"Good morning, good morning!"

Morning indeed. Ellie had gone back to sleep and slept the morning away, which was disgraceful. She was on the four-to eleven shift today as a customer service rep for the insurance company, so she wasn't late for work, but even so...

Song dashed away and returned with her favorite toy, a much-slobbered-over football. Chimes licked Ellie's hand. Music barked to go out. Ellie tried to attend to all of them at once, laughing at their antics. Scornfully she thought of her co-workers at the office, yammering on about TV shows and dates and clubbing in D.C. Who needed inane sitcoms or cheating men or noisy clubs? She had everything she wanted right here, with her precious friends whose lives she had saved.

Ellie opened the door to let the dogs out into the backyard. Somewhere a siren began to sound, but she barely noticed.

Steve Harper sat in his bedroom, listening to the phone ring. It was his mother, and he should answer it. She'd lost Davey, too, and he should be there for her. But he couldn't. He couldn't do anything but sit here, seeing over and over again the same image, *the brown mastiff with a single long string of saliva and blood hanging from its mouth onto Davey's body...*

Steve put his hands over his face. The phone went on ringing and ringing.

» 15

Allen Levy sat watching TV in the family room, waiting for 3:00, the remains of his lunch on a plate beside him. At 2:57, his mother bustled in. "Allen, it's time for my show."

"Oh, Mom, *pleeeessssse!* I'm right in the middle of *Star Wars!* Look!"

"You've seen it before, and you know I only watch this *one* show, Allen. *Star Wars* can wait an hour."

"No, it can't, I haven't seen it before, we never got the DVD, Jimmy gave it to me! *Pleeeessse!* I'm so bored!"

Mrs. Levy frowned. "This isn't like you, Allen. As I said, I only watch one show every day and – "

"Then can I go outside to play? It's so nice out, look!"

Allen pointed to the window, but his mother just kept gazing at him. He tried to look pathetic. Finally she sighed. "All right, I'll watch TV upstairs. But you stay right here, you hear me? And turn it down a bit."

"Thanks, Mom!" Allen turned back to the screen and inched toward it happily. He didn't touch the sound. On screen, the Sith blew up something.

When his mother had gone upstairs, he waited a few minutes. She didn't come down. She'd been watching her afternoon show, which seemed to involve grown-ups crying and screaming at each other a lot, as long as Allen could remember. It was very important to her. Allen crept quietly from the family room to the basement door.

He couldn't hear Susie through the door. All night he'd heard her, whimpering and barking because she wasn't where she was supposed to be, at the foot of Allen's bed. Instead she was locked in the basement, where it was dark and cold. She might even have eaten all her food by now. Allen's mother said she'd given Susie a lot of food, but his mother didn't always tell him the truth. Just last week she said Allen couldn't go over to his friend Jimmy's to play because Jimmy's mother had the flu, but the truth was that Jimmy's mother was drunk again. Jimmy had told him later.

"Susie," Allen whispered through the door. Nothing. He tried again, louder, hoping the noise from *Star Wars* covered him. "Susie!" Still nothing.

What if she really was sick from this dog disease? Then they should take her to the doctor, get her the right medicine. Not just leave her lying alone down there on the cement floor! What if she was dying, all alone?

Tears filled Allen's eyes. He tried the doorknob, but the cellar door was locked. Quickly, before he could think about it, he opened the front door and slipped outside.

It was cold out but not too bad, and anyway he didn't care. The sun was warm. Allen rounded the house, ducked behind the bushes, and put his face smack up against a basement window.

Susie lay on an old blanket his father must have put there, and for a heart-freezing moment Allen thought she was dead. But then she heard him, jumped to her feet, and gazed upward at the small window, her short tail wagging joyously. Through the glass, Allen heard her give her happy bark.

But her water dish was empty. That wasn't right! Dogs had to have water, everybody knew that. And Allen's father wasn't due home until after dark. Allen put his hand on the window glass, hesitated, and then pushed. The window, too, was locked.

Again he thought he might cry. Breaking a window was a sin, for sure. But so was punishing a dog that hadn't done anything wrong, that might even die if she didn't get water. Which sin was bigger?

Well, *duh.*

He went back inside, then returned. It took only one swing with his baseball bat to break a different window, one in the laundry part of the cellar, which was separate from the part Susie was in. Allen held his breath but his mother didn't come. Even from outside he could hear *Star Wars* playing loudly. With the blanket he'd brought from the house wrapped around his arm, he pushed all the rest of the broken glass away from the window, then dropped the blanket over the pieces of glass on top of the dryer. That's the way they did it on *Law & Order.* Allen slid onto the dryer and jumped onto the floor.

Susie was thrilled to see him! He hugged her, filled her water dish, and gave her the Cheerios he'd saved in his pocket from breakfast. Then he left the cocker spaniel in her part of the basement, carefully closed the door to the laundry-room part, and wriggled back up through the window.

A half-hour later his mother came downstairs. "How you doing, sweetie? Is *Star Wars* over?"

"Oh, I turned it off," Allen said. "It was boring."

» 16

In the early winter dusk Jess pulled the truck into the parking lot of the Cedar Springs Motel. The motel had no cedars and no springs. What it did have was the CDC. The motel was located just outside town on what passed for a highway, which made it easy to reach from D.C. – or, at least, as easy as anything else in Tyler. The motel's wide parking lot overflowed with vehicles. The largest was the CDC mobile lab, which had extended itself with an accordion-like structure to twice its traveling length. It looked intimidating, like some giant alien metallic worm.

In a field across the road, kept there by two scowling cops, were reporters from KJV-TV and a few newspapers. So far, Jess noted, no national media, although that wouldn't be far behind. "Goddamn vultures," Billy said, without rancor. "But hey, look at that babe with the microphone – isn't that Annie Farnham from the ten o'clock news?"

"I don't know," Jess said. "If it is, she probably knows more than we do at this point."

"Well, that's why we're here, right? Check in, get all the poop? And drop off the dogs, of course. Man, even in that coat, she's got tits out to here."

One of the cops – Jess saw that it was young Brian Carby – waved the animal-control truck through. Jess threaded his way among the huge CDC mobile lab, a sheriff's patrol car, and a black stretch limo with D.C. plates that hadn't been there on his last trip in. He parked behind the motel. Any dogs in the back of the truck that hadn't already been snarling and barking started up again.

"I'm going to find out if the protocol's changed," Jess said to Billy. "Can you start unloading the smaller cages by yourself?"

"Sure thing." Billy pulled on thickly padded handler's gloves and hopped out. "Still put the cages in rooms 10 and 11?"

"Far as I know," Jess said, although rooms 10 and 11 had been filling up fast. "We're going to need more help, Billy. Maybe we can get some citizen volunteers, like we did for that deer thinning two years ago. How about Miguel Del Toro? He breeds dogs."

"He got bit this morning."

"Jesus," Jess said. He went along the back of the motel to room 1, designated "critical-incident headquarters," a term that sounded to Jess as if the dogs were all hostages. The double beds had been removed and tables brought in from other rooms. Computers, faxes, and printouts covered most surfaces.

"Jess," Dr. Latkin said, looking as fresh and intense as he had this morning, "I'm glad to see you. Any changes out there?"

What had he expected to change? Jess said, "No. We just brought in sixteen more dogs. Six benign but on the street, four from reported bites, six who haven't bitten anybody but are showing unusual signs of aggression, so their owners called in. Billy's putting them in rooms 10 and 11."

"No space left. The animal control people we borrowed from Flatsburgh were just here. We're using rooms 8 and 9 now, 8 for infected, 9 for benign."

"I'll tell Billy."

"I'll go with you," Dr. Latkin said. "I want to see the infected dogs. We have a new symptom. First, though, let me introduce you to Joanne Flaherty from the White House. Joanne, this is the Tyler animal control officer, Jess Langstrom."

Jess shook hands, studying her. Thirties, carefully groomed, overdressed for Tyler in the sort of expensive red suit Jess associated with Nancy Reagan. Undoubtedly she had come in the limo, which was also overdressed for Tyler, and that was her uniformed driver reading the *Post* in the corner. Jess had never heard of Joanne Flaherty, which meant exactly nothing. *"From the While House"* could mean anything from the Chief of Staff down to a run-of-the-mill flunky. Although if she had an important title, Latkin would probably have used it.

She said, "I'm here at the direct request of Terence Porter, Mr. Langstrom. He'd like my assessment of your situation here in Tyler, and I'd like yours."

Reasonable, straight-forward...except that Jess had never heard of Terence Porter and this woman's tone was so self-important, her smile so condescending. It conveyed that the president was waiting breathlessly in the Oval Office for Joanne Flaherty's report, and that Jess was incredibly fortunate that his opinion would be part of it. She...oh, shit, those perceptions all might just be Jess himself. His own prejudices. He didn't like politicians.

"Ms. Flaherty, I don't know what I can tell you that Dr. Latkin hasn't. I think it's only going to get worse here. There are a lot of dogs in Tyler, and I hear a lot of them snarling and barking, shut up in garages and basements. People will call for us to go get them, or the dogs will get loose, or the owners will get bitten when they try to feed them. We're running out of room to put the ones we have rounded up. I think – oh, shit!"

Ms. Flaherty and Dr. Latkin both looked startled by Jess's outburst, as well they might. A television sat in one corner, volume on mute, and Jess had seen Billy walk on screen, pounced on by the blonde KJV-TV reporter. Jess said, "Excuse me, that's my assistant, he shouldn't be talking to reporters, I didn't tell him that because I never thought he – "

"Saul," Dr. Latkin said to a young man hovering nearby, "get that animal control officer away from that reporter. Now."

"No, it's all right," Ms. Flaherty said, surprising both Jess and Dr. Latkin, who stared at her from his pale eyes. "Media attention on this is inevitable, I'm afraid. Mr. Langstrom, Dr. Latkin said it's your recommendation that we quarantine Tyler. Is that true?"

She leaned forward slightly on the balls of her feet, Jess noticed, almost like a fighter ready for a bout. She wanted not only media attention but a quarantine – why? It was almost enough to turn him away from the idea, but that was dumb. He said carefully, "I think it would be very difficult to do, but things will be more difficult if any of these dogs infect animals from Flatsburgh or Linville and the infection – is it an infection, Doctor?"

Latkin said, "We haven't isolated the pathogen from any of the dogs' brains yet, but we've only had nine hours so far."

Joanne Flaherty said, "Do you want more people on this, Doctor?"

Latkin blinked. Of course he wanted more people, Jess thought – government agencies always wanted more people on their projects. More people meant more support, more budget, more importance.

"If you think that's possible, Joanne."

"It may be. And once again, Mr. Langstrom, do you agree with Dr. Latkin that a quarantine is necessary here?"

"Yes," Jess said, at the same moment that Latkin said, "I'm not sure I'm ready to go on record at this point as definitely – "

"Good," she said. "Doctor, may I see the mobile lab now? I have to be back in Washington in an hour and a half. The White House is expecting me."

Which, again, could mean anything. Jess didn't like Joanne Flaherty. Not that it mattered; he would never see her again. He walked to the TV and turned up the volume just in time to hear Billy say, "Got her right between the eyes, Annie. At least one ol' bitch won't be biting any more kids. And your pretty little self is safer, too." Billy grinned lasciviously and Jess groaned.

"Please tell me who's in charge here," another voice said, and Jess turned to see another woman stride into the room, followed by a furious and very young sheriff's deputy that Jess didn't recognize.

"I'm sorry, sir, she just kept on walking and I didn't want to...says she's FBI."

"No, I said a 'former FBI agent' and now a citizen of Tyler and a dog owner, so naturally I want straight information and not rumors," the woman said. She had short black hair with gel-goop in it; the hair looked even blacker against her pale skin. Her gaze passed dismissingly over Joanne Flaherty and lighted unerringly on Latkin, which amused Jess. "Are you the principal investigator from the CDC?"

"Dr. Joseph Latkin. But this is a restricted area, ma'am. You'll have to leave."

"Certainly," Tessa said, "as soon as you tell me what's going on here, and how I can best help. Are you deputizing citizens? I'm a former FBI agent with firearms training. Have you got a police officer to run my creds? Where's the critical-incident commander?" She held out various papers and a passport.

Latkin, irritated, said, "No one is deputizing citizens, ma'am, and –" at the same moment that Jess said, "I am."

He wasn't sure why he did it. They did need extra help, and an ex-FBI agent would be as good as anyone, maybe better. But mostly it was because he disliked Joanne Flaherty and because even Latkin, with his take-charge demeanor after less than a day in Tyler, was getting to Jess. Or maybe he was just tired.

The woman smiled at him, the first time he'd seen her do that. Five-foot-six, maybe 140 pounds, a lot of muscle. She wore jeans, an open jacket, and a wedding ring. Jess would bet she was packing. Somehow she had that look.

Latkin said, frowning, "I don't think –"

"No, it's fine," Joanne Flaherty said briskly. "Local law enforcement often recruits other branches of law enforcement during crises. The aftermath of Hurricane Katrina, for instance." She seemed pleased, which disappointed Jess. It puzzled him, too. She seemed to want as big a show as possible – why?

Jess turned to his brand new deputy. "Sheriff just pulled in. He can run your creds. Why are you ex-FBI?"

"Quit. Personal reasons."

"You have to sign a liability waiver."

"Of course."

"You have any experience with dogs?"

"Some."

That could mean anything. But she wouldn't have to do much except help lift cages and take reports, riding with Jess or Billy. He looked at her again. Not a raving beauty, but pretty enough. She better not ride with Billy.

"What's your name?"

"Tessa Sanderson," she said.

INTERIM

Deputy Chief of Staff Terence Porter looked up irritably from his desk in the West Wing of the White House. It was eight P.M. *and he would have liked to go home, but the president was still working in the Oval and that meant everybody was working late. "Yes, Kathy?"*

"Joanne Flaherty is still waiting to see you," his secretary said.

"Who?"

"Joanne Flaherty. You sent her out to Tyler this afternoon."

"Oh, right. Well...all right, show her in."

Flaherty bustled in. The deputy rose. "I'm sorry you had to wait, Joanne. We're right in the middle of–well, it's always something. You know," he said, including her among those who knew, smiling wryly. The deputy was known for his charm.

"Oh, yes, of course," she said cozily, and he remembered why he disliked her. "But I think you'll want to hear what's going on in Tyler. There's a real opportunity here, Terry."

It was not her place to tell him what was an opportunity, and he had not asked her to use his first name. He folded his arms across his chest and waited. Oblivious, she told her story. When she finished, he said, "Well, that's interesting. Thank you, Joanne, I appreciate your effort." He smiled and sat down, busying himself with papers on his desk.

"But...shall I go back to Tyler tomorrow?"

"No, that's all right. Good night, and thanks again."

Flustered and angry, she left. The deputy picked up the phone and asked to see the Chief of Staff. Ten minutes later he was shown into Hugh Martin's office. "Hugh, something I think we should pay attention to. An opportunity."

"What's that?" Hugh Martin, the president's long-time friend and former campaign manager, had one of the best political minds of his generation. He could, the Washington whispers went, have gotten a chicken sandwich elected president if he'd really wanted to. The president's detractors said that he already had.

The deputy repeated Joanne Flaherty's report on Tyler, adding, "This is a chance for FEMA *to redeem its reputation a bit, after that piss-poor perfor-*

mance with...well, you know. Send Scott Lurie down there, protect citizens proactively, better safe than sorry. The locals themselves are recommending quarantine, I checked on that, and some are being deputized, which really lends credence to their wanting help. And if there is any terrorist involvement – "

Hugh said sharply, "Any indication of that?"

"Not that I know of. But I can check with the intelligence director."

"Do that. And check with the intel agencies separately, too – communication inter-agency still isn't what it should be." Martin rose. "You come with me."

"Now?"

"He's wrapping up in there. We'll just take three minutes to brief him on Tyler, then I'll make the calls."

The deputy straightened his tie, ran his hand over his hair, and followed Hugh Martin into the Oval Office.

SATURDAY

» 17

When Cami Johnson woke early Saturday morning, having slept eleven hours straight, everything had changed.

She turned on KJV-TV on the small television on her dresser. The station was doing a weather report. She switched to CNN, not expecting much, and saw with a shock that Janet Belville stood in the lobby of Tyler Community Hospital. Cami, near-sighted without her contacts, rushed to the screen and practically pressed her nose against it. Yes, that was the hospital lobby, the gift shop behind Janet, the reception desk, the bright arrows on the walls pointing to the cafeteria, to the lab, to the pharmacy. Two men in uniform took hold of Janet's elbows and began walking her forward.

"– forced to leave this emergency situation by FEMA, in control here in Tyler since six A.M. this morning. Although I want to emphasize again –" a camera followed her as she was eased toward the door "– that no one is actually leaving Tyler until the CDC has determined how contagious this pathogen may be, both to animals and to humans. 'Nobody out,' was the terse statement from FEMA critical-incident manager Scott Lurie. This is the same Lurie who came under heavy fire last year for his handling of –" The uniformed men pushed her through the door.

Cami put her hand to her mouth. Scott Lurie, she vaguely remembered, was the head of FEMA, or maybe of Homeland Security. Or something. And Janet Belville was one of the CNN reporters who usually covered *wars*. And 'Nobody out'? How bad was the situation at the hospital? Cami better get over there right away. This was supposed to be her day off but it sounded as if they were going to need all the ER help they could find. She threw on scrubs, ran a comb through her hair, and opened the bedroom door to go brush her teeth.

Belle stood in the hallway, snarling.

For the long moment before she slammed the door, Cami stood still, in shock. Belle! The gentlest dog in the world... Belle, infected and ready to attack!

The gentlest dog in the world, but also the frailest. And Cami had a job to do.

She yanked the quilted comforter off her bed, opened the door again, and threw the thick spread over Belle. The dog growled and thrashed, but she was old and arthritic and couldn't get free. With one strong tug Cami rolled Belle over, hauled the quilt through to the bedroom, and closed Belle in. As she grabbed her car keys and purse, Cami could hear her pet working her way out of the comforter, barking and snapping. Cami ran out of the apartment. Belle had had access to food and water all night; she would be all right in the bedroom until Cami could figure out what to do next about her.

But in the hallway she stopped at 2-B. Last night she really hadn't explained the whole situation to Mr. Anselm – well, to be fair, she hadn't known the whole situation. She still didn't! But if he tried to go outside, walk to the store or anything... Cami knocked on the door.

No answer. Had he already gone out? Oh, God, if he had just his cane and Captain...the police were rounding up dogs. They might even be euthanizing them. But it would be worse if Mr. Anselm had gone out with just his cane. He did that sometimes. Then he'd have nothing to warn him of any strays.

Cami knocked louder. "Mr. Anselm! Are you there?"

Still no sound from within. They must have both gone out. Maybe there was some clue as to where they'd gone, an empty milk carton in the sink or something. If she knew, she could try to find him before she reported in to work. Cami tried the doorknob; it turned under her hand. She opened the door and went in.

Captain waited at his usual place just inside the door, his seeing-eye harness buckled on. Briefly he looked past Cami as a door opened somewhere in the corridor behind her and someone shouted. Cami herself barely had time to glimpse Mr. Anselm's body, the throat torn out, before the German shepherd sprang onto her and she went down.

» 18

Tessa stood brushing her teeth in the living room, grimacing around the toothbrush at the stupidity on the TV. Jess Langstrom wasn't going to pick her up until 7:00 A.M. and it was only 6:00, but she couldn't sleep. Last night it had taken the local cops two solid hours to clear her credentials, and by that time an exhausted Langstrom had gone home to sleep, which apparently he hadn't been doing too much of. The delay in a critical situation was enough to make Tessa drastically lower her opinion of locals – not that the FBI hadn't done the same thing too many times, God knows. In fact, the only people acting decisively seemed to be FEMA, who were erring in the other direction, for once. That idiot Scott Lurie had actually called Tyler "a possible act of terrorism." Terrorism! Give me a break. There was no evidence of that, none whatsoever, and of the newscasts Tessa had scanned so far, only Janet Belville of CNN seemed to acknowledge and recognize that fact.

FEMA, of course, was simply exploiting this mutated virus, or whatever it was, to counterbalance their dismal performance in last year's California earthquake. But Tessa had been watching TV for an hour and had heard no contradictions from the FBI, CIA, Homeland Security, or the White House. Bernini and Maddox must be tearing their eyes out at being muffled like this.

The problem with working counter-terrorism, Tessa had long since learned, was the tendency to see anything that happened in terrorist terms. An Amtrak train hits a cow and derails – was it a "deliberate disruption of transport"? Was that top adviser's suicide actually an assassination? She knew of CT agents who suspected that levees breached by a hurricane were the work of al-Qaeda.

"What do you think, Minette?" Tessa asked the toy poodle, who stared at her disdainfully and walked to the front door to be let out. Tessa scooped her up and carried her, protesting, to the back door. They slipped outside, where Minette piddled and shit before immediately being carried back in.

Tessa had no fear of Minette's being infected. Since coming to Tyler three weeks ago, Minette had had zero interaction with any other dogs, not even so much as a friendly butt sniff. Unless this thing were airborne, of course, in which case the entire country was in deep trouble indeed. But nothing Tessa had seen, read, or pried out of Jess Langstrom indicated that.

She still had nearly an hour until he showed up. Tessa meditated briefly and unsatisfactorily, then checked her email. Still no reply from Salah's second, unknown correspondent. Maybe she could have his or her original email translated from Arabic. She printed it out, finishing just as Jess's truck pulled up. Tessa shoved the paper into her jeans pocket and ran outside.

"Morning," Jess said grimly. He looked a little better than last night, but not much. Weariness shadowed his eyes and deepened the lines from nose to chin. He hadn't shaved and his beard, darker than the thick salt-and-pepper hair on his head, gave him the disreputable look of a parka-clad pirate. He had a nice voice, though, deep and calm even when he sounded grim.

"Good morning," Tessa said. "What's on the agenda?"

"FEMA's here, setting up a quarantine around the whole town."

"So I saw on CNN. Why do you look so disapproving? I thought it was your idea."

"It was. But I wasn't envisioning this kind of circus." He started the truck. "It's like they're deliberately fanning the panic."

"They are," Tessa said. "It's a political opportunity." He didn't know that? "FEMA consistently comes under fire for focusing on terrorism at the expense of natural disasters. Lurie will try to change that perception by playing this dog thing for all it's worth."

Jess shrugged. "If you say so. Today I have new orders. We're not just answering calls anymore, we're picking up every single dog in Tyler township and bringing them in. That's 1,402 dogs, according to the dog licenses issued last year. Here, take the list of addresses, courtesy of our town clerk."

"People are just going to hand over their pet dogs?"

"Some are, some aren't."

"Who else is going to help collect all those dogs? And where are you going to put them all?"

Jess waved at a passing cop car. "This Scott Lurie has brought in teams of dog handlers, animal control officers, vets, and qualified temporary deputies. We start by taking all the animals to the motel, and then they get them ferried to wherever after that."

"You have 1,402 crates?"

"Well, not on me," Jess said, but he didn't smile. "FEMA's getting them, I guess. They're getting whatever they want. And now they're jawing about this being a terrorist attack." He glanced sideways, as if to see the effect of this on her.

"I know," Tessa said.

"You don't miss much, do you?"

She said quietly, "I was an FBI agent."

Maybe he picked up her tone – *Don't ask me any questions* – because he said nothing until they turned down a long driveway bordered by trees. Then he changed the subject. "Dr. Latkin told me this morning that there's a new symptom. The infected dogs are developing a sort of milky film over both eyes. He thinks it means the pathogen might be affecting the endocrine system that affects the tear-duct system, or something like that. I didn't quite get it all, but we're supposed to watch out for milky eye films even if the dogs act normally."

"Okay," Tessa said. "Are the dogs actually going blind?"

"I don't know. Anyway, the strategy is for the pick-up teams to start at the edges of town and work inward, to keep animals from escaping."

The house at the end of the long driveway was impressive: stone and brick, three stories, covered with dormant ivy. Jess said, "Mr. and Mrs. James Gorman. A male Lab and a female Irish setter."

Tessa said, "I'll bet they're named Brandy and Whiskey. Rich people like to give their dogs alcoholic names." Jess laughed reluctantly.

Mr. and Mrs. Gorman were both home and neither was happy. "Are you here about this ridiculous rule that if I go to my office I can't return to Tyler tonight?" James Gorman demanded. He wore a business suit and carried a briefcase, standing in his black-and-white-marble foyer as if already in his office.

"No, sir, we're from Animal Control," Jess said. "We're required to take temporary custody of your two dogs until further notice. The animals will be well cared for, unharmed, and returned to you as soon as it's safe."

The Gormans exchanged stupefied looks. Tessa wondered what they'd thought the two wire cages sitting on the porch were for. Mrs. Gorman, a carefully groomed blonde still in her housecoat, said, "Take Schnapps and Applejack?"

"Yes, ma'am," Jess said.

"Now, see here –" Mr. Gorman began, but Tessa interrupted him.

"By order of the president of the United States, Mr. Gorman."

He stopped protesting, glared at her, and stomped off. Jess shot her an admiring glance: *Where did you learn to do that?* She said again, "I was an FBI agent," behind the Gormans' retreating backs.

Mrs. Gorman said over her shoulder, "Come this way, please." Her tone had faded from outraged to distant, as if Jess and Tessa were two more routine workmen, plumbers or refrigerator repairmen.

The dogs were in a guest room on the first floor. Jess went in with padded gloves and face mask, but neither animal seemed infected. They wagged their well-groomed tails at Jess, and dog biscuits lured them easily into the wire crates. Jess tagged the cages and carried them to the truck while Tessa filled out the paperwork. She would have bet her Smith & Wesson that someone at FEMA had invented this form overnight and run off a few thousand copies on a photocopier someplace. Emergency situations tended to generate paper, like a bonfire throwing off sparks.

"That was easy enough," she said to Jess as the truck pulled away, Schnapps and Applejack content in the back.

"They won't all be," he said, his face grim. "You can assist at the next stop but not at the one after that. You stay in the truck on that one, Tessa."

In a pig's eye. She wasn't here to sit in a truck.

So why was she here, other than the purely patriotic desire to help out her country in a time of natural disaster, yadda yadda and so forth?

"Jess, do you happen to read Arabic?"

He shot her an incredulous look. "*Arabic?* No. Why would you ask that?"

"No reason," she said.

» 19

Allen was good at sneaking into rooms and listening to his parents before they realized he was there. It was the only way he ever learned some important things. Like, when his Aunt Nicole died at college from a drug overdose, Allen's mother didn't even tell him for two days and then she said Aunt Nicole was hit by a car. You couldn't trust grown-ups to tell you the truth about anything.

So now he stood in the kitchen in his pajamas, hand on the refrigerator door so he could say he just came downstairs for a glass of milk, and listened to his parents in the dining room.

"Don't go, Peter," his mother said. "The office can do without you for one day! If you leave, they won't let you back into Tyler, and Allen and I will be here all alone!"

"You're overreacting again," Allen's father said coldly. "You and Allen are in no danger as long as you stay indoors and out of the basement until the authorities come for the dog. I'm needed at the office, even though once again you're dismissing my importance to the firm...I wish you would stop that, Amy. It's I who supports this family, after all."

"But if – "

"I can stay overnight at Tim's if I have to, or find a hotel."

"Are you sure it's Tim you'd be staying with?" Allen's mother said in her dangerous voice. But the words barely registered on Allen. "*Until the authorities come for the dog*"! They were going to take Susie away somewhere, maybe kill her like they did to sick dogs at the pound!

His father said, "That was uncalled for, Amy, and I think you know it. I told you that other thing is all over. If you don't choose to believe me, that's your problem." A moment later, the front door closed.

Allen was sure his mother would rush past him now toward the stairs, but she didn't. He heard the phone in the kitchen make its faint musical notes and then she said shakily, "Linda? It's me. You won't believe the scene we just...I can't take any more of this, I really can't, he – "

Allen crept back upstairs and dressed as fast as he could. In his parents' bathroom he balanced on the laundry hamper and took the drug bottle from the top shelf of the medicine cabinet, behind the Listerine. He put it in his pocket. In his own room he added a Reese's Peanut Butter Cup that Jimmy had given him. Allen wasn't allowed candy at his house. Silently he padded back downstairs in his socks. His mother was still on the phone with her friend, so he couldn't use the kitchen door.

Easing open the front door, Allen winced at the noise it made. But she didn't notice.

"– bad enough about his sluts, but at least at *home* he used to treat me as if –"

The morning was colder than yesterday. Allen shivered as he slipped around the house to the broken window. Probably all the heat in the house was rushing out the window and heating the whole outdoors – that's what his father said whenever his mother opened a window. But this was different. This was an emergency.

He slid down onto the dryer and then jumped to the floor. A shard of glass pierced his foot and he cried out. But he could take care of that later. Right now Susie was what mattered.

She lay beside her empty dishes on the old blanket. Daddy hadn't even given her more water! Well, she wouldn't need it now. Allen crouched behind her, petting her long silky ears, and she wagged her tail and put her head on his knee. It was then that he noticed her eyes: sort of unfocused and covered with white stuff like spilled milk.

"Poor Susie, you're getting so old," he whispered, hugging her fiercely. "But I still love you, Suze."

Susie licked his hand. Allen took the candy from his pocket and unwrapped it. Susie got eagerly to her feet, tail wagging harder. "Just a minute, Suze. Good dog."

He opened the pill bottle: PHENOBARBITAL. How much should Susie have? Allen wasn't even sure how many his mother took to put herself to sleep. However, Susie was a lot smaller than his mother. He better start with one and see what happened.

He poked the pill into the peanut butter cup and Susie gobbled it eagerly. Allen sat stroking her until she fell asleep. Then he pushed her onto the blanket and dragged it across the basement to the tall filing cabinet in the corner. The bottom drawer, labeled TAX INFO 2000-2005, was full of papers. Allen cleaned them out and stuffed them into a box with fake Christmas garlands. He lifted Susie in her blanket into the drawer and closed it, leaving a tiny slit for air. She just fit. And with her eyes closed, he couldn't see that weird milky white stuff in her eyes.

He was careful to leave the laundry-room door open. When the pound people came, they'd think that Susie had escaped through the window. Allen climbed through it himself, crept quietly through the bushes, and sneaked back inside the house.

Sometimes his mother slept for ten hours after she took those pills. Maybe by that time the pound people would have come and gone. If not, Allen would think up something else.

He was good at thinking things up. The way he figured it, he had to be, or he'd never get his own way in this house. Not at all, ever.

» 20

Jess and Tessa walked up the porch of the old farmhouse and rang the bell. Jess noticed that she put the extra-large cage on the floor of the porch and held her hands loose and free, even though he'd told her there was no danger here. Sunlight flashed suddenly on her wedding ring. Did her husband know she'd volunteered for this deputizing? Did he mind?

The door was opened by a little girl with bright red hair in pigtails. She took one look at the cages and burst into loud wails. "No, no, you can't take them! *Nnooooo!*"

An old woman hobbled from the kitchen. "Jess, I'm sorry, I *told* her, but she – oh, dear!"

Jess knelt down and tried to put his arms around Hannah but she pushed him away. "You can't take them!"

"I have to, dear heart," he said gently. "But I promise I'll watch over them with extra special care. And maybe it will only be for a little while."

Hannah cried, "You're mean and I hate you! I hate you forever!" and ran out of the room.

"I am sorry, Jess. I tried to explain it to her, but...I did try."

"It's all right, Aunt Kitty," Jess said. His throat hurt. "Where are they?"

"In the basement. I thought it best."

"Come on, Tessa," Jess said, leading the way. He drew his gun, just in case, but Aunt Kitty had said there was no change in behavior, and what Aunt Kitty didn't know about living creatures wasn't worth knowing.

She'd handled farm animals for seventy years.

"'Aunt Kitty'?" Tessa said behind him. He heard the cage thump against the stairwell wall and guessed she was carrying it one-handed, the other still free.

"My great aunt. Hannah was visiting her great-grandma when FEMA put up this quarantine, and now she can't return to her parents, who are frantic in D.C. Aunt Kitty told me all this on the phone this morning. She – there you are, Missy!"

The collie lay in a big, low-sided box beside the furnace, nursing four mongrel puppies. She wagged her tail at Jess, regarding him trustingly from big eyes the color of caramels. The eyes were unclouded. Missy let him pick up all four puppies, which looked like the father might have had some German shepherd in him, and transfer them to a towel on the floor of the cage. Then Missy followed them inside, lay down, and resumed nursing.

"Too bad they're not all this docile," Tessa said.

"Then we wouldn't have a plague, would we? There, Missy, good girl, good dog."

Tessa said abruptly, "Do you have a dog?"

"No."

"I do."

Jess rose so fast that Missy shifted uneasily. "You have a dog? And you didn't think to mention this before? Where is it?"

"I'm mentioning it now," Tessa said evenly. "It's in my house. She's a toy poodle, about as menacing as a gerbil, and she has not encountered any other dogs in Tyler since I moved her three weeks ago. Zero. Zilch. None."

"That doesn't exempt you from bringing her in with the others, as I suspect you know very well. Was that why you volunteered to be deputized? So you could evade the rules?"

"If I wanted to do that, I wouldn't be telling you about her now, would I? She's not on your county list because she's still licensed in D.C. Don't tell me how to obey the law, Jess Langstrom. I was an FBI agent."

"But you're not now, are you?" he said pointedly. She turned and walked up the stairs.

He followed with the cage, set it in the truck with Schnapps and Applejack, and went back inside. Tessa sat at the kitchen table with Aunt Kitty, completing the quarantine form. Aunt Kitty said, "Would you two like some coffee and cake before you go on? I just baked it this morning."

"I'm sorry, we can't," Jess said. "Short on time."

"And temper," Tessa added sweetly. "Good-bye, Mrs. Jamison. It was a pleasure to meet you."

"You too, dear."

In the truck Tessa demanded, "What was that all about in there?"

"Nothing," Jess said shortly. "Forget it."

They drove in silence, Jess wondering: What *had* all that been about in there? Yes, she hadn't told him upfront about her dog. Yes, years of Billy had made him suspicious of even simple omissions because they usually meant greater omissions. Yes, he realized that his insistence on deputizing her, just to get back at an officious politician and an M.D., who made him feel inferior, had been childish, and the realization made him feel dumb. But all that wasn't really it. The problem was that Jess was attracted to her, and not only was she married, but he didn't want to be attracted to anybody. Not since Elizabeth, not ever again.

"What is this place?" Tessa said as he stopped the truck at the road. "I don't see a house."

"It's back there." Jess waved at the faint dirt track leading back from a battered mailbox. "Here is the place we meet my partner."

She looked confused, as well she might. A very dirty white van pulled up, Billy at the wheel with a man beside him. From the van, unlike Jess's truck, came howling and barking. Billy jumped out, grinning. "Hey, Jess, how you doing so far? This is Ken Pilton from Flatsburgh, he's a new vet. Hey, Tessa."

Through the truck window Tessa gave Billy a do-I-know-you look. He didn't know her but obviously had heard about her, and that was enough for Billy. Ken Pilton, a nervous and bespectacled man in his early twenties, got out behind Billy. Jess took one look at him and made his decision. "Okay, Dr. Pilton, you stay here. You, too, Tessa – stay with the truck. We'll take the van. If we need you to do anything we'll call, so keep near the radio. If we don't come out in ten minutes, notify Sheriff DiBella. You got that?"

Pilton nodded. Tessa looked stony. Jess got behind the wheel.

Billy said, "You really think ol' Vic's going to open fire? He's nuts but he ain't that nuts."

"Are you positive about that?"

"No. Damn, if he lets those Rottweilers loose on us I'm gonna just purely enjoy plugging them. You remember when one of them mauled his girlfriend, that brunette waitress, last year?"

"I remember," Jess said. "Put on your helmet, Billy."

In full gear, they pulled up to Victor Balonov's ramshackle house. Rumors about Balonov formed one of Tyler's chief entertainments. A Russian immigrant, he was supposed to be former KGB, supposed to have tried to assassinate President Clinton in 1994, supposed to have been descended from tsarist royalty. Six four, three hundred pounds, he spoke broken English at the top of his lungs. The fish-and-game boys had arrested him twice for shooting deer out of season. At the second arrest, Balonov had set a Rottweiler on Sam Fields, which is how Jess became involved. The county list showed Balonov as owning two more Rottweilers, but Jess wouldn't have been surprised to find one, or three, or ten.

The dogs were clearly audible in the basement of the house. Jess and Billy waited in the van for Balonov to appear. When he didn't, they called out, then waited some more.

"Maybe the dogs got him already," Billy said.

"Maybe." It would solve a lot of problems. Finally Jess called through his bullhorn in his most soothing voice – although it was hard to sound soothing through a bullhorn – "Mr. Balonov, I'm Jess Langstrom from Animal Control. Please come out so we can talk to you."

Victor Balonov, in a parka suitable for crossing the Siberian tundra, finally appeared on the porch. Negligently, as if an afterthought, a twelve-gauge shotgun dangled from his right hand. From inside the van Jess repeated, "Mr. Balonov, I'm Jess Langstrom from Animal Control, and as you probably know we have orders from the government to bring in all dogs until this quarantine is over. Your animals will be well treated and will be returned to you when this is over. My partner and

I have cages in the back, safe and clean. The dogs will be treated with every respect."

"Yes, I know this," Balonov said in his heavy accent.

"You agree to let us take the dogs?"

"Yes. These dogs, a demon has entered into them."

This was a new wrinkle. Billy whistled low between his teeth. Jess, feeling helpless, said, "A demon?"

"Sometimes it happens, da? The demons of hell, they entered into pigs in the Bible."

Jess vaguely remembered something about possessed pigs in one of the Gospels – hadn't Jesus driven them off a cliff or something? This whole scene was starting to feel unreal. He said, "Mr. Balonov, please toss the shotgun off the porch into the bushes."

Balonov rose and Jess tensed. Billy had his gun already drawn. But Balonov tossed his weapon over the rotting porch rail into a mass of thorny, spindly, leafless rose bushes that might be either dormant or dead.

"Thank you," Jess said, and climbed reluctantly out of the van, Billy following. Keeping his eyes on Balonov every second, Jess opened the back of the van. Immediately the infected dogs within redoubled their snarling and barking, which caused the dogs inside the house to increase theirs. Over the noise Jess called, "How many dogs do you have, Mr. Balonov?"

"I have two. Two dogs with demons!"

Billy pulled out two cages. Balonov let them get halfway to the front steps before he pulled out a semi-automatic and fired.

Jess and Billy hit the ground rolling. Jess made it behind the truck, but Billy screamed, hit somewhere. Jess pulled out his own gun and took aim. He missed; he'd never been the shot that Billy was. Victor Balonov fired twice more at Billy, who kept rolling, and missed both times. How many rounds did the gun hold? Maybe eight, maybe ten. Jess fired again, missed. Now Balonov leapt down the steps, running toward Billy; he wouldn't miss again. "And demons in people!" Balonov shouted, and aimed. Jess, desperate, dodged around the truck to squeeze off another shot. No time, he didn't have enough time –

Balonov froze in midair, looking almost comical in his surprise, and toppled over onto Billy.

Jess looked at his gun. He hadn't fired.

Then he was running toward them just as Billy, cursing and shouting, was struggling out from under Balonov's motionless bulk, and Tessa was saying calmly from where she stood at the side of the house, "It's all right, Jess, he's dead." She stood in perfect regulation shooting stance, legs apart and two hands steady on her gun, the winter breeze gently ruffling her shiny black hair.

» 21

The bastards were coming for all the dogs and taking them away!

Ed Dormund scowled at the TV. That tit-heavy reporter, Annie Farnham, had just made the announcement on KJV-TV. Every dog in Tyler was supposed to be hauled off to God-knew-where, so the government could do whatever it wanted with them. And no people who left town could return. It was a goddamn fascist state, that's what it was. What was next, concentration camps for everybody who owned a pet?

Not if Ed Dormund had anything to say about it.

"I paid three hundred bucks for each of my dogs!" he said aloud, before he knew he was going to say anything at all.

"What?" Cora said blearily. "Can't you turn that damn TV down?"

"Nag, nag, nag. Go back in the bedroom if you don't like it."

"I got as much right to be here as you do." She plopped onto the sofa.

Ed ignored her. Outside, Jake and Petey and Rex had started to bark and snarl again. Ed didn't like to admit even to himself that he was afraid to open the door.

But that didn't matter. What mattered was that these dogs were *his*, and no pansy government was going to take them away. Ed knew his rights. This was supposed to be a free country, right?

Just let them try.

Del Lassiter opened the door to the two animal control officers. Brenda was asleep again, and Del hadn't told her what was happening. Time enough when she felt a little stronger.

He let the men in and handed over Folly, who looked miniscule in the cage they put her in. The Chihuahua looked at him reproachfully and started to shiver. Del had to turn away to hide the tears in his eyes.

The desk officer looked up as Steve Harper walked into the barracks. Steve saw the feelings flicker over Giametti's face: surprise then pity then the embarrassment people felt talking to somebody whose kid had died. Steve didn't give Giametti time to say anything dumb.

"I'm back for duty, Jack."

"But I thought – "

"I'm back for duty." Steve hoped his tone would end any objections here and now. He had to get back to work or go nuts, had to have something to do besides stare at the image in his brain. *The brown mastiff, a single long string of saliva and blood hanging from its mouth onto Davey's body...*

"Well, sure, okay," Giametti said uneasily. "We can use you. I'll call the sheriff."

"Good," Steve said.

Ellie Caine drove home as fast as she could, pushing red lights, peeling into her driveway. She'd heard the news at work and had instantly left her desk and raced to the parking lot.

It couldn't be true! No one would be so cruel as to take away her greyhounds, who had already had such crappy lives, to put them in cages. Maybe even euthanize them. Maybe even experiment on them! Ellie had read what happened to animals in so-called medical experiments.

The four greyhounds swarmed around her. Ellie looked frantically around her tiny house. Where could she hide them, *where...?*

There was no place. She didn't even have a basement.

Ellie dropped to the floor and hugged Song, Chimes, Music, and Butterfly. Sensing her distress, they pressed into her body, licking her face and hands. Her babies, her friends. To be staked out, shot up with ketamine, vivisected...

No.

Ellie got to her feet. The dogs followed her through the kitchen into the backyard. At the far corner, under the maple tree, was a gate giving onto open fields and then the woods along Black Creek. Ellie led the dogs through the gate, then darted back into the yard and locked them out.

For a moment she hesitated. How could they survive outside her care? She could feed them at night, of course, but rescued dogs had all sorts of strange issues. Kept in dog runs from an early age, they weren't exposed to the normal things that other dogs adjusted to. Song freaked out whenever he saw a ceiling fan, reacting as if it were a giant bird of prey. Chimes attacked all laundry baskets. Music was terrified of sloping land. How would they –

There was no choice.

"Run!" she cried, and the greyhounds, obeying a call familiar from their puppyhood and intoxicated by the sudden freedom, streaked joyously over the brown field toward the woods.

» 22

Cami woke on a strange, hard bed, and somehow her bedroom was filled with people – how could that be? How had they gotten in, and what if they were burglars? She cried out and tried to sit up.

"She's awake," someone said.

"Goddamn it, sedate her again! She's next in line for the OR!"

Someone dressed like a duck – *that couldn't be right* – tried to stab her. Cami heard weird, strangled noises coming from someone. She realized it was herself just before she slid away again into sleep.

When she woke again, she recognized that she lay on a gurney in a hospital hallway. The attack by Mr. Anselm's dog came flooding back, but not anything after that. A nurse whom Cami didn't know, a middle-aged woman dressed in scrubs printed with ducks, hurried by.

"Wait...wait..." Her voice came out faint and scratchy but the woman heard it and stopped. Deep circles ringed her eyes. "What...happened... me?"

"You've been operated on, honey. Compound tibial/fibular fracture.

You should be in Recovery but there's no more room."

"Wait..."

"I can't stop to talk, honey. All I know is that you were attacked by a dog and some sheriff's deputies interrupted the attack and brought you in."

"Mr....Anselm?" But the nurse was already gone.

A man lay on another gurney beside her, his shoulder thick with dressings, blond stubble on his face. He watched her from merry hazel eyes. "Hey, little thing, it ain't as bad as all that."

"I..." She felt tears start.

"Aw, don't cry, pretty girl like you, after the dog missed your face it'd be a shame to ruin all that make-up."

That made Cami smile; she never wore make-up. How could this man look so happy? "You...dog..."

"Not me, no dog bite here, I got shot," he said cheerfully. "Meanest dog owner in Tyler didn't want to give up his little ol' vicious pets. I'm an animal control officer. Billy Davis."

"Cami. Johnson...nurse."

"A nurse, huh? Well, then, that dog oughta missed you altogether, we need you too much...oh, shit, Cami, don't cry. What can I get you to make you feel better?"

He looked as if he shouldn't move himself, let alone get her anything. But maybe, since he was an animal control officer, he knew people. She managed to get out, "Belle..."

"You want a bell? What for? You gonna ring in the new year? Missed it by a month and a half, sweetheart."

"My dog..."

"Belle's your dog? That who bit you?"

Exhausted from talking, she tried to shake her head, which made it ache so violently that she cried out and everything went black. The next thing she knew the duck-scrubbed nurse was bending over her but scolding Billy Davis. "Mr. Davis, I told you twice not to get up! Miss Johnson, *you* should know better than to try to move. Now lie still, both of you!"

"Wicked Witch of the West," Billy said when she'd left, "'cept this is east Tyler. Listen, Nurse Cami, I'll find out about your Belle."

And he did. Everybody that went past, Billy harassed by name. "Hey, Rod, you bring in another load? Can you find out from Jess about a dog named Belle from the Magnolia Apartments? Sure appreciate any information... Hey, Burt...naw, I'm fine, takes more 'n a Russian semi to keep me down but I tell you, Jess and me got egg on our faces the way that FBI girl saved our bacon...Listen, there's a dog named Belle – "

Cami slept. When she woke, she felt marginally better. Billy Davis was being wheeled away by a tired-looking orderly who nonetheless was shaking his head and smiling. Billy saw that her eyes were open and said, "Your dog Belle's an old collie, right? She's safe at the tent that FEMA put up 'cross from the Cedar Springs Motel, for dog overflow. Bye, Nurse Cami, I'm gonna see you again, you can bet on it!"

Belle was safe. What a nice guy to find that out for her! When Cami had finished nursing school in West Virginia, become bored with her hometown, and taken the job at Tyler Community Hospital, her mother had warned her that even though Tyler, too, was a small town it was pretty near to Washington. Cami should watch out for those oversexed city boys with their smooth talk. But here was Billy Davis, as nice and real as possible, finding out about her dog just so Cami wouldn't worry. A thorough gentleman.

She drifted off to sleep, smiling.

» 23

Even in the middle of a natural disaster, Jess realized, you cannot kill somebody without repercussions. Not if you're deputized, and the federal government is trying to do everything right to make up for what it hasn't done right in the past, and the national media is slavering for news. And if you're the idiot who deputized the shooter, you're involved, too.

Not that he wasn't grateful. Without Tessa's interference, Billy would be dead, and it's possible Jess would have had to shoot Victor Balonov. Jess had never killed a man before. Something made him suspect that Tessa had. So Jess was grateful, and was slightly humiliated, and was kept hanging around critical-incident headquarters until sundown when what he wanted was to be back out on the street picking up dogs.

"You need to stick around, Jess, until Mr. Lurie says you can go," the sheriff told him.

"Don, they need me out there. You know that. What's Lurie got to do with this? It's local law enforcement – your jurisdiction, not FEMA's."

"You know that, and I know that, but Washington doesn't know that, and Lurie's in charge of everything by direct order of the White House."

Jess saw the conflict on Don DiBella's honest, exhausted face; DiBella had voted for this administration. Jess had not. But Don was a good man trying to make the best of a bad situation. Jess said, "I want to go by the hospital to check on Billy."

"Billy's fine. Burt just called in – Billy was badgering him about some girl's dog. A girl on the bed next to him." Don smiled, apparently despite himself. "Same old Billy. Anyway, I have your statement, it sure sounds like a justifiable shooting to me, so just stay around here until they're done with the lady FBI agent, in case Lurie's guys have more questions." Don glanced around, leaned forward, and whispered, "Between you and me, I think it's a goddamn turf war. FEMA doesn't want the Fibbies here."

"She's an ex-agent," Jess felt compelled to say, although he couldn't have given a reason for saying it.

"Whatever. Just stick around."

Jess left the Cedar Springs Motel room that served as temporary law-enforcement headquarters, blinking in the afternoon sunlight. The motel, he decided, was one ring of a three-ring circus, the ring where exhausted humans capered and jumped through hoops. Ring number 2, across the street in an empty field, belonged to the dogs; huge Army-issue tents were being set up to house all the caged animals taken from Tyler. In Ring number 3 the microbes performed, or maybe didn't. The CDC, the United States Army Medical Research Institute for Infectious Diseases, and FEMA's National Disaster Medical System each had huge trailers flanked by more tents for their respective personnel.

The entire circus was in turn ringed by the media, gawkers, and protestors, kept at bay by troops from the Maryland Guard. Reporters that had ventured into Tyler were now stuck here, although hastily printed "authorization passes" had been issued to crisis personnel. Occasionally someone from the motel would venture into the slavering audience of media and throw them tidbits of news, shouting to be heard over the hundreds of snarling, barking, and snapping dogs in the tents. And somewhere in the woods and fields all around Tyler were more troops, ready to shoot any escaping dogs, with or without owners. Already they'd captured two teenage girls and a middle-aged man, each trying to get out of Tyler with a pet dog.

Whatever Jess had envisioned when he'd suggested a quarantine, it hadn't been this.

He caught sight of Dr. Latkin crossing the parking lot toward the CDC mobile lab and strode toward him. "Dr. Latkin! Joe!"

Latkin turned, looking as harried and tired as everyone else. "Oh, hi, Jess. Great job you're doing bringing in the dogs." It was said mechanically; for all Latkin actually knew, Jess could have taken to setting every animal free.

"Thanks. Look, I know you're busy but I just want to know how the pathogen search is coming."

Latkin smiled wryly. "You know, I think you're one of the few people genuinely interested? Scott Lurie wants a scapegoat, a resolution, and a gold star, not medical information." All at once something new seemed to occur to him. His pale eyes sharpened, like water crystallizing into ice. "Come in here for a minute. I want to show you something."

Jess followed Latkin into the mobile lab, the first time he'd been inside. Somehow it looked even bigger within. The back third was sealed off. A door said:

INFECTIOUS AREA
NO UNAUTHORIZED ENTRY
TO OPEN THIS DOOR
PLACE I.D. CARD ON SENSOR

The first two-thirds of the lab was jammed with more counters, equipment, and people than Jess could have imagined would fit. Latkin led him to a woman in her forties, wearing a white lab coat and frowning at computer displays.

"Jess, this is Dr. Deborah Preston, our principal investigator, from Special Pathogens. Deb, Jess Langstrom, Tyler Animal Control."

"Hello," she said wearily. "So you're the one bringing us all these specimens. Did you haul in the boxer on Prozac?"

"The what?"

"Some hysterical woman wouldn't let her boxer come in because she was afraid we wouldn't give him his regular doses of Prozac and the dog was seriously depressed without it. I heard the animal people had to have *her* sedated."

"Sounds apocryphal," Latkin said.

Not to Jess. People got very strange about their dogs. If Jess hadn't been so depressed himself, he'd have told them about Victor Balonov's demon-possessed Rottweilers. Instead he said awkwardly, "Are you... you scientists finding the cause of this thing?"

"Could be. Take a look," Deborah said, getting up from her stool and motioning at the screen. Jess moved into position and stared at what looked to him like a lot of blue peppercorns wriggling frantically in orange sauce.

"That's false color, of course," Deborah continued. "The thing is, this is an unknown pathogen but not a very complicated one. It's relatively large as these things go, which is a good thing or we'd still be looking for it. Well, I shouldn't say it's totally unknown, it seems to be related to a class of canine viruses found mostly in Africa, although it's not identical to them. Mutated, most likely. It can cross the blood-brain barrier – like rabies, you know. It lodges in the amygdala, a part of the brain that contributes to aggression. There it just disrupts neural firing until *kaboom!* A regular electrical storm and a fried dog brain."

Jess fumbled for the right questions. "Can people get it?"

"Unknown. We have amygdalae, too, although the odds are they're not receptive to this particular microbe, at least not in this particular form. Some hot agents learn to jump species – avian flu, for instance – but it takes time. That's the good news."

"What's the bad news?"

Deborah looked at Latkin, and suddenly Jess had the feeling that this conversation was staged. Why? Tessa would have known. Jess wasn't good at this political stuff.

Latkin said, "The bad news is that this isn't something for which we can whip up either a cure or a vaccine in twenty-four hours. It's too new. The only way we might speed up the process is to find a dog with a natural immunity. Build on its immune-system defenses. That's why if you find such an animal, one infected but not aggressive, we need to know *immediately*. If you can let the other animal control officers know that, it would help a lot. I'm putting out the word on this but everyone is so exhausted and stuff doesn't always get read, and FEMA is trying to control information flow completely. Official channels, protocols, blah blah blah. They're making this a political situation first and a medical one only as an afterthought."

"I see," Jess said. "Got it."

"Thanks," Deborah Preston said, and went back to her wiggling blue peppercorns. But Jess wasn't done.

"How did the germ get here from Africa?"

Latkin steered him gently by the elbow, toward the door. "We don't know for sure that it was Africa. And it could have gotten here any number of ways. The most likely is a traveling pet who picked it up, but Scott Lurie tells me they've checked passports and no dog from Tyler has traveled out of this country in the last six months. We don't yet know the incubation period, but it's probably not that long."

"So how else could – "

"We just don't know," Latkin said grimly. "Thanks again, Jess."

He was dismissed. Jess walked back to the motel. Maybe the officials were all done with Tessa, which meant both of them could finally leave. This encampment gave him the creeps.

It had finally dawned on him, far later than it should have, that those wiggling blue microbes had to have come from some dog's brain. Probably more than one dog's brain, because wasn't that what science did? It duplicated experiments, to be sure the answers were right. Had they dissected brains from dogs that had already been shot, like the pit bull that attacked young A.J. Wright on his own sink or that dachshund, Schopenhauer? Or did they need freshly killed dogs?

Were those peppercorn-shaped viruses from his little cousin's collie?

Or from the sweet, overly pampered Schnapps and Applejack, which Jess had personally assured their owner would be returned to her unharmed?

Or from the toy poodle Tessa had belatedly confessed to owning, which might easily have been picked up by some other team while Tessa was away from home, explaining over and over how she'd saved Billy's life?

The sun was still warm. But Jess turned up his collar as he walked back to the motel to await whatever grimness came next.

» 24

Allen was worried about Susie. He hadn't been able to manage a trip to the basement to check on her because his mother, after she finished crying on the phone in the morning, insisted on spending the rest of the day with Allen. "We'll have fun!" she'd cried, with two weird spots of red high on her cheeks. "We'll play Candy Land!"

Candy Land was way too babyish for Allen, but his mother didn't know how to play Nintendo and didn't want to learn. They settled on Parcheesi, which was really boring, and Allen was just about to invent a social studies project he had to do for school, when the doorbell rang.

"Finally!" his mother said, which was weird because she'd been telling him all day that nobody was allowed outside, so how come she was expecting company? "Come in," she said to the two people standing there, and as soon as Allen saw how they were dressed, his stomach shot up into his chest and he thought he might be sick.

"The dog is in the basement," his mother said. "Just follow me. Allen, stay here in the dining room, please. Do you hear me?"

As they clomped through the room in their thick pants and parkas and gloves, carrying helmets and a cage, the woman stopped and spoke to Allen. "Don't worry, kid, we'll bring your dog back after this is all over. Meanwhile he'll be safe with us."

"It's a she."

"She, then." They clomped on. Allen hated both of them.

All three of them.

He waited until they reached the bottom of the cellar stairs and then crept down after them, trying not to throw up.

"I don't *understand*, she was right here, my husband put her down here! She wasn't acting aggressive, but he said just in case she – Allen, go back upstairs, do you hear me!"

Allen sat defiantly on a step halfway down. He made himself not look at the filing cabinet in the corner.

The man pound-person moved cautiously into the laundry room and then said, "Karen. Come look at this." The woman followed, and then Allen's mother. Allen stayed where he was. If he strained his ears, he could hear them.

"Did Susie escape through the *window?"* his mother said.

"Yeah, right, and first she knocked out every bit of glass and put a blanket on the dryer. Ma'am, did you or your husband let this dog loose?"

"No! We called you, remember?"

Allen closed his eyes. His stomach hurt really bad now. The three adults moved back into the main part of the cellar. The man said roughly, "When did you let your dog out, son?"

"Yesterday," Allen said. "She's gone."

"Son of a bitch," the man said, and Allen waited for his mother to tell him we don't use that language in this house. But she didn't. Instead she stared at Allen, and all at once he didn't want the pound-people to leave, because of what his mother would say then.

Which was nothing compared to what his father would do when he got home.

But Allen didn't really care, because Susie was safe, and that was all that mattered. And now that his parents thought she was gone, it would be easier for Allen to go down to the cellar to feed her, give her water, and make sure she had more of the pills Allen had in his jeans pocket from the little bottle in the medicine cabinet.

It was a good thing that Susie had Allen. He was the only one who cared.

» 25

They wouldn't let Tessa leave until after 6:00 P.M., when the February sun had just slipped below the horizon and the sky was still fiery red. Trying to be cooperative, she told her story to four different small groups of people, from four different agencies. The last group, who did not identify themselves, was not from FEMA, nor from law-enforcement; Tessa suspected they came from one of the intelligence agencies. She became sure when one of them said casually, "Wasn't your husband an Arab?" and Tessa finally lost her temper.

"Why aren't all you people off dealing with the dog crisis instead of with me? Never mind, I know the answer. You screwed up too much with past national crises and you don't want to screw up with this one. Well, guys, guess what? I don't represent a threat to you. I didn't screw up. I shot in defense of my partner, however temporary that partnership was. You're in the clear. And no, goddammit, for the sixth time, I don't need a lawyer! I *was* a lawyer, remember? I went to law school and then I became an FBI agent, and now I'm a temporary animal-control deputy."

"Not anymore," the man said, which didn't come as much of a surprise.

"I think Ms. Sanderson can go now," said a woman who hadn't spoken before. Tessa had pegged her for government counsel the second she laid eyes on her. "She should perhaps have an escort off incident headquarters."

"Jess Langstrom is out there, in case we need him," someone else said. "He can take her home."

"Yes," Tessa agreed sarcastically, "that would look good to the media. Show of solidarity."

There was a certain freedom of speech in no longer working for the government.

Jess was indeed waiting outside, looking impatient and weary and disturbed all at once, an interesting look to pull off. He said, "Tessa?"

"No charges, but they want me out of here. How's Billy?"

"Fine. I called the hospital. Victor Balonov didn't hit anything important."

"No wonder the Soviet Union fell," she said, and felt slightly warmed by Jess's reluctant laugh. "I guess you better follow orders and take me home. God, look at this spectacle here."

"Just what *I* thought. But at least the scientists are doing useful work." As he told her what Joe Latkin and Deborah Preston had said about the virus, Tessa got a sick feeling in her stomach.

"How are they choosing the dogs to kill for brain tissue?"

"I don't know. Please don't tell me you're among the more lunatic animal-rights activists."

"No. Just a dog owner," she said, and noted that he frowned. "Look, I'm sorry I didn't tell you about Minette. But anyway, now the powers-that-be have ended my deputyship."

"Sort of figured they would. Can't have you shooting any more exemplary Maryland citizens."

She laughed, although it didn't really make her feel any better. It was never easy to kill a man, not even when you'd had no choice. Tessa knew she was not unduly sensitive. But she also knew that Victor Balonov's dead face would turn up in her dreams for months. That was the price you paid.

They rode in silence through the streets, empty except for official vehicles. It looked as if every cop in the entire state had converged on Tyler. If they were all picking up dogs, there couldn't be any left. Her stomach tightened as they pulled into her driveway.

But Minette was still there, barking joyously as Tessa opened the door, seven pounds of thrilled ecstasy. Tessa picked her up with one hand and turned her to study the little poodle's eyes. "None of that milky film you said the researchers found in infected dogs."

"I still have to take her in, Tessa."

"I know you do." She hated the pleading note in her voice. "But can you somehow tag her to not be…so they choose some other dog for… shit!"

"I can try," he said, so gently that she was moved. He looked exhausted. They were both exhausted. She said, "When did you eat last?

Breakfast? If I heat up something in the microwave, will you eat?"

He hesitated, then smiled. "Sure. If it's quick."

"I don't cook anything not quick." Salah, strangely enough for an Arab male, had loved cooking. He'd prepared most of the meals they didn't eat in restaurants. His paella had been incredible. *Salah...*

Jess said, "Where's the bathroom?"

She told him, transferred two single-serving pizzas from the freezer to the microwave, and checked her Caller I.D. Five calls, all from Ellen, who was probably worried out of her mind. Tessa would call her sister right after dinner. But first she darted into the other bathroom, the one adjoining her bedroom.

Sitting on the toilet, and prompted by the memory of Salah, she suddenly recalled the printed email she'd shoved into her jeans pocket early this morning. She pulled it out and looked at it. Too bad she couldn't read Arabic. Although she'd picked up a few spoken phrases, the foreign alphabet had always defeated her. All these squiggles looked so much alike –

Too much alike.

For the first time, Tessa paid really close attention to the paper in her hand. It wasn't, as she'd assumed, a string of varied Arabic characters. It was one set of characters, maybe one word, repeated over and over:

كلب

Tessa went back into the kitchen. She turned on Salah's laptop, still set up on the messy kitchen table beside her own, and accessed its Arabic-English dictionary.

Jess emerged from the other bathroom. "Tessa, there wasn't any soap or towel in – wait, here's some by your kitchen sink."

She typed in كلب. Jess washed his hands. The microwave hummed. The translation dictionary gave her a single word.

Dog.

Repeated over and over in an email to Salah, just a few days before he died.

"Tessa? I think the pizzas are done."

She said numbly, "Plates in that box on the floor."

Dog.

Salah's email account had been closed when he died. Feverishly Tessa shifted to her own laptop and checked her email.

"Tessa? Is anything wrong?"

"No, not at all. There's beer in the fridge."

"Okay...Guinness, nice. You want one, too?"

"Yes." She didn't know what she'd just agreed to. Her whole attention scanned the email list. And there it was. She opened it.

> TO: tsand61@hotmail.com
> FROM: dkd78@vvvmail.com
> SUBJECT: dogs
>
> Tessa – Yes, Salah is dead, which is unfortunate, but it's fine that you are not. I'm perfectly willing to go on working with just you. He owes me this, he wanted it for me. Did you ever study the Bible? Solomon said, "A living dog is better than a dead lion." But I prefer 2Kings 8:13.

All at once her mind cleared, snapped into professional mode. It wasn't the message that did that, or even the time it had been sent: less than half an hour ago. It was the COPY TO line in the email: COPY TO: john_maddox@fbi.gov.

"Can I move some of this stuff off the table?" Jess said. "There doesn't seem to be much room to eat."

"Yes, of course," Tessa said. A detached part of her mind marveled at how calm she sounded, how normal. "That big box is my grandmother's china, it's heavy."

The phone rang. Tessa looked at Caller I.D. Maddox.

If she let the answering machine pick it up, Jess would hear. Tessa said, "Sorry," picked up the phone, and held it tight to her ear.

"Tessa, this is John Maddox. Listen, something's come up here and we need a bit more information. I've got two agents on the way to Tyler. Will you please stay at home until they get there?"

"Yes, of course, John. I got the email, too."

"We saw that you did. Just stay put."

"I will." He hung up.

Jess said around his pizza, "A problem?"

Tessa covered the dead phone. "No. Or at least, not a big one. That was my sister's husband, Jim. He's having a little trouble with my sister because...well, I don't want to go into it, but I do have to talk to him a bit in private. Will you stay here while I take this? I have to look up something on this laptop for him. I promise I won't be long."

"Okay. This pizza is good."

She unplugged the laptop and carried it and the phone into the front hall, picked up Jess's coat and her purse, and continued to her bedroom. Minette cast her one longing look but stayed with Jess and the hope of pizza. Tessa closed the bedroom door and took her gun from the bedside table. She opened the window, climbed out, circled the house, and started Jess's truck with the keys in his coat pocket.

The kitchen was in the back of the house. And Jess was not, unfortunately for him, a suspicious person. He'd have made a bad special agent. John Maddox, however, was a good one. He would have Tessa held as a material-witness detainee while the Bureau investigated this. Maddox would have little choice, not with Bernini as A-DIC, and not in the current political climate. Tessa and Maddox both had received mail that seemed to implicate Salah and her in something connected with dogs. Salah had received the "كلب" email. Salah's computer now resided securely under the truck seat, but the Bureau's computer analysts might be able to locate the original email on the Internet. And the sender might email again. Most of all, Salah had been an Arab. She remembered what Jess told her that Dr. Latkin had said: *Scott Lurie wants a scapegoat, a resolution, and a gold star.*

Tessa and Salah would make very good scapegoats.

The government could detain material witnesses, unlike someone actually charged with a crime, indefinitely. Behind bars, Tessa would have no chance to clear her name or Salah's. She needed to talk to people, some of them overseas, and once she was an official material witness, no one was going to let her do that. No way. Nor did she trust Bernini to do it for her.

She drove Jess's truck, mercifully empty of dogs, carefully through Tyler to the town's west checkpoint, on Route 63. When she stopped at the makeshift barrier, a soldier in camouflage shone a flashlight into the cab and said, "Sorry, ma'am, no one leaves Tyler."

"I'm an animal control officer, sent to bring more dog cages from Flatsburgh. Jessie Langstrom. Here's my authorization." She passed over the hastily assembled set of papers, stamped FEMA, that Jess had shown her before stuffing them under the truck seat. *"You'd think we were at war,"* he'd said, bemused.

The young guard studied the papers and Tessa held her breath. But many people must be going in and out of Tyler. She would bet her life that the politicos she'd talked to this afternoon were not putting up in either of Tyler's two motels, one of which smelled like dog.

"Pass," the soldier said, and she drove on.

By now Jess would realize she'd taken the truck. Maddox's agents would be entering Tyler from the southeast. Tessa didn't have much time.

She drove a mile, then steered the truck down a side road and forced it into a thick clump of trees. In the darkness, broken only by the flashlight in her purse, she ran back to the highway, Salah's laptop in the roomy pocket of Jess's too-big parka, and crossed the road to face east. Fluffing up her hair, she opened her coat and put on fresh lipstick. Then she stood as close to the road as possible. Six minutes later a six-wheeler, with KESSEL SHORT-TERM MOVING painted on its side, stopped for her. Tessa checked her gun and smiled brightly.

The driver, a short, thick man with a hair line like an inverted U, said "Where you heading?"

"Frederick."

"I go right through there. Hop in, honey. Though we gotta detour around that mess in Tyler."

"Perfect," Tessa said.

» 26

Jess didn't like to feed pets without their owners' permission, but Minette looked up at him from pleading black eyes, sitting on her little haunches in that dog stance that meant *I'm being so obedient, aren't you going to reward me?*

"Not without Tessa's say-so," he told the toy poodle. She wagged her tiny docked tail with the fervor of a tent-revival evangelist seeking souls. Five minutes later no pizza remained. Minette had not taken her gaze off him for an instant and Tessa had not returned. Whatever domestic crisis was going on with her sister and the sister's husband was apparently lengthy. Jess was glad he no longer had in-laws.

Liar.

Another five minutes. This was getting ridiculous. Tessa's brother-in-law might not know that she'd been involved in a shooting today, but wasn't the guy sensitive enough to realize that Tessa, stuck smack in the middle of quarantined Tyler, might have a few things on her mind besides other people's domestic issues? Some people were just oblivious.

Tessa's pizza was cold. Jess picked off a corner, fed it to Minette, and wandered into the living room. A wilderness of unpacked boxes, except for a small table under a window. On the table sat a statue of some sort, a many-armed god or goddess. It seemed an odd thing for an ex-FBI agent to have. He picked it up for a closer examination. Heavy, finely detailed, brass or copper or –

His truck was gone from the driveway.

"Son of a bitch!" He tore through the front hall to the closed bedroom door, didn't bother knocking. The bedroom was empty, but the window wasn't locked. Jess flung it open and saw her boot prints in the soft mud of the flower bed.

He went back to the kitchen and hit Caller I.D. harder than necessary, pulling up her call record. The most recent entry said JOHN MADDOX, followed by a Washington number. This told him nothing.

He had to report the theft of the truck before she got out of Tyler. But to whom? His list of critical-incident command numbers was in the truck. Hot with fury and embarrassment, he called Don DiBella's cell on his own. The sheriff answered, sounding weary. "Jess? What is it? Can it wait?"

"Afraid not," Jess said. Christ, this was going to sound stupid! And Jess had always ragged on *Billy* for hapless behavior... "I have a problem here, Don. That ex-FBI agent, Tessa Sanderson, just stole my truck. I think she might try to get out of Tyler with the FEMA passes. I showed them to her."

Silence. Jess closed his eyes, hating every second of this. Then DiBella said, "Stole your truck? Why would she do that?"

"I don't know. But somebody should alert the checkpoints, I guess."

"*You* wanted to deputize her!"

"I know. The...aw, shit."

"Shit? What shit? What's happening now, Jess?"

"I think the FBI is here." He gazed out at the two long black cars pulling up before Tessa's bare winter lawn. "Just notify FEMA, okay?"

He clicked off. Minette, hearing someone coming to the house, raced ecstatically to the front door.

It occurred to Jess, the way that black humor sometimes did at totally inappropriate moments, that he could hold off the FBI by telling them that Minette was infected. That it would be really funny if a seven-pound toy poodle could take them all down and, a canine angel of mercy, somehow set Jess Langstrom free.

"Tell us again," said the big, good-looking man who seemed to be in charge. Maddox. "Once more, just to be sure we have all the details, Mr. Langstrom. Start with Tessa Sanderson's first appearance at critical-incident headquarters. What was the first thing you heard her say?"

So he went through it all again, his anger banked by now, his humiliation dulled by the simple sheer repetition of his own gullibility. She'd played him for a fool. He saw that Maddox thought so, too, but that Maddox was making allowance for Jess as a non-Bureau civilian. And something else: Jess had the impression that Maddox knew Tessa already, and very well. Was it remotely possible that this was her husband? Agents, he'd heard, sometimes married each other. Maddox wore a wedding ring, but didn't seem to live in Tyler. Estranged husband? Ex-boss? Had he forced Tessa out of the FBI?

They sat in the living room on chairs hastily denuded of boxes, Maddox in a wing chair and Jess on the sofa while another, totally silent, agent sat beside him. As he talked, Jess kept his eyes fixed on the brass statue of the many-armed god. He'd just reached the part of his sorry-ass story where Tessa shot Victor Balonov, when another agent came in from the kitchen. "Sir, we have the warrant. 'All relevant or possibly relevant articles, information, or materials.'"

"Then start on the computer, Lee. Evan, Molly, you start in the bedroom."

Jess talked on, hearing boxes being ripped open beyond the wall, drawers opened, furniture moved. Almost immediately a printer hummed in the kitchen and Agent Lee (first name? last name?) came in with a sheet of paper. "Original of the email we were copied on, sir. English. I'll do a complete checking."

English. Something jogged in Jess's brain. "Wait... There is something I just remembered."

Maddox turned to Jess.

"Something Tessa asked me. I didn't think anything of it, but you said to remember everything – " He stopped. Was this going to get Tessa into more trouble?

"Go on," Maddox said, patient and intent and predatory.

Tessa hadn't hesitated to get Jess in trouble, now, had she? And anyway, this was – could be – a matter of national security. *Oh, God* – for the first time he actually believed that. This could be a matter of national security.

Maddox said, "What did Tessa ask you, Mr. Langstrom?"

"She asked me if I could read Arabic."

» 27

Tessa made random conversation with the driver of the KESSEL SHORT-TERM MOVING truck until she spotted what she wanted. She knew the small city of Frederick, not well but enough, from driving up to visit Ellen. "Could you drop me in that mall, please?"

"Sure, honey. Pleasure to have you aboard, like the airlines say." He laughed, the deep chuckle of a happy, dim, easily pleased man. Tessa envied him. She hopped out of the truck and waved.

On a Saturday night, the small strip mall was mostly closed. But cars clustered at one end, under a multiplex sign listing ten different movies. Beside this were a pizza place, a Starbucks, and a video arcade. Teenagers hung around outside, smoking. Tessa pulled up the hood of Jess's jacket and went into the arcade. At the inevitable change machine she got forty dollars' worth of quarters. Then she ducked into the Starbucks, which heavily advertised wireless Internet for its patrons. She ordered a latte and turned on Salah's laptop.

Solomon said, "A living dog is better than a dead lion." But I prefer 2Kings 8:13.

No new email to her account from dkd78@vvvmail.com. The address, Google informed her, was a mixmaster remailer, which meant the email could have come from anybody, anywhere in the world. Mixmaster remailers couldn't be traced without subpoenaing the remailer records, and many of those places didn't keep records. Many were located in foreign countries.

2Kings 8:13 read: "Is thy servant a dog, that he should do this great thing?"

Tessa scowled at the laptop. Dogs as servants, doing "great things" – she was dealing with a religious lunatic. Or with someone pretending to be a religious lunatic, which could be far worse.

If she had received only the second email, she would have assumed it had come from someone capitalizing on the Tyler plague in order to harass her. As an agent, she had worked on a number of task forces that had thwarted or put away a number of home-grown crazies bent on domestic terrorism. They were certainly out there; Timothy McVeigh and David Koresh had a lot of company. And it was not unheard of for freed convicts, or their unjailed friends or relatives, to mount a vendetta against the FBI agents who'd investigated their cases.

But the first email, the one in her jeans pocket, the one repeating كلب over and over again – dkd78 had sent that one to Salah three months ago. The email might merely have been a repetitious insult; "dog" was a common epithet throughout the Middle East. But it could be more. It could suggest he or she knew that the canine plague was coming.

Tessa would have to tell Maddox about this. Maddox had the second email but not the first. And Tessa *would* tell him – but not just yet. If Maddox knew that Salah had received a December email saying "dog" in Arabic, it would only serve to deepen Bureau suspicions that he had somehow been involved in the "attack."

Back at the arcade, covered by the jangling noise of machines and kids, Tessa found the public phone. Nobody paid her the slightest attention. She got the operator, requested international directory assistance for London, and prepared to feed quarters into the pay phone.

"*Ahlan? Ahlan?*" The guttural voice sounded alarmed, as well he might. It was one in the morning in London.

"Ruzbihan al-Ashan, please. This is Tessa Mahjoub, the wife of Salah Mahjoub."

Silence. Then, "I am Ruzbihan. We have sent email, yes?"

"Yes, and I'm sorry to call you so late," Tessa said, speaking slowly and carefully, praying that Ruzbihan's English was good enough for this conversation. "It is an emergency."

"Emergency?" Bewilderment, wariness. "It is Salah's family? Aisha?"

So Ruzbihan knew Salah's sister. Of course he did. They had all grown up together, in that Tunisian childhood she could not even imagine.

"Aisha and Fatima are well. I'm calling to ask about an email I received and one Salah received. They – "

"You call me now to ask after some email? Now?"

"Please, Ruzbihan, it's very important. I think I am in danger from an email in Arabic. It was sent to Salah on December 17 and said only one word: the Arabic for dog. Over and over. Do – "

"You think I have sent this email to Salah?"

"No. But I'm hoping you can identify the email address for me. The person sent me a second email with threats in it. Threats of danger." Had news of the dog plague reached London? Of course it had; anything on CNN was known to the world. "The address is 'dkd78@vvvmail.'"

"I do not know this address. What says this email?"

Tessa squeezed her eyes closed. All at once she was dizzy – when had she last eaten? She fought off the vertigo and recited as accurately as she could remember.

"The email said, 'Salah is dead, which is unfortunate, but I will work with just you instead, Tessa. He owes me this. He wanted it for me. Did you study your Bible? Solomon said that a living dog is better than a dead lion. But I prefer 2Kings 8:13.' That's a Bible verse about using dogs as servants to – Ruzbihan, are you there?"

Silence, and then over the new buzzing on the line, his voice again, loud and sharp in Arabic. She recognized the curse. It was one Salah had used only in extreme situations, and had looked shame-faced afterward.

"Ruzbihan?"

"The Christian Bible," he said, his accent abruptly thicker, so that Tessa had to strain to catch the words. "The email, it comes then from that one."

"Which one? Who?"

"Our classmate. Richard Ebenfield. He has converted Salah at the Sorbonne, that one, from Islam to Christianity. He is very crazy."

"Crazy? How? Is he by any chance a microbiologist?"

"What?"

"A...a scientist. Who works with diseases, maybe."

Ruzbihan made a rude sound. "He was not. He was nothing. He did not go to the classes, did not sit the examinations, did not finish his studies. Tessa – you are FBI?"

"No. I quit. Left. This danger is personal."

"Go back to your FBI. Tell them all this. Also, Tessa – "

"Yes?"

"Do not say my name to your FBI, please. I have talked with you because you were Salah's wife. But do not say my name to your FBI, or to the London authorities. Do you understand this?"

And Tessa did. Ethnic paranoia cut both ways. "Yes," she said.

"You promise me this?"

"I promise. One more question, please, Ruzbihan. Do you know where Ebenfield is now?"

"I have not seen Richard since Mogumbutuno a few years ago. I do not want to see him. Good-bye, Tessa. Please do not call again."

"But you – "

"Good-bye." The phone clicked.

Perhaps his paranoia was justified. On the other hand, perhaps she had not shown enough paranoia. Richard Ebenfield, crazy American who had not finished his studies at the Sorbonne, could probably not have gotten Tessa's and Salah's name into the intel chatter in the Mid

East. Ruzbihan, a well-connected Arab whom Tessa had never met, might have been able to do so. Ruzbihan's family dealt internationally in copper. They had influence and connections. Was everything Ruzbihan had just told her a lie?

Or was she the paranoid?

She fished out the rest of her quarters and called Switzerland.

No answer at Aisha's apartment in Geneva. Aisha was with a medical team at the World Health Organization; she could have been sent anywhere in the world. And it was 2:00 A.M. in Geneva. Tessa was not going to get any more information there tonight.

She went back to Starbucks, set up the laptop again, and searched the web for "Richard Ebenfield." Nothing. No address, no search-engine hits, no Web presence at all. Electronically, Ebenfield didn't exist, at least not under that name.

The cell phone in her purse rang. Damn – she had forgotten to turn it off! That meant that Maddox could find out exactly where she was. She pulled out the phone; it displayed her own number. The damage was already done, so she answered.

"Tessa? What the hell do you think you're doing?"

"Trying to find information, John. And I have some for you. That email may have come from one Richard Ebenfield, an American who was Salah's roommate at the Sorbonne, and whom Salah hadn't seen since. Ebenfield may be a religious nut of some variety, and I have it on good authority that he may be crazed. Check him out."

"On what good authority? Who did you talk to?"

"I can't tell you that," Tessa said, and knew how it sounded. She was already under suspicion. This could only make it worse. But the Bureau had resources she did not. They could find Ebenfield.

Maybe.

"I'm sending a car for you," Maddox said. "Give me your address and stay right there."

"I can't do that, John," Tessa said. She was already turning off the laptop, sliding it into the pocket of Jess's coat, moving toward the door. "Think – if I had stayed at my house, you wouldn't even have Ebenfield's name. I couldn't have gotten it with you watching suspiciously over my shoulder. And I'll feed you anything else I discover, I promise. But I'm not coming in."

"Damn it, that's an order!"

"But I'm not an agent anymore." Then she was gone, walking rapidly toward the door, sliding her cell phone into the trash bin on the way out the door, disappearing around the corner of the building into the night.

Short-term moving, she thought, picturing the jovial truck driver who'd given her the ride into Frederick. Now she was running, making good time on the cold deserted streets, sure of at least her next stop.

If not of anything else.

» 28

Allen lay quietly in bed, his face turned to the wall. Waiting. When the door finally opened, he watched the growing line of light slide down his clown wallpaper. Red clown hair, ruffled shirt, big fake hands holding a balloon, baggy pants...the wallpaper was too babyish and anyway Allen hated clowns.

"Allen? Are you asleep?"

He scrunched his eyes shut and blew softly through his nose.

Satisfied, his mother went quietly from the room and closed the door. Allen felt bad, in a way; he could hear from her voice that she'd been crying again. His father wasn't home because nobody was allowed back into Tyler, and his parents had had a big fight on the phone about that, although Allen couldn't see that it was Daddy's fault. The government *said*. Still, Allen knew he should have stayed up and comforted his mother, like the other times his parents fought, but he just couldn't. Not this time.

He gave her more achingly long time to take her pills and get to sleep. What if she noticed that the bottle held less pills than it was supposed to? But he guessed that she didn't notice because she didn't come back into his room, and eventually he decided she must be asleep by now.

It hurt to walk. When he'd stepped on that shard of glass in the basement, going down to Susie, a piece of it had gone through his sock and into his foot. Allen had locked himself in the bathroom and tried to wash it with soap and warm water, but the soap stung too much. Now his foot was swelling up and the skin around the cut was red, hard, and hot. He forced his foot into a hard-soled slipper, nearly crying out with pain, and kept going. Down the stairs, across the foyer, out the front door.

Outside it was spooky and much colder. Allen was afraid to walk behind the bushes – anything might be in there! – but he made himself do it so he could crawl through the basement window. His mother hadn't tried to fix the glass. That was the kind of thing his father always did. When Allen dropped onto the dryer he *did* yell, it hurt his foot so much. Tears sprang into his eyes. But he had to keep going.

Susie was awake inside the filing cabinet, whimpering and barking softly. Good thing he came when he did! He pulled open the drawer and she stumbled out. Allen put his arms around her.

"Susie, Suze – are you okay? Can you see, girl, can you?" The weird, milky film was still in her eyes. But she didn't seem blind. She whined and licked his face and gave her bark – two short quick yaps – that said she had to go out.

"I can't take you out, Suze, I can't. There are mean dogs out there. Come on, girl, come over here." He led her to a far corner of the cellar. "Go on, Susie, piddle here. It's okay."

Susie raised her eyes doubtfully to his.

"I know you don't like to piddle inside the house, but this time you have to. You have to!"

Susie whined and jiggled her hind legs.

Allen looked desperately around the basement. Nothing he could see, nothing he could...wait!

Hobbling to the pile of boxes filled with Christmas decorations, plus all the wadded tax forms he'd scooped out of the filing cabinet, Allen pulled open box after box until he found the pine garlands his mother put on the mantel every year. They were special garlands, very expensive she said, so soft and springy they looked real. Allen spread them in a little mat on the floor and pushed Susie onto it.

"See, girl, grass! Piddle on the grass!"

Susie gazed at him with disdain and whined again.

Allen jiggled her collar a few times, but she wasn't a toilet and this produced no water. He didn't know what to do. Susie had to piddle – and maybe poop, too – or she'd burst. But where? How?

He stuffed the garlands back into the Christmas box, which was patterned with elves smiling like stupid clowns. By now Allen had to stand on one foot, the other hurt so much. He just slightly touched the toes of his slipper to the floor for balance.

"Come on, Suze." The dog followed him to the laundry room. Allen closed the door while he swept all the glass into a corner. On the other side of the door Susie barked so loud he was sure somebody would hear. But no one came and he finished sweeping as fast as he could on one foot. Then he let Susie in, lifted her onto the dryer, climbed painfully up himself, and shoved her through the window, keeping a firm grip on her collar.

Immediately she squatted in the bushes, piddled, and pooped.

When she was finished, Allen pulled her by her collar back through the window. But Susie didn't want to come back in. She squealed and tugged backward against her collar. What if she escaped? A sick dog could bite her, even kill her! Allen gave the collar a frantic pull and Susie tumbled into him through the window, harder and heavier than he expected. He lost his balance and fell off the dryer, and both of them crashed to the floor.

Allen screamed. It *hurt*. For a second everything went black, but then it got better and he could see again. Susie! The dog lay on her side next to him, whimpering, and when he tried to touch her she growled at him.

"Susie! Is anything broken? Are you all right? *Susie...*" It was an anguished howl.

Susie inched toward him and licked his hand.

Slowly Allen got to his knees. He couldn't get any higher. Susie stood, too. From his pocket Allen took another pill and a piece of cheese. After she'd gobbled it down, he struggled, still on his knees, out of the laundry room to the filing cabinet.

But Susie wouldn't get in. She growled and even snapped when he tried to make her. So he sat by the metal cabinet, the dog on his lap, until she fell asleep, and then he stuffed her back in the bottom drawer. He could hardly do it, his body hurt so much. Every time he breathed, his chest hurt him. He tried to breathe just a little bit, because that was less painful.

Somehow he got back up on the dryer, through the window, and into the house. By then he was crying. Allen burrowed into his bed and pulled the covers over his head, praying desperately to God that his chest would stop hurting, that Susie hadn't broken any of her old bones, that pretty soon everything would somehow be all right.

» 29

Tessa ran the mile and a half through the dark residential streets of Frederick to her sister's house on Delmore Lane. She had only a limited time before Maddox thought to send agents to Ellen's house. Halfway there, she stopped to bend over briefly and breathe. Her stride was off from carrying Salah's laptop.

Ellen and Jim's fifties-style split level sat on a side street, shaded by now bare maples, bordered by the flower beds Ellen loved. The house showed only one light, in the living room. Tessa approached from the backyard next door, scanning for possible Bucars. None yet, as far as she could tell. The living room curtains weren't drawn. From one side she peered carefully into the window.

A teenage girl lolled on the sofa, eating nachos from a bag and watching television. A babysitter. Better than Tessa had hoped.

Both front and back doors were locked, as were all the windows. But sometimes people weren't so careful with the second story. It had been warm earlier today – warm enough to leave the backyard littered with toys – and Ellen might have opened windows to air out bedrooms. All that infant vomiting.

In the darkest corner of the backyard, Tessa shrugged out of Jess Langstrom's jacket, pushed it and the laptop under a bush, and brought a tricycle close to the back wall under a window. Balancing on the bicycle seat, she could just reach the eaves of the house's lowest, half-underground level. Her feet found the narrow upper window framing and she pulled herself to the roof, panting a bit.

She used to be better at this. At twenty-eight, she'd qualified for elite hostage-rescue training. But thirty-five wasn't twenty-eight and there had been slacker – not slack, but slacker – years in between.

The roof gave onto no windows, but there was one just around the corner, at the house's front. More dangerously visible, but necessary. Tessa reached around and felt with her fingers. The window wasn't locked.

Careless, Ellen, careless. I could be a thief.

She shoved the window open, hoping no neighbors called the cops, and pulled hard at the screen. It came away in her hand. Dropping it to the shrubbery below, Tessa oozed around the corner of the house and through the opening.

Two children lay asleep in the room, the baby in his crib and Tessa's three-year-old niece, Sally, in a toddler bed. The little girl didn't stir.

Carefully Tessa opened the door and crept down the half-flight of stairs. She couldn't see the living room from the hallway, which was good because it meant the babysitter couldn't see her. But light from the living room faded after she turned the corner and eased down the second half-flight, and she reached the basement level in darkness. Two rooms here, a large space land-mined with toys and child-sized furniture and, beyond, Jim's study.

It had to be there. It had to be.

Inside the study she closed the door and risked the light. Jim was not a methodical man. But even so, this was the logical place, and not among the piles of papers and books and rolled-up architectural drawings. Tessa opened the desk drawers, one after another, rifling efficiently through each. In the lower right drawer, she struck pay dirt.

Halfway back up the stairs, and the phone rang. The babysitter leapt off the couch and raced for the kitchen, on the other side of the hallway.

Tessa had no time. She slipped silently into the miniscule powder room, not daring to close the door, and pressed herself against the wall.

"Hello?" the girl said eagerly. "Blakely residence, Emily speaking!... Oh, hello, Mrs. Blakely."

Despite herself, Tessa grinned. The girl's disappointment was so unhidden, so artless. She'd been expecting some acned Romeo and instead had gotten Ellen.

"No, nobody's called, Mrs. Blakely, not your sister or anybody... The kids are all fine. They're asleep...okay. Bye." She dragged back to the living room.

And then started up the stairs.

Tessa caught her breath. She'd left the window in the kids' room open, planning to be only a moment, knowing that cold air seldom broke the sound sleep of the very young. Now Emily would see the window and the missing screen and, if she had half the sense she was born with, call the cops. Tessa bolted for the kitchen door.

Hand on the knob, however, she decided to risk waiting. Maybe the girl wouldn't notice the open window behind its filmy curtains, wouldn't go far enough into the room to feel the cold air coming in. Or maybe she'd think it had been open all along. There was probably a phone in Jim and Ellen's bedroom, but Emily wouldn't use that one. Babysitters didn't trespass into the master bedroom. She'd come back downstairs, use the kitchen phone to call 911...

Tessa slipped behind the open powder-room door and waited.

Emily came back downstairs, went into the living room, and resumed watching TV.

Ellen should get a more observant babysitter. Well, eventually Tessa might be able to tell her sister that.

When she was sure Emily was settled, Tessa crept back upstairs and out the window, awkwardly closing it behind her. She couldn't do anything about the screen, but screens fell out all the time. She hoped. Lightly she got to the ground, retrieved coat and laptop, and began running again. Not bad – the first of Maddox's agents hadn't shown up.

She caught another hitch on Route 15. This trucker was headed north but north was all right to leave Frederick. He could leave her at the big truck stop just before the Pennsylvania line, and she'd easily be able to pick up an anonymous ride back to Baltimore and BWI.

"I gotta have more coffee," the trucker said fifteen minutes later. They were the first words he'd spoken. Tessa didn't know why such silent types picked up riders at all, but they usually did. Perhaps they just wanted another body in the cab, mute evidence that they were not the only breathing life in a world of moving metal.

She said, "If you find a Starbucks, I'll treat."

He snorted. "I don't need no designer coffee."

"Listen...do you have a cell phone?"

He glanced at her suspiciously. "Yeah, why? You need to call somebody?"

"Sort of. Does your cell phone have data service on your calling plan?"

"Have *what?*"

"I mean, can you access the Internet from your cell phone?"

He peered at her. "Girlie, what do you think this is, a fucking war room? I got calls on my calling plan, period."

"There's a Starbucks!"

He sighed and pulled onto the exit. Tessa bought him a double mocha latte and a cheese Danish. She opened the laptop – still some battery left – and accessed her email account through the Web. Jess would have told Maddox that Tessa took a laptop with her. Maddox might communicate with her this way – and vice-versa.

But her one new message was not from Maddox.

> TO: tsand61@hotmail.com
> FROM: dkd78@vvvmail.com
> SUBJECT: dogs
>
> Nice try, Tessa. Ruzbihan wasn't helpful enough, you couldn't reach Aisha, and so you're preparing for the worst. What did you take from your sister's house? Not a gun, you already have one. My guess is a passport. The two of you look so much alike – and "Ellen Blakely" wouldn't be on a no-fly list, would she? But we're partners in this, you and I, you know that. I can't let you back out now. It wouldn't be fair. Not after all that Salah and I meant to each other. And where are you trying to go? To Aisha? You're right; she knows a lot. But not enough.
>
> Check out 1Kings 21:23.
>
> Fondly,
>
> Richard

He had been there. In the video arcade, listening to her call Ruzbihan, trying to call Aisha. He had been there, close enough to listen, and she hadn't noticed him, hadn't been looking... He had to have followed her from Tyler, followed KESSEL SHORT-TERM MOVING. And followed her run through the darkness to Ellen's house...

Despite her training, Tessa shuddered. She had never been undercover, had always worked counter-terrorism from the open. But she should have noticed him, among the masses of kids seething around the arcade. She hadn't been wary enough, hadn't expected to be followed except possibly by Maddox's men.

She didn't even know what Ebenfield looked like.

"Anything good on that contraption?" said the silent trucker.

"No," she said numbly. "Nothing good at all."

INTERIM

At midnight he sat in a dingy motel room north of Route 70. In the ashtray beside his laptop there burned a stick of incense, a smoky and pungent smell, not altogether pleasant. But he needed it. It distracted from that other smell, the necessary but terrible one, the price he had to pay. There was always a price. The incense was also supposed to help with the itching, at least that's what they'd said in Mogumbutuno, but the man hadn't found that to be true. Not everything they said was true.

The laptop screen showed no reply to his email.

That was all right. She'd reply when she was ready. He'd lost her after Frederick, lost her physically, but that was all right, too. There was no way she could truly escape him. No way any of them could. He was owed this.

The man leaned forward to relight the incense, which had gone out. When he did so, he caught a glimpse of his own face reflected in the computer screen. He closed the laptop so quickly that the sound echoed in the small room.

Soon.

SUNDAY

» 30

Cami woke before dawn, still lying on the gurney in the hospital corridor. The lights hadn't been turned up yet and the hallway had that night hush, broken only by the soft pinging of monitors and the even softer breathing of other patients on other gurneys. In the distance Cami, whose hearing seemed preternaturally sharp, picked up the footsteps of rubber-soled nurses' shoes, fading even as she listened.

And then another sound: a child whimpering.

Slowly Cami sat up. Her head felt clear and nothing hurt. Her leg was in a heavy cast, which suggested a serious fracture. For the first time she could recall the attack: Captain springing at her, her own reflexive kick and scream, the powerful jaws closing on her leg even as she stared, unable to either look away or stop screaming, and Mr. Anselm's bloody body. Then people behind her, shouts, a gunshot. Then nothing.

I went into shock, she thought, and felt obscurely ashamed. She was a nurse, after all.

A fracture would not keep her in the hospital very long. It might be followed by long physical therapy–Cami knew just how much that could involve – but that she was still here suggested other possibilities. Were they monitoring her for infection? Or did this dog plague lead to something in humans that could...she didn't know. Maybe nobody knew yet.

Tears blurred her vision. She was about to get severe with herself when she suddenly noticed two more things. The first was writing on her white cast. Small writing, upside down to her sight, in red pen. Cami squinted and twisted until she could make it out:

Your asleep. Back later! – Billy

She smiled even as the second thing distracted her: that faint sound of a child whimpering.

Cami inched her legs over the edge of the gurney. That was, of course, the great thing about a rigid cast: your limb was safe from further injury, unless you fell hard. She wasn't going to fall. There was a wheelchair not far from her gurney. Carefully, holding herself up against the wall, Cami reached it, plopped herself down, and wheeled slowly away.

The little girl lay on a gurney parked just inside a room with three other children. Between the two regular beds a woman sat asleep in a chair, head thrown back and mouth open, one hand touching each child in the beds. A second gurney had been shoved in the far corner and on it an older child, to judge from the dim outline under the blanket, also slept. But no one sat with this little girl. What was wrong with some parents?

"Hi, sweetheart, do you need anything?" Cami whispered.

The little girl, who looked about four, ignored her, sobbing softly. One half of her head was bandaged, covering her right cheek and eye. Cami could visualize what lay beneath and her whole body, even inside the cast, seemed to give a little shudder, like something touched by an electric current.

"My name is Cami, what's yours?"

"Poo-poo," the girl moaned, and Cami was about to become indignant at the absent parents all over again, but then she spotted the mangy stuffed kitten on the floor. Laboriously she bent and fished at it until she caught one ear.

"Poo-poo," the child said, snatched it from Cami, and stuck it under the covers.

"Poo-poo just fell off the bed. He's fine. Where's your mommy, honey?"

"Dead," the little girl said, with such stark finality that Cami was startled. "Snowy ate my mommy."

"*Ate*...Snowy is...was...your dog?" Fresh horror filled her.

"Snowy got dead, too." The whimpering began again.

A movement from the other bed caught her attention. A boy, nine or ten, rolled over and stared from suspicious brown eyes. "Stop bothering her!"

"I'm not bothering, I'm...are you her brother?"

"Yeah. Go away."

"I'm a nurse."

"Oh." He seemed to consider this. "Then why are you in a wheelchair?"

The woman hanging onto the other two children – *hanging on for dear life* is the way Cami thought of it – gave a sudden loud snore. Cami said over the noise, "A dog bit me." *Captain leaping and herself kicking and Mr. Anselm's body...*

"Us, too," the boy said. "What kind of dog was yours? Did anybody shoot it?"

Cami pushed away her own memory and looked more closely at the boy, now sitting up on his gurney. One arm was in a plaster cast. His face had a sickly, pale shininess, and his eyes gleamed feverishly. She recognized what she was looking at. This child was caught in his memory of the attack, enmeshed in it, in danger of being crushed by it.

"What kind of dog?" the boy demanded, and Cami said, "Mostly collie."

"Ours was a Newfoundland. He – "

Dear God, those animals were huge. *Snowy ate my mommy.* And the children trying to interfere, trying to stop the attack....

" – bit her on the neck and bit her on the head and bit her on the shoulder and – "

The little girl whimpered louder. These children should not be together right now, even though that was standard protocol. But right now they had vastly different psychological needs, they –

" – on the back and on the – "

"What's your name?" Cami said firmly. "Tell me your name."

"Jason."

"Where's your father?"

"No father."

"Okay, Jason, you come with me. I need you to...to push me down the hall. And you can tell me about Snowy, as much as you like."

Jason climbed easily out of his bed and walked over. Up close, his eyes shone even more wildly, darting around the room. Cami said to the girl, "You hold Poo-poo and I'll be back soon. Okay?"

She didn't answer, just lay there whimpering, eyes closed.

Cami got Jason out of the room. She started to push the wheels of her chair but Jason seized the chair with his good hand, nearly tipping her over. Strength, she suspected, born of almost intolerable tension. She said emphatically, "Be careful, Jason. Wheel me this way. It's a short distance and then you can tell me what happened. All of it."

"Okay!"

She guided him toward the meditation chapel at the end of the hall, hoping that it wasn't filled with gurneys. With the hope came another feeling: an easing of her own horror. This child needed her. That steadied her, always steadied her. It was why she'd become a nurse.

If she could help him and his little sister, Cami herself might be all right.

» 31

Jess said to Billy, "Why don't you have anything to eat in your refrigerator?"

"I do," Billy said. "Don't I?"

"Bottle of catsup, bottle of mustard, and two more six-packs."

"So what's your problem? There's a pizza in the freezer. I think."

Jess had spent Saturday night at Billy's, a sobering experience. After the FBI had finished grilling him at Tessa's house, an agent had driven Jess home. As Jess was stripping for the shower, Billy called from the hospital, sounding remarkably cheerful for someone who'd been shot. "They're throwing me outta here, Jess. Can you come get me?"

Jess groaned. "Can't one of your girls do it?"

"I'm done with all of them. Met the sweetest angel you ever saw, right here in the bone shop. Can you come right now?"

"Call Suzanne." A man who'd been shot in the line of duty – there's nothing Suzanne would like better. She'd eat Billy up.

"Not me, not that little tart," Billy said virtuously. "You come, Jess."

So he'd driven his own car, the seldom used and very battered Ford, to the hospital, picked up Billy, driven him home, and then had a beer with him. The beer turned into two, then a lot more than two, and Jess woke on Billy's floor after troubling dreams he couldn't quite remember. Billy's second-floor apartment, which faced the animal control offices across the street, consisted of one large room pre-furnished with a sofa bed that was never closed, some mismatched and ramshackle chairs, a table with one leg propped up on a tuna-fish can, and a gorgeous teak gun cabinet filled with assorted weaponry. Jess had slept on the floor in a none-too-clean sleeping bag.

He microwaved the pizza for breakfast. Billy, arm in a cast and sling, watched closely. "So what happened?"

"About what? Jesus, Billy, don't you ever clean your microwave?"

"No. What happened to make you look like a dog turd? And aren't you going in to work?"

"Yes. Now shut up and don't ask me anything else." Jess yanked out the pizza. Hot tomato sauce burned his hand.

"It was that FBI agent, wasn't it?" Billy said. "Her shooting up Victor Balonov. Stupid fucking feds – don't they see she had to shoot?"

Maddox had told Jess not to say anything about Tessa, not anything at all, not to anyone. Jess was tempted to do so just from sheer perversity, but he recognized how childish that would be, and anyway, anyone who expected Billy to keep a confidence was certifiable. So all he said was, "I don't know what they think."

"Well, it seems to me that the...*listen*."

A moment later Jess heard it, too: dogs, baying singly and then together. A lot of dogs – a very lot – had not been at home when Animal Control tried to pick them up. The dogs had suddenly "run away" or "died two months ago" or "were spending the week with my kids at my ex-husband's in North Carolina."

The baying grew louder. Billy said quietly, "They formed packs. Hunting."

Jess peered out the kitchen window. On this side of town, comparatively flat farmland gave way to woods and ridges rising up the mountains. Somewhere in that early morning light, Maryland Guardsmen ringed the town – but how close together? And with what cover?

"Let's hope those soldier boys know enough to keep guard from trees," Billy said. "The Guard posted singly or in pairs, Jess?"

"I don't know."

Jess cut the pizza in half and dumped one section in front of Billy, who picked it up awkwardly with his left hand. Last night's beer bottles littered the table. The sound of the dog pack suddenly changed. Not baying anymore. Lower noises, spaced apart, calling.

"They've got something surrounded," Billy said. "Fuck Victor Balonov, din't he just have to hit my right arm – Jess, *look*."

They both crowded near the kitchen window. A doe broke from the woods, speeding straight toward Billy's complex. It seemed to Jess that he could feel her panic right through the glass, a vibration like lightening in summer air. At the last minute the doe swerved and ran around the side of the building, toward the road. Two dogs raced out of the trees. A German shepherd and – Jesus! – a Bernese mountain dog the size of a small arm chair.

Jess's gun lay on the table. He grabbed it while Billy tore open the window. But when Jess got back, the dogs had followed the doe around to the front of the apartment building.

By the time he and Billy reached the front door, the doe lay thrashing on the ground, blood staining the small patches of snow. Five dogs tore at her: the shepherd, the Bernese mountain, two mutts, and a small terrier of some type. "Right there in the front yard!" Billy said, and there was a note of admiration in his voice, so dumb-ass and so Billy that Jess scowled at him. People had appeared in doorways along the corridor and at the top of the stairs to the second floor. Some stupid woman kept screaming. Somehow in Jess's mind the screaming became the doe's, not human. He opened the door, stepped out on the porch, and fired.

"Damn! Missed!" Billy said. "Maybe you need lessons from that FBI girl."

The dogs had scattered at the sound of the gun – all except two. The Bernese mountain turned and charged directly at Jess.

He threw himself backward into the hallway and slammed the door. It was metal, the better to thwart thieves, but the entire thing shuddered when a hundred pounds of enraged dog hit it. Instinctively, Jess leaned against the door. The screaming around him had intensified. Billy howled, "Shut up!" which only added to the noise.

The Bernese turned and followed the rest of the pack into the woods, except for the terrier cowering under the bank of mailboxes by the road.

Cautiously Jess opened the door, gun ready (like it had done him a lot of good so far!). There was something different about this dog. It had hunted with the pack, or maybe just trailed it, but it wasn't attacking now. Nor was it trying any longer to feed on the mangled doe. Jess took a careful step forward, then another, then two more. The dog under the mailbox neither attacked nor bolted. Not far out of puppyhood, it had short, wiry, shit-brown hair, a flat-topped head, and overly long legs, a genuine mixed ancestry that somehow gave it the look of a tipsy end table.

"Hey, boy," Jess said experimentally, ready to shoot if he had to.

The dog wagged its stubby tail.

Then, as if remembering that Jess was the enemy, it turned and raced across the road, around the Animal-Control building, and into the woods where the rest of the pack had gone.

"You coulda got *that* one, at least!" Billy called derisively. But Jess wasn't listening. He'd gotten close enough to the misshapen dog to see its eyes. The animal hadn't been aggressive, but its light-brown eyes nonetheless had that same milky film as the dogs that had been mangling people for days now. The terrier-mix was infected, all right – but not vicious. Just what Dr. Latkin had said the scientists might be able to use to find a defense against this disease.

Finding that small misbegotten terrier had suddenly become Jess's number-one priority.

» 32

Steve Harper slammed into DiBella's office, the notice in his hand. "What the hell is this shit, Don?"

The sheriff stood, but calmly. "It should be clear what it is, Steve. You're on temporary suspension."

"Now? When we need everybody possible on the street, shutting down these fucking dogs?"

DiBella searched among the debris on his messy desk. He looked as if he hadn't slept in way too long. Well, guess what – nobody else was sleeping either. This was a fucking *crisis.*

DiBella found the paper he was looking for. "You signed off on this statement, Steve. You really shot an uninfected dog less than two feet from its owner?"

"I didn't know it was uninfected!"

"She said she told you so."

Steve slammed his right fist into his left palm. "So what? They lie, you know that, they just want to protect their damn pets no matter who else dies. We should shoot every fucking dog on sight!"

DiBella gazed at him, and all at once Steve heard himself. So he wasn't advocating the "temperate and appropriate response" – so what? The time for a temperate response wasn't in the middle of a natural disaster!

DiBella said, "This is about Davey, isn't it? Your judgment is impaired just now. That's natural, given...everything. But I can't have you out there in the field like this. The temporary suspension stands."

"But – "

"That's all. Leave your badge and gun at the desk."

Steve slammed out of DiBella's office. DiBella was an idiot. *Now*, when every officer was urgently needed on the street, now in the middle of a huge threat... *"This is about Davey."*

Of course it was about Davey. Everything was about Davey. Steve couldn't eat, couldn't sleep, couldn't console his mother, who'd lost her only grandchild. When he stopped working, stopped moving for ten minutes, all he could see was *the brown mastiff with a single long string of saliva and blood hanging from its mouth onto Davey's body...* What did DiBella expect Steve to do with his rage if he couldn't help rid Tyler of the dogs destroying it?

What?

» 33

When Tessa's latest ride let her out at Terminal A of Baltimore-Washington Airport, she found a phone bank and stuck in her credit card – no help for it, this time. She was nearly out of cash. Maddox would trace it, but not instantly.

Still no answer at Aisha's Geneva apartment, so Tessa called the World Health Organization. It was past noon in Switzerland, and even on a Sunday someone should be answering. Global medical emergencies did not cease during weekends.

"Organisation mondiale de la Santé."

"Do you speak English?" Tessa asked.

"Yes. May I help you?" The French accent was strong.

"I need to reach Dr. Aisha Jamilla bint Mohammed Mahjoub. This is her sister-in-law in America and there is a family emergency. It's urgent, involving her mother, Fatima. I *must* speak to her immediately."

"Dr. Mahjoub...one moment, *s'il vous plaît*...She has gone on assignment from Headquarters."

"Gone where?"

"I cannot give to you that information."

A sensible safety precaution. Under any other circumstances, Tessa would have approved. "Please, I need to reach her...it's her mother. Is she somewhere reachable by phone? Can you give her a message?"

"Yes, that I may do."

"Tell her – tell her right away – to call Tessa about her mother, Fatima. Call at this number." Tessa read off the pay-phone number, adding the international code for the United States.

"I will do this."

"Thank you." She tried to sound urgent but not annoyed. The FBI kept airport spotters at BWI. Maddox could have her picked up in two minutes if he knew she was here. She sat, in Jess's too-big coat and her own sunglasses, in the chair closest to the phone bank, reading an abandoned copy of the *Baltimore Sun*.

DOG PLAGUE DEATH TOLL AT 36

PRESIDENT DECLARES FEDERAL DISASTER AREA

"FINDING THE PATHOGEN DOESN'T MEAN FINDING THE CURE," SAYS TOP CDC INVESTIGATOR

MUTATION OR TERRORIST ACT?

Tell me something I don't know.

Aisha called forty-five minutes later. "Tessa! *Qu'est-ce que c'est?* They said...maman..."

"It's not Fatima," Tessa said quickly. "I had to say that to get WHO to contact you, but it *is* urgent, Aisha, as urgent as possible. You know of the dog plague here in Maryland?"

"Of course." She sounded bewildered but there was a sharp undertone of resentment as well, and Tessa realized how badly she'd scared Aisha. "We at WHO were notified about the plague by the CDC, and now it is on CNN as well. We are sending observers, but not me, I am now – "

"I was in the middle of the plague. I live in Tyler, Maryland, now. And I've been getting email messages with cryptic references – "

" 'Cryptic'?"

It was rare that Aisha didn't understand an English word, but it happened. All at once, unbidden, a memory took over Tessa's mind and Salah was solidly before her in his gray suit, curly black hair, dark expressive eyes:

"You look so dapper tonight, Salah."

"Dapper'? What is 'dapper'?"

"Tessa? Are you there?"

"Yes. Sorry. Strange messages, with references to dogs, from Richard Ebenfield. He was – "

"I know who he is." Said in a tone that could freeze glaciers.

"Aisha, he sent Salah email with the word 'dog' in Arabic, over and over, three months ago. Long before the plague broke."

"The plague?" Now Aisha sounded bewildered again. "Richard could have nothing to do with this dog plague."

"Why not?"

"He is not...I have not seen him for fifteen years, the year after Salah finished his studies at the Sorbonne. Richard had rooms near Salah's and knew Salah and his friend Ruzbihan, Ruzbihan al-Ashan, he was – "

"I've spoken to Ruzbihan. Ebenfield emailed him last year asking for Salah's email address, and Salah said to give it to him. But Ebenfield didn't contact Salah until December."

Aisha sighed, a soft sibilant sound continents away. "Richard was...*le dommage*...a nuisance. He followed around Salah and Ruzbihan, but especially Salah. He was so jealous of Salah! Salah was everything Richard was not. Handsome, intelligent, successful. And rich, of course. Richard would dress like Salah, try to act like him.... It was pathetic. But Richard could have nothing to do with your plague. He did not finish his studies, he did not attend his lectures, he was... thin. Papery. No – the word – light of weight. Not a person of substance. If you think he could, perhaps, genetically engineer a microorganism to infect these dogs' brains, you are wrong. He could not."

It was the same thing Ruzbihan had said about Ebenfield.

Tessa listened very carefully, balancing Aisha's words against her vicious tone. Aisha, who was usually as easy-going as her brother, as generous of spirit. "What did Ebenfield do to you, Aisha?"

Silence.

"Please."

"He tried to rape me."

Tessa gaped. She knew what rape meant for an Arab woman, even a modern Arab woman like Aisha: ostracism, blame, shame that could be erased by nothing short of murder.

"When he could not become Salah, he came for me. I was at the Sorbonne then, and Salah had finished his studies. I would not go out with Richard, would not dance with him, would do nothing with him. He caught me one night outside my dormitory and – he could not do even that successfully, Tessa. He failed at the act of rape as he failed, always, at everything. Richard is weak, Tessa, but the weak can nonetheless be dangerous. A contemptible man. Just be careful."

"Did you report the attempted rape?" Tessa said, and immediately regretted the question. Of course she had not. "Aisha, I am so sorry – "

"This was fifteen years ago, and he did not succeed. I am all right. Richard fled immediately, to Africa, I believe. He joined the Catholics, les Frères de l'Espoir céleste, and none of us heard from him again."

The Catholics. 2Kings 8:13. "Okay, Aisha, thank you. I'm sorry to have frightened you about Fatima."

"Are you in some trouble, Tessa? You said you live in the middle of the dog plague?"

"I'm fine, Aisha. They're getting it under control, and my dog Minette is not infected." Tessa suddenly saw Minette, a loving bundle of silvery fur. No one would ever know how much Minette had kept Tessa sane in the first terrible days after Salah's death. It was only with Minette that Tessa had been able to cry, able to let out the terrible storm of tears and rage. *The things we owe to dogs.*

"That is good. Good-bye, Tessa. Allah be with you."

"And you."

She hung up, hitched her purse onto the shoulder of Jess's coat, and walked toward the counter for British Air. Maddox would have a trace soon on her credit card, and by that time she had to be out of BWI. She had to be on her way, to the one person who might be able to tell her what he certainly would never tell anyone else.

"None of us heard from him again," Aisha had said. But that was not strictly true. Ruzbihan's email to Tessa said he had not seen Richard Ebenfield "since many, many years." But on the phone, in the stress of a midnight call that he wanted kept secret, Ruzbihan had mentioned seeing Ebenfield in Mogumbutuno "a few years ago." Mogumbutuno was the capital of a West African country remarkable even on that beleaguered continent for the number of its revolutions. Mogumbutuno, Tessa happened to know, had been open to the West only briefly, between civil conflicts, two years ago. Before that, the country had been closed for two decades. So two years ago was the only time Richard Ebenfield and Ruzbihan al-Ashan could have been there at the same time – which was not "since many, many years."

She went to study the DEPARTURES board for the next flight to London.

» 34

Allen's foot wouldn't stop hurting. Every time he moved it under the covers, he almost screamed out loud. But he couldn't do that because then his mother would...do what? Take him to the doctor? Nobody in Tyler was supposed to leave their houses. But if she knew about his foot...

Gross, greenish-yellow stuff was oozing out of the foot. And under the covers, it smelled really bad.

He pinched his arm hard to keep himself from crying. Sometimes that was the only thing that helped. He had to stay home and get down to the basement and give Susie food and water and a sleeping pill. He *had* to.

"Allen? Are you awake, sweetie?" She stood in the doorway in her robe, her hair all mussed up, her eyes red and swollen. So she'd been fighting on the phone with his dad. Probably Allen's father hadn't come home again last night because of the quarantine.

"I'm awake."

"What shall we do today? Would you like to help me make chocolate chip cookies? Yum!"

"Maybe later. I don't feel so good."

Instantly she was by his bed, putting a hand on his forehead. "Why, you have a fever! Does your stomach hurt?"

"No," Allen lied, and promptly threw up.

His mother made little mother-noises and wiped his mouth with a corner of the blanket, which was pretty gross except he saw he'd already gotten puke on the blanket. Now his head started to hurt really bad. At first Allen didn't realize that she was pulling the blanket and sheet off his bed, and when he did, he tried to grab them and pull them back. "No! No!"

"Sweetie, it's okay, I'll just wash the...*Allen!*"

Now the green, awful-smelling stuff coming out of his foot had blood in it. The smell made him want to throw up again. His mother, her eyes big and scared, touched the foot and Allen screamed and started to cry.

In the hospital he slept, maybe a long time, and when he woke up, he didn't hurt so much anymore. He lay on a skinny white bed with his mother sitting beside him. He couldn't ever get away from her, it seemed, and then felt bad because it wasn't a nice thought. His mother had carried him out to the car even though sick dogs could have attacked them. They had not, in fact, even seen any dogs, sick or well, but it *could have* happened. Then his mother yelled at nurses and doctors until they paid enough attention to Allen, and then after that he didn't remember anymore.

His foot, wrapped in so many bandages it looked like a big pillow, was propped up on some rolled blankets. A bag on a big pole hung over his bed and a little hose ran from the bag into his arm. Beside the bed, Allen's mother snored in a chair. There were three other beds in the room, two with kids in them. One was a little girl holding some sort of babyish stuffed animal. The other was a boy about his age with his arm all bandaged up.

The boy said, "Go away. This is our room now."

"Is not," Allen said automatically.

"Is too. The other kids' mom took them away so it's ours."

"Is not."

"Is too. Is that your mother?"

Allen looked at his mom, asleep hunched over in the chair, as if he'd never seen her before. "Yeah."

"Our mom's dead. Our dog ate her."

Allen said, "Liar."

"No, he really did," the boy said, so seriously that Allen felt sick. Maybe it was true. *A dog could eat a mother.* There was something wrong with the boy's brown eyes. They were too shiny or something. "He bit her on the neck and bit her on the head and bit her on the shoulder and bit –"

Allen said, to stop him, "*My* dog would never hurt anybody. She's a good dog."

"Snowy was a good dog!"

"Oh, right – a good dog who kills people!"

The other boy jumped out of bed, ran over to Allen's bed, and socked him on the arm. Allen swung back, missing wildly. They spat at each other, globs of white hock that landed on the bed. Amazingly, Allen's mother slept on. The other boy tried to hit Allen in the face, but smacked his arm against the metal bed railing, and cried out.

"Jason! You stop that!"

A woman in a wheelchair pushed past the little girl's bed over to Allen's. He expected her to look mad but instead she smiled at Jason and put out one arm to touch him lightly on the hip. He scowled, and looked away, then moved defiantly behind the wheelchair. "Where do you need to go, Cami? I'll take you!"

Cami's eyes moved over Allen to his mother. All at once Allen felt a need to defend his mother, sleeping there sagged over like some skinny broken doll. "She's real tired," he said angrily. "She was up all night!" Which might even have been true, he realized. Crying or fighting on the phone or walking up and down the way she did.

"And you're nice to worry about her," Cami said, smiling at him.

Jason was scowling again. "Come on, Cami! Where you want to go?"

The little girl spoke for the first time. "You said you'd read me a story!"

"I will, Lisa, I promise. But first I need to go to...to the gift shop and you know I can't go if Jason doesn't help me. He's my main man, aren't you, Jason?"

Jason had been mouthing *bit her on the neck and bit her on the head and bit her on* – but now he stopped. His good hand gripped the wheelchair hard and he yanked it backward toward the door. Cami said to the little girl, "I'll bring you something from the gift shop, Lisa."

Then they were gone. Allen settled back into his bed. He wanted Cami to bring *him* something from the gift shop. He wanted to be her main man. Which was stupid because she was a grown-up, too, but not a grown-up like his mother. Nothing like his mother.

Who had brought him to the hospital. If his mother hadn't of done that, maybe the doctors would have had to cut off his foot or something. That happened in a movie he saw once. His mother had probably saved his life, and he wished she wasn't here, and Cami was just this dopey adult (only she didn't look that old) in a wheelchair, and here Allen wanted to push her down to the gift shop....

It was too hard to think about. He gave it up and started to plot how to get Susie her food and water and pills, in the bottom drawer of his father's filing cabinet in the basement.

» 35

Jess drove his car, with Billy beside him, to the makeshift critical-incident headquarters. He hadn't wanted Billy to come along, but Billy had been insistent. "I gotta see about one little thing, and then I'll just sit in the car and wait for you, okay?"

"It turned a lot colder overnight. How long do you think you can sit in a freezing car?"

"How long are you gonna be?" Billy said blandly. "Come on, Jess, you know I'll go nuts if I just sit at home all day. And I told you, I gotta check on something."

"Oh, all right," Jess said, because he'd humored Billy their whole lives.

"Do you remember," Billy said as Jess drove, "that year in high school when you were a senior and I was a sophomore and we were running around with crazy Desmond and his crowd?"

Of course Jess remembered. That was the year he'd met Elizabeth, Desmond's sister. He said nothing.

"We had some great times, didn't we, Jess, huh?"

Jess recognized this opening. "What do you want, Billy?"

"I want you to help me," Billy said, which was so unprecedented that Jess blinked and glanced over. Billy gazed at him seriously, parka open over his sling, shirt misbuttoned.

"Help you with *what?*"

"Help me court a girl. No, don't laugh, Jess, I mean it – not like I usually do, you know, lick 'em and stick 'em, but a *real* courtship. I was thinking you and some woman could, like, ask us to dinner. A dinner party. You know how to cook. I could bring a bottle of wine or something."

Now Jess stared so hard at Billy that he nearly ran the car off the road. Billy began to really get into his fantasy. "Maybe you could ask that FBI girl. She's pretty. Yeah, 'Jess and Tess' – it's made for you!"

"It's 'Tessa,' she's married, and you're a lunatic, Billy. A raving lunatic."

Billy said quietly, "You been alone too long, Jess. Elizabeth left a long time ago."

"We're here." Jess stopped the car in front of a uniformed Guardsman. Immediately the car was surrounded by reporters.

"Mr. Langstrom, are dogs hunting in packs?"

"Is it true that yesterday you fatally shot a citizen who wouldn't surrender his dogs?"

"Mr. Langstrom! Mr. Langstrom!"

"Jesus Christ," Billy said. From the expression on the Guardsman's face, Jess could tell that he'd heard the story – or some version of the story – about Victor Balonov. But the soldier waved him through when Jess said, "I have to talk to Dr. Latkin. In an official capacity." For half a second he considered Tessa's formula – *By order of the president of the United States* – but thought better of this.

Jess parked beside the Cedar Springs Motel lot. In the fields around it had sprung up, overnight, an entire city of large Army-issue tents. Billy ambled off toward the dog shelter and Jess knocked on the CDC mobile van. A girl in a white lab coat went to fetch Joe Latkin. When the scientist appeared, Jess said without preamble, "I saw something. I think it was a dog with symptoms of infection but no aggression."

Latkin stared at him. Finally he said, "There's coffee in the mess tent. This way."

After Jess told Latkin about the shit-brown terrier mix with milky eyes but no aggression, Latkin made five cell-phone calls. Jess said as mildly as possible, "I want to be part of this search, Joe," and Latkin nodded absently. Jess took that as authorization and went to search for Don DiBella. Scott Lurie, the FEMA incident chief, would be officially in charge of the search for the terrier, but he knew neither the landscape nor the men who did. Sheriff DiBella would make any decisions that counted.

DiBella was already busy summoning people. Evidently he had not heard about Tessa's flight, although he had heard about the rest of it. "Hey, Jess, we need you to organize a search for some dog that Dr. Latkin has identified. He says it could be important. Are you still working with that FBI agent who shot Balonov?"

"No."

"Oh. Well, let me describe this dog to you and tell you what we're looking for and why. Then we'll meet at the north checkpoint in an hour and form teams. You better get breakfast first, if you haven't already – going to be a long day. Mess tent is over there."

"Okay," Jess said. That was the third person today to tell him things he already knew, if you counted Billy.

Billy, of course, was not waiting in the car as he'd promised. Jess found him in the dog tent, which was significantly colder than yesterday. Rows and rows of dog crates, ranging from the size of a laundry basket to that of a small bathroom, sat on the grass. Dogs snarled or barked or slept or whimpered. The noise was terrifying, as was the smell. Volunteers hosed down cages with warm water without removing the dangerous dogs. More volunteers poured in kibble through chutes that kept them a foot away from the bars. It was a canine version of hell.

But a much smaller hell than it should have been. There were still a lot of loose dogs out there.

Billy was pushing bits of a cookie through the cage bars of a feebly snapping, ancient-looking, clearly arthritic collie. Jess said sharply, "Don't do that, Billy."

"Don't do no harm." He crooned at the dog, "She's a good ol' girl, aren't you, pretty Belle?"

"I have to take you home, then come back here for duty. We need to find that terrier mix."

"Just give me another minute with Belle. I gotta report on her to Cami."

Jess walked the rows of cages. He found Minette in a far section against the tent wall, with a wide swath of withered grass between these cages and the rest. He said to a man inspecting the dogs, "Why are these dogs separate?"

"Who are you?" the man said, voice raised to be heard over all the dogs. The shouting made the question sound belligerent.

"Tyler Township Senior Animal Control Officer."

"Oh. Well, these animals aren't infected yet. We need to see if the virus is airborne, and if so, what the range is." He moved on.

So Minette was a guinea pig. The toy poodle wagged her tail at him, pushing against the bars of her cage. Her eyes were clear. On the label giving Minette's particulars, Jess noticed a red stick-on dot with the number "2." Other cages in this section bore yellow or blue dots. He found the inspector again.

"What does the system of dots mean?"

The man didn't look up as he shouted his answer. "Red has had the shortest airborne exposure in the tent here, blue next, yellow longest. Numbers mean order of sacrifice for dissection, if we need to do that."

"Thanks."

Jess went back to Minette. He wished he'd brought a cookie, like Billy had. Minette barked hopefully, tail going like a pendulum on speed. Jess inspected all the other red-dotted cages. Then he carefully peeled off Minette's red dot with the number "2" and exchanged it for another dot on another cage with the number "8," the highest he could find.

She was still wagging her tail when he left.

» 36

Tessa waited until an hour before British Air flight 0043 was due to take off for London. That was as long as she dared delay. Earlier she'd phoned the ticket counter from a pay phone and discovered that seats were available, but she would need time to make it over to International Departures. It was going to be close.

In the meantime, she took Salah's laptop into a pay-to-use data booth and accessed her email account on the Web. Her throat spasmed. Two new emails: Ebenfield and Maddox.

> TO: tsand61@hotmail.com
> FROM: dkd@vvvmail.com
> SUBJECT: You
> Tessa – Where are you now? Where are any of us in this rotten world? Thousand-year Reichs fall, civilizations crumble, everyone dies. In the end, it all means nothing, and yet still we strive to right the balance. Email me back, Tessa.
> كلب الرئيس

Cheap and lunatic philosophical maundering. *This* idiot was somehow connected with a deadly plague?

> TO: tsand61@hotmail.com
> FROM: john_maddox@FBI.gov

SUBJECT: Contact

Tessa – Where are you? Things are growing critical. Contact me now.

Maddox

For a lunatic moment the similarity between the two emails made a rising bubble of hysteria in Tessa. She fought it down. At least this time Ebenfield had spared her any more Biblical references. On a translation site she looked up each Arabic word of Ebenfield's new sign-off, remembering that Arabic was read right to left. She got "dog" and "first." Dogs first?

Before she left the booth, Tessa also Googled Ebenfield's previous citation, 1Kings 21:23:

"The dogs shall eat Jezebel by the wall of Jezreel."

Beautiful.

She stayed in the booth another fifteen minutes, researching. Then she made herself eat a tasteless and overpriced hamburger. In a stall in the ladies' room, she wrapped her Smith & Wesson in the take-out food bag, padded with half a dispenser's worth of paper towels. Regretfully she shoved the gun into the trash. For the second time this morning, she dialed the British Air ticket counter, pitching her voice high and flustered. "Hello? Hello?"

"Yes, ma'am, how may I help you?" One of those cool English voices that said *I'm unflappable and you're not.*

"It's my daughter! She's on the way to the airport – she has to go to London – her husband is British and his mother is ill well not ill exactly she fell down a flight of stairs and broke every bone in her body practically the doctor says – "

"Ma'am? How may I help you?"

"My daughter has to go to London! I want to buy her ticket over the phone on your next flight – she just called on the cell phone she's parking the car I thought it might save time if I – "

"One ticket on British Air flight 0043. The passenger's name, please?"

"Ellen Blakely. But the ticket will go on my credit card, that's a different name she – "

"Yes, ma'am. Please spell the passenger's last name."

Tessa did, then held her breath. She wasn't sure where the no-fly list was actually checked, at ticket purchase or at the gate.

The clipped English voice said, "And the name on the credit card, please?"

"Tessa Sanderson. S-A-N-D-E-R-S-O-N."

"And the number?"

The card cleared. Five minutes later Tessa walked to the ticket counter, produced Ellen's passport, and claimed the ticket.

"Luggage to check?"

"No. Just a carry-on."

"International Departures are from – "

"I know. Thank you."

She cleared Security, her breath tangled in her throat, her face displaying nothing, and was the last passenger aboard the plane. It was half-empty; most people preferred overnight flights to Europe. Salah always had. Tessa sank into a window seat, leaned her head against the cold glass of the window, and tried to organize her thoughts for London.

She might get no farther than Heathrow. Maddox might have her picked up at the gate. Or he might have her followed, hoping she would lead agents to something even more interesting. Or Maddox might conclude that he had had it wrong and that the Bureau had made a massive, humiliating mistake with her.

Certainly it had happened before. Aldrich Ames had sold out the CIA to the Russians, and Robert Hanssen had done the same to the FBI. Tessa, Maddox might figure, had been lured into suspect activities through love of her husband, and Salah Mahjoub had indeed been a very clever, until-now undetected terrorist.

And there lay the heart of the question.

The American public thought that either you were a terrorist or you were not. But in reality, it was never that simple. A terrorist organization, large or small, is still an organization. Like any other organization, it needs supplying from the outside. Is the man who sells arms to a terrorist group, knowing its purpose, a terrorist himself? Yes. But what of the humble man who sells it blankets, or fish, or stone to build a hut in Afghanistan or Iraq or Syria? Is he, too, a terrorist?

And what of the man who supplies information?

The Mideast was rich in information brokers. All kinds of brokers, all kinds of information. If you sold information about an oil refinery to what you thought was simply the refinery's business competitor, and later a terrorist group blew up that same refinery, did that make you, too, a terrorist? What if you were merely the person who'd sold the information to the person who sold the information?

Ruzbihan al-Ashan's family dealt in copper. They had powerful international business connections, including in Africa. A lot of copper came from West Africa. And a lot of copper was, presumably, sold in North Africa, and not only in Ruzbihan's native Tunis. Also in Rabat, in Algiers, in Cairo.

What did Ruzbihan know? Did his firm deal with the World Bank, where Salah had worked? And what – oh, God, she hated herself for even thinking this question! – had Ruzbihan been able to convince Salah to do?

"Please fasten your seat belts and return your tray tables to their upright positions," said a dazzlingly handsome young flight attendant. "We'll be taking off in just a few moments. We thank you for flying British Air, and we hope your trip is a pleasant one."

» 37

Ed Dormund got the call right after he and Cora had another fight. There was no bread for sandwiches and Cora was too chicken to go out and buy some. "There's dangerous dogs out there!" she said. "You go!"

"Like I don't already do everything around here while you sit on your fat ass and cry," Ed snarled. Christ, being cooped up with her like this was driving him nuts. He couldn't go to work because if he left Tyler the fascist government wouldn't let him back in, and then where would he go? It wasn't like he had money for luxuries like motels. Cora spent all his money on her so-called therapy and her depression drugs and her stupid crafts.

"Hey, Ed," Dennis Riley said on the phone, "they get your dogs?"

"No. I set them free."

"Good for you," Dennis said, and Ed felt a flush of pleasure. It *had* been ingenious, the way he'd figured out how to lift the gate latch without leaving the house. He'd duct-taped together the broom handle, mop handle, and vacuum-cleaner extension and had thrust the whole thing through an open window. Jake and Petey and Rex had rushed right out. Now at least they had a fighting chance. Dennis's praise helped push down the thought that he should have just shot the animal control goons demanding his dogs, but then the authorities would have arrested Ed *and* his Samoyeds, and what good would that do?

Dennis said, "They got my Lab, Ninja. I wasn't home and Barb gave him up, she didn't know what else to do. I don't blame her, but Ninja didn't have no plague and there's a bunch of us that don't like this goddamn government thinking they can get away with seizing private property without even warrants."

"Yeah. I know."

Dennis's voice dropped several tones. "A bunch of us are going to do something about it, Ed. Are you with us?"

Ed drew a deep breath. In the next room he could hear Cora, moaning again. Rage rose in him, the rage he felt so much nowadays, for just about everything: for Cora and his lousy job and the economy and the government that never did anything to help people like him, only took away everything it could in taxes and fees and penalties and speed traps. And now even dogs.

"Yeah," Ed said, "whatever you're planning, count me in."

» 38

Jess stood in the lightly falling snow beside Rick Carlin, a nineteen-year-old whom Jess had known since he was an infant. Jess and Billy had gone to high school with Rick's parents. *If things had turned out differently*, Jess thought as he checked his rifle, *this could be my son.* Sophomore year he had dated Linda Carlin, who was then Linda Nellis. Why had they broken up? He couldn't remember. Although he had a vague idea that Linda had dumped him.

"Okay, you all have your assignments, let's do it," Don DiBella said. "Everybody clear?"

No one was unclear, or at least no one said anything. Men and women began to disperse, the town teams more lightly clad than the countryside ones. The town teams would search street by street for the shit-brown terrier with milky white eyes but no sign of aggression, while other volunteers began a telephone tree to ask if anyone had seen the dog. Jess and Rick, a countryside team, drove to the last place the terrier had been seen, the woods behind the Animal Control building.

"Do you think we'll find him?" Rick said. Jess glanced over. The boy looked excited, nervous, and self-important, all at once. Nineteen.

"Dunno, Rick."

"What does it mean if we do?"

"I'm not sure of that, either, except that Dr. Latkin thinks it may speed up finding a cure or a vaccine or something." This sounded vague even to Jess, but he didn't understand the science here. Increasingly, he thought that he didn't understand much of anything.

"Dad said there are dog packs still hunting out here. Packs you were supposed to catch but didn't yet."

It sounded like an accusation but Jess knew it wasn't. Rick's voice had grown thick, and he stared determinedly out the passenger window. Jess said gently, "You have a dog missing, Rick?"

"Zorro. Our Bernese mountain."

Who had done its best to attack Jess earlier that morning. He didn't say this, or anything. The terrier was hunting with that pack. The countryside search teams had orders to shoot any dog they saw except the terrier. Rick shouldn't be out here, but there was no way he could send the boy back now. That would only make it worse for him. Damn, Jess needed Billy. Billy, unlike Jess, could put a bullet cleanly wherever he chose.

Jess parked the car and they started into the woods on foot. It wasn't hard to follow the pack, which had gone barreling through the brush, breaking twigs and leaving footprints and marking territory. A light snow began to fall.

When they came to Black Creek, here a wide, shallow swath murmuring over icy stones, Jess lost the trail. He looked at Rick. "Any ideas?"

The boy scanned everything carefully, and Jess had a powerful image of Rick's father Buddy at this age. Buddy Carlin had been a wonderful tracker, back when Tyler had been smaller and sleepier than it was now, with no commuters, no Wal-Mart, no plague.

"I think they went up the bank," Rick said. "That way."

They climbed the bank, steeper on this side of the creek than the other, and headed west. If dogs were going to escape the Tyler township limits, this was the direction they were going to do it. At the top of the bank the woods were mostly white pine, birch, and oak, miles of them spreading toward West Virginia. Somewhere out there were supposed to be Maryland Guardsmen, preventing dogs from escaping Tyler. Yeah, right.

"They were here," Rick said, pointing to a pile of half-frozen turds under a bush. Jess would have missed it. He sighed.

They walked another forty minutes before he heard baying, so faint he had to strain to catch the sound.

"Northwest," Rick said. "But look over there, Mr. Langstrom."

"Jess," he said automatically. And then, "Bear."

The brush had been raked back as the bear dug for mast. Jess saw signs of acorns, too. Lately bears had been wandering in from West Virginia with greater frequency. Female bears would be denned with newborn cubs; this was probably a male, newly up for the too-early spring, scrounging for food. Hungry.

Rick said, "Dad told me once his dogs ran a bear for ten miles before he shot it." He glanced at Jess's face and said, "Not here, of course. Somewhere it was legal. A long, long time ago."

Jess said nothing. The dog pack bayed again, closer.

He followed Rick through the forest. As they ascended steep ground, the trees thinned a little, letting the light snow drift lazily onto Jess's shoulders. He wasn't in as good shape as he should be, and he tried to keep the boy from noticing that his breathing had become labored. Rick climbed lightly, constantly gazing around, determined to miss nothing.

But it was Jess who first spotted the blood. A few drops, brownish-red on the lighter brown pine needles. Then more. When he stooped to examine it, his chest tightened. "Not bear."

"Uh-uh," Rick said. The few hairs matted in the blood were short, wiry, shit-brown.

They found the terrier a hundred yards on, after more blood. The little body was mangled so badly that at first Jess wasn't even sure it was the terrier. A foot lay in one direction, a haunch in another. Slowly Jess examined each piece, not touching them, until he was sure.

"Bear," Rick said.

"Yes." And not a male. This was the thorough work of a female with cubs nearby. "We need the head, Rick. With the brain."

They hunted for thirty minutes, but didn't find it. *Shit, shit, shit.*

The dog pack burst from cover before either of them was aware of it. Four of the five that had brought down the doe early that morning. The dogs stopped and circled, growling. Among them was the Bernese mountain.

Jess and Rick stood back to back, rifles raised and cocked. The dogs continued to circle. *It would be the Doberman,* Jess decided; that was the leader. He put the dog in his sights and fired.

The Doberman dropped. The other dogs scattered, howling. Jess aimed at the German shepherd, fired, and missed. Behind him a second shot sounded, echoing off the side of the mountain as if reluctant to end.

Then silence.

Jess turned slowly. At the edge of the woods, almost back in the safety of its cover, lay the Bernese mountain. Zorro. The dog had been fleeing, no longer attacking. Rick stood with his rifle still raised, his young body completely motionless, taut as piano wire. He stayed that way, a boy who had just shot his own dog, until Jess spoke as softly as he could.

"Rick?"

Finally the boy moved. "We had orders. *Orders.*" He resumed looking for the head of the mangled terrier.

Jess was careful not to look at Rick, not to notice whether there were tears freezing on his face. Rick's movements were steady. All at once Jess remembered why Linda Nellis had dumped him in high school in favor of Buddy Carlin. *"I'm sorry, Jess,"* she'd said. *"You're just too…I don't know…wishy-washy for me."*

He searched for the head of the terrier without any real hope that they'd find it.

INTERIM

Newspaper in hand, the deputy knocked on Hugh Martin's door. The White House Chief of Staff looked up and said, "Yes? Is this urgent, Terry?"

"It's the Baltimore Sun, *Hugh. They got a reporter through the quarantine cordon in Tyler."*

"How the hell did they do that?"

"He sneaked through, sir, from the West Virginia side. You can only cover those mountains so well." He handed his boss the newspaper and Martin scanned it while Porter gazed out the window at the frozen Rose Garden. The reporter, one Rudy Lundeen, had made the best of his scoop: three separate articles and an editorial.

Martin said sourly, "Where's Lundeen?"

"Under arrest for federal trespass. Apparently he thought it was worth it."

"Apparently. So now the world knows that there are still a lot of loose dog packs down there, that FEMA *has trucked in enough porta-potties and heaters, and that the* CDC *still doesn't have any effective medical protocols. So what?"*

Porter didn't answer. They both knew that the factual reports from inside Tyler weren't the point. The editorial was.

Martin said, "If we give the order to destroy over a thousand dogs, half of them not even infected, the political fallout is going to be bad."

"Avian flu has led to millions of chickens being destroyed all around the world."

"Chickens aren't dogs. Do you know how Americans feel about their dogs?"

Porter didn't, actually. He didn't own a pet, and never had much liked dogs, who peed and barked and chewed shoes. Terry Porter wore eight-hundred-dollar Italian loafers.

"Americans spend thirty-four billion dollars a year on pets. They sleep with them and travel with them and go to therapists when their dogs die. Hold off on this order, Terry. We'll just have to ride it out."

"If even one single infected dog gets out of Tyler – "

"I know. Just hold off a while longer. And tell Scott Lurie to shoot those

damn roving packs. He ought to at least be able to do that."

Porter left. Martin looked at the fresh intelligence report on his desk. Terry didn't know it yet, but a lot worse things were coming out of Tyler than a single biting dog.

MONDAY

» 39

Allen woke in the hospital very early. His foot was still propped up at the end of his bed, but his mother wasn't sitting in the chair, crying. Cami had persuaded her that she should go home for the night. Something was still wrong with Allen's foot and he couldn't go home yet, but at least he could do stuff this morning without his mother there.

He hoped he could do stuff.

The awful Jason was still asleep. That was good. Lisa was awake, holding her stuffed animal tight, her eyes on the door. She was watching for Cami, Allen knew. Lisa wouldn't talk much except to say "Poo-poo," but she liked Cami to read to her, stupid stuff about bunnies or princesses. Yesterday Cami had read to Lisa for *hours*, when Allen needed her himself. Still, Lisa was just a little kid and she'd seen her mother eaten by their dog so, grudgingly, Allen guessed it was fair that she came first.

Today, however, was *his* turn with Cami. She would help him with Susie, he knew she would. That's what she did: she helped people. She told Lisa and Jason that yesterday. Allen's mom just made people do things they didn't want to do, and then asked if they'd heard her. *That* was no help.

When Cami finally came, she was in her wheelchair but she had regular clothes on, not a hospital gown. Allen whispered loudly, "Cami!"

"Good morning, Allen. Good morning, Lisa. How's Poo-poo today?"

Lisa didn't answer – she never answered anything Cami asked – and she didn't smile, either. But she gripped Poo-poo harder and sort of wiggled her body toward Cami, and Allen knew he better act quick or it would be Lisa, Lisa, Lisa again most of the day.

"Cami, I need help!"

"Okay," she said. "But it will have to be now, Allen, because they're sending me home soon."

Home? She was going home? Instantly Allen revised his plan. He'd been going to ask for her cell phone, but this might be even better. People could overhear you on a cell phone.

Cami was talking to Lisa, saying in a low voice that she would come back and visit, visit every single day, she promised, and when Lisa was well again –

"Cami!"

"What, Allen?"

"Do you have paper and a pencil?"

"I can get them for you."

"Please! And then when you go home will you take a note to my best friend, Jimmy Doake? It's really, really, really important!"

"Of course I will. But you know, I can't drive, so I have to ask the friend who's taking me home. But I'm sure he'll help, too."

Cami's face sort of glowed when she said "friend." Allen ignored this. "Could I have the paper and pencil now? The nurses are probably too busy, they're always too busy." He tried to sound sad.

"I can get paper at the nurses' station. Back in a minute."

When she returned, Allen pushed the button to make the top part of his bed go up, balanced the paper on his good leg, and wrote. His teacher at school had taught them correct letter form:

> Dear Jimmy,
>
> How are you? I am fine only Im in the hospitel. You have to do something VERY IMPORTENT!!!! Belle is in my seller in the file droor and she needs food and water NOW. Also to go out. She will not bite you! She is sick but not biting. Please do this now and DON'T TELL ANYBODY!!!!
>
> Your frend,
> Allen

"Writing to a girl?" Jason said. He poked his neck toward Allen's note. "A girl, a girl, Allen's got a girlfriend!"

"It's not to a girl!" Allen said furiously. He turned the note over.

"A girlfriend, a girlfriend, a hairy ugly girlfriend named Jimmy!"

A chill ran through Allen. If Jason had seen the name, he might also have read some of the note. Jason was a total loser but he was smart. Allen scowled at Jason's stupid, taunting face and folded the note into a very small bundle.

"Here, Cami. It goes to Jimmy Doake, 146 Cobbler Drive. Remember – you promised!"

"I promise," Cami said, smiling. "Jason, don't tease so."

"He's a nerd."

"Am not!" Allen said hotly, although in his secret heart he knew he was.

"Are too!"

"Am not!"

"A fight this early in the morning?" said a new voice. "Hot dog, let's sell tickets!"

In the doorway stood a man with his arm in a sling. His hair was wet, like he'd just washed and combed it, he had on a dress-up coat like Allen's father wore to the office, and he carried a bunch of red flowers. Behind him stood another man in regular clothes with, Allen saw, a gun on his hip. Ordinarily this would have been thrilling, as thrilling as the gun Jimmy's dad kept under his bed, but now it gave Allen a sick feeling. People with guns were taking dogs away to the pound.

"Ready to go, beautiful?" the man with the flowers said to Cami, and she got that glow again. But she had good manners.

"Billy, these are my friends Jason, Lisa, and Allen. Kids, this is Mr. Davis and...."

"Jess Langstrom," said the other man, who looked very tired. "Chauffeur."

None of the three children smiled at the men.

Cami kissed Lisa and said, "I promise I'll be back soon, Allen, Lisa, Jason. Meanwhile, get well."

Lisa started to cry, silent tears rolling down on Poo-poo, and for a hopeful minute Allen thought maybe that would make Cami stay. But it didn't. Mr. Davis rolled her chair away from them and down the hall. But at least Cami had Allen's note to Jimmy, and at the last minute she looked over her shoulder, held up the note, and smiled at Allen.

That would have to do for now.

» 40

Tessa's plane landed at Heathrow shortly after midnight, London time. She'd slept a little on the plane, but not much. Trudging along the jetway to Terminal 4, Tessa could feel every muscle in her body tense. By now Maddox knew that the British Air ticket for "Ellen Blakely" had been purchased on Tessa's American Express card. If he was going to have her picked up, it would most likely be at Customs.

He didn't. That probably meant Door Number Two: Maddox was gambling that she'd lead him to someone else. Now a lot would depend on how many agents Maddox had been able to assign last-minute to this, and how good they were.

Plus, of course, how good Tessa herself was.

She walked purposefully through the terminal, knowing that she would not be able to spot the agents following her. The Underground stopped running at midnight; Maddox would expect either a cab or the N9 night bus. He would have a team of agents in a car, ready to follow either.

She drew out euros from an ATM; her American Express card was already compromised, so what the hell. Outside the weather was cold and rainy, London at its most unpleasant. Tessa told the cabbie, "Charing Cross Road, please, at Shaftesbury."

"Clubbing, then, is it?" he said pleasantly, but Tessa didn't answer. During the ride in to London she leaned back and closed her eyes, not trying to identify her tail, but once they reached Soho she was alert again, watching for her chance.

She'd been here with Salah. He didn't know London the way he knew Paris, but he'd loved it. He had loved so much, been so delighted with the world... Tessa pushed away her memories. *Not now.*

Soho was difficult for even Londoners to navigate. Narrow, winding streets jammed with shops, pubs, restaurants, clubs, and, even after midnight on a rainy Sunday, people. Tessa directed the cabbie, "Turn right here, now left...another left..." Midway down a tiny street she saw her chance, thrust money at the driver, and jumped out. She just glimpsed the two agents leaping from the car two vehicles behind.

Tessa darted into a club and pushed her way through the dancers. In jeans and Jess's parka, she was spectacularly conspicuous among the short skirts and satin camisoles. The music pulsed and roared. Tessa kept close to the wall, moving fast, then hunkered down and doubled back as soon as she'd spotted the agent moving in the other direction. She was back outside the front door before the man racing after her realized what she was doing. A female agent waited outside, covering the door. *Thank you, Lord,* Tessa said inside her head. If the second agent had been male, this would be a lot harder.

As soon as she laid eyes on the agent, Tessa charged her and kicked. The woman had out her gun but didn't get to use it, and she wouldn't have shot to kill anyway. Tessa wasn't Victor Balonov. Her kick caught the woman square on the chest and she went down.

A third agent abandoned the car, causing horns to beep in the narrow streets behind him. Time had slowed down for Tessa now, in that strange way it had always done during hard physical training. She was around the corner and into an alleyway – no, a *mews,* this was London – before the first agent had exited the club. Dodging, weaving, she made it to Piccadilly Circus and flagged one of the many cabs. One of the agents was close enough behind her to actually slap the back of the cab. He couldn't stop it, but he had the number.

"Beat out that man for my cab, did you?" the driver said sourly. "Where to, then?"

"Shoreham. Quickly."

It was two more changes of cab before Tessa was sure she'd lost all the agents. Leaning back in the last cab, she clasped her shaking hands together hard, and thought that she'd have to tell Bernini to up the training requirements for the London Legat.

Ruzbihan al-Ashan lived in the East End, once the home of Jack the Ripper and still a stew of poverty, gentrification, immigrants, gangs, boutiques, and unrest. His firm's world headquarters were in the City, moved ten years ago from Tunis. If you are that rich, your address is never an electronic secret. The house was large, surrounded by the high solid wall so popular with both Brits and Tunisians, and even at 1:30 in the morning, two men stood in the small, lighted guardhouse inside the iron gate.

Tessa pressed the intercom. "I am here to see Ruzbihan al-Ashan. He is not expecting me, but he will agree to see me. My name is Tessa Sanderson Mahjoub."

The answering voice was heavily accented, and heavily sarcastic. "You demand to see al-ustaath al-Ashan at such this hour? Go away, woman."

"If you do not tell him who I am and that I am here, he will be very angry."

Silence.

She added, "You must tell him that I have come about Salah and Richard, and that others know where I am and why."

"You threaten me?" Ruzbihan said quietly. "In my own house you threaten me?"

"No," Tessa said. "It was only to gain admittance, Ruzbihan. No one else knows I'm here. Please…may I sit down?"

He motioned to a floor cushion. They stood in a small room directly off the spacious entry hall, furnished in the old Tunisian style with rugs, oversize cushions, and low tables of hammered brass inlaid with silver and gold in intricate designs. The white walls were hung with antique copper trays and yet more exquisite, hand-woven rugs. On the nearest table sat a brass coffee service. Tessa wondered if the entire house was decorated this way, or if Ruzbihan had deliberately chosen to see her in a room that might have existed when he and Salah had been boys together in Carthage. The security camera, which of course must be present, was not visible.

She sat on a bright cushion and studied Ruzbihan. Smaller and darker than Salah, he had a neat, compact body dressed now in a Western bathrobe over pajamas. Black curly hair, thick dark beard, and green eyes that, like so many Tunisians, suggested Berbers somewhere in his ancestral past. His expression gave her nothing.

"I am sorry to come here like this at this hour," Tessa said. "I would have hoped to meet Salah's boyhood friend under different circumstances. This is not...I'm sorry. But I have no choice. Something is happening to me in the United States, and I think it is connected somehow with Richard Ebenfield."

"Richard has nothing to do with me. I have told you this since before."

"I loved Salah very much," Tessa said. A completely uncharacteristic thing for her to say to a stranger – not to mention being a complete non sequitur – but the moment after she said it, Tessa knew why she had. Ruzbihan must believe that she did not suspect Salah of anything underhanded. That she had trusted him, and was prepared to trust Ruzbihan...if he would let her.

He shifted on his cushion but answered nothing, his dark eyes wary.

She smiled slightly. "You don't approve of my coming here alone, in the middle of the night."

"It is not safe for a woman. Salah has before permitted this behavior for his wife?"

She saw the gulf then, between the Salah she had known and the heritage he must have shared with Ruzbihan. But there was no way to tell this man how much his childhood friend must have changed, how little the concept of "permission" had had to do with her marriage. Instead she said quietly, "You told me, Ruzbihan, that you had not seen Richard Ebenfield for 'many, many years.' But you also told me you'd seen him in Africa, in Mogumbutuno. That city was open to Westerners only briefly, two years ago. That's not 'many, many years.' Can you tell me which is true?"

Tessa watched him carefully; she was trained to detect lying. But Ruzbihan did not change expression at all. "My English is sometimes not too good. I have perhaps spoken wrongly."

"Were you in Mogumbutuno two years ago? And saw Ebenfield there?"

"Yes." This time something moved behind his eyes, but it might just have been resentment at being questioned like this, in the middle of the night, in his own home, by a woman he could not in a million years understand or approve of. "I had business in Africa. Richard saw my name in the local paper and came to my hotel."

"Why was he in Africa, do you know?"

"He said he was with les Frères de l'Espoir céleste."

The Brothers of Heavenly Hope, a Catholic missionary order. It was the same thing Aisha had told her. "Was Ebenfield a monk, then?"

For the first time, Ruzbihan smiled, a cold smile that made Tessa suddenly feel she would not like to cross him in business. "Richard was not a monk. He was nothing, a failure. Never has he done anything with success, never for his entire life."

"Aisha said that, too."

"You have spoken with Aisha?"

"Yes. Yesterday."

"She is well?"

"Yes," Tessa said.

"And Fatima? She too is well?"

"As far as I know."

Then Ruzbihan did give her a full smile, full of such sudden warmth and charm that Tessa's heart was pierced. This must have been the Ruzbihan that Salah had known, that he had played with and laughed with and loved. Ruzbihan said, "Fatima has thought you a strange daughter-in-law, yes?"

"Yes," Tessa said, smiling.

"You have won her heart after time?"

"No, I'm afraid not. But we managed."

"Salah, he has loved his mother but he has gone on your side, the side of his wife," Ruzbihan said shrewdly. "He was always brave, my good friend."

"And it *was* bravery." Tessa laughed. "He never said so, but I think that getting me away from Fatima was one reason he was willing to move to America."

"'*Une femme formidable,*'" Ruzbihan said, with such a good imitation of Salah that Tessa laughed again, in startled bittersweet memory. Ruzbihan seemed to understand. He smiled at her with sad sympathy, and out of that shared moment she began her hardest and most crucial question.

"Ruzbihan, your name – " The door flew open.

Tessa, facing the doorway, saw the young man first. Ruzbihan had his back to the door, but she saw from his face that he knew who it was even before he turned around. The boy was in his late teens, maybe as old as twenty-one. He was as short as Ruzbihan but much more muscular, as if he worked out daily, and without Ruzbihan's green eyes. This boy's eyes were very dark, burning with anger. He wore a traditional djellabah, perhaps thrown on hastily over whatever he slept in. Tessa's first thought was that he was part of Ruzbihan's security detail, but Ruzbihan's expression, and the boy's, told her different.

The young man said something in Arabic, a staccato burst that made Ruzbihan scowl. He said, with great deliberation, "Tessa, may I introduce my son, Abd-Al Adil. This is Tessa Sanderson, the wife of the friend of my youth, Salah Mahjoub. I have spoken of Salah to you."

The boy ignored Tessa, once more speaking angrily in Arabic. Now Ruzbihan spoke sharply in that language to his son, perhaps reprimanding him for his behavior. Abd-Al Adil snapped back and then left the room, shutting the door loudly.

Ruzbihan turned back to Tessa, once again coldly formal. "I apologize for my son. The youth, they have not the manners, it does not matter sometimes what one says at them. I am sorry."

"It's all right," Tessa said, trying to smile. "Kids will be kids."

"He has wanted my car and driver this night and I have said no, because of some previous bad behavior. Again, I apologize."

He was lying.

Tessa felt it as strongly as if Ruzbihan had just sent a polygraph stylus zinging off the charts. Their moment of shared warmth had vanished the second Abd-Al Adil entered the room. In fact, what had just happened was more than vanished camaraderie. The small room, with its Arabic furnishings and the quick and un-Anglo emotional warmth, had changed in a second. It had become alien, foreign, a miniature version of that other Middle East, the one where nothing was quite as it seemed. The Mideast full of hair-trigger convolutions no Westerner ever really understood, and where no distinctions were made among business, politics, religion, and family. No Arab belonged to himself; he was part of a vast interconnected web where everything he did brought honor or catastrophe to all. Whatever Abd-Al Adil had been arguing about with his father, it hadn't been the family car.

The moment to ask her pivotal question was lost. And all at once Tessa knew this was a good thing, that if she *had* voiced her question, disaster would have followed. She couldn't have named that disaster, but it would have come. Ruzbihan watched her closely, waiting. She said instead, "Your name was 'Ruzbihan bin Fahoud al-Ashan' when you were a boy, Salah said, but now you use 'Robert Ashan.' If I hadn't known how Arabic names worked, I'd have never found your address in the London directory."

Did something in his face relax an infinitesimal amount? She couldn't be sure. He shrugged and said, "Salah did the same, has he not told you this? His name was 'Salah bin Mohammed bin Karim al-Mahjoub.' He has changed his at the Sorbonne, because he has thought that 'al-Mahjoub' is too much an aristocrat for him. The family estates at Mahjoub has gone from the family since very long time ago. And 'bin Mohammed bin Karim' he has dropped because Salah has not liked too much formality, not because he has disrespect of his father Mohammed and his grandfather Karim."

"But that wasn't why you changed your name," Tessa said.

They gazed at each other. Finally Ruzbihan said, "No. I wish for business a name less Arabic. In business in London I am Robert Ashan. With my own people, I remain Ruzbihan bin Fahoud bin Ahmed bin Aziz al-Ashan. This is the world we live in now."

"I know," Tessa said. He had given her the opening she wanted. "I have felt some of that myself, married to an Arab. That prejudice is the reason I left the FBI. When you asked me not to give your name to the FBI, I understood why. And I have honored your wishes."

"Thank you," Ruzbihan said. She felt his wariness grow; he was too experienced not to know that this was preliminary negotiation. She wanted something. "Why are you in London, Tessa? Why do you ask after Richard Ebenfield?"

"He has sent me threatening emails. The emails also soil Salah's name. I am very angry. I wish to stop this, and to punish him for it."

Ruzbihan studied her. On the one hand, he understood the avenging of honor, as perhaps few Americans could. On the other hand, he knew she was an American, and a woman. On a mythical third hand, he also knew he did not understand American women, particularly one who would choose to become an FBI agent. She watched him weigh these considerations, and she saw the moment Ruzbihan chose to believe her.

It was the same moment she knew he was not in collusion with Richard Ebenfield, and that this trip had been a dead end.

He said, "What is it you want from me?"

"I came here on a stolen passport, my sister's. I cannot return on it. By now the FBI is looking for me. They don't believe a few emails are reason to take action against a crazy American. They don't understand what he has said about Salah." Tessa hesitated, averted her face, and repeated the filthiest epithets in Arabic. She had made Salah, against his better judgment, teach them to her.

Ruzbihan was silent. Then he said, "You should have borne a son to do this someday for you."

"We were married only five years."

"And you had no husband before Salah? You are...thirty maybe?"

"Thirty-five. No, I had no husband before Salah."

Ruzbihan shook his head over the mating customs of Americans. Then his demeanor shifted once again, becoming all business. "You want from me what?"

"A passport and airline ticket to Pittsburgh, going first to Toronto. The Bureau will have spotters with my picture at all the Washington airports. I know you can do this, Ruzbihan. In Tunis, business is conducted like...I know you can get me a passport in another name, with my picture. With a date of issue that predates all the new embedded chips. Then I will be away from London and out of your hair, and I can find Ebenfield in the States."

"Why have you thought he is there? His emails have come from someplace near you?"

"No. They came through a mixmaster remailer."

"He may be anywhere in the world."

"No," Tessa said, not surprised that Ruzbihan knew the English for "mixmaster remailer." She would bet that on occasion he used them himself. "Ebenfield has already emailed that he watched me once."

He frowned. "And your authorities do nothing for this? It is not a crime?"

"It is, yes. Stalking. But the authorities are too busy with major problems to investigate a stalker who doesn't actually make death threats."

Ruzbihan nodded. Authorities who were "too busy" for their duties were an old story in Tunisia. But he said, "I cannot give you a false passport, Tessa."

She faced him squarely. "Yes, you can. You are saying that you will not."

He regarded her thoughtfully. Suddenly she understood. "Ruzbihan, I no longer work for the FBI and I am not wearing any electronic devices. Send a woman of your household to search me, to take all my clothes. You want me out of London, because it's not good for anyone to know you even talked to someone who used to work for the FBI. That's why you didn't want me to tell them your name in the first place. It must be some questionable business deal, because I know you are not a terrorist."

"How can you know this?"

"I worked domestic counter-terrorism for the Bureau. We investigated American crazies who want to blow up their own government. But it's more than that. When I married Salah, the Bureau did a thorough background check on his life. You were checked out then. You came up politically clean.

"And also – you were Salah's *friend.* He would have wanted you to help me. We can help each other. You want me out of London before your business associates hear about me, maybe because Mogumbutuno is closed again to any signatory of the 2004 International Trade Agreements ... it doesn't matter why you don't want anyone to know I visited you. I want *you* to know it doesn't matter to me. You want me out. I want to be back in the States. All I need is a passport and an airline ticket."

A long moment passed. Finally Ruzbihan repeated, with a mixture of anger and disapproval and admiration, "You *should* have borne a son. Wait here." He left the room.

Tessa was suddenly exhausted. Sleep was out of the question, but she lay on the floor with her head on her cushion. Damn the security camera. Let Ruzbihan bin Fahoud bin Ahmed bin Aziz al-Ashan's security detail think she was disgraceful. Undoubtedly they already did.

Ruzbihan did not return. Eventually Tessa fell into a light, fitful doze. She dreamed that she stood braced to shoot her gun at Victor Balonov, who in turn aimed at Billy. She fired, but when the body toppled forward, she saw that it was not Balonov but Salah, and that she had killed him. She cried out, waking drenched in sweat in the small room with its bright Arabic rugs on the pristine white walls.

» 41

Cami sat in the back seat of the car with Billy, while his friend Jess Langstrom drove them. That made Cami feel weird, as if this were a date or something and Jess really was just what he'd said, the chauffeur. He seemed to be a very quiet man, maybe a little depressed. Billy, however, talked nonstop.

"You been in Tyler long, Nurse Cami?"

"No, I just came here from Benton, in West Virginia. That was my first hospital, but I wanted something more exciting."

"*Tyler* is more exciting? You gotta be sh...kidding me!"

"Well, Benton is pretty small. And Tyler is so much closer to Washington."

"You been down to D.C.?"

"Not yet, but –"

"I'll take you," Billy said. "We'll do the night life."

"Well, maybe." He was starting to scare her a little, the intense way he leaned toward her, the eagerness on his face. He seemed to understand that, though, because he leaned back and his voice got calmer.

"I'm sorry I couldn't drive you home myself, but in a coupla days I'll be just fine, the doc said. Or almost, anyway. You ever been to the Moonlight Lounge? Right here in Tyler?"

"No. No, I haven't." But she'd heard about it. A wild place.

"Or maybe we could just go to the movies," Billy said, and he looked so hopeful and little-boy, with his face all eager and his hair slicked down with water, that she melted again.

"Oh, I'd like to go to the movies." In the front seat, Jess Langstrom glanced back at her in the rearview mirror. He was smiling slightly and shaking his head...why?

Billy said, "And maybe in a few days you'll get your dog back."

Jess's smile vanished.

Cami said, "Oh, that reminds me... Jess, would you mind making one more stop? I'm really sorry to put you to the trouble, but I promised a little boy at the hospital. The address is 146 Cobbler Drive. I'm really sorry."

"No problem," Jess said.

"I just have to give this note to his friend. I did promise."

"No problem," he repeated.

Billy said, "Now you're a post office as well as a nurse, hahaha."

"Well, when it's for a child... Billy, you wouldn't believe what some of these dog-bite victims have been through! Those poor children!"

"Tell me," Billy said, and even though that too-eager look was back again, this time Cami didn't mind so much because the look was for the kids, not herself. So she told him about Jason and Lisa and Allen, until the car stopped in front of a small, dingy house with sagging shutters and a chicken-wire fence broken down at one corner. All at once Cami realized that Billy was no longer listening to her. Both men had turned their heads toward the woods.

"Another dog pack," Billy said. "Damn it, Jess, they got umpteen volunteers out there plus the whole goddamn Maryland Guard and they can't nail a few renegade hounds? If I could shoot..."

"I know, you'd take them all down single-handed. Actually," Jess said, turning to Cami, "Billy's probably the best shot in Tyler. Very handy if you need a rhino stopped at your door. What do you need to do at the Dokes'? I think it would be better if you stayed in the car and let me do it."

Cami hesitated. "Well...all right, I guess. It's a note that Allen wanted delivered to his friend Jimmy." She passed over the tightly folded piece of paper.

"Why didn't Allen just call Jimmy from the hospital? I'm sure you'd have helped him do that."

"Of course! But you know kids...they like to be secretive."

Jess fingered the note he'd taken from her. For a moment she thought he was going to open it, and she braced herself to protest. Kids should be allowed their little secrets! But then he nodded and took the note to the door.

Billy said, "Your hospital kid has some strange friends."

"What do you mean?"

"Like Jess said, that's the Doakes' house. Sheriff is there three, four times a year for domestic disturbance, oldest kid is truant from school all the time, Jess and I been called in for animal abuse."

"Animal abuse!"

"Well, more like neglect. They got a passel of cats and somebody called 'em in for shutting the cats outside in really cold weather. The cats were howling their heads off, so maybe it was really more like a noise violation. Don't look like that, Cami, nobody was torturing animals. Least, not here."

Cami watched the house. The door was opened by a woman in jeans, baggy sweatshirt, and oversize slippers. Three kids crowded behind her, one a boy of about Allen's age, a skinny red-head in a torn Eminem T-shirt. After some discussion, Jess handed the boy Allen's note and the woman slammed the door.

Billy was asking her about Belle, and Cami answered mechanically. Ordinarily she loved talking about Belle, but now she had the strongest possible feeling about that note. It was so silly, completely irrational, and even as she answered Billy, a part of her mind tried to suppress the feeling. But it only grew, no matter how much she told herself that it would have been wrong, unethical, unfair to Allen.

She felt that she should have read the note before Jess gave it to Jimmy.

» 42

Tessa left Ruzbihan's house a little after noon. Much earlier an old woman in traditional dress had come to the small anteroom, silently gestured for Tessa to remove all her clothes, and watched while Tessa did so. The woman then ran her hands through Tessa's short, dirty hair, searching for, presumably, recording devices. Finally she handed Tessa a bundle, which turned out to be all men's clothing: jockey shorts, jeans, T-shirt, socks, boots, and a hand-tailored jacket lined in fur. The boots were a bit too big, the jeans a bit too tight. Tessa managed. She guessed that the clothes belonged to the boy she had seen, Ruzbihan's surly son. She and he were about the same height.

The crone picked up Jess's old parka, holding it by one finger, as if it were filth. In the pocket was Salah's old laptop. Tessa had known she wouldn't be allowed to keep it, there was no help for that, but she felt a pang. The woman also took Tessa's purse but left her wallet. Great – she could continue to take out books from the D.C. Public Library.

From some inner fold of her abbayah the unsmiling woman produced a small camera, snapped Tessa's photo, and left. Shortly after, a younger Arab woman in a Western skirt and blouse entered with steaming coffee, hot rolls, and cheese.

"*Ahlan*," Tessa said. The girl put the food on the low table. "*Bonjour*," Tessa tried. "Hello." The girl ignored her and left.

Hours of boredom and anxiety later, Ruzbihan returned with an envelope. "Tessa. Here is passport and money. Also your own credit card and driver's license. You have waited for you at Heathrow an electronic ticket for flights to Toronto and Pittsburgh, as I have wrote here. A taxi is outside. You go now directly to Heathrow, no stops, and wait there. Yes?"

"Thank you, Ruzbihan. I'll get out of London, and you have my promise to say nothing about you to my government."

"Good-bye, Tessa. *Marhaba*."

Salah had taught her that word; it meant "Blessings be upon you."

"*Marhaba*, Ruzbihan."

"One more thing," he said. "Do not visit Tunisia anytime soon. Maybe anytime ever."

That was unexpected. She peered at him, but his face gave away nothing. After a moment she nodded.

The rain had stopped. London had produced a rarity, a sparklingly clear winter day. Children ran and shouted in several languages. The cab pulled away without asking her destination.

She let it get several blocks away before she said, "Victoria Station, please."

"Not Heathrow?"

"No. Victoria Station."

Once there, she immediately got into another cab. The first cabbie might very well have reported back to Ruzbihan. She said, "One six nine Ogilvie Road, please."

She had promised Ruzbihan to get out of London. She had not agreed to his statement that she would go directly to Heathrow.

Les Frères de l'Espoir céleste occupied a crumbling brick building in a bad neighborhood. Tessa said to the man who opened the door, "Hello. My name is Jane Caldwell and I need to see your abbé on a matter of great importance. Will you please tell him it's about a man named Richard Ebenfield?"

The man studied her. He wore jeans and a black T-shirt, not at all monk-like, but les Frères de l'Espoir céleste, Tessa had discovered on the Internet, was an order devoted to helping the very poor. They cared for the dying, ran orphanages, dug wells in the poorest countries on Earth. Finally the monk said, "I may see identification, please?" His accent was German.

Tessa produced her brand-new passport and he studied it. "Wait here."

The man who eventually came to the foyer did wear a rough brown robe. Seniority, or PR? But then she was ashamed of her cynicism.

"Madame Caldwell, I am Abbé Guillaume LeFort. You wish to ask about Richard Ebenfield? And who are you?"

"I'm an American who knew Richard a long time ago, at the Sorbonne. I've heard through mutual friends that he's in trouble. They've been getting strange emails from him. But the last address any of them had for him was here. I was in London on business and I volunteered to see if he can be located. It's a matter of some urgency, but I can't tell you the details, I'm afraid."

"In London on business," LeFort repeated. His French accent was very strong, and he had a remote, austere air. He studied Tessa's expensive jacket and men's boots. "What business is this?"

She smiled slightly. "I'm with the World Bank. But later today I'm driving north to hike the Dales."

He shrugged, a very Gallic gesture, and Tessa could almost hear him think: *Americans.* "I do not know the present address for Richard Ebenfield. The last time I saw him was in Africa, in Mbandaka, six years ago."

"In Congo? What was he doing there?"

Again the abbé shrugged. "You must understand, madame, that a missionary order like ours attracts many kinds of people. There are the brothers, of course, committed to helping the suffering poor. So, also, are many others who have not a vocation but who are filled with the grace of compassion. But we also have...*les partisans temporaires...*"

"Hangers-on?" Tessa suggested.

"You speak French, madame?"

"No. Only a little."

"Ah. *Dis donc,* Richard Ebenfield was such a one. They come and go, helping a little at one mission for some time, going into the bush, coming sometimes years later to another mission, drifting again down the river. Many are lost souls. Many drink. Eventually most die of diseases or are killed in civil fighting or robberies. Your friend may have drifted down the river to almost anywhere. In the jungle, borders disappear. Others of our order may have seen him since, or not. I cannot say."

"When he was with you, did he ever mention Salah Mahjoub?"

For the first time, the abbé's remoteness disappeared. "Yes, he did. Very often. Salah Mahjoub was Richard's besetting sin."

Startled, Tessa said, "His sin?"

"Yes. We all have our besetting sin, and his was envy. He envied this man, talked about him with much bitterness. You are a friend of M'sieu Mahjoub?"

"Yes," Tessa said, her chest tightening. "Can you tell me anything more about what Ebenfield did in Africa?"

"I cannot."

"Can anyone else here?"

The remoteness was back. "Mademoiselle, we are an order charged by God to relieve suffering. We are not an information bureau."

"I understand. But here, this is my email address." She thrust toward him a paper torn from the envelope Ruzbihan had given her, written on with a pencil borrowed from the cabbie. "If you or anyone else thinks of anything more about Ebenfield, would you please email me?"

Reluctantly he took the paper. Tessa said, without knowing she was going to, "My late husband was a Catholic. Not very practicing, I'm afraid, but when he died... He was killed in a car crash and there was about twenty minutes before he... I've always hoped his religion was some comfort to him at the end."

"You were there with him, madame?"

"No. I didn't...I didn't get there in time. No, please don't...I'm all right. But I would appreciate it if you would email me anything you learn about Ebenfield." Tessa moved quickly to the door, and the abbé didn't try to stop her.

The cab had, per instructions, waited for her. Moving toward it, Tessa was ashamed of herself. What had moved her to tell LeFort about Salah's death? She had been *using* that monstrous tragedy. Or maybe not, the words had just seemed to well up out of her, as tears were doing now, fuck it –

She didn't even see the men in the racing black car until the first shot rang out.

The black car sped past Tessa and the shot pierced the gray London afternoon. She heard the bullet ricochet off the stucco wall surrounding the monastery. *Close, very close.* She dropped to the ground but there was no place to hide, nothing...down the street a child was screaming, a witness, she must make sure the child wasn't hit...nowhere to hide, nowhere to run and the wall was too high to scale quickly...

The car had stopped and was backing up fast.

Tessa scrambled to her feet. But she really had no chance. The thick walls that privacy-loving Londoners so favored lined both sides of the street, which was too narrow to permit parked cars that she might have used as cover. The iron gate of les Frères de l'Espoir céleste had locked behind her. There was only the hope of reaching the corner but it was no hope at all, it was too far away...

The car slowed more and she glimpsed the interior: driver and shooter, both in masks, the shooter's semi-automatic aimed out the window. At her.

She rolled toward the car, making his shot more difficult, a downward trajectory. If she could scramble behind the car, dodge it that way... It wasn't going to work. The car came to a full stop, the door opened, and the shooter leaned out into the street. He knew she wasn't armed! He had a clear shot, Tessa couldn't dodge fast enough...

The shooter's head exploded.

He collapsed back onto the passenger seat, bits of blood and brain spattering Tessa below. The driver accelerated abruptly and the car's forward motion slammed shut the passenger-side door, bearing away its grisly burden. Tessa looked around, dazed; a man stood lowering his gun from between the iron gate bars, *inside* les Frères de l'Espoir céleste. He wore a ski mask. Armed and deadly *monks?*

The child down the street was still screaming, and now a woman ran outside, snatched it up, and disappeared behind another of the ubiquitous walls. Another car pulled up. The shooter disappeared from the gate and a moment later leapt lightly down from the wall. A ladder, there had to be a ladder on the other side or something to...it didn't matter, she wasn't thinking clearly...

The shooter took her arm and shoved her into the car. Tessa resisted, grabbing the car's frame and preparing to kick, but the man said, "I come from Ruzbihan. This time you're bloody well going to the airport."

"From Ruzbihan? Who – "

He shoved her again, and she got into the car. All at once it seemed safer than being on the street. The car sped away.

"Who are you?"

"I told you," he said impatiently. His eyes through the slits of the mask were bright blue. His speech sounded like Manchester, or Liverpool...She wasn't good at British accents. "Ruzbihan sent me. You were supposed to go directly to Heathrow. You didn't. Now you will."

"How did Ruzbihan know I would – "

He made a rude noise and pulled a bandana from his pocket. Tessa let him blindfold her, understanding the necessity. Nor did she resist when soon the car pulled into a structure of some sort and she was led, stumbling, to a different vehicle. If these men were going to kill her, she would already be dead.

So who had tried to kill her? And was this car really going to Heathrow?

Out of sight of her captors, she clenched her fist tightly, hoping to stop her hands from shaking.

An interminable time later, the car stopped. Tessa heard honking, vehicles starting and stopping. A moment later the blindfold was pulled from her eyes and she was pushed out the door at International Departures, Heathrow.

"It's 3:28," the blue-eyed Brit said. "Your flight is at 6:10, isn't it. Be on it. You'll be watched." The car pulled away. Tessa memorized the license number, knowing it would do her no good whatsoever.

Then she was inside the airport, walking to the counter, claiming her ticket, acting as if this was all normal and she was actually "Jane Caldwell," a weary American whose luggage had been lost. An American returning from an emergency trip to London for her mother-in-law's funeral.

Normal.

Yeah, right.

Tessa closed her eyes until her stomach had calmed. Then she turned back to the counter attendant, a pretty redhead with warm brown eyes. "Can you please tell me if Heathrow has a cyber café, or data center, or some such equivalent where people without their own laptops can send and receive email?"

» 43

Ellie heard the dog before she saw him. Twilight had fallen and the backyard was wrapped in deep shadow, but she would recognize that bark anywhere. Song!

She grabbed a package of deli roast beef from the fridge, yanked on her coat, and ran through the backyard. There he was, just beyond the fence, a slim gray shape lighter than the dark field and woods behind him.

"Song! Oh, I'm so glad to see you!"

But where were Music and Chimes and Butterfly? The four always stayed together – *always.* Ellie's heart clutched. Could the other three greyhounds have been captured, or even shot?

"You came home, I knew you would, I have a treat for you...*treat* – " She stopped abruptly.

Song drew back his lips, showing all his long teeth, and snarled.

Oh, God, no –

Ellie took a step backward. This couldn't be happening. Not her dog, her baby, that she'd rescued and nurtured and loved so much, not...

Out of the darkness, Butterfly came running toward her at full speed. The swiftest and most muscular of Elli's dogs, Butterfly covered the frozen ground so fast that he seemed to be flying. *Yes, that's why I named...* She had no time to finish the thought.

In complete silence, and all the more terrible for that, Butterfly launched himself off the ground toward the fence. Ellie saw the graceful light shape, ears back and teeth bared, hurtle toward her through the gloom. She felt paralyzed, unable to turn or run, and so she had to witness it all.

Butterfly didn't make it. His body fell onto the top of the fence, where the chain link rose to sharp metal points to keep out intruders. The dog screamed – that was the only word for it – a sound so human and horrifying that Ellie cried out, too. Then somehow she was moving, trying to tug the dog's impaled body off the fence, trying to avoid the snapping jaws, while a foot away Song leapt and barked.

Butterfly bit her coat, his teeth sinking into the thick fabric just short of her arm.

Ellie shrugged out of the coat just as Butterfly freed himself and fell, with a sickening thud, into the yard. Blood flew off his body. Ellie ran. She could hear Butterfly behind her, but the greyhound was badly enough injured to slow him dramatically. Ellie reached the house, ran inside, and slammed the door. She began to cry.

Her dogs, her pets, her babies...

Somewhere outside a siren sounded, neared, stopped.

She had to help Butterfly, had to...had to...

Sobbing, Ellie nonetheless heard the men shouting outside, heard the single rifle shot. Her sobs increased until she was crying hysterically, ignoring the doorbell, wailing for Butterfly, for Song, for the missing Chimes and Music, for a world where nothing any longer made sense.

» 44

Something was going on underground in Tyler. Jess could feel it when he rang doorbells to ask questions about dogs, when he paid for gas at the Kwik-Fill, when he picked up groceries for dinner. People wouldn't meet his eyes, or gazed at him too steadily, or said hello with false heartiness. He tried, and failed, to find a name for what he sensed. Suspicion. Fear. Anger. It was all of these, and something more.

Nearly 400 dogs were unaccounted for. Jess suspected a lot of those had been deliberately let loose by their owners, people like Ed Dormund. Dormund smirked at him at the gas station, as if he knew something that Jess did not.

The short winter afternoon was darkening when Jess put his key into the front door, scooped two days' worth of *Washington Posts* off the porch, and put a Hungry-Man TV dinner into the microwave. As it heated, he pulled the latest newspaper from its plastic bag and scanned the headlines.

TEDIC CALLS FOR DESTRUCTION OF ALL INFECTED DOGS

House Minority Leader Albert Tedic (D-Ohio) today called for the destruction of all dogs infected with canine plague in quarantined Tyler, Maryland. "Have we learned nothing from the bird flu?" Tedic asked dramatically on the House floor. "The safety of all Americans must and will be our first priority, not the sentiments of a handful of pet owners. It's not impossible that this thing could go airborne – why is the current administration taking this risk with American lives?"

The battle in Washington power circles over the best way to handle canine plague has heated up in the last few days as various party –

Jess grimaced. Not that he hadn't seen it coming. In one way, Tedic was right. The dogs in those open cages were a potential menace, and people went in and out of the tents all the time. Christ, people still went in and out of *Tyler* all the time. Tessa Sanderson certainly had. If the wiggling blue viruses that Dr. Latkin had shown him did mutate...

But Tedic was wrong, too. It wasn't just "the sentiments of a handful of pet owners" that were keeping those dogs alive. Dr. Latkin needed them for research, had a whole sequential order set up to kill them for their brains. The public didn't know that yet. Or maybe they did, it had been three days since Jess had really attended to any news that wasn't right under his nose, so –

His phone rang. "Jess? Billy. Listen, did you hear?"

"Hear what? I just got home."

"Then come back. They'll want you. One got out."

"One what?" Jess said, a second before he realized that it was maybe the stupidest question of his entire life. But he'd thought immediately of Tessa, who'd gotten out of Tyler: *One got out...*

"One *dog*," Billy said. "Game warden over the state line shot a Doberman that brought down a doe. Didn't get it clean, and when he went closer to finish it off, he saw that white film on the eyes. Dog was snarling and lunging like a son-of-a-bitch, even shot in the leg it tried to attack. Warden got back-up and they're bringing the Doberman into Tyler."

"Was the dog wearing tags?"

"Hell, I don't know, you think they tell me everything? I just happened to be with Don DiBella when the call come. Better get in here."

Jess shoved three spoonfuls of Hungry-Man Steak Tips into his mouth, burned his tongue, and headed back out again.

An escaped dog. The FEMA cordon, the Maryland Guard, the hunting teams...none of it had worked. And how many other dogs had the Doberman infected, roaming around the West Virginia hills for the last however many days?

It wasn't over yet. In one awful sense, it might be just beginning.

INTERIM

He was late going out to feed the dogs. It was the fucking rash – it had kept him up half the night. And the smell was getting worse, much worse. Why should he have to suffer this way? But, no, that was wrong thinking. Suffering made a man strong. Suffering was a test, and a glory.

Still, the itching had gotten so much worse it made it hard to sleep.

So he stumbled out at mid-morning toward the dog shed. The mountains, so different from those of his real country, shone with sunlight on snow. He hated that; the dazzle hurt his eyes. Which also itched. He carried the bucket of kibble to the dog pen, ignoring the growling and snarling, and saw that one of them was missing.

The man stood very still, dread seeping along his spine. He'd been told to not let this happen. He'd been told...*frantically he searched along the fence. The hole dug under it hadn't been there yesterday. It was small, and deep, and bloody. The dog had dug it overnight and squeezed under, tearing his own flesh. The others hadn't followed, not yet.*

He brought stones and dirt and filled the hole. He fed the remaining three dogs. He scratched the rash on his face until it bled, and through all of it his rage grew, replacing the dread. Rage was better. Rage was heartening. Rage let him be in command, no matter what the others said. And command was his right. He'd been denied it all those years by all those soft elite bastards, and now it was his right, because unlike those others, he was not soft. He was a true man.

Leaving the dazzle of the day that so hurt his eyes, he went back into the dark cabin and sat at the laptop to compose email messages. Later, he would drive to some place with wireless capacity, sit outside in his car, and send them.

And very soon now he would have his reward.

TUESDAY

» 45

Ed Dormund slipped through the back door of Tom Martinez's house at four in the morning. It was a relief to finally get out of his own place and away from Cora. They were all meeting at Tom's because he lived out in the country and didn't have a wife, lucky bastard.

Dennis Riley was already there, along with two other friends of his, Sam Jones and Leo Somebody, plus a guy Ed didn't know. Dennis said, "This is Brad Karsky. He used to work with me at Slocum. He's an explosives expert."

Instantly the air in the dim kitchen tautened. Brad was older than the rest of them, maybe in his fifties, with drooping jowls and a deliberate, almost fussy manner. Ed felt a kind of coldness coming off the man, something you could almost touch. Weird.

Dennis said, "Slocum Mining really screwed Brad over but good. Fifteen years he puts in without a single mining accident for his explosives and – "

Brad cut in with, "That isn't relevant here, Dennis," and immediately Dennis shut up.

"What matters," Brad said in his heavy way, "is that we do this right. First a warning explosion, because that may be enough to achieve our goal. And no one gets hurt. That's an absolute must. We want safe destruction of a meaningful target. We want to be absolutely positive that no one is inside the building. We want the explosion followed by a clear and untraceable phone message stating the activity the authorities should take."

"'Free the uninfected dogs,'" Tom said. "Short and sweet."

Brad said, "Better would be 'Return all uninfected dogs to their owners within the next twenty-four hours.'"

Ed nodded. This Brad guy was smart.

Sam said, "What's the explosive?"

Brad said, "An RDX compound with blasting cap and remote detonator."

"How'd you get RDX out of Slocum?" Leo asked. "I thought all that stuff was controlled."

"It is. But it's not hard to fill out the forms for a certain amount of explosives needed for secondary rock breakage and then use a little less. The blasting caps and detonators I make myself."

Dennis said, "I thought Congress got all itchy about terrorism and made the manufacturers embed plastic I.D. tags in all that stuff."

"True," Brad said. "But my supply predates those regulations."

Feeling left out, Ed demanded, "You sure your stuff is still good?"

"I'm sure."

Tom said, "So what's our target?"

Brad told them.

» 46

Jess started out at first light for the West Virginia mountains, one of five cars slipping unobtrusively and separately out of Tyler. Each car held one or two men, animal-control officers or deputies. "Attract as little attention as possible," Sheriff DiBella had said, "but find out if you can where that Doberman came from, if it happens that the damn thing *didn't* escape from Tyler. Find out if anyone's missing a dog, find out if anybody's been attacked."

"Anybody been attacked, they'd of reported it," deputy Ed Ames objected.

"Not necessarily," DiBella said. "If the Doberman bit a commuting soccer mom, you bet your buns we'd know about it by now. But you know how secretive and clannish some of those hill folk are. Or maybe you don't. Our story is that Flatsburgh Animal Control has a Doberman that was bringing down deer and does anyone know where it belongs. Keep your eyes peeled for anyone who acts like he knows more than he's saying."

The eight men shifted their booted feet uneasily. Finally Ames said, "Sheriff, are we looking for a terrorist?"

"No. Jesus H. Christ, Ames, there's no terrorist out there! You been watching too much bad TV. There's a dog that either got infected in Tyler and wandered out, or a West Virginia dog that caught this thing some other way. We're just trying to find out which. Now everybody get out there, and be careful what you say."

Jess headed for his truck. *Or a West Virginia dog that caught this thing some other way*, DiBella had said, and that was the real terror. DiBella meant an air-borne germ of some kind. DiBella meant that the thing might have spread away from Tyler, wafting through the air like lethal snowflakes, infecting neighboring counties. DiBella meant an out-of-control pandemic, spread by dogs. DiBella meant mass plague and mass hysteria.

No. It hadn't happened yet. Don't borrow trouble.

Jess snorted at his own thin optimism and showed his papers at the checkpoint out of Tyler.

Up in the West Virginia mountains, most radio stations disappeared. The truck was down to two, both of which ran heavily to country-and-western music and announcements of car-dealership events. Finally he caught WKBL from Keyser. A very angry woman from some animal-protection organization was being interviewed.

"Nearly all of the dogs in detention in Tyler are *not* infected, and they're beloved members of families, and. Even if – " Jess dipped over the top of the rise and down a steep slope, and the station dissolved into static.

Something bright orange lay in the snow behind a stand of bare trees.

Jess stopped the car, backed up carefully, and pulled over. He tried the binoculars but the orange splotch was hidden from this position; he'd caught it only by chance when he'd glanced into the rearview mirror at just the right point. Carefully Jess waded across a small stream, the icy water not quite reaching the top of his boots, and under trees that gave onto a snowy upland field.

The hiker had been dead a while. She lay looking up at the gray sky, half her face torn away. Her orange jacket was soaked with dried blood; the rest of the blood had been covered by the falling snow. From the part of her face that was left, he could see that the girl had been young, twenties maybe. Her eyes were blue, her hair light brown. She'd been pretty.

Jess pulled out his cell phone. He'd keyed in most DiBella's number when he saw the dog.

It lay about thirty feet away, partially covered by drifting snow, as dead as its mistress. A King Charles spaniel, not really a hiking dog at all. Jess squatted beside him and stared into the dog's open eyes. No milky white film. The spaniel's body wasn't mauled, but the head lay at a strange angle, as if the dog's neck had been broken. The girl might have landed a lucky kick, but Jess doubted that's what had happened. This spaniel had been a victim, not an attacker.

Cell reception was bad up here in the mountains, and non-existent back at his truck. Jess had to tramp over half the field before he got a staticky, intermittent call through.

"DiBella here."

"Don, I've – "

"What? What? I can't hear you!"

"It's Jess!" he shouted, as if shouting would help. He moved to another, higher section of the field. His boot prints made a mess of the pristine snow. "I got something. Dead hiker alone in a field, female, throat torn out. Maybe yesterday, I can't be sure. Also dead is a dog, King Charles spaniel, not mauled. I think I should – "

"Wait a minute," DiBella said, in a voice not his own. "I'm standing here with Mr. Lurie and Dr. Latkin. Let me...wait a minute."

Jess waited, gazing across the snow at the body. It looked very small and very alone.

Finally DiBella said something garbled by static.

"What?"

"I said, what's your position?"

Jess gave the GPS coordinates memorized in his truck.

"Okay, that's Bonchester jurisdiction. Call the sheriff's office there and report the ...no, just a minute, Mr. Lurie wants to talk to you."

It was the first time Jess had had a direct conversation with the FEMA chief. He said with a belligerency that Jess didn't like, "Who'd you tell about this, Langstrom?"

"Nobody. I only just found – "

"What? *Who*'d you tell?"

"*Nobody!*"

"Who's with you?"

"No one."

"You touch anything?"

"Of course not."

"Well, don't," Lurie said. "We'll have people there in an hour. Stay with the body. Don't call anyone, and...*what is it?*...just a minute, Langstrom."

A long minute, filled with static. Jess fought with his temper. Like all weak men, Lurie thought that strength consisted of treating everyone else like idiots. But the next voice was Dr. Latkin's.

"Jess, Joe Latkin. Listen, I'd like you to bring the dog here in your own truck, separate from whatever they do with the hiker. The dog – "

"It doesn't have the milky white stuff in its eyes, doctor."

"No. But that dissolves right after death, when the proteins are no longer being produced. That dog could be infected but not aggressive, at least if you're sure it wasn't what killed the hiker."

"I'm sure." Then what Latkin had said hit Jess: The milky film in infected dogs went away right after death. They knew that because they'd killed some dogs already.

"Can you get the dog into your truck right away, before the FBI arrives?"

The FBI. Scott Lurie was going to bypass local authorities. "I'm breaking West Virginia law if I don't report the death, aren't I?"

Silence. Then Lurie again, brusquely, "Don't worry about that, Langstrom. We'll take care of it. Just *don't talk to anyone and bring Latkin the dog.*"

Jess said curtly, "Right." Suddenly a loud noise came, clear and hard, over the phone. "What was that? It sounded like an explosion!"

The connection was dead.

An explosion. In Tyler? Jess must have been mistaken.

He carried the spaniel, a stiff mass of frozen bloody tissue, to his trunk and put him in back, covered by a tarp. Then he went back to wait beside the body of the girl who had died so horribly on a walk with her dog. It was cold in the field but Jess couldn't leave her there, alone. She'd died alone; that was bad enough.

The first victim to die of canine plague outside of Tyler, Maryland. She and her pet. From nowhere his mind pulled up an old Will Rogers quote: *"If there are no dogs in heaven, then when I die I want to go where they are."*

Jess hoped they were both there now.

» 47

By the miracle of modern flight, Tessa had left London at 6:10 on Monday and arrived in Toronto before 9:00 P.M., flying steadily backwards through the time zones. No one in Toronto paid her any attention. She changed the very generous stack of bills Ruzbihan had given her into American dollars, waited out her lay-over, and flew to Pittsburgh, landing at two in the morning. Someday, she thought wearily, it would be nice to arrive in some city when it wasn't the middle of the night.

The problem was transportation. Ruzbihan had provided "Jane Caldwell" with a passport but not a driver's license, so she could not rent a car. She spent the rest of the night sleeping upright in a plastic chair at the airport. Tuesday morning she took a cab, choosing the driver carefully. She passed him fifty dollars and asked for "a place where I can buy a used car, even if the place doesn't have such a good reputation." They sparred a little, but Tessa knew the right words. He dropped her at a chop shop where the dealer/owner hadn't shaved, leered at her, and tried to show her a car whose engine had been badly camouflaged after a major wreck. Perfect.

She didn't buy that one. Her dead father had, long ago, tried to teach both Tessa and Ellen about cars. Ellen hadn't been interested. Tessa had learned. Now she bought a fifteen-year-old Toyota with 103,000 miles, paying twice what the criminal asked in exchange for his asking nothing else. They came to this agreement without either openly acknowledging it was happening, and she felt a certain tired, grudging admiration for his underhanded skill.

With stolen plates still on the Toyota, she drove to the public library.

When she'd accessed the Internet at Heathrow, there had been no email from Ebenfield, which surprised her. Nor had there been any when she'd checked at the airport in Toronto. Maddox, however, had emailed her:

> Stop this immediately, Tessa. You don't know what you're dealing with. Wherever you went in London after you eluded our agents, it isn't worth it. Come in, and stop being such a goddamn fool. We can protect you. CALL ME.

Tessa snorted. She typed back to Maddox:

> I will call you on your cell at noon today, Tuesday. Be ready.

Tessa left the library. At a nearby convenience store she bought five pre-paid phone cards, and at a Verizon store she bought a cell phone in her own name, using her own American Express card and driver's license. She made sure the phone was turned off and left Pittsburgh, driving north. At a gas station in a small town she didn't catch the name of, she found an outside phone kiosk out of earshot of anyone pumping gas. Tessa loitered inside, drinking coffee, until noon. Then she called Maddox. He answered on the first ring.

"It's Tessa, John."

"Where are you?"

"Doesn't matter." He'd have the cell-phone registration traced soon enough. "I have some things to tell you, so listen carefully. Someone tried to kill me in London after I lost your agents. Two people, failed drive-by. Another group rescued me. That second group of three included a blue-eyed male with a British accent, Liverpool or Manchester by my best guesstimate. Maybe five-nine, a hundred and seventy pounds. Not much to go on, but if they were ours or the Brits', you at least have something to recognize. The –"

"Goddammit, Tessa, what the hell do you think you're doing? You're not even an agent anymore, and you were never undercover! Do you –"

"Shut up and listen to me, John! Have you found Richard Ebenfield? Have you?"

"After you've – "

"Fine, don't tell me. But if you haven't found him, *keep looking*. I still think he's connected somehow to this dog plague, although I don't know how. But I do know he was in Mogumbutuno two years ago. He'd had a loose affiliation for years with a Catholic missionary organization, les Frères de l'Espoir céleste. Check with Bernini on our intelligence presence in Mogumbutuno and run Ebenfield's name by them. Although he might have been using an alias. He might be using one now, if you haven't found him. Have you checked everyone in Tyler itself? It wouldn't be unknown for principals to hang around to observe the effects of their operations."

"Don't tell me how – "

"Shit, John, it took us five years to find Eric Rudolph and eighteen years to find Ted Kaczynski! Look inside the cordon around Tyler! I don't have any more information for you, but I do have a question. When I escaped your agents in London, was that staged? Did you let me get away so you could follow me and see where I led you? Do you actually know where I went, and is this whole thing an elaborate charade? John, are you using me?"

Silence. But was it guilt, or shock at Tessa's paranoia? Finally Maddox said, "Come on in, Tessa. *Now*."

"I can't."

"We can protect you."

"Oh, sure. You can protect me in a nice safe jail cell, right? Evading arrest, traveling on a false passport, maybe even obstructing justice, just for good measure."

He said evenly, "What do you want? A deal?"

"Eventually, but I'll make one with a good lawyer sitting right next to me. Someone a lot better at ass-covering than I am. Meanwhile, I'm giving you information for free."

"We can gather information better than you can."

"Really? You haven't so far. And the last time I saw figures, John, the Bureau had over 120,000 hours of untranslated surveillance tapes in Arabic. You know and I know that you just don't have the manpower to keep up. What's on those tapes that might have tipped you off about this whole situation – other than my name and Salah's, I mean. I can do this better alone."

"Do *what* better?" he snapped, and she hung up.

She got back in the car. Maddox would know soon enough where she'd been, but he didn't know what she was driving. The big danger was the car's being stopped due to the stolen plates. A chance she'd have to take.

Was she being paranoid about the FBI?

Since last week, it paid to be paranoid about everything.

After an hour she exited the expressway at another small town, found the library, and accessed her email. Still nothing from Ebenfield. That surprised her a little. Usually fanatics, especially amateurs, loved to explain their demented "causes," and Ebenfield had a secure means to do so. She sent him another email:

Richard –

I still want to hear from you. And I want to talk to you. Send me a pay-phone number and a time to call, and I'll phone you.

After a moment's hesitation she added a proverb common throughout the MidEast, one Salah had been fond of. She had to guess at the phonetic spelling, but, then, Ebenfield was no Arabic scholar. Maybe he'd recognize the syllables, or be intrigued enough to find a translation on the Web, or even be pushed to phone her. Carefully she typed: "Kul kahlb beiji youmo."

Every dog must have its day.

She got back in the car and pointed it toward Maryland.

» 48

On the way back to Tyler with the dead King Charles spaniel in his truck, Jess was stopped twice before he even reached the edge of town. At the state line, Maryland troopers waved him on after a cursory look at his FEMA pass and driver's license. The whole thing took maybe thirty seconds and looked to Jess like a routine stop-and-scrutinize, a net to catch whatever violations happened to turn up.

By the second stop, he knew better.

Just beyond the sign proclaiming WELCOME TO TYLER TOWNSHIP, traffic backed up nearly a quarter mile. Vehicles were being turned away. Jess studied the drivers' angry faces as they headed back along the highway. When his turn came, a soldier in full battle gear demanded his authorization. More unsmiling soldiers – Army, not Maryland Guard – stood beside a concrete barricade that spanned most of the road.

"Jess Langstrom, Tyler Animal Control Officer, this is my FEMA pass."

"Wait here."

In the near distance, troops lounged behind sand-bag fortifications. Jess, incredulous, spotted a sniper prone on a tree platform. Since this morning, Tyler had changed from a quarantine site to a city under martial law.

The soldier returned with Jess's pass. "Proceed into Tyler at no more than twenty miles per hour, Mr. Langstrom, and report directly to Dr. Latkin."

"Yes." It had almost come out *Yes, sir.*

Half a mile beyond the checkpoint, Jess saw the burned building. He stopped the truck – the soldier hadn't said he couldn't proceed at *less* than twenty miles per hour – and stared. What had been the Stop 'n' Shop, owned by Mayor Hafner's son Carl, was now blackened timber and twisted metal. Debris lay, as if hurled, fifty feet away from the ruins. No ordinary fire did that. Yellow police tape circled the scene. A cop strode forward, sunlight glinting off his mirror shades.

"Please leave this area immed – oh, hi, Jess."

"Eric. Was it a bomb?"

"Yeah." Eric Lavida took off his shades. Beneath the brim of his hat, his sunburned young face was grim. "You been out of town?"

"For DiBella."

"Find anything?"

"No. Anybody hurt here?"

"No. They phoned in a warning, gave the clerk plenty of time to get out. Janie Wilcox, Mike's girl. She was the only one in the store."

"Any suspects?"

"Not yet. But the caller said, 'Mr. Mayor, return all uninfected dogs to their owners within the next twenty-four hours, or this will happen again.'"

Jess stared at the burned Stop 'n' Shop. Things like this didn't happen in his hometown, which had suddenly become a place he didn't know.

"Later," Eric said, and the word was more than a casual leave-taking.

Getting into critical-incident headquarters meant another cordon of troops, another showing of his flimsy FEMA pass. Finally Jess was allowed to pull into the parking lot of the Cedar Springs Motel and deliver the hiker's dead spaniel to Dr. Latkin, whose face was gray with exhaustion.

"Doctor," Jess asked as he passed the little tarp-covered body to Latkin, "will this really help?"

"We don't know what will help!" Latkin snapped. He closed his eyes and breathed deeply. "Sorry, Jess. Pretty tense around here. This dog might or might not give us new information about mutations, immunities, branching, or brain effects. We won't know until we do the procedures. Meanwhile, FEMA –" He broke off, shaking his head.

Jess said, "When did Tyler get all these troops?"

"This morning, after the explosion. Scott Lurie's hell-bent on nobody's saying FEMA isn't doing a total job on *his* watch. He's overcompensating, if you ask me, for all of the agency's past screw-ups. Trying so hard to keep the epidemic contained in Tyler that he's bound to create a backlash. When he heard about the West Virginia Doberman, he went ballistic."

"Joe, what do you think will –"

"I don't know," Dr. Latkin said, pulling his hands over the gray skin on his face as if to force some life into it. "I've seen Ebola in Africa and Marburg in the Philippines and cholera in South America and we got them all under control, but none of them involved eradicating people's pets. People just aren't rational about their pets!"

Jess had been an animal control officer for twenty years. He didn't need a CDC doctor with a lot of advanced degrees to tell him that. And since Joe Latkin didn't seem able to tell him anything else, he got back in his truck and headed for West Virginia and the fruitless search for the home of the escaped Doberman that, Jess increasingly suspected, they were not going to be able to find.

» 49

Tessa checked into a Maryland motel a few miles south of the Pennsylvania state line. That was as close as she could get to Tyler because every other place displayed NO VACANCY signs, full of reporters and gawkers and Tyler citizens exiled from their town for the duration of the quarantine. The motel featured bullet-proof plastic between the desk clerk and his patrons, accepted cash, and didn't question her story that she had no car. Bars shielded the windows. The sink ran a trickle of rust-colored water. The phone allowed only local calls.

She showered, a much overdue necessity, retrieved her car from the supermarket parking lot down the road, and found the local library. She was getting tired of rural libraries.

One of its two Internet terminals was down. Tessa waited while three teenage girls noisily used the other one, emailing somebody named Zach that somebody else named Emily was secretly in love with him. Finally the librarian chased them away. Tessa accessed her email.

> My dear Tessa,
>
> You asked about my "cause." How laughably naïve you are. First, to think that I don't know what you're doing. You think the more you know about me the easier it will be to find me. You are mistaken. Second, you are naïve to think that I have a single "cause," as if there is only one thing wrong with the world.
>
> You, and all like you, will soon learn otherwise. The decline of the United States has many causes, but all come back to one thing: we have become soft. Don't you read the newspapers, my Tessa? Men no longer stand up, take command, do whatever proves necessary to bring about a righteous society. Soft men – even women – take office and then can't even hold their own positions, let alone bring forward those who truly deserve to hold power. Our politicians cannot rule. Our soldiers cannot fight. Our children cannot compete. Softness has nearly

destroyed us. I have seen the world, and I see how we are despised by those that *we* should despise.

But not for much longer. A New Order is coming. The soft elite shall fall, and the true men come out of the shadows and rule. I am owed this. I have earned it.

More later.

Richard

كلب الرئيس

"Ma'am, are you almost finished? I got a term paper due tomorrow."

Tessa looked up at the girl. Thin, tall, shy, with accusing blue eyes. The same blue, she thought numbly and irrelevantly, as the eyes of the Brit shooter in London. Small world.

"Just let me print this, and...just let me print it in private, okay?"

The girl moved to the side of the computer station, but kept staring balefully at Tessa. She hit PRINT, heard the communal printer whirr behind her, and was about to log off when the PC announced, "You've got mail!" The girl sighed.

Madame,

I have received what follows from frère Luc-Claude of our order. Since you have said your French is not good, I will tell you what he tells to me.

Tessa glanced at the message reprinted at bottom of the email; it was long, detailed, and in complex French. She returned to Abbé LeFort's summary.

Richard Ebenfield was indeed with les Frères de l'Espoir céleste in Mogumbutuno two years ago. He was very ill and our order cared for him until he recovered. He told frère Luc-Claude that he has been into the jungle, at a village besieged by wild dogs. There Richard was bitten. When he came to les frères, he had a very strong fever but this passed away after some days and Richard once more left. He seemed then

> once more healthy. Frère Luc-Claude has not seen him ever since. He adds only that in his fever Richard said many violent things about both the United States and the man named Salah.
>
> I wish you success under God in your endeavors.
>
> Abbé Guillaume LeFort
>
> les Frères de l'Espoir céleste

The girl whined, "It's a term paper on *Faulkner*. And he's *hard*."

"Just another few minutes," Tessa said, and somehow the words came out normally. The girl scowled and flounced off.

She printed the email. The girl reappeared with a middle-aged woman. "Ma'am," the librarian said, "there's a ten-minute limit on use of the Internet connections, and Sarah here says you've exceeded your limit. Is that true?"

"No," Tessa said. "I've got two minutes left." She had no idea how long she'd been on.

"Sarah, dear, I think you can wait two more minutes."

"She's lying! She's been on longer than ten minutes already!"

Tessa forwarded both Ebenfield's and the abbé's email to Maddox with the heading "VERY IMPORTANT!" She signed off, grabbed her printouts, and matched the girl's scowl. She wanted to tell the brat, "I hope you flunk your SAT's." She didn't say it; she'd already drawn enough attention to herself.

Tessa drove back to a public phone. Using one of her phone cards, she called Maddox's cell. He answered instantly.

"John, Tessa again. I just sent you email. See that the medical information gets to that CDC doctor, Laskit or whatever his name was. Tell him to watch the dog-bite victims who didn't die, looking out for high fever. And –"

"Tessa, where are you?"

"– and *find Ebenfield*." She hung up. Nowhere near time for a trace.

She parked the Toyota on a carefully-chosen residential street, where it was less likely to be noticed overnight than in the supermarket parking lot, and walked through the cold winter night to her ratty motel. The

TV was broken. Too exhausted to look for a bar with a television, she fell into bed and slept like a stone, without dreams.

INTERIM

He sat alone in his house, smoking, gazing out the window. The foliage was withered and sere. It would come back in the spring, of course, but spring seemed, at that moment, a long time away.

It was not supposed to come to this.

He had been very careful. Launching the rapid but still meticulous investigation since the woman's visit, since she had planted the suspicion. He had used every resource at his command, gathering information until he was sure, hoping all the while that he was mistaken. Hoping that no one connected to him could be that stupid. And, when he finally knew there had been no mistake, enduring the heartache.

It was not supposed to come to this, and he did not want to do what was required.

But his flesh, his bone, his blood...his son.

Ruzbihan al-Ashan stubbed out the cigarette, picked up the house phone, and gave the order.

WEDNESDAY

» 50

Cami woke with a headache worse than she had ever had in her life.

Ordinarily she didn't get sick. At her high school graduation, she'd won the perfect attendance award for never missing a single day from kindergarten through grade twelve. Nor had she ever called in sick to work, not even once, and she'd been a little shocked at the nurses who called in to take "mental health days." But now Cami felt really awful.

Getting out of bed only made her head hurt worse. Throwing off the bedclothes – they were so hot! – she stumbled into the bathroom and groped in the medicine cabinet for her thermometer. One hundred one point five.

She barely made it to the toilet to vomit.

It might be some kind of flu. Or an infection from the bite of Mr. Anselm's dog. Or...oh, dear Lord, no...something transmitted by the bite, something unknown. If so –

She vomited again.

Her head feeling as if it would shatter, Cami made it back to the bedroom. Her nightgown was soaked with sweat. She got it off and pulled on a light T-shirt plus sweat pants, all that would fit over the dressings on her leg. Almost immediately sweat soaked the tee. She lay on the bed and fumbled for the phone.

"Billy? It's – "

"Cami! 'Morning, beautiful!"

"I'm sorry to bother you so early – " What time was it? She had no idea. " – but I – "

"What is it? What's wrong, darlin'?"

"I'm...I'm sick. I have to go to the ER and I can't drive. I'm sorry to bother you but – "

"I'll be there in ten minutes. Just stay still and...and do whatever it is you're supposed to. I'll get Jess and we'll be right there."

She lay on the bed, feeling the sweat bead and roll down her forehead, her breasts, her belly. The door...she had to unlock the front door for Billy and Jess. He was so good to come get her...this was probably just the flu, the flu season wasn't really over yet although it had been a light year for flu oh she was so *hot!* She had to unlock the door for Billy had to get up and unlock the door...Billy and Jess so good to come right away –

But it wasn't Jess who came. Billy alone burst through the door, making so much noise that Cami's headache spiked into unbearable pain and she cried out from her slumped position against the wall. Billy stopped, stared, and then knelt beside her.

"Well, you really are hurtin', nurse Cami," he said in the softest voice she'd ever heard from him. "But it's gonna be okay, everything's gonna be just fine, darlin'. Now I can't lift you, worse luck with my damn arm, but I'm gonna pull you up slowly and you're gonna lean on me down to the car. Can you do that, beautiful? Here we go."

He got them both through the door, down the steps, outside. The cold air felt wonderful. But she didn't have on a coat or shoes...when had she put slippers on? Had Billy done it? She couldn't remember. Billy was easing her into the car, Billy was –

"Where's Jess?"

"Not home. I'm driving you." The car lurched forward as Billy maneuvered it with his left hand on the steering wheel.

"But I have to see Allen! I promised!"

Billy scowled. "Who's Allen?"

"Allen! I promised! At the hospital!"

Billy's face cleared. "Oh, the kid. Right."

"I promised! I promised!"

Something was wrong; someone was screaming. And then she cried, "Fire!" because all at once flames were dancing along her arms, red and blue and orange and cold...but the weird thing was that they didn't hurt. How could flames not hurt? The car went forward. Belle...was Belle all right? Why were there flames? She had to see Allen, she'd promised!

"Steady, Cami, we're here," somebody said, and the flames surged once more before someone did something and she slid down into the blessed cool dark.

—

Billy was scared.

He couldn't remember the last time he'd been scared. Not when this dog plague had started with young A.J. Wright and his dad's pit bull. Not even when that fucking lunatic Victor Balonov had shot Billy. But turning Cami, twitching and raving about Allen, over to the ER nurse, Billy was terrified.

The ER was full of people again, and Billy recognized nearly all of them. They were the same people who had come in with dog bites and had since gone home, been moved upstairs to ICU, or died. Now here they were back again, minus the dead ones, and most of them were screaming or twitching or raving like Cami. There was old Mrs. Carby and the Wingerson kid and Jayne Steadman and one of the little Gladwell twins…

Everybody who got bit was now getting sick.

Helplessly he watched Cami being wheeled away. Now there was probably something in her brain, like Dr. Latkin said was in the dogs' brains. Oh, Christ, were all the infected people going to die? Or – and this was what twisted Billy's stomach into what felt like the mother of all knots – were they going to start acting like the infected dogs, trying to bite people and so spread the disease?

And if people could get the plague – if that could happen, Billy couldn't imagine what on God's green-and-shit-smeared Earth could happen next.

» 51

Jess woke late on Wednesday, to gunfire.

He leapt out of bed and hit the floor before his sleep-clogged brain registered that the shots were outside, close but not immediately outside his window. They'd been rapid-fire, as if from an automatic weapon – the Guards? Some maniac with an AK-47? Nearly twenty-four hours had passed since the bombing of the Stop 'n' Shop, and FEMA had not returned the uninfected dogs to their owners.

9:30 A.M. He'd slept through his alarm. Or turned it off in his sleep, or something.

Throwing on yesterday's jeans and sweater, lacing up his boots with unsteady fingers, Jess grabbed his gun and raced to the front door. The snowy street outside was deserted and absolutely quiet. He saw nothing amiss. But then he heard a single dog, somewhere a few streets over. It was giving out the single saddest sound a dog can make, two or three quick barks ending in a long howl, what some people called the "death howl" of a dog in mourning.

Jess got into his truck and drove to look for the dog. The Guard troops that circled Tyler like a noose weren't evident in this residential section, but neither was anyone else. Jess's was the only vehicle disturbing the pristine layer of snow on the street. But he saw curtains pulled back and faces at windows as he passed.

He found the dog, a brown-and-white beagle, sitting on its haunches on the open front porch of a house that appeared to be deserted. Soggy newspapers dotted lawn. Some people had chosen to leave Tyler as soon as the epidemic had started, even when that meant leaving pets behind. The beagle howled again, a long mournful cry with no hint of aggression in it. Its coat was filthy; blood spotted one hind leg. Somewhere the beagle had lost its collar. Jess wasn't close enough to see if its eyes were filmed with white.

He called the Animal Control office on his cell. "Suzanne, I need –"

"Where *are* you? We're backed up with calls!"

"Overslept. I'll be in soon but right now I need a dog I.D. for 627 Herlinger Street. Get it off the computer."

"Okay, 627 Herlinger...That's the Dorsey residence. They show a licensed male two-year-old beagle named Hearsay."

"Hearsay?"

"Maybe he's a lawyer?"

Jess buckled on his protective gear, got a medium-sized crate from his truck, and started toward the house, gun in his right hand and crate in his left. Hearsay turned and wagged his tail. His brown eyes were clear. In all Jess's years working with animals, beagles were about the only breed he hadn't seen bite anybody. He always thought that if he ever got another dog, it would be a beagle.

"Hey, Hearsay. Here, good dog."

The beagle wagged his tail harder and tried to drag himself toward Jess. It was obvious that his bloody hind leg hurt him. Jess was three or four feet from the dog, just setting down the crate, when a single shot sounded. Hearsay screamed and dropped. A pool of blood spread onto the porch.

Jess wheeled around and shouted, "Who fired that!" A nanosecond later it occurred to him that he was a target and there was an armed nut out there, but he didn't move. Scanning the street, he saw nothing. The shooter was hidden.

His cell rang, an unfamiliar number. Even before he answered, he knew.

"Langstrom," a male voice said, "If you and the whole damn federal government can't kill these vicious dogs, we'll do it for you. No more kids are going to die because you guys won't do what you fucking well should," Click.

Jess stood motionless. The voice was vaguely familiar, but he couldn't place it. DiBella could have the call traced.

The cell rang again, but this time he recognized the number: Latkin. "Jess? Joe Latkin. Listen, my team and I spent all night with that spaniel you brought us, the one killed with the hiker in West Virginia. Thank God the media haven't got that yet. The spaniel wasn't infected, but the neck-bite area held the virus in saliva, and it seems to have come from a primary, not a secondary."

"I don't understand that, doctor." And why was Latkin telling Jess? He scanned the street for something, anything, that might tell him where the shooter was. Nothing.

"Let me give it to you briefly," Latkin said. "The virus is highly mutable, which shows through the way it manifests in different animals. There are very tiny changes with each transmission. It's called branching, and it lets us construct a diagram: A bit B, and B bit C and D and F, and then C bit G and so on. It's not a perfect history but it's not bad, either. We think your King Charles spaniel was bitten by the original source of the plague, not by another dog somewhere down the line."

Jess tried to concentrate. "You mean the Doberman captured in West Virginia was the source of the plague?"

"Yes. But that Doberman wasn't the one that bit the spaniel. The salivas don't match."

"You mean there's *another* source out there?"

"Yes. Another primary source of the virus. And I need you and DiBella, plus whoever else you trust one hundred percent, to go look for it."

"Why me, Joe? God, you've told the FBI and FEMA, right? The feds'll comb those hills."

"Yes. But they won't know where to look because they don't know the terrain, and they won't get anyone to tell them anything because they don't know the people. Scott Lurie won't use local help, Maryland or West Virginian, because he's a supercilious son-of-a-bitch who thinks you're all a bunch of bumpkins. I'm outside my own sphere of authority here, but God, I can't work if they won't let me get at the right material! I need you to go back up to West Virginia and find that other dog. You know animals, and you know whom you can trust to look along with you. I *need* that other primary source."

"Is it another Doberman?"

"Can't tell. Can you? You saw the hiker."

Jess said, "It could be any big breed. But I looked at her carefully and I didn't see any hairs, and the spaniel's neck was snapped with a single shake, so probably a short-hair with really strong jaws."

"See what I mean? You know what you're doing. How many FBI agents would know all that? Do you know what story the family of the dead hiker was told? That she was killed by a bear."

Jess thought of the West Virginia medical examiner, the undertaker who would prepare the corpse, the family who would view her for identification of the body. *A bear, my ass.* That story would dissolve like sugar in rain.

Latkin said, "Will you do it, Jess?"

"Yes."

"Good. Bye."

Jess put Hearsay's body in the crate. From his truck he called DiBella, told him what had happened, and read him the phone number from his cell's call record. DiBella swore for a full, creative fifteen seconds. "Jess, last night we broke up a bad fight at the Moonlight Lounge. Dennis

Riley and them want their dogs back. The other group of drunks wanted every last dog in Tyler killed yesterday to keep the people safe. The fight got really ugly. FEMA hasn't returned the uninfected dogs like the bombers demanded – well, Lurie can't do that, of course. But FEMA's just making the whole situation worse by locking the whole town up tighter than a virgin's ass... I'll get on that phone number."

"Thanks, Don."

Jess drove to the Animal Control office. He saw no one on the deserted streets but he could feel eyes on him, hear uncaptured dogs baying in the distance, could smell the tension like fumes in the air, gasoline too close to way too many sparks.

» 52

Tessa woke early Wednesday morning, hiked to the library, and waited impatiently for it to open. A different librarian was on duty and, this time, the local kids were in school instead of waiting to use the Internet. She had email from both Maddox and Ebenfield. Maddox merely repeated his demand that she come inside. Ebenfield's email was in the form of a 200-kilobyte attachment. At least fifty pages.

She scanned it quickly, grimacing. It was a political screed, railing against the United States government, big corporations, the corrupt medical establishment, political parties, and science. Tessa caught phrases here and there: "soft-bellied elite," "godless values," "corruption at the core," "suffering of the poor," "necessary downfall," "choosing easy pleasure over hard necessity," "duty to destroy." She'd heard this mish-mash before, from other domestic terrorists. Different lyrics, same tune.

It wasn't until the end that Ebenfield turned personal:

> So, my Tessa, now you understand. If you understand, you must come to me, because that is what is right. First destruction of the soft and corrupt Old Order, then the rightful ascension of those meant to rule. And just as you were first with the enemy Salah, now you will be with me. Everything

goes full circle. Where are you? Give me a phone number and I will call you.

Richard

كلب الرئيس

Give me a phone number.

So this was it – decision time. She stared a few seconds at the Arabic below his name: "Dogs first," again. Then she typed back, "This is my cell-phone number. But I'm not going to turn it on until 3:00 P.M. today. We can talk then."

To Maddox she typed, "Call you at noon. Be ready. Tessa."

Outside, Tessa wrapped her head in the scarf she'd bought with pretty much the last of Ruzbihan's money and walked back toward the side street where she'd left the Toyota. She approached cautiously, slipping into a backyard from an adjacent street, watching a while from behind a hedge. This lower-middle-class neighborhood was deserted in the day, kids at school and adults at work. So it wasn't hard to spot the FBI agents.

They'd traced the hot car. They'd taken a chance that she might have bought a car in the same city she'd used her American Express card to buy the cell phone, and they'd come up lucky.

Carefully Tessa backed out of the hedge, out of the yard, out of the neighborhood. She walked to the highway, took a deep breath, and caught a ride with a man heading east. He leered at her and she told him her husband was a cop and she was leaving him because he turned violent at the slightest provocation. In fact, he'd already be in jail for assaulting someone if his buddies on the force hadn't protected him. He'd accused her, Gina, of having an affair with the guy, which was ridiculous because she'd never been unfaithful, *never*, but her husband was so insanely jealous and vindictive she just had to get away. Although it was possible her husband would follow her. The driver stopped leering.

She left him at a truck stop in West Virginia, a small seedy place with minimal facilities. It was twenty minutes to noon. She called Maddox from a pay phone, using one of her prepaid phone cards.

"John, it's Tessa. Did you get that long manifesto from Ebenfield?"

"Yes. Tessa –"

"Have you found him?"

"No. Where are you?"

"He's going to call me at 3:00. I'll call you after that, Bye."

"Wait! Tessa, just a minute. I want to run some names by you again. You –"

"I can't –"

"Just *listen*, for once! Do you know anything about any of these people? Hakeem bin Ahmed al-Fulani?"

"No." Was he trying to keep her on the line long enough to trace the call? But he must know she wouldn't fall for that.

"Aktar Erekat?"

"No."

"Sometimes he uses the name Abd-Al Adil Erekat."

Abd-Al Adil. The name of Ruzbihan's son. But that wasn't an uncommon name in Tunisia, and Erekat was not among Ruzbihan's surnames.

"No."

"Tessa –"

She hung up.

For the next few hours, she drank coffee quietly at a table in the truck stop, reading discarded newspapers, her chilly manner a clear warning to leave her alone. At two-thirty she started watching the truckers coming and going. She picked an older man, kindly looking, fairly slightly built, went over to his table, and asked him for a ride when he left.

"Sorry, no." He kept shoveling in his hot roast-beef sandwich.

"Why not?"

"Don't take women. Don't want any trouble."

"I won't be any trouble. I just need to get to Tyler, Maryland or as close as I can!"

Now she had his attention. "Tyler? Where the dog plague is?"

"My mom's in that town, caught in the quarantine. She's got diabetes and high blood pressure and I don't know what else. I know they won't let me in but I need to get as close as I can, for when the quarantine is lifted!"

"Isn't gonna be lifted. Not soon, anyway. Not now that they're killing dogs and blowing up buildings."

Tessa felt as if she'd been punched. "Killing dogs? Blowing up buildings?"

"Haven't you seen no news, girlie?"

"No! What's happening?"

"Just what I said. If you ask me, they shoulda killed those dogs before this. We could have ourselves some kind of bird flu, only with dogs. Can't risk it. But protestors don't see it that way – they want their precious little pets back. Hey, don't look so – did your mom get bit?"

"No."

"Then she's probably all right. Oh, come on, girlie, your mom'll be fine."

"Please take me to Tyler! Or as close as you're going!"

"I…oh, what the hell. You look like a nice enough girl. What you doing thumbing it, anyway? It's dangerous."

"I don't have any money." She tried to smile. "A little down on my luck."

"Been there, done that. You hungry?"

His eyes on her were so kind that Tessa nodded, even though she wasn't hungry. He ordered her the same thing he was having, without asking her first – clearly he was used to being in charge of women. She smiled tremulously and ate a few bites, dawdling to get the timing right. At 2:55 he said, "You gonna actually eat that or can we go?"

"I'll eat." A few more bites and she said, in a voice more girlish than her own, "Can you ask the waitress to put it in a doggie bag for me? And can I use the rest room a minute?"

"If you gotta go, you gotta," he grumbled.

The ladies' room was empty. Tessa took a deep breath and turned on her cell phone. The tiny screen displayed the icon that meant the phone was searching for a transmission tower.

…and searching…

...and searching.

NO COVERAGE AT THIS TIME.

Tessa stared at the phone. Numbly – stupidly – she shook it, which of course did nothing. Ebenfield was probably trying to contact her, and she was going to miss her one chance to talk to him.

She raced out of the ladies' room and cried, "Let's go now! Please! Now!"

The old trucker got slowly to his feet, shaking his head at the unpredictability of women.

Tessa sat tensely in the cab of the semi, staring at the cell phone display. No little tower appeared. Still too many mountains here

...and here....

...and here...

"Leaning forward like that ain't gonna make us get there any faster," the old trucker said. "Neither's glaring at that there phone."

"Do you know when we come back into an area of cell coverage?" Tessa asked. He glanced over at her and she realized she'd dropped the voice and diction of the distraught, not-too-bright woman rushing to her ailing mom in Tyler. Well, there was a reason Tessa had never worked undercover.

"Top of that peak ahead, might be your phone'll work."

"Thank you." She continued to watch the display, but now she also watched the road signs and tried to measure the distance to the place he'd indicated. Fifteen minutes, twenty? How long would Richard Ebenfield try to call her before he decided she wasn't going to answer?

The trucker said dryly, "Your mom really needs to talk to you, huh?"

"I told you she's sick."

"You told me a lot of things."

When her cell phone finally chimed cheerily and the tower icon flashed on, Tessa said, "Please let me out here!"

"Here? Ain't nothing here."

"But I want to get out. Please!"

The old man sighed, pulled onto the shoulder, and said, "Miss, I think maybe you should take your medication more regular-like."

"Thank you! I really appreciate the ride! I'll call for someone to come get me!"

He sighed again and drove away. Tessa stood in the snow by the side of the road in front of a clump of bushes and stared at the cell phone. *Call, Ebenfield, damn you. Call.*

He didn't. She'd missed the three o'clock appointment and he wasn't going to keep trying. She had to get to a computer, had to email him what had happened... A car rounded the top of the steep rise in the road and she drew back into some bushes, out of sight. The last thing she wanted right now was the distraction of persuading some Good Samaritan that she didn't need a ride out of the West Virginia mountains.

But the car slowed, then stopped. Tessa stared from behind her bushes. The cover they provided was incomplete but still the driver shouldn't have been able to see her from the road...The door opened and a man stepped out.

"Tessa?"

The smell hit her then, brought on a sudden gust of winter wind, the sickly-sweet smell of living rot. The man wore a strange headgear over his face, a loose white square of cotton held in place with a ring of knotted cord. She realized suddenly that it was supposed to look like an Arab headdress worn backward, cut with eyeholes.

Then she saw the gun.

"Get in the car, my Tessa," Ebenfield said. "No, you can't escape. And there's something I've waited such a long time to show you."

She rushed him, prepared to kick. But then something happened, something she had only read about. A wave of nausea and disorientation hit her, so strong that the mountains wavered in her sight. She fell backward onto the snowy ground.

When she came to, she lay in the open trunk of his car. Her ankles and wrist were bound and on her feet she wore only socks. In the small enclosed space, the smell of decaying flesh was so strong that Tessa gagged. Ebenfield suddenly loomed above her. He used the sonic-wave gun again and a second wave of nausea and blackness took her, but not before she saw the terrible abomination that was his face.

» 53

Ed Dormund sat in his living room, watching TV. A pleasurable glow wrapped him, composed of accomplishment over the successful bombing, anticipation of what might happen next, and an entire six-pack of beer. On CNN, Janet Belville intoned, "pressure from both sides – to destroy all dogs in Tyler, Maryland as a way of combating and containing the epidemic, or to continue with the present policy of capturing and holding both infected and uninfected dogs. Since there have been no new dog attacks reported since yesterday, according to FEMA spokespersons, it may that the president will wait for – "

Ed snorted. That wimpy president wasn't ever going to make a decision, just like FEMA didn't make the right decision and return the dogs after the bombing. So Ed and the others were going to make those decisions for them. After all, this was still a free country!

He drained the last beer as Cora emerged from her crafts room. "Ed! You left rings on the coffee table again! Couldn't you at least – "

"Don't start," Ed snarled. All at once his pleasant, interested mood vanished. She ruined it, just like she always did, ruining everything, wrecking his life.

"Look at this place!" Cora shrilled. "Chips all over the rug, if you think I'm going to clean it up you got another think coming! Get up off your lazy ass and vacuum up that rug!"

Ed stood, intending to...what? Wooziness took him and he grabbed at something to stay upright. His fingers closed on the lamp on the end table beside the couch. It and he crashed to the floor.

Cora laughed bitterly. "Look at you! Can't even stand up!" She stomped off into the kitchen and slammed the door.

Could he stand? All at once it was an interesting question, almost as interesting as what the White House was going to try to do about the dogs. Carefully Ed pulled himself to his feet and swayed, triumphant.

He heard barking.

Jake! Ed staggered to the window and there they were, all three of them, Petey and Rex and Jake. At the sight of Ed they bared their impressive teeth and snarled, but Ed wasn't fooled. Good ol' Jake! Ed knew the dogs loved him even though they temporarily had this disease. That wasn't their fault. Ed knew how it was when you caught a disease. Hadn't he had pneumonia once?

Tears filled his eyes, the easy tears of the very drunk. The dogs were probably hungry, that's why they came home. He could get them dog food from the kitchen, pour it out the window under the sink. Yeah, food...

Cora reappeared, dragging the vacuum cleaner. "So it's me cleaning up after you again, you worthless, drunken piece of garbage, you never do anything around here."

At the sight of Cora's smirk, Ed ignited. All the weepy love he'd felt for Jake and Rex and Petey turned in a single instant to white-burning hatred of Cora, this bitch who ruined everything, who never let him enjoy anything, who was always at him and at him and *at him* and never left him alone –

He could be alone.

It wasn't a thought but a force, inevitable as thunder after lightening. You couldn't stop thunder from coming, and Ed didn't try. All you could do with a force of nature was go with it. He lurched across the room and grabbed Cora.

She shrieked and struggled, but Ed didn't even slow. He outweighed her by fifty pounds and anyway, this was thunder here. In less than thirty seconds he'd dragged her through the kitchen to the garage door. He pushed her forward and she stumbled down the two shallow steps to the garage. Ed hit the automatic garage door opener, then slammed and locked the kitchen door.

Cora screamed. Jake and Petey and Rex, as they'd done their entire lives, responded to the sound of the garage door and raced around the house. Cora screamed again, a different sound, horrible! Ed resisted the urge to cover his ears. Instead he stumbled to the phone and dialed 911.

"My wife! My wife! The dogs –"

"What is it, sir? Calm down, can you tell me your name and address?"

"Ed Dormund! 693 Asbury Street! My wife went into the garage to get into the car, she must of hit the garage door opener by mistake, the dogs came in – oh God!"

"The police will come immediately." Horror in the young voice, and struggle to stay calm.

"Yes, yes, oh my God – " Ed heard his own horror, his own excitement. Yes. Just right.

Cora had stopped screaming.

Gently Ed lowered himself to the kitchen table. His moment was slipping away; he could feel it going. No matter. He could do this. He could do anything he wanted to. He just needed to get his story straight. The argument over the vacuuming. Cora mad. She says she's going to her mother's. Car in the garage, no danger, go right into her mother's garage, mother would have been ready to open and close door after Cora called her on her cell. The way people were managing all over Tyler. Cora angry at Ed, didn't stop even for her coat. But –

Ed staggered to his feet and unlocked the kitchen door. Before he could hesitate, he opened the door, hurled Cora's purse into the garage, and slammed the door. The dogs, occupied, didn't try to come in. He gagged at the sounds out there now.

But he could do this, he *could* –

Police sirens, coming closer.

Good ol' Jake!

» 54

Tessa didn't know how long she'd been locked in the reeking trunk, or how far they'd driven while she'd been unconscious. Finally the car stopped and the trunk opened. She managed to say, "Richard Ebenfield."

"My Tessa." He lifted her and she had to force herself to neither gag nor recoil. The skin on his face had rotted. Pieces had fallen off, leaving exposed, oozing purplish patches like those of leprosy. But this was not leprosy; his features were all intact and apparently only his face was affected since he didn't seem in pain where her body unwillingly pressed against his. He staggered under her weight. This was not an athlete.

Somewhere nearby, dogs howled.

Snowy mountains and pine woods pressed close. Under the thick pines, the sunshine was muted. Ebenfield kicked open the door of a small wooden shed and dropped Tessa on a pile of very dirty straw. Lighting a Coleman lantern, he closed the door. The shed was windowless. Turds littered the corners. A rat scurried away from Tessa and disappeared down a hole.

She said, as evenly as she could manage, "The tracker was in one of my boots, wasn't it. The boots I was given in London. The signal is encrypted and goes through satellite. The metal detectors at the airport didn't pick up the tracker so it's state-of-the-art, ceramics or plastic. And that sonic stunner you used on me is military-grade. Who are you and Abd Al-Adil working with, Ebenfield?"

"Ah, my Tessa, I knew you were as smart as you are beautiful. Salah chose wisely for me."

"For *you*?"

"But of course. He was the precursor, the forerunner. John the Baptist, if you like."

Which cast Ebenfield as Jesus Christ.

Tessa stifled her grimace of disgust. "Who are you working with?"

"Those the Lord has sent me as minions, as servants, as means to carry out the design of Heaven."

She stared levelly at him. "You don't believe that Biblical stuff. Not really. I can detect lying."

He laughed, a horrible distortion of his scabrous face. "You're right. I've grown past that. The Bible was useful to me once, but now my path has taken me beyond it. Religion, like government and economy, is nothing more than a way to keep the true men from claiming their rightful power."

He was as loopy as tangled yarn. "And what's your rightful place, Ebenfield?"

"You already know, my Tessa."

"I don't. Tell me."

Ebenfield didn't answer. Moving to the far wall of the filthy shed, he fumbled at something on the wall. Tessa took advantage of his turned back to strain at the rope that bound her wrists behind her. It didn't give. All she succeeded in doing was sinking her body deeper into the stinking straw.

Sudden light flooded the shed.

Ebenfield had unfastened and lifted away a section of the wall, a solid piece of wood maybe five feet square that began at the dirt floor. Behind the opening was strong chain-link fencing, through which poured weak late-afternoon light filtered through pine boughs and air even colder than that in the shed. Behind the fence snarled and jumped three huge dogs. One black-and-tan Doberman. The other two of some all-black breed with snouts like pigs, heavily muscled legs, and long, saliva-flecked teeth. The dogs' eyes were all filmed with milky white.

The chain-link fence had a latch that opened it into the shed.

Ebenfield turned back toward her, the line of light from the opening cutting like a knife across his rotting face. *A knife would have been more merciful*, Tessa thought. But Ebenfield's voice was triumphant.

"Behold my servants. Not the first ones, but my servants nonetheless."

"They're dogs." It sounded stupid, but how did you talk to the certifiably, dangerously mad? She had to keep him talking, had to hope that something he said could somehow be used to her advantage. "Where did the dogs come from, Richard?"

"They are mine. Of my making, under my control."

"They're infected with canine plague, aren't they." It wasn't a question. "Where did the infection come from?"

"Provided for the restoration of the true men." He moved away from the opening – and toward her. The awful smell of him, strong even over the dog turds and pissed-soaked straw, intensified.

"Provided through you," Tessa said. "You were infected in Africa, weren't you? When you were bitten by wild dogs in that jungle village. Monks cared for you afterward. Les Frères de l'Espoir céleste."

She'd hoped to stop him cold with this but he only nodded, as if of course she would already have that information. He stopped at her feet and gazed dreamily down at her.

Tessa said desperately, "You recovered from the dog bites, the monks said. Then what? How did you infect these dogs here? You didn't bring them with you from Africa."

"Don't you know, my Tessa?"

"No. I don't know. Tell me." She was babbling, anything to keep him motionless. "You were sick from the wild dog bites, the monks nursed you –"

"I was sick before the wild dog bites. The brothers only made me sicker. But the dogs cured me, which is how I knew they were on my side. Beasts are never fooled, my Tessa. They can always recognize the natural rulers of the Earth."

Sick before the wild dog bites. He had had one type of illness, maybe a virulent flu, and the dog-bite pathogen had mixed with it and...Her mind was skittering around. Ebenfield raised the hem of his jacket and unbuckled his belt. *Aisha.* With Aisha he had tried to –

"But wait, Richard, how did you...I want to hear everything, I want to know, don't stop talking now, tell me how you did it. How?"

He pulled off his belt and dropped it into the straw. "I'll show you."

She stopped breathing, but he came no closer. Instead he turned and left the shed. Again she strained at her bonds; again they refused to budge. Beyond the fence the dogs howled, jumping hysterically at the chain links, their teeth white in their black mouths. Two minutes later Ebenfield returned, carrying something under his jacket. He closed the shed door and smiled at her.

"You see, my Tessa, the power was always there for the true aristocrats. All we had to do was see clearly the terrible injustice that has deceived the world. That injustice is this: *The wrong men rule.* Soft, rich men who don't deserve their riches. Men like Salah and his friends. What did Salah ever do to have all that money, all those friends, women like you? He inherited it, is all. A perpetuation of a corrupt system. But when true men genuinely recognize their own power, nothing can stop them from claiming what is rightfully ours. Because we are *not* soft, not corrupted by pampered ease. We are willing to do anything to reclaim our rightful control. Anything."

From under his jacket he drew out a puppy.

Eight weeks old, Tessa guessed numbly; ten at the most. A small wiggling ball of black fur. The dogs behind her went crazy, leaping and snarling. Probably one of them was the puppy's mother. Ebenfield smiled at her again, raised the puppy to his mouth, and bit it hard.

The animal yelped. Ebenfield tossed it into a corner, where it cowered and cried. Blood and dog hair smeared Ebenfield's lips.

"You see, my Tessa, how I make the beasts of the Earth mine, to do my bidding and to correct the errors of the Old Order."

She fought to keep her voice steady, to inject into it cold contempt. "But you aren't correcting those errors alone, are you, Ebenfield? Someone else is using you. To bring the dog plague to the United States, to commit an act of terrorism here where they couldn't go but you can. They're *using* you, don't you understand that – "

She couldn't deflect him. It was as if he didn't even hear her. The dreamy expression had returned to his face. He unzipped and pulled down his pants and briefs, exposing his penis, engorged purplish-red. Below it, his spindly legs puckered into goose pimples from the cold.

"Don't you understand? They *used* you! You were convenient, an American who could go anywhere in the U.S. without suspicion, a vector no different from the mosquitoes that carry malaria or dengue fever – "

He smiled at her and knelt in the straw. His voice held caresses. "Yes, it must happen here, in the sight of my servants. Salah was first, but only as the precursor to me. Ah, my Tessa, I have waited so long – but the true men always triumph in the end."

Gently – the gentleness was an obscenity in itself – Ebenfield reached for the button on her jeans.

The moment he leaned over her, Tessa arched her entire body and thrust her knees upward. The blow caught him in the balls and sent him, shrieking, backwards against the wooden wall. The dogs went crazy, barking hysterically, snapping their sharp teeth.

Frantically Tessa tried to spin herself in the straw to aim a kick at him from her bound feet, but he wasn't disabled long enough. Gasping in pain, his rotting face contorted, he nonetheless scrambled over to her and punched her hard in the face.

"You've ruined it! You've ruined everything! You bitch, you whore! You're supposed to be mine, not his! Everything is supposed to be mine now!" He made as if to punch her again but instead collapsed against the far wall and began to cry.

Tessa tasted blood. Her ears rang. But her jaw wasn't broken; the deep straw had absorbed some of the impact.

Ebenfield sobbed for what seemed like a long time. Cold seeped into Tessa's bones. She couldn't reach him and she didn't want to provoke another blow. This time he might kill her.

But when he finally got to his feet, she saw with amazement that his erection had actually returned. Again he knelt, this time beside her where she couldn't reach him, and yanked her jeans and underwear to her ankles. Hope surged through her. If he meant to spread her legs to rape her, he'd have to cut the rope around her ankles and if her legs were free to really kick…he was weak, and she was trained to fight.

However, he didn't cut the rope. Instead he lay on top of her. She felt his hard penis thrust between her bare legs – and felt, too, its quick deflation into soft, limp jelly.

"He…couldn't," Aisha had said.

Ebenfield rubbed himself against her, trying to regain his erection. It didn't happen. Tessa braced herself for the blow, but he didn't hit her again.

In a voice full of more quiet anguish, of genuine despair, than she had imagined him capable of, Ebenfield uttered a single word. Then he rose and dressed quickly, not looking at her. He put out the lantern. For a moment his hand strayed near the latch on the fence, and Tessa closed her eyes. *No.* But of course he wouldn't let the dogs in from into the shed while he himself was in it. He would go outside, spring the latch with some remote mechanism…

He left the shed, but the fence stayed closed. Tessa couldn't hear where he went. All she could hear as she lay naked from waist to ankles in the reeking cold were the dogs and, even louder than the dogs in her head, that one word Ebenfield had whispered. Not with hatred this time, nor even with bitter envy, but with agonized longing for what he could never be, never have.

Salah.

» 55

Frantically Tessa chafed against her ropes until her wrists bled. When Ebenfield returned, once his momentary anguish had passed, he would almost certainly kill her. He'd failed to rape her, failed to make Salah's woman his own, and his humiliation would turn to rage.

She couldn't get free of her bonds. She did manage to get to her feet and hobble to the shed door, but Ebenfield had locked it from the outside. If she could find a nail or rough edge of wood, rub the ropes against it to weaken them...but that didn't work, either, because she didn't have enough time. The light from the dog enclosure faded into red sunset.

In the corner the bitten puppy whimpered.

Tessa, naked from waist to ankles, started to shiver. God, it was cold! Frostbite, hypothermia...Her teeth chattered.

All at once, the dogs raced away from the shed opening.

Tessa went completely still, straining to hear whatever had alerted the dogs. After a moment she caught it: voices! Maddox must have traced her!

She almost called out, but long training restrained her. And a moment later, the voices became clearer as they neared the shed. They were speaking Arabic.

Tessa dropped back onto the filthy straw and forced her icy body to shimmy from side to side. To the left, to the right, left, right... Straw drifted over her face, her belly, her exposed public hair. As quickly and silently as she could, she burrowed deep into the straw. A dog turd fell onto her face. She heard another rat somewhere, scurrying away from her.

The back of her head scraped concrete just as the shed door opened.

Tessa lay covered by straw. Completely covered? She couldn't tell and couldn't check. All she could do was concentrate on not making the straw quiver by trying fiercely to control her shivering. That, and hope that the fading light made visibility difficult.

The men spoke Arabic and she understood none of it. But she heard their voices muffle as once again the door closed. After a moment, the voices again grew louder and so did the barking and howling. The men had come around to the side of the shed that abutted the dog pen. And now one voice spoke English. Ebenfield, yelling in hysteria.

"No you can't – no! Abd-Al Adil promised – he told me – no you don't understand *no* – "

Something hit the ground hard. The dogs' howling rose to a frenzy. Then the screaming began.

Tessa squeezed her eyes shut. The agonized screams seemed to go on forever, although it was probably just a few minutes. The tearing of flesh lasted much longer. Over those terrible sounds, Tessa just distinguished another voice she recognized, also speaking English.

"Come on, then. The bloody Yanks'll be here soon."

Manchester or Liverpool.

"The true men," Ebenfield had said to Tessa. The ones who could claim, rule, protect what was rightfully theirs. The masters.

Ruzbihan bin Fahoud bin Ahmed bin Aziz al-Ashan had protected his renegade son.

Tessa, lying buried and half naked in the straw, heard the car drive up to the shed, then a last volley of gunfire, and then the car roaring away. The gunfire bewildered her – what had they shot at? Not the dogs; she could still hear them outside, tearing at Ebenfield's body. Ripping, slavering, sucking: noises that Tessa knew she would hear in her head for the rest of her life.

Again she hauled herself out of the straw and onto her feet. Her jeans puddled above the ropes binding her ankles. She found a protruding bent nail and rubbed her wrist cord over it, again and again. It took a long time to weaken the rope, and it was full dark before it gave way. Cold seeped into her very bones.

With numb fingers Tessa fumbled for and lit the lantern, untied the cord around her ankles, and pulled up her jeans. That didn't warm her much. She did jumping jacks until she could feel circulation return to her limbs. Then she laid one hand on the shed door, hoping the blue-eyed Brit had left it unlocked.

He had, but as soon as she cracked the door, she heard panting in the dark and slammed it again. The dogs were loose.

That last volley of gunfire – Ruzbihan's men had, from the safety of their car, shot off the lock on the dog pen. Why? Perhaps to let the infected dogs scatter, making it harder for anyone to notice this place from the air, although the thick pine cover already contributed to that. Or perhaps just from malice.

Tessa put her ear to the door. Quiet breathing. They were waiting for her to come out.

A violent shiver rattled her teeth. She couldn't stay in here; she'd freeze. The temperature must be in the twenties. Already her toes, despite the jumping jacks, felt like ice cubes. They might even have frostbite.

She walked to the open wall, where Ebenfield had removed a five-foot section to expose the dog fence, and slipped her hand between the fence and the outside wall of the shed to see how high the fence rose. Only a few inches higher. And the roof of the crude wooden shed rose maybe another foot and half above that.

One dog came back into the enclosure. The other two had disappeared. This one stood beside the mangled thing that had been Ebenfield, a darker shape in the dark yard, and Tessa could feel it staring at her.

She grasped the sawn edge of the wooden wall just inside the fence and pulled inward. The wall didn't budge but the dog hurtled itself, snarling, at the fence. Tessa stumbled backward, shuddering. The fence held – she could see that it was strong and new – but her reaction was involuntary. That dark shape leaping at her out of the night: every primitive circuit in her hindbrain fired. *Danger danger run run...*

She couldn't run. Again she tried to pull boards above the fence free from the shed wall. The wall had been weakened when Ebenfield cut his removable panel; this time a board tore loose.

Five minutes later she had a hole a foot-and-a-half high between the top of the fence and the roof. But if she put one frozen foot into the chain link to climb, the dog would surely bite it. As Tessa pondered this, the moon rose over the mountains to the east, filtering silver light through the pines. Somehow, it cheered her. Not just for the light, which would be useful, but because that lopsided white orb seemed a witness to her efforts. She'd always done good work under close observation.

It took several vigorous, painful jumps on Ebenfield's wall panel to break it. When it finally cracked, Tessa hurled the largest piece at the dog, which dodged it. She thrust the second piece, sharp side down, into the snow on the other side of the fence. It shielded her foot from the dog's jaws when she stuck her toes through the fence and climbed it to the top.

Immediately the dog snarled and leapt. But it couldn't reach her, perched five feet above the ground. Tessa crouched, worked her body through the hole, and scrambled onto the roof of the shed, under the overhanging pine branches that hid the structure from any air surveillance.

Here the cold really hit her. She hadn't realized how much warmth the straw-filled cabin had actually held. But at least up here she didn't have to smell the filthy straw.

Ebenfield's cabin was about thirty feet away, under another thick stand of trees. Pines weren't ideal for climbing and Tessa's arms were stiff with cold. Nonetheless, she managed. As she swung out over the roof onto the second tree, the dogs went crazy. There were two of them down there now. *Keep moving, don't look down...* When she reached the roof of the cabin, her feet were so cold she nearly slipped off. There were no gutters to catch her. Spread-eagled on the steeply pitched roof, Tessa breathed deeply and forced herself to calm. "*The dogs shall eat Jezebel by the wall of Jezreel...*"

Not tonight.

Groping with extended arms over the eaves, Tessa found what seemed to be the cabin's only window, set high in the south wall. She used a branch broken from the pine tree overhead to break the glass and sweep the opening clear of all shards. *Almost there.* Lying on her stomach, she eased herself down the wall until her feet found the sill, teetered briefly, and slid inside, falling heavily and gracelessly onto Ebenfield's bed beneath the window. A few bits of glass pierced her clothing, but nothing serious.

Even with the broken window, the inside of the crude cabin was blessedly warm, heated with a propane stove. Bed, table, one chair, some rough open shelves. Ruzbihan's men had obviously been inside, and they had been thorough. No papers, no books, no cell phone, no medicines, no camera. No laptop, which Ebenfield must have charged and used at various wireless locations around West Virginia, since the cabin was without electricity. Tessa didn't even see any extra clothing. Just the crude furniture, a few basic tools, a fifty-pound bag of dry dog food, and, in the corner, a cardboard box with two more squealing black puppies.

Outside, the dogs growled and scratched at the door.

She nailed a blanket over the open window; at least it would stop the wind. The shelves held ten cans of beef stew, all the same brand, plastic jugs of water, and three packages of dried figs. *Figs.*

Salah and she at a market stall in the souks of Tunis, eating fresh figs sold still attached to the branch, fresh dates from the harvest at Nefta, the juice running down her chin and the warm fruit tasting like heaven.

"You bastard," she said aloud to Ebenfield. His figs defiled her memory.

She heated a can of stew and ate it, enduring the pain as feeling returned to her frozen toes. The puppies cried and she gave them some dog food mashed with stew gravy. Outside, one of the dogs howled at the moon. Another, maybe the puppies' mother, scratched relentlessly at the door. The third puppy, the one Ebenfield had bitten, would undoubtedly freeze to death in the shed.

Too exhausted to plan her next steps, Tessa wrapped herself in Ebenfield's remaining blankets – she couldn't bring herself to lie in his bed – and fell asleep on the floor beside the propane heater.

INTERIM

Chief of Medicine Bruce Olatic sat in the conference room at Tyler Community Hospital. The faces along the length of the table all wore the same expression: profound weariness. Olatic didn't blame them. He himself had been on duty twenty straight hours.

Luke Mendenhall said, "Tell me again – how many people left who were initially treated for dog bites but haven't yet come in with post-bite syndrome?"

"Only three," said Rosita Perez, "and they were the last three arrivals in the first wave. We've contacted them."

The first wave. Post-bite syndrome. A part of Olatic's tired mind noted how quickly new terminology attached itself to crisis situations. Lexicographic leeches.

Jennifer Peters said, "I called Joe Latkin again just before the meeting. He said he requested reports from the African village where Doctors Without Borders treated what sounds like the same dog-borne hot agent, but there's a delay because the reports have to be translated."

"From what?" Olatic asked.

"The village was Congolese. The reports are in Lingala."

"Christ," somebody said. "And how did the virus get HERE?"

Dr. Peters continued, "Joe also said they've confirmed the physical effects on the dogs' brains, specifically and especially on the amygdala, and found nothing to contradict the preliminary findings we all saw. But, of course, that's only for sacrificed subjects at given points in the disease progression. The CDC's watching more subjects to determine later cerebral changes or physical damage."

Young Dr. Klein said, "And the physical damage to human brains?"

No one answered. PET scans and MRIs could reveal just so much. The only real way to assess the effect of canine disease on the human brain was for an infected human to die.

THURSDAY

» 56

Allen had finally – about time! – been allowed to go home from the hospital, mostly because a lot of other sick people came in. While his mother watched her afternoon show and Allen himself was supposed to be asleep, he called Jimmy on the upstairs phone.

"Yeah?" said Jimmy's father, a big man who wore his undershirt around the house and only went to work sometimes. Allen was a little afraid of him.

"May I speak to Jimmy, please? This is Allen Levy."

"Jiiimmmmeeee!"

Jimmy took his time coming to the phone. Allen could hear the little kids shouting and a TV on loud. Finally Jimmy said, sounding just like his father, "Yeah?"

"It's Allen. I'm home. Did you feed Susie?"

"Yeah. I took her out, too, but she also pooped in that stupid file drawer so I didn't put her back there."

"You didn't? You mean Susie's loose in the *basement?*" His mother would hear her for sure unless Allen gave Susie more pills, and he couldn't walk much with his foot like this. His mother might even go down to do laundry, now that she thought all the dogs in Tyler had been captured, or she might hire somebody to fix the broken window. His father might even come home from the city!

"Naw," Jimmy said. "I could hear her from way outside with your cellar window busted. So I brought her to my house."

"To *your* house? Jimmy! Your parents – "

"It's okay, Allen. Chill. My dad helped me. He says Susie don't have anything wrong with her except she's going blind and the govmint don't have any business poking their fucking noses in our private lives."

That sounded like something Jimmy's dad would say, all right. Allen struggled to sort everything out. Susie at the Doakes... "Where is she?"

"In my bedroom. She sleeps with me and everything."

"She's *my* dog!"

"Hey, I'm helpin' you out here!"

"I know," Allen said, suddenly afraid of making Jimmy mad. Jimmy had Susie. "I know. Thanks. I just...take good care of her, okay, Jimmy?"

"'Course I will."

"Don't let Tammy and LaVerne try to ride on her again? Susie's so old!"

"I know. I'm keeping the little brats away. Don't worry, Allen."

"Do you have dog food? And her dishes? And – "

"Gotta go, my mom wants the phone. I got everything. See you later, dude."

Somewhere in Jimmy's house something crashed, and then the phone clicked.

Now how would Allen get to see Susie? He had to see her! But his mother wouldn't let him go to Jimmy's house. What could he do?

He still hadn't figured out anything when, just as his mother's show was ending, the doorbell rang.

"Yes?" his mother said. A big man stood in the doorway, letting in cold air and looking really unhappy.

"Hi, how ya doing? I'm Billy Davis, Cami Johnson's friend. We met at the hospital."

"Oh, yes," Billy's mother said uncertainly. "Can I help you, Mr. Davis?"

"I don't know. But Cami's sick and she said I should visit Allen instead of her." Mr. Davis sounded as if he'd really, really rather be someplace else. But all at once Allen saw his chance.

"Yes, mom! Cami was going to take me out for ice cream! She promised!"

"She did?" Mr. Davis said.

"Yes! Let's go!"

"Allen," his mother said, "could I see you in the other room? Please excuse us, Mr. Davis. Won't you just step inside and wait in the foyer?" In the dining room she whispered, "Allen, what is this all about?"

"Just like I said! Cami was going to take me for ice cream only she's sick so I want to go with Mr. Davis!"

"Sweetie, we hardly know him. And there are still dangerous dogs out there."

"But...but it's really fun to go out for ice cream. And Mr. Davis is a real animal control policeman! He does cool things with animals and everything!"

All at once his mother's face got a funny look. "It's really Mr. Davis you wanted to see, wasn't it? Because he talks about animals and other things that boys like? "

She didn't understand anything. But maybe that was good. He said, with just a touch of whining, "I like Mr. Davis. And it's...it's good to talk to, you know, grown-up men."

Again she stared at him, and Allen held his breath. Maybe he shouldn't have said that. Maybe it was too much. But he'd listened to her talking on the phone to her friend Linda: *"Allen needs male role models, God knows Peter isn't here enough to provide one, the two-timing bastard..."*

"Yes, sweetie," his mother said slowly, "it's good to talk to grown-up men. Okay, Mr. Davis can take you out for ice cream."

In the car, Mr. Davis said quietly, "You don't really want to go for ice cream, do you, kid? I mean, it's the middle of winter."

"I want to go to Jimmy Doakes' house."

"And your mama don't want you there."

"I just want to see Jimmy for a few minutes! He's my best friend!"

"And best friends are important." Mr. Davis sighed. "You know something, you remind me of me at your age. Hell bent for high water on what you want."

That was so stupid that Allen snorted before he could catch himself. He was nothing like Mr. Davis!

"Just don't let it carry you too far, kid. You can do stupid things when you're that way. Things you regret later in life."

Allen stared straight ahead out the window, and maybe Mr. Davis knew what a nerd he sounded like, because he didn't say anything else. He didn't even get out of the car when they got to Jimmy's.

Jimmy's parents weren't home and neither was his big brother, Wayne. The house smelled of cat pee. Jimmy, Tammy, and LaVerne sat on the saggy old sofa, watching TV and eating Fruit Loops out of the box. Jimmy jumped up.

"Hey, Allen! Come watch this really cool movie! This guy just stabbed all these girls and –"

"I want to see Susie."

"Oh, yeah, come on!"

Jimmy ran down a hallway. Allen hobbled after him, trying to keep his weight off his foot, trying not to fall. Jimmy's room had stuff all over the floor, torn curtains, two unmade beds. But Susie wasn't there. They found her on Jimmy's parents' bed, chewing on a red plastic ray gun. As soon as Susie saw Allen, she jumped up and her tail wagged so hard it looked like it might wag right off. Allen fell onto the bed and hugged her. "Susie!"

"She chewed up my gun! Awww! Bad dog!" Jimmy grabbed the gun and started hitting Susie's rear end with it. Allen shoved the plastic away and turned on Jimmy.

"Don't you dare hit her! She didn't know and anyway she's old and don't you dare hit her!"

"I didn't hurt her none," Jimmy said. "But she better leave my stuff alone or she's outta here!"

Allen went cold all over. What if Jimmy meant it? Allen had no place else to put Susie, no place that his mother wouldn't find her, or even Mr. Davis. And Susie didn't look good, neither. Her coat was all matted like nobody brushed her, and when she wiggled around licking Allen's face, she wobbled on only three legs.

"I'm sorry," Allen choked out. "Jimmy, look at her eyes...that white stuff is worse."

"She sees okay," Jimmy said. "Don't worry about it. But she better not chew my gun again."

"Is that a bruise on her leg? Did somebody *else* hit her?"

"She tried to eat my dad's shoe. But he just tapped her, Allen, honest."

"He hit Susie?"

"She really fucked up his shoe."

"And you hit her, too!"

"Aw, don't be such a wimp!"

Something broke in Allen. He hadn't been able to sleep or eat from worrying over Susie and here the Doakes were *hitting* her and his head all at once felt funny, like it had come loose and was floating above his shoulders. He'd been trying to protect Susie for so long! And they were *hitting* her – his *Susie* –

Allen launched himself at Jimmy, not even caring about the sudden pain in his foot, and beat on him with his fists. "Don't you people touch my dog!"

Jimmy, after an astonished moment, pounded back. Susie started to bark frantically, her old body circling the boys. Allen knew he was crying and didn't care. He just wanted to hit Jimmy, hit everything, everybody wanted to take Susie away from him, and now the news said they were going to kill all the dogs Allen had heard it this morning before his mother snapped the TV off and not Susie *not Susie* NOT SUSIE –

"What the hell is going on here?"

Both boys froze. *Mr. Davis.* Allen twisted around on the floor and there he was, staring at Susie like she was a crocodile or an elephant. He said, "Did that dog bite anybody since it got that weird white stuff in its eyes?"

Not Susie!

"Damn it, boys, this is important. Did that dog bite anybody since it got white in its eyes?"

Not Susie.

"Leave her alone, you!" Allen cried, reached under the bed, and pulled out Jimmy's dad's gun. "You just leave Susie alone!"

Mr. Davis stood very still. "Now, son, let's just calm down here, okay? I'm not gonna bother your dog."

"Yes, you will!" Mr. Davis was lying! He thought Allen was too stupid to know that a dog policeman *had* to take Susie away, *had* to get her killed – he thought Allen was stupid and he was lying, you couldn't trust anything any grown-up said to you not Allen's mother or his father or this terrible man who wanted to kill Susie – Susie, the only real friend Allen had...No. *No.*

He snapped the safety off the gun the way Jimmy had showed him, aimed at Mr. Davis, and fired.

» 57

Jess drove down a snowy Tyler street. The snow clouds had finally blown over and the sunset was bloody red over the West Virginia mountains. Somewhere a dog howled, announcing its presence, and from the distance came an answering howl.

Always from a distance. Jess hadn't captured a single dog all day, although he'd shot one. Maryland Guards had shot two more. The loose dogs, infected and not, had become wary of humans. They'd learned.

A third howl, to the east, prolonged and confident. *I'm heeeeerrre.* Despite himself, Jess shivered.

Lights came on along the street. Soon every house was ablaze. Floodlights, porch lights, room lights. The people inside, Jess knew, kept whatever weapons they owned loaded and handy. Many of them slept fully clothed. It wasn't rational, dogs couldn't open locked doors, but this went deeper than the rational. The beast beyond the door, the wolf just outside the circle of light.

A dog flashed across the road in front of Jess. Instinctively he slammed on the brakes, but it made no difference. The dog was gone. Large, light-colored – infected or not? No way to tell. He might as well go home; he wasn't going to catch any dogs in the dark. Not that he'd been doing so great in the light.

He made a U-turn and headed north, passing a Guards truck and a patrol car. Both hunting the hunters, both probably fruitlessly. Don DiBella had reported back to Jess on the phone call Jess had received after the sniper shot the beagle, Hearsay, practically in Jess's arms. The call had come from a pay phone across town, which meant the sniper had not been working alone. More bad news.

Three blocks over, he again caught the dog in his headlights, this time more clearly. Fawn-colored and huge, with some Great Dane in him somewhere. The dog ignored him and ran straight to the porch of a fifties-style ranch house. Jess stopped the car. People appeared in the big picture window, silhouetted by the lights behind them: a man gesturing wildly, waving his arms, and a woman who ran from the room, maybe to a phone. Kids.

Jess powered down his window and took aim. Now he could hear the dog growl low in its throat. *Infected.* The dog evidently heard the car window go down because he wheeled and ran off in the darkness.

Damn. Another chance gone. He powered the window back up.

Then the dog was back. It appeared from between two houses across the street, running at full speed. The thing was *fast.* Jess again reached for gun and window, but there was no time. The dog leapt with those powerful hind legs and threw himself full-force against the low picture window. Ninety pounds of dog hit the glass. The window shattered.

Glass and blood flew through the air, the glass twinkling in the bright lamplight within. The family screamed. *The dog was inside.*

Jess tore out of his truck, thinking crazily that he was nowhere near as fast as the dog, *those powerful muscular hind legs meant to rush prey run run* –

He reached the window. The dog – God, it was huge! – had fastened itself on one of the kids. The father beat on it, shouting. Jess screamed, "Get away! I need a clear shot!" The man looked up and had the presence of mind – how? – to spring away. Jess fired.

He got the dog in mid-body, as close as he dared come to the child. The dog howled, dropped its prey, and rushed toward Jess. He got it between the eyes.

There, Billy!

The dog crashed to the floor. The parents rushed to their son, who screamed and wailed but at least that meant he was alive. The living room seemed full of blood, although that was an illusion, there wasn't that much blood, how much blood was too much...

He was light-headed.

Jess grabbed the window sill, trying to steady himself. A shard of glass pierced his left hand, sinking deep. More blood. The dog lay still on the blue wall-to-wall carpet. Definitely mostly Great Dane, often praised as the "gentle giant" of the dog world.

Sure. Right.

» 58

Mr. Davis screamed, "What kind of idiot leaves a gun under a bed in a house full of *kids!*" Then he crashed to the floor.

Allen could barely hear him; the sound of the gun rang over and over in his ears. Then he saw blood on Mr. Davis's face. Oh God God God... he'd *killed* him! But Mr. Davis lurched to his knees, blood gushing from his head, and grabbed the gun away from Allen. "You okay, kid?"

"I...I...." Oh God God God....

"Stop blubbering, it just grazed me and anyway I been shot before. In fact, this is the second time in a week."

"Wow," Jimmy breathed, and despite his panic, Allen was impressed, too. But Mr. Davis's face was screwed up with pain and the blood still ran down his head. On the bed, Susie barked once, feebly, and leaned over to lick Allen's face.

Susie. They would take Susie and –

"Don't cry, all right?" Mr. Davis said. He swiped at the blood, smearing it on his hand but not stopping it at all. "Them girls are making enough noise already. Hey, stop it, you two!"

Tammy and LaVerne stood screaming in the doorway. Jimmy, suddenly taking charge, yelled at them, "Call 911! Get some towels!"

"No, don't call 911," Mr. Davis said irritably. "Just get the damn towels."

The twins didn't move. They didn't stop screaming, either. Jimmy pushed them aside, galloped off, and returned with two crumpled towels. Mr. Davis mopped at his head with one. The towel came away red, and he dropped it and wrapped the other one around his head.

Jimmy said, "You look dumb like that. Like a girl that just washed her hair or something. Are you going to give my dad his gun back?"

"Shut up," Mr. Davis said. "Allen, how long has your dog had that milky white stuff in her eyes?"

"He don't know, he hasn't been here," Jimmy said importantly. "I been taking care of Susie!"

Mr. Davis looked at Allen, who was too petrified to reply. What would they do to him? It was probably a crime to shoot someone – they might send him to jail! And then what would they do with Susie?

"Fine," Mr. Davis said, turning to Jimmy, "I'll talk to you. How long has the dog had that white milky stuff in its eyes?"

"Since the disease started – right, Allen?"

Allen found his voice. "Susie's not an 'it'!"

Mr. Davis briefly closed his eyes. "Fine. 'She.' Has Susie bitten anybody since the milky stuff appeared?"

"No," Jimmy said. "She don't even growl or snap."

"Not at all? Ever?"

"Not even once." Jimmy looked proud, as if this were his accomplishment.

Mr. Davis spoke to Allen. "How'd you keep her from being picked up when she was supposed to be? Did your parents help you?"

"No," Allen said. "I...I hid her in a file drawer and gave her sleeping pills to stay quiet, until I got hurt and had to go to the hospital. Then – "

"Then I brought her over here!" Jimmy said. "It was me!"

Tammy and LaVerne had stopped screaming and were listening now, their dirty faces under the tangled lank hair turning to gaze from one person to another. Allen said desperately, "Mr. Davis, you can't take Susie! You can't! She never bit anyone and she isn't dangerous and they'll kill her! Please leave her! I'm really sorry I shot you and I promise to never do it again but please leave Susie!"

"Son, I can't. But – no, listen to me, Allen, really listen – nobody is going to kill Susie. Dr. Latkin at the CDC wants her. He's been looking for a dog that's got the plague but isn't biting anybody so he can...I don't know. Something. But the doctors need her alive to study so nobody's going to hurt your dog."

Allen wanted desperately to believe him. But Mr. Davis's eyes, below the blood-soaked towel, slid sideways and didn't meet Allen's. Mr. Davis was just talking, the way Allen's dad did. He didn't know for sure what would happen to Susie.

"I'm going with her!" Allen said as Mr. Davis got cautiously to his feet. He still held Jimmy's father's gun. "You can't take her without me. If you try to I'll...I'll yell rape!"

"Do *what?*" Mr. Davis said. "You don't even know what that means, do you?"

Allen didn't; it was a threat he'd heard a girl make on TV. But Jimmy must of known because he had his hand clamped over his mouth, laughing. Allen felt tears fill his eyes.

"Come on, Allen, let's go," Mr. Davis said wearily. "Jimmy, your dad got a permit for this gun?"

"Sure he does."

"Uh-huh. I'm going to put it on the closet shelf where your little sisters can't get it, and you tell your dad I'm checking his registration, you hear me?" Mr. Davis shoved the gun behind a mass of sweaters on the highest closet shelf. Awkwardly he picked up Susie, balancing her on the arm in his sling. Susie grunted and licked his face. Jimmy and both twins started to giggle.

"Now what?" Mr. Davis said, as Allen stumbled to his feet and clutched at the hem of Mr. Davis's parka. He would just hang on wherever Mr. Davis took Susie, and not let go no matter what. Wherever Susie went, Allen was going, too.

Tammy piped up, "You look weird."

"With that towel and bloody head and dog!" Jimmy amplified.

Then Mr. Davis muttered something that didn't even make any sense. "Christ," he said, "I hope to hell Cami don't want any kids."

» 59

DiBella was speechless a full fifteen seconds after Jess called him about the attack by the Great Dane mix. Finally he said, "Jesus, Jess – through the *window?*"

"Yeah."

"I'll tell Lurie. We need to get the word out right away – board up windows, stay in windowless rooms, especially if you have an infected pet who might come home and...the kid okay?"

"I don't know. The ambulance just took him away."

"Hospital's buried in dog bite victims in the second phase."

Jess already knew this; Billy had called him about his new girlfriend, Cami Johnson.

DiBella said. "KJV-TV can help. And maybe – through the *window?"*

"Yes."

"This changes everything."

"I know."

At home, Jess bandaged his hand, which hurt like hell. He should probably get stitches but with all the second-wave dog-bite victims coming in, it would be hours before anybody in the ER got to him, if at all. He settled for hydrogen peroxide and enough gauze to stop the Johnstown Flood, then turned on the TV.

DiBella, or Lurie, or KJV-TV was efficient. The story was already there. "Breaking news...local man...FEMA recommends...all citizens of Tyler...please notify friends and neighbors...urgent breaking announcement...."

By now it would have begun. People would be nailing plywood to window frames, moving bedding and food and water to safe rooms on barricaded second floors. Building fortresses inside their own homes. Getting angrier, and more desperate, and more afraid.

And talking. They would call, email, blog. Jess wasn't a great user of the Internet, but he knew it was one way groups organized themselves. It was now much easier to find fellow believers, in any cause at all, than it had ever been before.

"Return all uninfected dogs to their owners within the next twenty-four hours, or this will happen again." And the dogs had not been returned.

"If you and the whole damn federal government can't kill these vicious dogs, we'll do it for you. No more kids are going to die because you guys won't do what you fucking well should." And the uninfected beagle Hearsay had been shot.

He stared helplessly at the his heavily bandaged hand in the blue glow of the television.

INTERIM

The president sat behind his desk in the oval office and scowled at his chief of staff. "A dog actually broke through a window to attack?"

"Yes, sir. Terry spoke directly to the local sheriff."

"Where's Scott Lurie?"

"He's there. And he concurs about what we have to do."

"I don't like it," the president said."

"No one does, sir." His tone held a sourness that the president didn't pick up. The leader of the free world, Martin thought, seemed even more out of touch than usual. Martin, who was never out of touch, had wanted to replace Lurie a year ago. Now he reflected, not for the first time, that "electable" and "capable" were words with far different roots.

"You told me, Hugh – you yourself! – that killing all the dogs would be a really unpopular move. That people love their pets and spend all that money on them and we should wait. You told me so right in this office!"

"We did wait, Mr. President. Now we have to act. And we have to do it quickly to show we recognize the gravity of people not being safe even in their own houses."

"But killing the well dogs, too, the ones that aren't infected – "

"Necessary, sir. Who knows what those dogs might have been exposed to? If we don't do a thorough cleansing euthanasia, we risk looking weak, and so does FEMA and Homeland Security. The country's had enough of that."

"Well..." The president shifted fitfully in his chair. In this mood, he could be impossible to deal with. Martin willed himself to patience.

"What about the dogs nobody's caught yet?" the president demanded. "And why the whole damned Maryland Guard plus all these animal people can't catch a bunch of Lassies and Rin Tin Tins...what does the governor say?"

"He agrees that the uncaught dogs are the reason we have to evacuate Tyler completely. This is our last chance to demonstrate that we will do anything necessary to protect our citizens, and that we'll do it pro-actively."

Not that that had worked very well so far.

"Evacuate. Jesus Christ, Hugh, I hate this. You know some of those people will resist. We can't even get everybody out when a volcano is going to blow."

"We still have to make the effort, sir."

"And what about that FBI agent, ex-agent, whatever she is?"

"We still haven't found her or Ebenfield."

"Why the hell not?"

There was no answer to that, so Martin waited. The president swiveled his chair and stared out at the dark Rose Garden.

"Hugh, you think it's possible she found Ebenfield?"

Martin hoped not, fervently. But again he said nothing.

"All right. All right. Give the orders."

"Yes, sir. The Army Veterinary Corps can go in to Tyler tomorrow and Scott can get the evacuation started. But Rob should brief the press tonight, late as it is, while we still have control of the story."

"All right. Do it. And Hugh – "

"Yes, sir?"

"Find the FBI agent NOW."

FRIDAY

» 60

At just after midnight, Ellie Caine sat slumped in a chair in her living room. On her lap rested Music's rawhide bone. Ellie had sat in the same position for hours, not eating or sleeping. What was the point? She was too depressed to even turn on the TV.

Butterfly was dead, the other three greyhounds lost to her. Locked up. Not dead – if they were dead, Ellie would know. In her heart she'd know.

She fingered the rawhide bone. Other toys littered the floor: Song's favorite ball, a stuffed alligator that Butterfly loved. Every time she looked at them, Ellie felt like crying all over again, but she had no tears left.

When the phone rang, Ellie jumped. Few people ever called her, usually just telemarketers, and not at midnight. Who...

"Ellie Caine? Is this Ellie Caine?"

"Yes."

"Ellie, my name is Jenna, you don't know me. I got your name from Larry Campos at the Greyhound Rescue League in Frederick. He said you adopted four greyhounds and are really zealous for the League."

"Yes..."

"Well, I live in Tyler, like you, and I have dogs I love. *Had* dogs. Jess Langstrom took my English setters last week and they were *not* infected. Now we have this awful announcement from the White House and – "

"What announcement? What are you talking about?"

"You haven't had the TV on?"

"No!"

Jenna said, "The president has ordered all the confiscated dogs in Tyler killed – sick and well dogs! – and the town evacuated, starting tomorrow. Because of that dog that crashed through a window and attacked a little boy."

Ellie hadn't heard about that either, but her mind barely registered it. All the dogs in Tyler killed! All!

"Some of us won't permit that," Jenna said, her voice hardening. "Our pets aren't infected and we won't let them be murdered. Even the infected dogs shouldn't die because the CDC might come up with a cure. So we. Will. Not. Permit. This."

Ellie stood very still, clutching the phone. A strange emotion leapt through her. Hope.

"What are you going to do?"

"Are you with us?"

"Yes! Oh, yes!"

"Larry vouched for you. Our organization is still pretty loose, and we don't have much time, but we're going to free our dogs. Do you own a gun?"

"No. But I can shoot." Her father had shown her once, fifteen years ago, the one time he'd paid any attention to her at all. Surely she could remember what he'd demonstrated.

"Good. Stay at home all day tomorrow and I'll call again with instructions. We're still getting our plans together. But I can tell you this – no uninfected dog in Tyler is going to die. Not one. Bye for now."

Ellie stood blinking in the middle of her kitchen. So much to take in. There would be danger, and she had never been particularly brave. But for Song and Chimes and Music, she could dare anything, even take on the government. And it wasn't like the government had ever done all that much for her. It hadn't protected her against her father or ever helped her find a job or sent her checks like those welfare deadbeats. Ellie Caine had always been on her own, and the greyhounds had given her all the love and comfort she ever got. She could do whatever was necessary to save them.

In her mind she rehearsed the steps to load, cock, and aim a gun.

Steve Harper stared at his TV. It was barely six in the morning, but he couldn't sleep. He'd spent the night in his recliner, dozing fitfully, only to wake from nightmares about Davey. *The brown mastiff with a single long string of saliva...*

Davey's toys spilled from the toy box in the corner; Steve hadn't been able to bring himself to remove them. Plastic stacking rings, red and blue and yellow. The dump truck. A stuffed pig. The miniature plastic baseball bat.

Whatever was on TV wasn't making enough distracting noise. Steve flipped through channels, coming to CNN. "–in Tyler, Maryland. Scott Lurie, FEMA director, announced last night that all dogs in Tyler will be euthanized in an attempt to control the canine plague. Many consider this a long-overdue move to–"

Damn right! Steve sat up straighter and clenched his fists. If they'd done that immediately, maybe more people wouldn't have died the way Davey did. Wusses. But at least they were doing it now.

"–emergency evacuation from Tyler. Volunteers from Tyler itself will help coordinate the evacuation. FEMA said it would provide buses for those unable to–"

An evacuation. That made sense. And they needed volunteers, probably to make sure no half-assed idiot tried to smuggle a dog out of town in their luggage. Steve could do that. And he fucking sure needed to do something.

Since DiBella had put him on temporary suspension, the only constructive thing he'd done was shoot that dog on Herlinger Street right out from under Jess Langstrom. Putting a bullet in at least one canine killer had been satisfying, but it wasn't enough, not nearly enough, to discharge his rage or grief. He needed to do *something.*

Just let anybody try to get a fucking dog past *his* checkpoint.

Del heard the announcement on the radio while he fixed Brenda's breakfast. He felt a pang for Folly, sweet little dog that she was. But the government had to think about everybody, had to look at the big picture. And maybe leaving Tyler would be for the best for him and Brenda, too. As long as they could switch Brenda's chemo to Frederick–and the doctor said just yesterday that they could–it might be better to be there with Chrissy. Their daughter always cheered up Del and kept Brenda interested in scrapbooking and all those other crafts they both liked. Yes, an evacuation was a good idea.

He was glad the government was finally bringing the crisis to a close.

» 61

Tessa, stiff and aching, woke on the floor of Ebenfield's cabin. Slowly she stood, stretching her sore body. Ebenfield's scabrous smell still hung in the small space. In the corner, the puppies whined in their box.

Outside, all was quiet.

She climbed onto the bed and untacked one corner of the blanket over the window. Bright sunlight struck her eyes; the window faced south, the only direction not thickly covered with pines. It was at least mid-morning. Overnight the cold front had passed and it was maybe forty degrees out there, maybe more. Water dripped from pine boughs. Ebenfield's car was pulled up under trees about thirty feet from the cabin, but open space lay between. The keys were either in his car or in a pocket on his mangled body. Tessa couldn't see any of the dogs – had they run off?

She heated water, mashed it into dry dog food, and put the mixture in the box. The puppies ate it eagerly. After she heated and ate a can of stew, she combed the cabin, inch by inch, looking for papers, CD-ROMS, memory stick, anything that Ebenfield might have hidden and Ruzbihan's men missed. Nothing.

Then she had to pee. The cabin had no chemical toilet; Ebenfield must have gone outside. Since that wasn't an option until she was sure where the dogs were, Tessa used a corner of the cabin, grimacing. As she finished, she climbed on the bed and peeked outside.

Two of the dogs stood between her and the car, facing the cabin window. Against the white snow their dark bodies bulked even larger than she remembered. When they glimpsed her face at the window, their ears pricked forward and muscles rippled in their powerful back legs, but they made no sound. The milky white film over their eyes made them look blind, but their heads followed her every shift in position.

The only way she was going to get out of this cabin was to kill them.

Oh, right. With what?

The dogs moved closer, and Tessa had to fight the impulse to leap backward off the bed. She was safe enough inside – but not indefinitely.

She'd found no spare canister of propane, and the stew and figs wouldn't last very long.

The dogs began to act weird.

First one, then the other, began snapping at empty air. Abruptly the larger dog leapt two feet off the ground and closed his powerful jaws on nothing. He did it again, this time with a twist in the air, as if to bite squarely into something slightly off-center from his leap. The other animal did the same, slavering and gnashing its fangs. The entire performance took place in total silence. Again and again they leapt, bit, fell, ignoring each other, neither of them looking at Tessa. What on Earth –

The dogs were attacking something that wasn't there.

Gooseflesh rose on Tessa's neck. There was something eerie, almost frightening, about the scene. The dogs whirling, jumping, biting at nothing – it was somehow worse than if there *had* been something solid there to attack. The animals' utter silence only deepened the eeriness, removing the dogs from their own nature and turning them into creatures moving in some unseen, spectral realm. Ghost dogs, half in this world and half in another, attacking demons visible to only their demented, filmy eyes…

Where they maybe hallucinating? *Could* dogs hallucinate?

A long shiver ran through her body, clear from neck to legs. *Ebenfield.* He'd been bitten in Africa by infected dogs. Initially, Frère Luc-Claude had said, Ebenfield had developed a high fever, then a coma, and then seeming recovery. But if the virus had remained in his brain – and some viruses could do that, Tessa knew – what then? Had the virus gone on eating slowly at Ebenfield's mind? Turning him into a human and therefore more complex version of these dogs – into an animal that senselessly fears, hates, attacks?

By his end, Ebenfield, like the dogs, had believed things that did not exist. He'd believed himself to be superior to Salah, an alpha male if there ever was one. A top dog.

لكلب الرئيس

In Arabic, the adjective went after the noun. Not "dogs first – "first dog."

Tessa stepped off the bed, sat on the edge, and allowed herself a moment to calm her ragged breathing. All of this was speculation; none of it might be true. Still...

She walked to the cabin door, slid back the bar, and cracked it an inch. If the dogs were now attacking things that didn't exist, perhaps they would ignore things that did exist. She stuck one hand through the crack.

The dogs raced around the side of the cabin, now growling and snarling audibly. Tessa slammed the door and slid the bar into place. Apparently if something solid moved into their awareness, the dogs reverted from their illusionary world to this one.

She was still trapped.

» 62

Jess called Billy to see how Cami was doing, but he got no answer on either Billy's cell or his home phone. Nor did anybody answer at the Animal Control Office – had Suzanne evacuated without telling him? Frustrated, Jess drove downtown.

Early as it was, a few cars crammed with luggage already moved toward the evacuation exit point. Maryland Guard trucks and police cars patrolled. Jess saw windows heavily curtained or already boarded up, as if expecting a hurricane. It gave Tyler an eerily deserted feel, as if everyone had already left, aided by a town-wide hushed silence.

Too much silence.

Jess stopped his truck, rolled down the window, and listened. No dogs.

All right, they were sleeping, hiding in the woods or in sheltering backyards, until dusk. But dogs, unlike cats, weren't really nocturnal. They usually hunted by day. And over three hundred dogs were unaccounted for and presumably out there somewhere. Their baying and barking and howling had been unsettling Tyler since the epidemic began. Why didn't he hear any of them now?

He hadn't come up with an answer when he pulled into Linda's Diner and stamped the slush off his feet. A dozen faces, mostly old men, watched him with careful blankness. Jess picked a table and watched

Linda approach with the coffee pot and a scowl.

"I'm not going, Jess."

"Not evacuating, you mean."

"That's right. You gonna try to make me?"

So that was the lay of the land. They associated him with FEMA. He said, "Not my job, Linda."

"You approve of telling everybody they got to get out?" She held the coffee pot out like a sword.

"Hasn't worked in most evacuations. There's always some who refuse to leave for a hurricane or flood or whatever, so I imagine they'll be some here, too. Maybe a lot."

He'd kept his tone mild, uninvolved. Linda gazed at him, nodded, and poured his coffee. "You want eggs?"

He'd passed the test. At other tables, conversation resumed. While eating his breakfast, Jess listened. That was why he'd come.

"– prob'ly carried by mosquitoes. You know, like malaria."

"Isn't neither. This is a terrorist act, Bill. It's plain as the nose on your face."

"Don't matter where the plague comes from, only matters where it goes. The government's going to try to put all the infected people in internment camps, like the Japs in the war. And then, just watch, they'll go for everybody who was even exposed to plague."

"Not internment camps. More like leprosy colonies."

"You're both full of it. Won't ever happen."

"You're too naïve, Vern. Always were. Might be the Army wants our land, build a supplement to Fort Detrick. This is a good way to just clear us out."

"– heard on the radio that it's Cubans in league with the Mafia. Like with JFK."

"– read on the Internet that the old KGB – "

"– Arab terrorists – "

"– Greenpeace and those environmental crazies – "

"– Aryan Nation – "

"– North Korea – "

Jess sipped his coffee. Rumors, conspiracy theories, hate reactions…

People would seize on anything to make sense of the unthinkable. They –

"Hey," Billy said, settling into the chair opposite Jess. "Saw your truck outside."

Jess stared at the left side of Billy's head, which was covered with a dressing the size of a toaster. "What the hell happened to you?"

"Accident. Gunshot."

"*Gunshot?*"

"Yeah. I was trying to clean my gun with my left hand and the sucker went off. I forgot it was loaded. Bullet just gazed my head. A lot of blood but no real damage and a few stitches just closed it right up."

Jess stared at him. Billy's lies were never smooth but usually they were vaguely plausible. There was no way that Billy, arm in a sling or not, had shot himself in the head. Like all good marksmen, he always knew the state of his guns and handled them with respect. Even drunk, Billy was deft with weapons, if with nothing else.

"You shot yourself?"

"Yup." Billy stared stonily, and Jess knew to drop it. He would never find out what had really happened. "You heard about the dog and the window?"

"It was on TV at the hospital. I been sitting with Cami all night."

"How is she?" Jess said. He'd never seen that expression on Billy's face before and it took him a moment to find the word for it: tenderness.

"Her fever broke and she's sleeping. Actually, it's more like a coma. The docs said the rest of them, the ones that got bit earlier than Cami, come out of the coma after a while, but nobody knows what's still in their brains."

Or in their saliva. Joe Latkin had told Jess that mutations in the virus could be tracked through differences in the dogs' saliva. What would happen if Billy kissed Cami? Could she infect him?

Billy said, "They're planning on evacuating the hospital patients when they get a plan together. I'll stay, Jess, till this thing's over, 'cause I know you need me. But the reason I come in here to see you is that something good happened yesterday."

"I'll listen to anything good," Jess said, wondering why Billy thought Jess needed a one-armed man who had supposedly shot himself in the head. "What is it?"

"They found a dog like we been hunting for, with anti...annie...those things that will help cure the plague. A dog with milky film in its eyes but no aggression."

"They did!"

"Yup. Actually, I found it. Right here in Tyler. The owner, a little kid Cami made friends with, has been hiding it and giving it his mother's sleeping pills to keep it quiet. I brought the dog to Doc Latkin."

Billy beamed. Jess saw where his thoughts were going. "That's great, but you know it takes a long time for science to make any kind of vaccine or cure for anything, and Joe Latkin only said that a dog with natural immunity might be useful to their research. *Might.* So don't count too much on them coming up with something right away for Cami's – "

"I got to go sleep," Billy said. "I been up all night."

"Okay. Bye. And Billy – "

"What?"

Jess hesitated. He wanted to mention the strange silence outside, the absence of howling and barking, but Billy looked so exhausted, so worried about Cami, so lopsided with his arm in a sling and his head in a bandage, that Jess let it go. All he said was, "Don't nap too long, Billy."

"Catch you later, dude."

Jess finished his cold coffee. When he left, he heard a single dog bark in the distance. The loose dog reassured him, which was messed-up all by itself. Everything had somehow gotten turned inside out. He listened to the dog for a long moment.

Why only one?

» 63

Ed Dormund got into his car in the closed garage without looking at the rust-colored stains on the floor. The medics had taken away Cora's body two days ago and Ed had thrown a few buckets of soapy water onto the floor, but blood did a real job on concrete. However, he had no time to think about that. Enough beers and he didn't think about Cora at all, but right now he was sober. There was a job to do.

He picked up Tom, Sam, and Leo at their doors. "How do we get past the Guards checkpoint?" Leo asked.

"We don't," Ed said. He was the only one in the car who knew the whole plan; Dennis had explained it to him last night. It wasn't that Dennis was any better than Ed – he didn't even own his own house, just rented – but whoever was running the bigger show had told Dennis what to do. And Dennis told Ed, which was fine with Ed as long as they got it done. The guys at the top were smart and organized.

He explained everything to the others, drove into the supermarket lot on Jamison Road, and waited for the other cars. The lot was full of cars from people stocking up on things either to evacuate or to resist evacuating. A driver would pull up as close to the door as possible, a passenger would jump out dash inside, and the driver would wait for a cell call to crowd the doorway again. Somebody told Ed that morning that the supermarket windows were reinforced against looters and so no dog could ever shatter them.

His cell phone rang twice, stopped, rang twice again. The signal. Ed said, "Let's go!"

Cars began to leave the parking lot. Ed watched the dashboard clock carefully. Everybody had to arrive at the same time. Over his shoulder he said, "None of you guys brought guns, right? Not for this part?"

"I don't like that," Tom said, "but, yeah, they're at home until tonight."

"Good."

They drove in silence to a point where the highway from the south turned sharply west around a thick stand of pine. The place was well inside the Maryland Guard checkpoint. Four cars already formed a barricade across the road, with more cars parked beyond the trees. Ed joined these and the four men pulled on ski masks. A few minutes later Leo said, "There they are! Go!"

That was for Ed to say, not Leo, but there was no time to argue. Forty people jumped out of cars and trucks and rushed the van as it stopped for the barricade. Everyone yelled and screamed, smashing the snowy silence.

The van coming from Fort Detrick in Frederick held a driver and a single Guard holding a rifle. The soldier raised his weapon and shouted something Ed couldn't hear. A few men hit the ground or ducked behind vehicles, but the majority kept going. In the red and black and orange ski masks Ed couldn't tell where Dennis or Brad were. A single shot rang out and someone screamed.

Ed's heart pounded and his blood raced. Then they were on the van, all of them, rocking it until it fell over, doors still locked. It took less than a minute. The driver and his passenger, Ed glimpsed briefly, struggled sideways in their seatbelts. He lost track of what happened up front as he joined the crowd in the back. Another minute and someone had blown open the lock – with what? Dennis hadn't told him.

Sixteen sealed cardboard boxes with the four-circle symbols for "Biohazard" on them. People grabbed. Ed actually got a box and ran with it full speed back to his car. "Get in! Get in!" he cried to the others. They were peeling out onto the road like kids, all of the other vehicles speeding off in every direction. The van, lying on its side with its trapped men, was alone on the highway.

"We did it!" Sam cried, ripping off his ski mask. He and Tom high-fived and then they were all laughing and talking and slapping each other on the shoulders, even Ed, who was driving.

Tom opened the box on the back seat. "Look at all these loaded needles!"

"They're called 'syringes,' dumb-ass," Sam said and Tom socked him playfully.

"Stuff would have killed our dogs," Leo said. "Just murdered them."

Leo was right. Ed thought of Petey and Rex and Jake...Jake tearing at Cora's flesh...*no, don't think of that.* Leo was right. Bastards wanted to kill his Jake, plus Tom's boxer and Leo's pug and Sam's Newfie. Ed had heard all about the others' dogs, at their first meeting. And now Ed had protected them all, and he didn't even have to go home to Cora. Life was different now, and Ed could get anything he wanted.

They continued to laugh and shout, reliving the glory, as Ed pulled into his driveway and the garage door rose majestically. Everybody tumbled out.

"What about the *syringes?*" Tom said. "What do we do with them?"

"Stick 'em in the president's ass!" Leo cried.

"I'll hide them," Ed said, "but keep your voices down! And hey, anybody want a beer?"

» 64

Del Lassiter helped Brenda out of the car at the evacuation checkpoint. Thank heavens this was one of her good days. Swelling from the radiation treatments had gone down with the increased steroids, and she could walk.

"Wait in that tent over there, sir," said the polite young soldier. "Wait is about two hours, I'm afraid."

"Why so long? My wife – "

"I'm sorry, sir, it's necessary."

"I'm fine, Del," Brenda said, taking his arm and smiling up at him. "Truly. And they have that whole enormous long line of cars to search."

The line of a few hundred cars had already backed far down the road. Del hoped it wasn't going to rain; clouds had rolled in overnight and the temperature risen to above freezing. He noticed that the evacuation buses whizzed right on through the checkpoint. But, then, he'd heard that those people and their luggage had been thoroughly searched as they were picked up at their homes. It was just wonderful how quickly FEMA had organized all this. And Del felt quite safe, even crossing the open stretch between his car and the tent, because many, many sharp shooters looked perfectly ready to stop any stray dog.

Although come to think of it, Del hadn't heard much howling or barking this morning.

The evacuation tent was large and warm, equipped with lawn chairs and volunteers serving coffee and bagels. Now, that was thoughtful! Del got Brenda settled in a chair. She winced as she lowered her poor body, but Brenda never complained. She was the bravest person he knew.

A large woman in a pink down coat sat down next to Brenda. "First they say we can't leave Tyler, then they say we can't stay. Be easier on all of us if they'd make up their damn minds."

Brenda laughed and the woman grinned. She said, "You going to kin?"

"Oh, yes, our daughter Chrissy in Frederick," Brenda said. "This is a good opportunity, really."

"I got my son in Hagerstown, going to meet me right after we clear the checkpoint. He's a CPA."

Del left them chatting and went to get coffee. It took him a moment to recognize the man behind the coffee urn: Officer Harper, who'd come to the house a few times when Del had called about noise from Ed Dormund's dogs. But why was a police officer serving coffee instead of out patrolling? Del decided it would be tactless to ask. Officer Harper didn't look good. He'd lost weight and anger radiated from him, like heat. Del could see it in the set of the young man's shoulders, the jerky way he poured coffee. Not really a good choice to aid shaky evacuees.

But perhaps a good choice for what nagged at Del's mind.

"Officer Harper?"

"Yeah." He looked sharply at Del. "Lassiter, right?"

"You have a good memory. Look, I'd like to report something that – "

"I can't help you." Harper scowled.

"Oh, I see," said Del, who didn't. "Then is there someone else here I can talk to? That I can report something to? It might be nothing, but I think..." He hesitated. Was this fair? But if it *was* connected... "I think I saw something that might be connected to that robbery this morning. Of the van carrying the euthanasia things for infected dogs."

Harper, who'd been turning away, snapped around. His eyes burned. "You saw something?"

"Yes. No. Not directly but...I'm not sure."

He wasn't sure he should tell this ferocious person, but after all, Harper was a cop. So Del followed him to a corner of the big tent filling up with evacuees and explained about Ed Dormund's leaving home half an hour before the robbery and returning with three other jubilant men. How Del, opening his kitchen window to ask them to please not wake Brenda with their noise, had caught the word "syringes" from Dormund's garage and had closed the window without speaking.

Harper said, "How'd you know about the robbery? It's not on TV yet."

"It's on-line," Del said. "The story's on-line already. That never takes long." He smiled apologetically, although he wasn't sure what he was apologizing for.

"Okay. Thanks, Lassiter." Harper turned away but Del laid a hand on his arm. "Officer, I want to emphasize that I don't *know* that Dormund is involved in anything wrong. I just thought – "

"You did the right thing." Harper strode away before Del could finish.

When Del returned to Brenda, she and the pink-coated woman were talking about their dogs that had been taken away. Brenda had tears in her eyes for poor Folly, but when she saw Del, she tried hard to smile.

"I want to emphasize that I don't know that Dormund is involved in anything wrong."

Well, Steve Harper damn well knew. He'd never believed for half a second that Ed Dormund had nothing to do with his wife's death, no matter what the know-it-all detectives decided. Steve had been to the Dormund house twice for domestic disturbance, plus noise caused by those fucking dogs. Dormund was a dirt bag, just the kind to "defend" their bullshit "right" to keep vicious dogs, no matter what the consequence.

The brown mastiff with a single long string of saliva and blood hanging from its mouth onto Davey's body...

Steve got into his car, first scanning full-circle for any sign of loose dogs. He was carrying, and if one of the jackals came anywhere near, the snipers wouldn't be the ones to take it out. Jess Langstrom and his boys were idiots, to not be able to shoot a bunch of dogs. That went for the Guard as well, and FEMA – telling him the best job for him was pouring coffee! – and most of all for Steve's boss, DiBella, who'd handed over his town without so much as a murmur. Well, he didn't have to go to DiBella – DiBella had put Steve on suspension.

Steve drove to his old friend Keith Rubelski's house, taking the back routes to avoid the cars heading for evacuation points. Steve's buddies on the Force couldn't be counted on, not for this. They didn't understand. But Keith had lost his wife to these uncontrolled animals, so Keith understood completely. He knew how it felt to hurt so much inside that you could hardly breathe and sometimes just taking a single step felt like it would shatter your whole body.

Since Davey's death, the only thing that had comforted Steve at all was the president's decision to kill all the dogs in Tyler. And now Dormund and his kind were trying to take that comfort away. Steve knew in his guts that they wouldn't stop with hijacking the Army Vet Corps truck with the euthanasia syringes. They would know that the Army would just send up more drugs from Fort Detrick, under stronger and more alert guard, and that a second hijacking wouldn't work. No, the jackal-lovers had to be planning something else, something bigger.

Let them. Steve knew people like Keith, who understood better than to count on FEMA, or even on the Maryland Guard. The individual soldiers might be good people – probably were – but the command wasn't strong enough to stop the jackal-lovers. Steve had heard talk around the police barracks, talk around town. The fucking feds were too afraid of another Kent State to fire on civilians, if it came to that. It was okay to let any number of kids die from dogs, but don't let a precious dog-protecting protestor die while breaking the law. Well, Steve would just see about that.

The perps who had blown up the Stop 'n' Shop weren't the only ones who knew about explosives. Keith was a trained and certified expert.

» 65

The canine silence in Tyler still bothered Jess. Throughout the day he heard a couple of hounds giving voice as they chased a rabbit or squirrel somewhere, and once a dog howled, a long drawn-out howl that raised the hairs on the back of his neck. It might have been one of the Nordic breeds, a Husky or Malamute, or even a wolf-dog hybrid. But that was all, all day.

On his way to critical incident headquarters he motioned down a patrol car with Eric Lavida and Neil Patman. "Hey, Jess."

"Hey. You guys have anything yet on who stole the Vet Corps syringes?"

"Not yet." Eric looked stony. Forty or fifty participants and no arrests yet. "Nobody's talking."

"Eric, something's brewing here."

"Don't I know it. We're looking."

"I hear anything, I'll give you a call."

"Good."

Headquarters had changed yet again. The road running between the Cedar Springs Motel and the fields across the street had become the border of a fortified enclave. People came and went freely into the motel parking lot, still dominated by the huge mobile labs. Every room in the motel had become an office for some agency: CDC, USAMRIID, FEMA, FBI, MNG, the entire alphabet soup of crisis. The motel had been supplemented by large Army-issue tents stretching down the road.

Across the street, military law prevailed. Guardsmen ringed more tents occupying at least fifteen acres. Two of the tents were gigantic. These housed dogs; Jess could hear the barking, snarling, yapping, growling, and baying that he'd missed all day in town. Around the two big tents sprouted a few dozen smaller ones. Above it all towered a forest of floodlight poles.

Jess knocked on the CDC lab door and was told by a weary, white-coated woman that Joe Latkin was in the mess tent. The mess tent was warmer than the outside but not really at room temperature, and Latkin wore an open parka. Even in the parka, his slight frame seemed even thinner than a few days ago. With his pale blue, almost white eyes, he looked like a ghost from some scientific afterlife.

"Hello, Jess."

"Hi, Joe. Listen, Billy told me he brought in a dog with milky film in its eyes but no signs of aggression."

"Yes, we're very pleased to have it." Latkin looked far too exhausted for pleasure. "But of course its antibodies may or may not provide us with additional clues to this thing, and a big factor is that viruses mutate constantly. By the time we determine what's going on with that dog's immunity at a cellular level, something entirely different might be going on. For instance...no, wait, come with me. I want to show you something."

Jess followed Latkin from the mess tent. The winter twilight had begun, a featureless gray under the cloud cover that had been building all day. Latkin strode across the road, where a rifle-carrying Guard stopped him. "This is a restricted area, sir."

"Oh, for God's sake, I'm Dr. Latkin, head of the CDC team, and this is Jess Langstrom, Tyler animal control officer!"

"I need to see your passes."

Jess didn't have the pass required, which was apparently a new one resulting from tighter security. Fuming, Latkin summoned a Guard officer, who made two cell calls before allowing them to cross the road. Then they had to sign in, signatures and time: 5:15 P.M.

"They keep changing the rules, the soldiers, and the whole damn protocol," Latkin seethed. "All the emphasis is on the wrong things. Forms, not substance. Of all the mismanaged...that's Tent A, Jess, where we have the infected dogs, and the other big one is B, uninfected. Come this way."

The floodlights came on, turning the field brighter than the gloomy day had been, as Latkin led him into a much smaller tent. It held a jumble of equipment, including an open laptop computer on an Army-issue folding metal table. A single large dog cage sat in the middle of the floor. In it was a male Doberman with a large dressing on its left hind leg and the funnel-shaped collar put on animals to keep them from biting off bandages or stitches. Despite the awkward collar and its damaged leg, the Doberman was going through some very peculiar motions. It leapt up as far as the cage would allow, closing its jaws on thin air, for all the world as if it were attacking invisible prey. Leaping, twisting, biting, tearing something only it could see, all in utter, eerie silence.

Jess felt cold around his bones. "What's it doing?"

"We don't know," Latkin said somberly. "The dog just started this behavior this morning, and so far it's the only one. This is the Doberman that was shot in West Virginia. The one whose saliva samples indicate it to be among the first infected. We're waiting to see if the other dogs present with this behavior, or if this dog progresses to something else. Meanwhile, we have had one piece of luck."

"What's that?" Jess said. He couldn't look away from the Doberman. Leaping, twisting, biting at things that didn't exist. At ghosts.

"Doctors Without Borders came across a similar virus in Africa, and somebody at their headquarters found saliva samples frozen in the specimen library. They're being flown to Atlanta now. Maybe a comparison will turn up something interesting."

"Hope so," Jess said, although he didn't understand how that would help. "Doctor, can I visit an uninfected dog? For just a minute?"

"Go ahead. I'm needed back at the lab."

At Tent B, Jess had to sign in on a clipboard hanging from a rope beside an unsmiling Guardsman. As he endured the soldier's hard stare, Jess tried to remember the time when it had been he who had jurisdiction over the animals in Tyler. All of ten days ago.

Tent B was brightly lit. The noise was incredible but mostly benign; hundreds of uninfected dogs barked or slept or lapped water or chewed on rawhide or tried vainly to get at each other. Jess was startled to realize how many he recognized from rounding them up all over Tyler.

Applejack and Schnapps. He heard Tessa's voice saying, "*Rich people like to give their dogs alcoholic names.*"

Daisy, giving off the soft, strange, yodeling sound that only Basenjis make.

Rio, a Bernese mountain, asleep in a huge cage.

Folly, a tiny Chihuahua, shivering on her mat.

Oxford College, the beagle belonging to a pair of over-educated commuters.

Jess couldn't find his great-niece Hannah's collie, Missy, or Missy's four pups. He hoped that didn't mean they'd already been "sacrificed" for research. Although what did it matter, since as soon as the Army Vet Corps could get enough sodium pentobarbital to Tyler, all these dogs were dead anyway.

He shouldn't have come in here.

Rounding a corner created by the stacked cages, he nearly bumped into a cluster of animal handlers deep in serious conversation. Jess heard "– have to remember to – "

"Mr. Langstrom!"

The group sprang apart. The girl who'd gasped his name was Melissa Taney, a twenty-something who worked with the county vet, Carl Venters. She looked as startled and upset as if Jess had caught her naked.

"Hi, Melissa. I'm looking for a specific dog, a toy poodle named Minette, address 142 Farley Street. Can you help me?"

"She's over there," a man volunteered. He was older than Melissa but not by much, and looked vaguely familiar to Jess. He realized that FEMA must be using locals for routine dog care. Well, that made sense – you didn't need highly trained K-9 specialists to clean cages and pour kibble.

"Thanks," Jess said. He walked in the direction the man pointed, feeling all their eyes on his back.

Minette lay asleep in her cage but woke as soon as Jess squatted beside it. As he squatted beside her, she barked and pushed against the bars to get close to him and feverishly licked his fingers. Did all this joy mean she remembered him, or would she have reacted the same to attention from anyone? He didn't know.

Jess stood, his eyes moist. Definitely he shouldn't have come. Probably right now a second van, under much heavier guard, was on its way from Fort Detrick.

Melissa stood beside him. "Mr. Langstrom, I'm sorry but you really should go now. This is a restricted area and we could get in trouble with Mr. Lurie."

He didn't want that. "All right, Melissa," he said in his deepest, most soothing voice, and then watched her mottle maroon. Something wasn't right here. "I certainly don't want to get anybody in trouble with Mr. Lurie."

She nodded, not meeting his eyes.

Jess walked back across the brightly lit field, signed himself out, and headed for the mess tent. Might as well have dinner there as at his silent apartment, and it seemed a good idea to stick around here for a while.

Just in case.

It was 5:37.

» 66

Tessa was running out of supplies. She'd eaten five cans of stew and one of the two packages of dried figs. Worse, the propane that heated Ebenfield's cabin was running out. He must have gone down the mountain every few days to buy supplies and steal wireless Internet service.

She stood on Ebenfield's bed, craning her neck out the window to watch the two dogs. The third one had never returned. Tessa's hope had been that the dogs' eerie behavior was the first sign of impending death, but so far this had not happened. The huge animals continued to bite and leap at the demons visible only to their diseased brains, but they did not die. Ebenfield's disease didn't kill them; the cold at night didn't kill them; they didn't kill each other.

So she would have to do it.

There was nothing in the cabin to help her. Saw, hammer, propane canister – but what could she do with them? Anything she threw, the dogs could dodge. Blowing up the place, with propane as the combustible, would probably kill her, too. She had no faith in the ability of any fiery, hand-carried torch to keep the dogs away from her long enough to reach Ebenfield's car. The car itself had antifreeze in it, which was poisonous to dogs; in fact, lapping antifreeze spilled on garage floors was a leading cause of death among pet dogs. But Tessa couldn't reach Ebenfield's car. Maybe she...

Poisonous to dogs.

Tessa bounded back to the window and stuck her head out the hole. Carefully she studied the ground, the trees, the bushes.

There.

It was easier getting back onto the roof than it had been getting off it before. She was rested now, fed, and not quite so cold. As soon as Tessa emerged from the cabin, balancing herself on the window ledge in her filthy socks, the dogs emerged from their trance and started lunging and growling at her. She forced herself to not look down. Even so, she could see the forty-two deadly teeth in each set of powerful jaws.

She got herself onto the roof and began the slow, agonizing transfer from pine tree to pine tree. Immediately she realized her mistake. This wasn't easier than her first trip, but harder. The melting snow made the pine branches slippery. As her socks became increasingly sodden, Tessa's toes lost their ability to judge the thickness and sturdiness of the branches beneath her feet.

Twenty feet from the cabin roof, she slipped off a wet branch.

Her left food slid sideways and she cried out. Below, the dogs jumped high. Had her right foot slipped, she would have fallen off the branch and onto the dogs. Instead, her legs parted to either side of the branch and her groin hit the wood. Hard. Despite the jolting pain, Tessa had just enough presence of mind to immediately jerk both feet upwards even as her arms clutched for the tree trunk. The jaws of the bigger dog missed her foot by inches.

Shaking, Tessa waited a long time to rise again. The sun filtered wanly through the dripping pines. Water dropped on her head. The part of her mind not occupied with either pain or fear realized what word she had cried out as she fell: "*Jess!*"

What the hell was that all about?

No time to wonder. Carefully, and twice as slowly, Tessa resumed her tree-to-tree transfer. When she finally reached her goal, the branch was too slight to support her weight. She was forced to go as far out on the thin limb of a neighboring maple as she dared, then grab for twigs and branches she could break off. The dogs, snarling, followed her every inch of the way.

The dogs shall eat Jezebel by the wall of–

Then came the journey back, slower and even more treacherous because of the load she carried. Her groin felt on fire; she must have bruised everything down there. As the roof of the cabin drew closer, Tessa knew that no matter what, she would not be able to make herself do this Tarzan act again. Twice, yes. But not a third time.

Back inside, she gave herself a moment to stop shaking, then stripped the bark from the yew and tore it into tiny pieces. The light outside was already fading, it would be a cloudy night, and she needed to get this done while she could still see outdoors. In Ebenfield's one saucepan she dumped the remaining cans of stew, heated them, and mixed in the yew bark. She dumped the whole mess out the window onto the melting snow.

"Come on, doggie, did-din, you hell-hound bastards!"

Both dogs raced over and gobbled the stew as if they were starving, which they probably were.

As Tessa watched, she silently thanked Minette. It was because of Minette that she'd researched canine toxins, because of Minette that she'd vowed to dig up all her lilies of the valley, come spring. Yew was much more toxic to animals than lily of the valley, than rhododendron, than begonia or daffodil bulbs or spinach plants. To die of yew poisoning, a dog needed to consume only one-tenth of one percent of its body weight.

That worked out to about one and half ounces per hell-hound outside the cabin.

Tessa peered out the window. But a part of her mind had snagged on something else. Ebenfield had said of these monstrous beasts that they were "not the first ones." That implied that he'd infected other dogs, earlier. If so, what had become of them?

She watched the dogs, and she waited.

» 67

Dennis Riley said, "Anybody want me to go over everything one more time?"

Ed Dormund fingered his old nine-millimeter in his coat pocket and eyed Dennis resentfully. Sure, Dennis had organized this "cell," as he called it, for tonight's action, but the meeting was being held at *Ed's* house. Dennis was acting like he was Big Boss here, and that wasn't right. Also, everybody practically bowed down to Brad Karsky.

Well, okay, there was reason for that. Ed wanted to be fair. Karsky had been the brains behind the Stop 'n' Shop bomb. But there were no explosives involved tonight, and this was *Ed's* house, so Dennis should just –

"Let's go," Leo said, standing up.

"It's too early," Ed said, and felt a little better when Leo sat down again.

The six men, all dressed in dark nondescript clothing, sat in Ed's living room, illuminated by a single lamp with a forty-watt bulb. Ed had drawn the thick drapes over the window and locked the doors. Nobody knew when the evacuation flunkeys would come around to start throwing citizens out of their homes, but if any FEMA fuckers came tonight, it would look like nobody was home. That had been Ed's idea.

He'd slept all afternoon after the morning's raid on the Army Vet

Corps van, and now he was energetic and ready. He had a sudden thought. "You know what? We're like Minutemen."

"Who?" Sam said.

"The guys who defended Boston and won the American Revolution for freedom," Ed explained, and when Brad and Dennis both nodded, Ed felt good again.

Dennis said, "It'll sure be good to have my Ninja back. I'll bet you miss Jake and them, too, Ed."

"You know it," Ed said. He did miss the Samoyeds. He hadn't told any of the men that his dogs had been infected, or about Cora's death, just saying for now that she was "away." Nobody questioned this. And anyway, maybe the Samoyeds hadn't really been infected after all. They'd never liked Cora.

"Be a lot of traffic," Tom said.

"That's true," Sam said. "All the lily-livered evacuees. But that's good. Our people will blend right in."

Brad nodded again. He said, "Ed, you work with me, okay?"

"Sure," Ed said, with a quick grin. "Maybe we should go. Traffic."

The men picked up their ski masks and headed for the garage.

Del and Brenda Lassiter sat in the kitchen of their daughter's house, finishing dinner. Brenda had eaten hardly anything. Chrissy, sweet girl that she was, fussed at her mother.

"Have a little meat, Mom."

Brenda smiled tremulously. "It's all so good, honey, but I just don't seem to have much appetite."

Chrissy glanced at Del, who shook his head slightly: *Don't force her.* Even before she was diagnosed, before the chemo, Brenda had never been able to eat when she was distressed.

"How about turning on the news to – " Chrissy began, caught herself, and flushed guiltily. Del, who'd told his daughter privately not to have the news playing near Brenda, said quickly, "Three-handed pinochle until Jack gets home from work? Honey?"

Brenda apparently hadn't been listening. She suddenly burst out, totally unlike herself, "I just don't understand! I just don't understand what the government...I just don't understand how anybody could hurt a dog!"

Kill every last dog before they all kill us.

Steve Harper had kept it small. Just him, Keith Rubelski, Ted Joyner, and Ted's girlfriend Cassie. Keith carried the explosives in a canvas bag that surprised Steve with its smallness and lightness. Thank God for Keith.

And for all the people who, Steve knew, would understand when this was over. He had faith that they were out there, those decent people who knew that children's lives mattered more than dogs. Not to mention those smart people who understood that unless you stopped a plague right away, you would get what the world got with Spanish flu in 1918.

"They'll try again," Steve had told Keith and Ted and Cassie, "and it'll be tonight. The jackal-lovers'll know that FEMA will bring in more euthanizing drugs tomorrow, and they won't wait. And the Guard won't do any more than they did when the van was robbed."

The others nodded. They understood. Cassie, whose sister had been killed by an infected Rottweiler, went further. "We owe it to the dead," she said.

We owe it to the dead. She was right. The mastiff standing over Davey's poor little body...

Steve checked his weapon yet again.

Billy sat by Cami's hospital bed. She still slept deeply, almost a coma, and her forehead felt clammy and cold. Her pretty hair lay all limp on the pillow and the nurse wouldn't even let him comb it.

"You shouldn't even be in here, Billy," she said. "You aren't family."

"Not yet," Billy said. Turned out the nurse was Donna Somebody, who used to hang out at the Moonlight Lounge when she was home from nursing school. Billy was pretty sure he'd never done her, which was good because now Donna let him put on a paper gown and mask and sit with Cami.

Donna said, "You two are a pair, all right. You with your arm in a sling and your head in a bandage, and Cami with her leg in a cast. I tell you, when she wakes up you'll be the most accident-prone couple in town."

When she wakes up. Billy knew Donna said that to cheer him up, and her kindness moved him. She was a great girl. Maybe her and Jess... Lately, Billy wanted the whole world to be in love.

"Look," Donna said, "I have to take Cami for another test and you should go down to the cafeteria and eat something. Cami and I'll be gone for over an hour. And I promise you the hospital won't start evacuating until tomorrow."

"Well..."

"Go eat, Billy."

He touched Cami's hair again and went, but the thought of more cafeteria food was puke-making. Billy called Jess on his cell. "Jess, want to grab a bite? Where are you?"

"At the CDC mess hall."

Billy heard something in Jess's voice. "Why? Is something happening?"

"Yes. No. It's nothing, Billy."

Billy didn't believe him. He'd known Jess all their lives. When Jess's voice went flat like that, when it got that particular tone in it, something was going down.

Donna said to go away for an hour, and everything in the hospital always took longer than they said it would. There was food in the CDC mess. Billy could eat there, check it out, and come back to the hospital. If something was happening at the CDC, maybe even something about the dog Billy had brought in, he wanted to know about it. After all, it might help Cami.

With his good hand, he punched the elevator button for the parking garage.

Ellie Caine inched her car into the intersection of Rutherford and Exchange. There were so many evacuees! Although not all of them were what they appeared.

Her chest tightened with fear. Never had she imagined herself doing anything like this. But she knew she could. Nervously she checked the time on the dashboard clock. Timing was important. Jenna, her contact, had emphasized that over and over. The timing was very carefully coordinated.

As she waited out the red light, Ellie felt in her pocket for the gun Jenna had showed her how to use. Her lips moved, rehearsing her small part in the events to come. No matter how afraid she felt, she had to do this. She would do this.

Dogs' lives were at stake.

» 68

Forty-five minutes after they'd eaten the stew mixed with yew bark, Ebenfield's Dobermans staggered. They took a few lurching steps before their hind legs buckled and they collapsed onto the melting snow. A few minutes later both dogs went into convulsions. In the growing twilight they looked as if being jerked by unseen ropes. Neither dog made a sound, which somehow made the brutal scene worse.

When she was sure they were both dead, Tessa picked up Ebenfield's hammer and unbarred the cabin door. With the hammer she could shatter Ebenfield's car window and then – she hoped – hot-wire the car. Or maybe the keys would be in the car. It's not as if he would have feared thieves. Or –

The dog came out of nowhere.

It was Ebenfield's third dog, the female Doberman that Tessa thought had run off. It hurtled out of the gloom almost before Tessa saw it. Tessa screamed and instinctively struck out, swinging her arm with all her strength. The hammer connected with the dog's neck.

The Doberman fell heavily to the ground, screaming a noise that Tessa would have thought dogs couldn't make, a high-pitch scream like a tortured child. Tessa ran, hoping the dog was too injured to follow. But after a moment the dog was up and pursuing. The moment was barely enough; Tessa flung open the door to Ebenfield's car and herself into it, slamming the door hard. A nanosecond later the Doberman smashed into the side of the car hard enough to dent it.

If Ebenfield had locked his car, Tessa would be dead.

No, not Ebenfield, she realized dazedly. Ruzbihan's men had searched the car, taking everything incriminating, just as they'd searched the cabin. The glove compartment gaped open and the contents of a first-aid kit lay strewn over all the seats. For the second time, Tessa owed her life to Ruzbihan's al-Ashan's thugs.

The Doberman threw itself at the car once more, then seemed to realize this was hopeless. It raced around the shed where Tessa had lain amid dog turds and rats and Ebenfield's smell and he had tried to… All at once, a huge and irrational rage filled her, the pent-up accumulation of everything that had happened. *Everything*, from Salah's pointless death onward. The rage was frightening in its intensity, a red mist soaking her brain. The keys were in the ignition. She started the car and hit the accelerator.

The car leapt forward as Tessa yanked the wheel to follow the Doberman. She made a wide circle in the clearing and then jammed her foot on the gas, aiming straight at the wooden shed.

The Doberman looked up as Tessa drove straight at her. The dog didn't move. Why didn't she *move?* The car slammed into the dog at maybe twenty miles per hour and kept going, pushing into the shed wall.

Tessa's teeth rattled in her head as she hit the steering wheel hard. The red mist vanished. *Stupid, stupid*—she could have killed herself! But although her chest ached where it had hit the wheel, she didn't seem to be seriously injured. All this she realized in the second before she turned off the engine and sat, panting and trembling, the car halfway through the shed wall.

Eventually she got out. A flashlight was among the items the blue-eyed Brit hadn't deigned to confiscate. In its conical beam Tessa saw the squashed body of the Doberman between the car's grill and the shed. And something else: the hole that the dog had dug, trying to burrow under the shed wall. The shed rested on an ancient, unsuspected concrete foundation, but that hadn't stopped the Doberman. Tessa saw how it had scraped and scraped at the crumbling concrete. It must have worked hour after tireless hour, bloodying its paws, ignoring Tessa in the cabin and even the smell of the stew she'd dumped out the window.

The Doberman had been trying to get at her puppy inside.

Tessa went around to the shed door. The puppy was dead, frozen.

She went back into the cabin and carried the box with the other two puppies out to the car, careful to not let them nip her fingers. Wedging the box into the trunk, she got back in the car and started down the mountain, to find her way back to civilization.

» 69

7:20 and full dark.

Ellie peeked again at the illuminated dial on her watch. She wasn't supposed to do that, but after one fast glimpse she lowered the sleeve of her coat over the watch, and anyway nobody could see her crouched here, not behind these bushes and in her dark clothing and ski masks. Nobody could see any of them. They waited in parked cars, behind building, in the woods. Ellie didn't know how many people. Jenna had simply said, "Lots."

7:25.

She, on the other hand, could see everything. Floodlights on tall poles showed her "Tent A," where the infected dogs were, Tent B, smaller tents, all the soldiers with rifles. The killing fields. That's what this was, yes – a killing field.

Her chest tightened, as if someone squeezed it with a vise.

7:28.

Ellie closed her eyes and covered them with her gloved hand as she'd been instructed, in order to adjust her pupils to darkness.

Now she couldn't peek at her watch. But she didn't need to. All she needed to do was wait for the signal.

The lights in the mess tent went out. Jess said, "What the –" and spilled his fresh cup of coffee. A tremendous noise began, bludgeoning him: the siren from the power factory.

Frantically he lurched in the direction of the door, crashing into a table until he remembered the flashlight, standard equipment for checking out skunks under houses, in his pocket. In its beam he gained the door and then stopped cold as he glimpsed, in sweeping conical flashes, the scene across the road. People running from everywhere, yelling their lungs out even as the siren blared, storming the dog tents. And the floodlight gone, all of the lights gone –

All at once Jess recalled picking up Gabe Bruhler's dog, an uninfected beagle. Gabe had argued and protested and resisted. And Gabe Bruhler was chief engineer at the #47 Cahoctin Power substation.

The young animal handlers in Tent B had pressured Jess to leave.

The siren and screaming – confuse the scene as much as possible, make it hard for the Guards to hear orders.

This was *big.*

And then he was running across the street, shining his ineffectual beam of light ahead of him, until someone rammed into him and snatched the flashlight away. "No lights!" the man cried, and was gone. A gunshot sounded, disconcertingly close, and Jess hit the ground.

Oh, God, no...the Guards had opened fire.

Jess crawled forward. There wasn't another rifle crack right away – were the Guards equipped with night-vision goggles and were they putting them on? The blackness was nearly total, as if they all scrabbled around at the bottom of a deep mine.

Another gunshot, farther away.

Jess kept crawling toward Tent B. He bumped into a boot and was hauled abruptly to his feet. A gun jammed into his ribs. "Don't shoot!" he cried. "I'm not armed! I'm with the CDC!"

The soldier's voice was young and scared. "Mr. Langstrom?"

"Yes!" Jess had no idea who he was.

"Get out of here!"

He dropped Jess, and Jess kept crawling.

A sudden, brief flash of light – from where? – gave him a nightmare glimpse of the field. People grappled with soldiers or ran blindly, crashing into each other. The faint light disappeared, then appeared again, then disappeared, and Jess realized it came from a flap of canvas on Tent B, swiftly being opened and then closed. From the slit poured dogs, racing wildly away. Another gun fired.

A dog leapt over him and kept going. Then another.

Another shot, and a high, agonized scream. Were these people firing on the *Maryland Guard?* Or the Guard on them? There was no way to tell what was happening, it was hellish bedlam, and only one thing was clear: the dogs were loose again. The handlers in Tent B were part of this...whatever it was.

The tent flap briefly opened, and before it closed, more dogs tore out. Then the light inside the tent ceased. Jess kept crawling forward. Someone stepped on his hand and he rolled away before whoever it was could fire downward.

He bumped into something...the tent wall. He felt along it until, a few feet on, he came to the door, opened it, and ducked inside, surprised to not find the door guarded. Were the soldiers already overpowered? Dead?

The inside of the tent was very faintly illuminated, and Jess realized his mistake. This wasn't Tent B. The light came from the screen of a laptop, which must have switched itself to battery. It lit close-together walls and a single big dog cage. This was the tent Joe Latkin had taken Jess to earlier this afternoon, with the West Virginia Doberman that had been attacking empty air.

He looked at the Doberman now and drew a sharp breath.

Steve Harper crouched low and raced in a zig-zag pattern through the lethal chaos, running interference for Keith Rubelski. The black-out had come as a surprise but a great one; he and Keith wore military-issue night-vision goggles. Somewhere to each side of them were Ted and Cassie, just in case, but Steve knew now that he and Keith wouldn't need them. They had it covered, unless one of the bozos firing out there hit them. But no shot could touch him, he could *feel* that certainty like a holy truth. Not now, when they were so close to justice.

Keith yelled something over the shouting and screaming, but Steve didn't catch it. A bullet whizzed past him and instantly he dropped, pulling Keith down with him and then shielding Keith with his own body. Something crashed into them...a fucking dog.

The rage was like a hot iron to his brain. But there was no time for rage, either.

He got Keith moving again. The closer they got to Tent B, the more the screaming and gunfire was behind them. All the jackal-lovers were at Tent A, fumbling and shooting and screaming and *letting loose the uninfected dogs.*

No time.

They slit the canvas of Tent A on the side farthest from the door and crawled through. The tent seemed empty, an unexpected piece of luck but it made sense. All the handlers were helping with the supposedly uninfected dogs. Steve switched on his flashlight and he and Keith made their way swiftly to the center of the tent. All around them dogs snarled and leapt and barked, and *the brown mastiff with a single long string of saliva and blood hanging from its mouth onto Davey's body...*

"Hey, Steve, you all right? Stay with me, man!"

"I'm on it," Steve got out. He left Keith setting the charge and made a swift tour of the tent to make sure it was empty. He passed several cages where the dogs lay quiet, despite the incredible noise – what the fuck was that all about, how could they lie so still in the middle of –

He spotted the girl.

She crouched behind a dog's cage, curled into a little ball, terrified eyes outward. As soon as she saw Steve she started screaming. He grabbed her and dragged her along, not bothering to explain. She was the only one in the tent, somehow not included in the others' plans. That might have made him feel tender toward her fear but she kept on screaming, and eventually he growled at her, "Be quiet! No one's going to hurt you!"

He met Keith back at the slit in the canvas and they plunged through, Steve still dragging the girl.

Ed charged with the others toward Tent B. He stumbled and for a moment fear grabbed him, but then he was on his feet again and it was all right even though he couldn't see anything. But the tent was over there, just straight ahead, and he could get this done. He could do anything. Hadn't he made Cora go away?

Good ol' Jake!

Jake deserved his help, all the dogs deserved his help (*but Jake was infected he isn't in Tent B* whispered a small part of his mind), all the dogs deserved life not death he could get this done nobody was going to tell them what to do with their own property –

Someone was screaming and someone was shooting and Ed didn't know which way to turn. Just keep going, this way, no that way, it was so fucking dark –

Suddenly all the lights went on.

Jess stared incredulously at the Doberman in the cage. It lay staring at him, completely still, as calm as if there were not shouting and gunfire and death rising to a crescendo ten feet away beyond the tent walls. And yet the animal wasn't dead. Its white-filmed eyes followed Jess as he moved, and Jess could see in the light from the computer screen that the dog breathed.

He picked up the metal chair beside the desk, thrust one leg through the bars of the cage, and poked the Doberman. Nothing. Jess poked harder. The dog registered no reaction.

Not dead, not asleep. The disease had entered some new phase, maybe, starting with the first dogs affected. That was why Jess had heard so little baying or barking all day from the dogs still at large in Tyler. Like this one, they'd started to go inert, each on its own virus-given schedule. And all the savagery outside, the shooting and killing –

Soon no dog would be a threat at all. Now the savagery now was all human.

Jess ran outside. "Stop!" he screamed, and a part of him knew this was the most futile act of his life, a pointless howl. No one could hear him or see him, no one knew he was there. "Stop! Stop! *Stop!*"

Two figures, bent low to the ground, zig-zagged by him. Jess heard one shout, "No, this way now!" and an electric jolt went through him. The voice was the one he'd heard on his cell phone as he stood on the steps and watched a harmless beagle named Hearsay die at his feet: *"If you and the whole damn federal government can't kill these vicious dogs, we'll do it for you."*

The two figures raced off into the darkness.

The lights came on.

—

Ed staggered to his knees. In the sudden shocking light he could see a woman holding her gun in one shaking hand. All that was visible within her ski mask were two eyes, wild and crazy like Cora's had been during a fight, Cora *you won't get me –*

"You won't get me!" he screamed and, still on his knees, drew his own gun. Before he could aim it, she shivered and –

– disoriented by the sudden light – there wasn't supposed to be light! – and terrified that he would kill her before she rescued Song and Chime and Music and Butterfly her wonderful greyhounds no no no –

Ellie Caine fired. She got him square in the face.

The lights were back on. Those jackal-lovers were so inept they hadn't sabotaged the back-up generators. Or maybe they had tried to and the Guards overpowered them. Either way, the floodlights blazed over a field chaotic with running people, prone bodies, dogs. Steve saw a Guard down. *Hell to pay.*

Once they were far enough from the tent, he let go of the girl, who immediately fell to the ground and curled back into her protective ball. Well, that would be as safe as anything, and they were far enough away now. He glanced over at Keith as they ran, and so saw the moment that Keith, still crouched low and running a good zig-zag pattern, pressed the detonator clutched in his right hand.

Tent A, with all its child-killing infected dogs, exploded into sound and fury. A moment later it began to rain down debris and metal bars and the pulpy bodies of incinerated dogs.

Jess, halfway across the field, was knocked to the ground by the blast shock. He fell heavily and felt something tear, but not before he saw Tent A blow up. A sound like a lightening crack shattered the air, followed seconds later by its echo: *Bbbooooooommmmm.* What was left of the tent's canvas walls began to burn.

The human sounds, shrieking and yelling, rose to a crescendo and then fell in a long, keening wail.

Jess covered his head, waiting for the second tent, the one with people in it, to also explode. It didn't. A horrible smell filled the air. Dog flesh, roasted in the blast. He gagged and tried to sit up, feeling his chest pull in sharp pain. He'd cracked a rib.

Nonetheless, he crept forward on his knees, toward a body ten feet away on the ground. He pulled off the ski mask and saw it was a middle-aged woman with bright red lipstick, as if she'd freshened up for this. She was dead.

Sirens sounded, coming closer, a whole other cacophony. Police, fire, maybe more Guards.

Too late for that. The field was emptying rapidly. People and dogs vanished into the woods, down the road, into the night. Some figures carried dog cages. Another dog jumped over Jess and kept running. Jess moved forward, to another body. This one was a Guardsman, not yet dead.

"Medic! Medic!" Jess screamed. He went on screaming it until there was no one moving but the newly arrived EMTS and one of them rushed over to the Guardsman. In the harsh glare of the floodlights and the flames at Tent A, the medics' faces were dead white.

Jess rose to his knees. Definitely a cracked rib. Holding his chest together, he staggered to his feet and gazed in despair over the terrible scene, how could this have happened, if the –

He saw Billy.

Carefully, as if any movement might startle that inert form lying on his back, eyes open to the sky, Jess walked toward Billy. He sank to his knees, put out one hand, withdrew it. Billy was dead. He'd been shot through the heart.

"Don't nap too long, Billy."

"Catch you later, dude."

Jess crouched by the body. He didn't shout or cry or even touch Billy. He just sat, while around him the medics and firefighters and cops and fresh Guards filled the field with as much noise as the departed terrorists and their departed dogs.

But not all departed. Jess felt something hurl against him. He looked down and there was Minette. Maybe because she recognized his smell, maybe because he was the only live human at her level on the ground. She huddled against him, shaking violently, ears so far back that they rested on her quivering little body. She was terrified by the noise and the fire and the guns, and as soon as Jess tried to pick her up, her terror made her growl and then bite him with her small, sharp, harmless teeth.

» 70

Tessa drove Ebenfield's car very slowly over the dark mountain roads. A part of her mind was genuinely surprised to see that her hands shook on the wheel. She hadn't eaten in – how long? She couldn't remember, couldn't think of anything but Ebenfield's screams as the dogs tore him apart, of the Doberman rushing straight at her as she yanked the car door, of the eerie leaping and twisting of the other huge dog as it snapped and fought with empty air, of the dog she had crushed against the shed...

Damn it, her hands shouldn't shake like this! She was – had been – an FBI agent.

The two puppies whimpered in the back seat. Tessa's feet, in socks sodden from her dash across the snow to Ebenfield's car, felt like ice. She turned up the heat as high as it would go and directed it downward. As the car warmed, the puppies fell asleep.

She had no idea where she was, or even if she was still in West Virginia, although she guessed the answer was yes. The dashboard display included a digital compass. Tessa headed west, searching for a highway. She turned on the radio, flipping through staticky country-and-western stations – she must really be far from civilization – until she came to the news, also staticky.

" – terrorist act that – crackle crackle – Tyler, Maryland. Initial reports – crackle – Guardsmen dead and – crackle – explosion that – "

Tessa reached the top of a hill and the broadcast abruptly cleared. She listened to all of it, parked by the side of the dark road under the high cold stars. The freed dogs, the Guard opening fire, the explosion, the stupid senseless slaughter Ebenfield had caused among innocent people. *"Is thy servant a dog, that he should do this great thing?"*

And...Minette?

Dr. Latkin?

Jess?

After another half hour, she came to a cluster of houses with a grocery store, a gas station, and a roadside diner/bar, McGarrity's. When she stopped the car, the puppies woke and barked feebly. Tessa shuddered, berated herself, and got out.

A big, middle-aged man in parka and a hat with ear flaps climbed out of a pick-up beside her. "Looks like you hit a deer."

"Yes." The car grille was smeared with blood and pulpy flesh, made even more hellish by the red neon glow from the bar.

The man peered at her. "You okay, miss?"

"I'm...I'm fine."

"Don't look fine. You need a doctor?"

"No."

"You don't got on shoes, you know."

"I know," Tessa said, managed a smile, and went inside.

A large dim room, tables covered in red oilcloth, pool table, bar. George Jones played, too loud. She ordered chicken wings and a Scotch, then padded in Ruzbihan's son's socks, cold and sodden again from the parking lot, to the phone in the corner. The big man watched her all the way, his face creased with concern.

She called Maddox's cell. He picked up immediately.

"This is Tessa," she said, and paused. Where to even start?

Maddox drew a sharp breath. "Where are you?"

"Somewhere in West Virginia, I think. Ebenfield's dead. He did start the plague and he nabbed me...I can't give it all to you here now on the phone. Bring me in, John. I'm at a bar called McGarrity's someplace on Route 50."

"I'll have a helicopter there inside an hour."

"Put a lawyer on the helicopter."

"Not necessary. Just *stay put*, Tessa."

"I'm not going anywhere. I heard on the radio...Tyler..."

"Yes. Just stay put."

She padded back to the bar, leaving wet footprints on the grimy floor. By now most of McGarrity's was watching her. Tessa leaned across the bar to speak to the woman behind it. "I have two puppies in the car.

They're in a box. Is it all right if I bring the box in here while I eat, so that the little dogs don't freeze?"

"Sure, honey," the woman said. "You okay?"

"Yes," Tessa said. "Just fine."

Maddox looked as tired as she felt. He met the helicopter as it landed in an empty field located somewhere, Tessa guessed, near Tyler but not too near. Had he driven up from Washington or had he already been in Tyler? Maddox was alone, no driver, although two other cars were part of the entourage, one of which immediately drove off with the box of puppies. Tessa knew she'd never see the dogs again. She and Maddox sat in the front seat of his car. He kept the heat running.

"Are you all right, Tessa? Do you need a doctor?"

"I need a lawyer."

"No, you don't. I'm going to record what's said here, all right?"

"Here? Now?"

"Yes. With your agreement, of course."

Because she wasn't an agent, just a civilian. "Tell me first why I don't need a lawyer. Off the record, John."

He hesitated and then, in the half-light from the dashboard, made his characteristic movement of eyes and mouth, that Maddox-grimace she knew so well from years of working together. She saw the moment he decided to trust her, as she was trusting him.

"You know what happened tonight in Tyler?"

"Yes. Or at least, what the radio reported."

"Probably accurate, although not the whole story."

"It never is."

Maddox turned in his seat to look her full in the face. She could see how carefully he was considering his words, and that he wanted her to see that carefulness. "You don't need a lawyer because you're going to come out the hero of this thing. Not publicly, of course. But the administration is going to need an intelligence hero, just like they're going to need an intelligence scapegoat, along with a public scapegoat. The whole thing's been mismanaged from beginning to end. The president is on the war path and Hugh Martin will be able to restrain him only so far."

Tessa nodded. The chief-of-staff's restraining of the president was an old story inside the Beltway.

"Scott Lurie will be fired," Maddox said, "and Bernini will resign."

"*Bernini?* The Assistant Director?"

Maddox nodded. "And you're going to be the unsung hero of the dog plague problem. Completely unsung, except at the top echelons, especially if you're right about Ebenfield. Now tell me where we can find his body. The CDC is going to need it." He reached for the recorder.

Tessa put a hand on his arm. "Just one more minute, John. And one more question." She gathered herself, knowing how critical her question was, how outrageous. But she had worked counter-terrorism for a long time. She knew the kind of people recruited as informers – and what often happened to them later, when they went off the rails and out on their own. *The whole thing's been mismanaged from beginning to end,* Maddox had said. How long a beginning?

She said, "Were we running Ebenfield originally? Not the Bureau, of course, but our friends across the river at Langley?"

Maddox looked at her. He made no answer – which was her answer.

Jesus Christ.

He said, "I'm going to start to record now."

She nodded, still stunned, but managed to say, "And I want to know what happened in Tyler."

"We have a lot to tell each other," Maddox said. He turned on the recorder.

INTERIM

The president, so angry he could not sit still, raged at his chief of staff. "God-damn it, Hugh, what a massive screw-up! How many dead?"

"Seven, sir. Three National Guard and four civilians. Plus five wounded." The number was right in front of them, displayed on CNN *in a huge headline behind a somber anchorman. Nothing else had played on all major networks all evening. Now it was nearly midnight and the full staff still worked the Oval Office.*

"Son of a bitch! Of all the mismanaged – I want Scott Lurie fired. Now."

"Yes, sir."

"Burial with full honors for the Guards – how many of the funerals should I attend?"

"All three, Mr. President."

The president scraped his hands across his face, pulling at the tired flesh. "And the civilians? Personal phone calls?"

"No. Everyone on that field in Tyler was engaging in an act of domestic terrorism, sir." Was it possible that the president didn't understand that this was the end of his presidency, there would be no second term, and that his legacy would be the "Tyler Massacre"? Was that – in the face of the screaming on TV*, in the papers, and from the Hill – even possible?*

Yes. It was possible.

"What are we doing with all the damn dogs?"

"The caged infected ones all died in the explosion. The loose infected ones are, according to the CDC*, slowly going inert and then dying. The ones set loose weren't infected so we're trying to round them up again and move them to a secure facility at Fort Detrick. Anything else would look like condoning terrorism."*

"Yes. I see."

The president didn't ask if the escaped dogs were actually being found in the round-up, and Hugh Martin didn't volunteer the information that no, of course they weren't. Animal handlers and law enforcement hadn't even found them all the first time, when at least some dog owners had been more willing to cooperate.

Martin said, "The good news is that all threat to the public seems to be over, which is what you'll say in your broadcast tomorrow morning. Also that there is cautious optimism from the CDC *about the dog-bite victims."*

"There is?"

"There's always cautious optimism, sir."

"There's always a good hard strike-back, too! I want everybody who organized that terrorist act to have the book thrown at them!"

"As soon as we identify them, sir."

Irritably the president snapped off CNN. *"And speaking of terrorism, what about that* FBI *agent? She came in, right? Can we charge her with anything?"*

"No, Mr. President. She led us to Ebenfield and the dogs that were the primary terrorist weapons. She's a hero."

"Oh." The president considered this. "Does she know anything about... you know."

"No, sir."

"I just don't want any loose ends here snapping back to hit us in the ass."

"There won't be."

"I want Lurie fired. And Bernini, too. He couldn't even find one of his own agents, for God's sake, let alone find Ebenfield!"

"Bernini will resign." Martin had already spoken to him. "Sir, the agent has no idea that originally we were running Ebenfield."

The president's thoughts had moved on. "That Arab cell that turned Ebenfield – how do we know he didn't tell them anything?"

"He didn't know anything, sir," Martin said patiently. They'd been over this before. Nor did Martin remind the president that Tessa Sanderson's late husband had also been an Arab. It would only confuse him. "Ultimately Ebenfield did what we wanted him to – he led us to Abd-Al Adil al-Ashan. Nobody could have predicted that on the way he would contract an infection from wild dogs."

"And then attack the United States with it. Damn, Hugh, I've got half a mind to hold Decker responsible, too."

James Decker was the head of the CIA, *which had recruited Ebenfield in Africa. Martin said, "I wouldn't advise that, sir. Decker's a good man."*

"If he was such a good man then we wouldn't have had a biological terrorist attack in the United States! And from dogs! The best surveillance techniques

in the world and we get zapped by a man who bites Lassie and Marmaduke!"

Martin said nothing. In this mood, the president couldn't be reasoned with. The best thing was to let the tantrum run its course.

"Was it the plague that turned Ebenfield into such a raging megalomaniac? The virus in his brain?"

"We don't know that yet, sir."

"And what about Abd-Ali...Abdul...whatever the hell his name is, the one with the alias 'Erekat.' Where is he and what are we doing about him?"

"He'll be neutralized in Tunis. It's being set up now."

"What about the father?"

"He's clean. The son apparently went off on his little jihad without paternal backing."

"All right." Abruptly the president calmed down. He sat behind his desk, looking presidential, a thing he did very well.

Too bad it was too late.

SATURDAY

» 71

Ellie Caine sat on the edge of her bed. Ten in the morning, she hadn't slept at all, and she couldn't stop shaking. No matter what she did – another blanket, warm milk, wine – she couldn't stop shaking.

She had shot and killed a man.

He had been going to shoot her, that man on his knees in the black ski mask. She was sure of that. He'd raised his gun and was bringing it up to point at her. So her shooting had been self-defense. But it had happened while she was committing a crime herself, so didn't that make it some sort of felony? Could she go to prison?

Who had he been?

When the doorbell rang, Ellie screamed and jumped. But it wasn't the police. Two Maryland Guards stood there with dog cages.

"Ellie Caine?"

"Yes...."

"Are you harboring any of the four dogs licensed to you, ma'am? The Greyhounds?"

"No." None of them had come home, not her beloved Song nor Chimes nor Music. Other dogs had come home, but not hers.

The soldier's gaze pushed hers. "Are you sure, ma'am?"

"I don't have my dogs."

"We have an emergency warrant to search."

"Go ahead," Ellie said, while a complicated wash of emotions went through her. Indignation. Grief. But, most of all, relief.

They had come for the dogs, not for her.

This time.

» 72

Steve Harper heard the knock on the door but didn't move. The people outside, cops or Guard or FBI, weren't looking for dogs; he didn't have a dog. They were looking for him. The door wasn't locked and if they had a warrant, they'd come in. If they didn't, they'd go away. It didn't really matter.

He and Keith had blown up Tent A, but the world was still full of dogs. He could hear them barking somewhere out there, filling up newscasts on TV, the endless subject of endless debates by talking heads. The world would always be full of dogs. Steve knew that now. And some people – enough people – would always value the lives of dogs over the lives of children.

The brown mastiff with a single long string of saliva and blood hanging from its mouth onto Davey's small body... No.

Steve couldn't think about that image anymore. Couldn't struggle any more. He was so tired inside.

Another knock on the door.

Let them take him. He'd done all he could. If they had a warrant, they'd come in. If they didn't, they'd go away.

He heard the doorknob turn.

» 73

Jess sat by Cami Johnson's hospital bed. Late afternoon sunlight slanted across the floor. Cami was still in a semi-coma, but the doctor had told him that it would end soon. The other dog-bite victims, the ones infected earlier than Cami, had already woken up. Unlike the dogs, the infected humans didn't die. Although God alone knew what was going on in their brains.

Jess put his hands flat on his knees and stared at the clumsy homemade bandage, the bitten nails. How was he going to tell Cami about Billy?

How was Jess himself going to manage without Billy, his only real friend?

"Don't nap too long, Billy."

"Catch you later, dude."

When Cami woke up, Jess was going to need the right words. He didn't have them, not for her and not for himself. The only sentence that kept coming to his mind, over and over, was completely selfish, not concerned with Billy at all. Or maybe it was.

I need to change my life.

On the hospital bed, Cami stirred and her eyelids fluttered like blue-veined butterflies.

» 74

"She's alive! She's alive!"

"Allen, be careful! Your foot – Allen, do you hear me?"

"Susie's alive!"

Amy Levy smiled wearily. It had been worth it, then, after all – all those phone calls and all that fake blustering. *"This is Mrs. Peter Levy, my husband is an attorney with Dalton, Arendt, Carruthers, and Levy, and I'm calling to find out –* " Yes, worth it, to see Allen's face like that.

Peter had called, finally, from D.C. He professed concern for his wife and son in what was practically a war zone, but it was too little concern too lately professed. Probably he was at his little tart's place. Anger and outrage and fear for the future boiled through Amy, but for this moment she pushed them all aside to savor Allen's joy.

He shouted, "When can we see her? When can we have Susie back?"

"We don't know that yet, honey. I told you."

"But you could make more calls and make them tell you!"

"Allen –"

"Susie's alive!"

APRIL

» 75

Jess stood on the porch of the Cape Cod and took a deep breath. In the twilight, porch lights were coming on along Farley Street but Tessa's light, he noted, had burned out. Leaves from last autumn littered corners of her porch, but tulips bloomed in the front yard. Feeling like a manipulative fool, Jess nonetheless unlatched the cage at his feet, lifted the wiggling little dog into his arms, and rang the doorbell.

"Minette! Oh, Minette!"

The poodle, barking frantically, leapt from him to Tessa. Tessa hugged her and turned away – to hide tears? This was an unexpected side of her. Uninvited, Jess stepped inside. "I thought I'd bring her myself. The dogs are all being released today."

"Thank you." She turned back – no tears after all. He admitted disappointment. Still, she said, "Would you like a cup of coffee? Or a beer?"

"Beer would be great."

She led him through the living room to the kitchen. No more cardboard boxes and, given the state of neglect outside, the rooms looked quite nice in an exotic, non-cozy sort of way. Straight curtains of some rough brown material, a gorgeous Oriental rug that looked wickedly expensive, one sofa and one chair with straight, low lines. Smaller rugs hung on the white walls. Instead of a coffee table she had a wide copper tray on a tripod, its intricate design inlaid with what looked like gold. The tray was surrounded by bright floor cushions. Despite the TV and a bookcase, this was definitely not your usual Tyler décor, which ran to plaid sofas and wreaths of dried flowers.

The kitchen was more familiar: American coffee pot on the counter, notes and cartoons stuck on the refrigerator with magnets, a package of Doritos open on the table. Jess glanced at the empty dog dishes on the floor.

"I never did put them away," Tessa confessed. She filled the bowls with kibble and water but Minette wouldn't leave her lap. As she and Jess sat at the table with their beers, the tiny dog pressed into Tessa as if trying to burrow into her belly.

"I heard you went back to work at the FBI," Jess said.

She paused with the beer halfway to her mouth. "How did you hear that?"

He smiled. "It's a small town. People talk all the time. You leave the house every morning before seven dressed in a dark pantsuit, you head toward D.C., you come home after eight at night. That's all it takes."

"Jesus Christ, federal intelligence should only be that good." She grinned at him over the edge of her beer glass and his heart skipped a beat.

"So are you at the FBI again?"

"Yes. I discovered I'm not the type to sit around Tyler and bake cookies."

Like there could ever have been any doubt. "So you're moving back to D.C.?"

"No. I like Tyler. Despite the gossips."

"Long commute."

"I can manage," she said stiffly. Somehow this had become a verbal contest, not at all what Jess intended. He held out his glass. "Can I have another beer?"

"Sure." She got him one from the fridge, and he noted the way her trim ass moved in her tight jeans. She was fitter than he was, richer, better educated, probably smarter, and certainly a better shot. But she was the only woman who'd stirred him at all since Elizabeth walked out. He pressed on.

"Your husband was Arabic, wasn't he?"

Her eyes narrowed. "Why do you say that?"

"You asked me once if I read Arabic, and Agent Maddox got really interested when I told him that. Also, you have all those things in the living room...Look, I don't know what happened with you during the dog plague, why you took my truck and disappeared, or where you went after that, or...anything. And I don't care. I was just asking to make conversation."

She nodded. Her eyes lost that hard look and hope sprouted in him. He said, "Tessa, would you have dinner with me?"

She took a long time to answer. "Yes, my late husband was Arabic. His name was Salah. He was killed five months ago by a drunk driver. I loved him very much."

The hope withered.

"Tessa – "

"Don't, Jess. Please...don't." She hesitated, weighing something in her mind, and apparently decided on honesty. Although he had no doubt she was capable of elaborate, perfectly delivered lies if she so chose.

"You don't want to get involved with me, Jess. Apart from the fact that my husband has been dead for only five months...Christ, there *is* no 'apart' from that. Not for me. How can I explain it so you...Since Salah's death, every day has been like striding along the street and all of a sudden you step in a pothole and go down. Again and again. Sometimes it's just a little stumble and it's relatively easy to get up without much pain. Other times it's pure torture. But it keeps happening, over and over, and you get so you half expect the ground to not hold under your feet. The damn *ground* isn't trustworthy any more. Yet there's no place else to walk."

She stared into her beer, stroking Minette with one hand. "And there's something else, too. During the dog-plague investigation, for reasons I won't go into, I came to doubt everybody. I doubted my boss and the Bureau. I doubted my sister-in-law overseas. I even doubted – briefly but it happened – my dead husband. Do you understand – *I doubted Salah.* I can't trust my own judgment in personal matters, and I don't want anyone else trusting it, either. I don't want the responsibility. Can you understand that?"

He could. All at once, he saw why she'd returned to work in D.C. It wasn't because she was bored baking cookies in Tyler. It was because she needed impersonal work, twelve-hour days of it, to protect her against feeling and emotion. That was also the reason she was staying in Tyler. Her friends, her old life of emotional connections, was in D.C.

Jess spoke, and it felt like an enormous risk, a lot more dangerous than rounding up infected dogs. "I know something about relying on work to blunt pain. I know because...well, I did the same thing after my wife walked out on me. It didn't work so well."

She looked up from Minette. "You were married?"

"Yes, until Elizabeth left with my best friend. Besides Billy, I mean. I thought my life was over except for my job. I went on thinking that for a real long time. But now I know better."

"How?"

It seemed a genuine question, not mere chatter. Jess tried to give a genuine answer. "Billy. Billy's death. I need to..." Christ, it was hard to find the right words! "...to connect again."

"Starting with me?"

"I like you, Tessa."

She looked away, and Jess knew how much of an ass he'd made of himself. So he said, as lightly as he could manage, "I talked to Joe Latkin this afternoon, when the dog release was okayed."

"Oh?" Her tone held relief at the change of subject. "What did he say about a vaccine or a cure?"

"They're working on it. He told me – " Jess concentrated, retrieving Latkin's exact words " – that the CDC has finished sequencing the plague virus. He said that it's very similar to both the 1918 Spanish influenza and to avian flu, with alterations in just...let me see...in thirty-eight of the virus's 4,400 amino acids. He said for the already infected, the CDC's best shot was drugs to slow down viral replication, based partly on the antibodies of a dog with natural immunity. While also...let me think... oh yeah, while also managing the virus as it mutates. He also said that we're charmed that the transmission vector was dog bites, and not airborne like the 1918 epidemic. "

"'Charmed'?" Tessa said. She tried to smile. "That was Latkin's word?"

"Yes."

"The virus is still in the saliva of the people who were bitten. And in their brains."

"Yes," Jess said. "Thanks for the beer."

"You're welcome."

She walked him to the door. He managed to avoid looking at her.

As he left he said, "See you around, Tessa."

"Wait. Jess...I would like to have dinner with you."

"You would?"

"Yes." Her eyes met his straight on. "But just dinner. It's still too soon for me to...just dinner. Are there any good restaurants in Tyler?"

"No. But we can drive to Frederick. On Saturday?"

"Okay."

A cool breeze stirred the dead leaves on the porch. It ruffled Tessa's dark hair as she stood on tiptoe and kissed him briefly on the cheek. Warmth surged through him.

At the curb he looked back, but she'd already gone inside. However, he saw Minette at the window, barking silently behind the glass, wagging her negligible tail with sheer pleasure at being alive and being home.

» 76

"What if she's not there?" Allen said anxiously.

"She's there," said the young man in the white coat. He smiled down at Allen with that look grown-ups got when they saw him on crutches. It was a sappy look but good for getting things, if you answered right. Today Allen didn't care how he answered. He was too excited.

"Which building? Which *one?*"

"That brick one over there, behind the big tree."

"Allen," his mother said, "slow down, you're still not used to your crutches. Allen, do you hear me?"

Allen didn't want to slow down. As fast as he could, he swung himself along the path that wound among the CDC buildings. It was warmer here in Atlanta than at home, and the grass was lots greener, but he didn't care about that, either.

"Sometimes I can't do a thing with him," Mrs. Levy apologized.

"Well... kids," said the attendant, who was all of twenty-two.

"Since his father left, that bastard...never mind, I'm sorry." She fumbled in her purse for a tissue, still walking rapidly to keep up with Allen, while the attendant looked delicately away.

Allen burst through the doors of the building. It smelled wonderful, of dogs and cats and maybe even something exciting like monkeys. He'd read on-line that the CDC had monkeys. But today not even a monkey could deter him.

"This way," the attendant said. "Down this elevator."

An elevator, another corridor – Allen was moving so fast his crutches almost slipped on the slick floor – and another door, and then there she was!

"Susie!" He hurled himself to the floor.

The attendant opened the cage and Susie ran out, nearly knocking Allen over. Her tail wagged non-stop and she barked and whined and climbed clumsily all over him.

"Allen, watch your leg, do you hear me?"

"She's got on a muzzle! Why does she got on a muzzle! Take it off!"

"I'm sorry but I can't," the young man said. "She's still infected, you know. If she bit you – "

"She would never bite me!"

"I'm sorry," the attendant said in a tone that said he wasn't budging. Allen scowled at him but after a second he forgot the muzzle. He was with Susie again! A long plane ride and the night in the hotel and listening to his mother cry when she thought Allen was asleep...it was all horrible but here was Susie, and she was safe and whole.

"Susie," he crooned as she pressed into him, uttering little yelps of joy. "Susie, Susie..."

The attendant looked mistily down at them. "I had a dog when I was a child."

Allen's mother didn't answer.

"A boy and his dog. Such a simple, easy relationship. Nothing but pure love, no messy human complications."

"Oh, shut up," Amy Levy said.

JULY

EPILOGUE: PHILADELPHIA, PENNSYLVANIA

It happened so fast that only one person actually saw it. The little boy squatted in the sandbox, digging with a red plastic shovel. His mother sat two feet away on a park bench, talking with the mother of the baby in the carriage and the mother of the little girl driving everybody crazy by demanding that the adults dance with her, and screaming at the top of her lungs if they didn't.

"Dance! Dance with me!"

"Not just now, darling, Mama's tired."

"Dance!"

"Later."

The child let out an ear-stabbing yowl that made the other two women jump. They exchanged covert, disapproving looks. What an obnoxious kid!

Wearily the girl's mother got up to dance with her beside the park bench.

The dog came out of nowhere, a bouncy red-gold Labrador retriever that dashed up to the boy in the sandbox and leapt onto his lap. The two-year-old screamed and did something, and the dog howled and snapped. The boy's mother snatched him up just as the dog owner, a young man in dirty khaki shorts and scraggly blond beard, sauntered up.

"Your dog is supposed to be on a leash!" the mother screamed, frantically jiggling her son in her arms.

"Hey, chill, Garcia never bites," the man said. Languidly he took a leash from his pocket and fastened it on the dog, who stood trembling at his feet, his broad tail tucked between his legs. "Hey, Garcia, it's all right, boy...wow, he's really upset."

"*He's* upset," said the mother of the dancing girl. "We should report you to the police!"

"Whatever," said the young man, leading his dog away.

"We *should* report him!"

"Well, maybe," said third woman, who was the group's peacemaker, "but Labs are pretty peaceful dogs. We always had them when I was growing up. He didn't bite Robbie, did he?"

"No, I don't think so," Robbie's mother said. The child had stopped crying and was clambering to return to the sandbox. There were no rips in his Oshkosh overalls or little red T-shirt, nor any punctures on his chubby hands.

His mother hugged him tight. No, she wasn't going to say anything... she *wasn't.* She and Bob had lost so many of their old friends, from fear or pity or something. It was so unfair because they were doing everything right: checking in with the CDC every three months, keeping all those charts and records of Robbie's health. Giving Robbie the experimental drugs. Since their move to Philly, she'd been really lonely until she met these two women in the park. Sarah, the mother of the infant, might even become a real friend. And although it was true that lately Robbie had been biting everything in sight – toys, spoons, his babysitter, the cat – she hadn't actually *seen* him bite the Labrador. Chances were, he hadn't. She didn't want to throw away these precious mornings in the park – nobody knew how hard it was to raise a child without the companionship of other women! – for an accident that most likely hadn't even happened. After all, she deserved a life, too.

"Dance!" demanded the little girl.

Robbie's mother set him back down in the sandbox. Such a happy baby, usually. And the scar under his shirt was fading more every day. She was very lucky. When you think of all the children that hadn't survived the dog bites...

"*Dance!*" shrieked the little monster in the pink sundress. "*Now!*"

The red-gold lab whimpered on its leash. The young man didn't notice. He had left the park and was ambling toward the supermarket, whistling tunelessly. Garcia trotted obediently beside him, the teeth marks hidden by the thick, red-gold fur on his tail. They reached the curb and disappeared into the crowd on the city street.